Praise for *Drea...*

"Readers will enjoy the easy pac...
waiting for the grand finale, and v...

...terviews and Reviews

"Amanda Cabot's new novel, *Dreams Rekindled*, is a wonderfully entertaining and inherently absorbing read from cover to cover."

Midwest Book Reviews

Praise for *Out of the Embers*

"Cabot expertly combines suspense with a pleasant romance to create a moving and uplifting tale."

Booklist

"Cabot transports readers to 1850s Texas in the enjoyable first installment to her Mesquite Springs series."

Publishers Weekly

"If you like adventure, drama, danger, mystery, and a clean romance, then this is the book for you."

Interviews and Reviews

"*Out of the Embers* is part prairie romance, part romantic suspense. I can't remember when I've enjoyed a book more. Amanda Cabot has written an intriguing, chilling mystery, and she winds it through the pages of a sweet romance in a way that made me keep turning the pages fast to see what was going to happen next. An absolutely excellent read. And now I'm hungry for oatmeal pecan pie!"

Mary Connealy, author of *Aiming for Love*, book 1 in the *Brides of Hope Mountain* series

Praise for Amanda Cabot

"Broad appeal for fans of historical fiction as well as romance and even westerns."

Booklist on *A Tender Hope*

"Filled with complex emotion and beautiful prose."

Woman's World Magazine on *A Tender Hope*

"Another deftly crafted gem of a novel by a true master of the romance genre."

Midwest Book Review on *A Borrowed Dream*

Books by Amanda Cabot

Historical Romance

MESQUITE SPRINGS SERIES

Out of the Embers
Dreams Rekindled

TEXAS DREAMS SERIES

Paper Roses
Scattered Petals
Tomorrow's Garden

WESTWARD WINDS SERIES

Summer of Promise
Waiting for Spring
With Autumn's Return

CIMARRON CREEK TRILOGY

A Stolen Heart
A Borrowed Dream
A Tender Hope

Christmas Roses
One Little Word: A Sincerely Yours Novella

Contemporary Romance

TEXAS CROSSROADS SERIES

At Bluebonnet Lake
In Firefly Valley
On Lone Star Trail

The SPARK *of* LOVE

AMANDA CABOT

Revell
a division of Baker Publishing Group
Grand Rapids, Michigan

© 2022 by Amanda Cabot

Published by Revell
a division of Baker Publishing Group
PO Box 6287, Grand Rapids, MI 49516-6287
www.revellbooks.com

Printed in the United States of America

Library of Congress Cataloging-in-Publication Data
Names: Cabot, Amanda, 1948- author.
Title: The spark of love / Amanda Cabot.
Description: Grand Rapids : Revell, a division of Baker Publishing Group, [2022] |
    Series: Mesquite Springs ; 3
Identifiers: LCCN 2021020271 | ISBN 9780800735371 | ISBN 9780800741037
    (casebound) | ISBN 9781493434138 (ebook)
Subjects: GSAFD: Love stories.
Classification: LCC PS3603.A35 S63 2022 | DDC 813/.6--dc23
LC record available at https://lccn.loc.gov/2021020271

Baker Publishing Group publications use paper produced from sustainable forestry practices and post-consumer waste whenever possible.

22 23 24 25 26 27 28   7 6 5 4 3 2 1

For Catherine, my first and forever friend.
I'm so glad you're my sister.

MESQUITE SPRINGS, TX

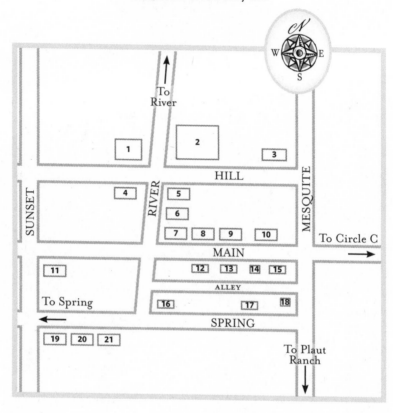

1 – Cemetery
2 – Park
3 – King's Hotel
4 – Downeys' House/Alexandra's Home
5 – School
6 – Parsonage
7 – Church
8 – Mayor's Office/Wyatt and Evelyn's House
9 – Sam Plaut's Law Office/Sam and Gabe's Home
10 – Dressmaker's Shop
11 – Saloon
12 – Mercantile
13 – Polly's Place
14 – Post Office
15 – Sheriff's Office and House
16 – *Chronicle* Office/Dorothy and Brandon's House
17 – Boardinghouse
18 – Doc Dawson's Office and House
19 – Smiths' House
20 – Blacksmith Shop
21 – Livery

CHAPTER

One

APRIL 1857

She had to leave.

Alexandra Tarkington tried to bite back her anger as she removed the tray from the smaller of her trunks, laying it carefully on the floor. This shouldn't be happening, but it was. Though she was grateful today was her maid's half day and she wouldn't have to deflect Bridget's curiosity, Alexandra had never before packed a trunk or even a valise. Then again, she'd never before been forced to flee.

"What are you doing?"

She looked up, startled by her great-aunt's approach. Aunt Helen was showing signs of her seventy-one years and moved slowly, but the sound of her cane on the hardwood floors should have alerted Alexandra. It *would* have alerted her if she hadn't been so preoccupied.

"Tell me, child."

Alexandra winced at the final word. Aunt Helen might believe she was still a child who needed to be protected, but the truth was, Helen was the one who needed protection. While she might seem formidable to those who sought her favor, Helen Cameron's bones were fragile. If Franklin resorted to the physical violence he had threatened and Aunt Helen tried to protect Alexandra, she might be injured. Alexandra couldn't take that chance.

"I'm going to the Springs." Once Alexandra left New York, her aunt would be safe.

"Because of Franklin." Aunt Helen made it a statement, not a question.

"Yes," she admitted, "but how did you know?"

Her aunt wrinkled her nose as she settled onto a chair. "I may be hard of hearing, but I'm not deaf, and he was shouting." She leaned forward and laid her hand on Alexandra's. "No matter what he threatens, Franklin can't touch your trust. Your grandmother hired the best attorneys in the city to make sure your mother and now you were protected. Even after you marry, the money is yours, not your husband's. You can use it, but you can't give it to him. It can only go to your daughter. Still, after hearing Franklin last night, I think you're wise to get away for a while."

Though she knew that, Alexandra railed at the necessity. "I hate feeling like I'm running away."

She'd heard whispers that Franklin was a violent man, but she hadn't believed them. Until last night, he'd been a perfect gentleman. Until last night.

"You're being wise," Aunt Helen repeated, making Alexandra wonder if she'd overheard Franklin's threats. "Besides, your cousin will enjoy your company. It's been a long time since you and Opal were together."

"That's true." Alexandra hated deception, but her aunt would be safer if she believed that the springs Alexandra planned to visit were Saratoga, not Mesquite. The charade wouldn't last forever, but it should give her enough time to reach Texas. Even if Franklin discovered where she'd gone, he wouldn't follow her, not when he realized Papa would be there to defend her.

Alexandra took a deep breath, wishing she could believe that, but the assurance she sought was overwhelmed by the memory of Franklin's fury. Tamping down the fear that threatened her composure, she tried to smile.

"Don't worry if I don't write. I imagine I'll be so busy I won't have much time." If she didn't receive a letter, Aunt Helen could honestly say she didn't know where Alexandra had gone if Franklin asked. *When* Franklin asked. Alexandra was certain he would.

Once again, Aunt Helen inclined her head, her gesture as regal as her coronet of braids. "Especially if you find new things to paint. You're taking your watercolors, aren't you?"

"Of course." Alexandra would not consider leaving behind the one thing that had comforted her during the lonely times.

"Well, then, I shan't worry about you." Aunt Helen smiled. "You'll be safe and happy at the Springs."

Alexandra could only hope that was true.

~~~~~~

"She's gone!"

Jason Biddle stared at the man who'd been his closest friend from childhood, the man who'd convinced Father there was no reason for him to stay in that horrible place. It wasn't like Franklin to show his anger. Normally, though he seethed inwardly, Franklin maintained a calm exterior. Not today. Today he was pacing his office, reminding Jason of the dogs that raced around the perimeter fence at Serenity House, growling at anyone who dared to walk too close.

"What do you mean, gone?"

"Don't be a simpleton, Jason. Surely you understand the English language." Franklin poured himself a healthy serving of whiskey and emptied it in one swallow. After he laid the glass back on the table, he glared at Jason. "Let me phrase it differently. Alexandra Tarkington, the woman whose fortune was supposed to pay my debts and make me a rich man, has disappeared. Her aunt said she went to the Springs, but no one in Saratoga has seen her."

"I'm sorry to hear that." And even sorrier to be here. Being with

Franklin Beckman on the rare occasions when his anger erupted was not a pleasant experience. Though women had told Jason they admired his muscular body, he was no match for Franklin. The man outweighed him by fifty pounds, and every one of those pounds was pure muscle. The scuffles they'd had over the years had invariably left Jason battered and bloody, and he had no intention of provoking another fight.

"I knew you'd want to help." Apparently, the conciliatory expression he'd feigned had convinced Franklin, because he nodded as if Jason had agreed to do whatever he wanted. "That's why you're here. The chit won't talk to me, but everyone knows you're good at charming the ladies. Find her and talk her into coming back and marrying me."

"What if I can't?" Though Jason had not been introduced to the Tarkington heiress, she was reputed to be a determined woman. If she'd refused Franklin's suit, she must have had a reason.

The scowl that marred Franklin's face deepened. "If she won't marry me, I want her gone. I don't want some other man getting all that money."

"I don't want to sound like a simpleton"—the word rankled, but Jason used it deliberately, knowing it would help placate Franklin—"but how am I supposed to find her?" It was easier to focus on that challenge rather than what he might be expected to do. It was one thing to kill a man when he'd been angry. The cold-blooded murder of a woman was different.

"You always claimed to be the smart one. Prove it. Find her. Convince her I'm the man for her."

"And if I can't?"

"I'll tell the police what happened at Chadds Ford."

"How would you like to be a rich man?"

Sonny stared at the man who knew just how far from rich he was. Even though the man paid him well, it would take Sonny years—maybe even the rest of his life—to repay his debts. "You know I need money, Mr. Drummond, sir." The old man liked being addressed that way.

"If you do what I say, we'll both get what we want. You'll be able to repay me, and I'll be one step closer to having it all. I want it all." The old man pounded his fist on the larger desk, the one he dared not occupy even when his partner was absent, as if a solid thumping would change the fact that he was the junior partner.

"It should be yours. You're the one behind its success." Sonny doubted that was true, but he knew Drummond liked to be flattered.

"It will be. Soon. If you do what I say, we'll both be rich and I'll be the senior partner."

Sonny blinked in surprise. The other assignments had brought in some money, but nothing like what Drummond was suggesting. "What do you want me to do?" The sooner he knew, the sooner he could get started.

The old man gazed at the door, though there was no chance his partner would suddenly materialize, then lowered himself into the forbidden chair, propped his feet on the desk, and stared at Sonny, daring him to say something. "The girl's the first step. Find her, and then here's what you need to do." He lowered his voice.

Sonny's surprise increased, and he started to laugh. He'd done many things for the old man, but never that.

"I heard you're as good as a Pinkerton."

"I've had my share of successes," Gabriel Seymour said as he assessed the man seated across the table from him. Four or five inches shorter than his own six feet, the man was blond with eyes several shades lighter blue than his. His clothing was obviously expensive, his cuff links gold. But, despite the outward trappings of wealth, Jason Biddle would blend into any crowd, unnoticed by all but the most astute observers. If Everyman had a face, it would be this one.

His appearance was ordinary; his demeanor was not. Though Biddle's voice was calm enough that he could have been discussing the weather, his eyes betrayed both fear and anger, telling Gabe he had a personal stake in whatever it was he wanted him to investigate. Gabe's office, which looked more like a parlor, was designed to put his clients at ease, but Biddle's shoulders and neck were tense.

"What can I do for you, Mr. Biddle?"

The man, who'd declined Gabe's offer of coffee, leaned forward. "I want you to find Calvin Tarkington and put him behind bars."

Gabe didn't recognize the name, but that wasn't unusual. The majority of his cases involved average citizens, not men whose names were prominent in society circles or newspaper articles. Whether they were famous, infamous, or somewhere in between, Gabe rarely failed in finding them. That was his job. Prosecuting them was not.

"I'm not a policeman, Mr. Biddle. I'm an investigator." And this man's accent, though he tried to disguise it, was East Coast, setting Gabe's antennae quivering and making him wonder why he'd traveled to Columbus to hire him. Gabe was good at his job, but there were equally good investigators closer to Biddle's home.

Gabe's potential client nodded. "I know that, but if you can find evidence that Tarkington is swindling innocent people, he'll go to jail."

"Possibly." Gabe refused to offer false promises, particularly when he wasn't certain he'd agree to help this man. While Biddle sounded sincere, Gabe's instincts told him this man was hiding something important, and that made him cautious. "I can't guarantee the results of the judicial system. Juries can be convinced to let flagrant criminals go free."

When Biddle indicated his understanding, Gabe continued. "Tell me what you know about Tarkington and why he's important to you."

Biddle's eyes flashed with anger. "He killed my father."

Anger instead of sorrow. Gabe made a mental note of his client's emotion. Anger was understandable, particularly if the killing was recent and Biddle hadn't had time for grief to settle in. But it would, and when it did, it was there to stay. Gabe knew all too well that though the pain would ebb eventually, it would never disappear.

He fixed his gaze on Biddle. "How did Calvin Tarkington murder your father? I thought you said he was a swindler."

"He is. And, no, he didn't pull the trigger, but he might as well have." Biddle's voice, no longer calm, rose as his anger turned to fury. "That lying, swindling, no-count—"

Gabe held up a hand. "I get the idea. What exactly did he do?"

"He convinced my father to invest in a new shipping line. He claimed the shares would double—maybe triple—in value in the first year. That's why only a few men were being invited to invest at the beginning."

Gabe's heart lurched at the painfully familiar story. Substitute "bank" for "shipping line," and you had the scheme that had bankrupted Pa.

"My father invested every penny he owned, then borrowed from his friends." Biddle's face contorted with pain. "He even pawned my mother's jewelry so he could buy more shares."

Fortunately, Pa hadn't gone that far. He'd lost only his own savings in the investment that was supposed to pay for the expensive treatments Ma needed. Rather than let Biddle continue, Gabe completed the story. "It was all a sham. There was no shipping line, and the only person who made money was Calvin Tarkington. No one could prove it, though, because his name wasn't on any of the documents."

Biddle nodded. "Precisely. How did you know?"

Because it was my father's story and the reason I became an investigator. Because schemes like that made me realize that the only way to ensure justice prevails is to help root out dishonesty.

Biddle didn't need to know how closely his story mirrored Gabe's, so Gabe said only, "It's a common enough ploy."

Biddle crossed and uncrossed his legs, then began to tap the floor with one foot. "How common is it for men to shoot themselves because they're ashamed of how gullible they were?"

"I don't know." Pa hadn't done that. He'd simply faded away after Ma's death, losing the will to live along with his wife and his savings. Though not as dramatic as the elder Biddle's suicide, it had still been a tragedy.

"I want justice, Mr. Seymour. I want Calvin Tarkington stopped before he can destroy another family. I want him to rot in jail while he pays for the damage he's already done." Biddle rose and looked down at Gabe. "Will you help me?"

His previous doubts vanished, leaving only one possible answer. Gabe couldn't change what had happened to either his father or Jason Biddle's, but maybe if he stopped Calvin Tarkington from continuing his deceptions, Biddle would be able to put his anger aside, and maybe—just maybe—Gabe would find the peace that had eluded him for so long.

"I'll do my best."

CHAPTER

Two

*L*ooky here, Clint. Sure as shootin', it's my lucky day. That purdy lady's going our way."

Alexandra tried not to shudder as the cowboy nudged his companion and pointed at her. Even from this distance, the odors of horse, sweat, and things she didn't want to identify rolled off them. Though she'd seen the duo milling around in front of the hotel as she waited for the stagecoach that would take her on the final leg of her journey, she'd hoped—foolishly, it appeared—they were simply passing by.

"What do you mean, your lucky day?" Clint slapped the first cowboy on the shoulder. "'Pears the filly's got an eye for me."

The men were closer now, close enough that there was no mistaking the glint in their eyes. Alexandra had seen the same expression on Franklin's face the night he'd demanded she marry him. That had alarmed her. This was worse, because there were two of them, neither with the veneer of gentility that had often disguised Franklin's emotions.

As the sound of horses and wheels rumbling across the hardpacked dirt announced the approach of the stagecoach, Alexandra looked around, searching for an older woman or a family she could join to put some distance between her and the cowboys. She had left New York determined to avoid this kind of attention, and so far she had succeeded, but the thought of sitting next to or, even worse, between them all the way from Dallas to Mesquite Springs made her skin crawl.

She took a shallow breath as she edged toward the coach. At least if she boarded first, she'd be able to choose a seat by a window and would not be sandwiched between the men. It would be bad enough having them close by, undoubtedly continuing to leer at her.

This was partly her fault, she admitted. She knew the risks of traveling alone. Until today, there had been no problems. She'd bought a ticket to Saratoga Springs, spending a few extra seconds to chat with the ticket agent so he'd be certain to remember her, boarded the train, then disembarked well before it reached Saratoga to begin her journey southwest.

Despite the many detours she'd taken, the journey had been uneventful, perhaps because she'd done everything she could to appear unattractive. She'd arranged her hair in a style that would have made Bridget shriek with horror, even rubbing dust into it to dull the shine. When she'd exchanged her fashionable frock for the almost shapeless black bombazine dress she'd found in a trunk in Aunt Helen's attic, Alexandra had replaced her corset with padding around her waist to hide the curves men seemed to find appealing. The frumpy look had protected her from unwanted attention until now, but Clint and his companion were problems from the top of their shabby hats to the tips of their scuffed boots.

As the driver descended from his perch, Alexandra took a step toward the stagecoach.

"Hey, little lady, let me help you with that." The first of the cowboys reached for the small valise that Alexandra refused to relegate to trains' luggage compartments or the back of a stagecoach. Containing a few toiletry items, a book to while away the long hours, her Bible, and her watercolors, it was one thing she had no intention of losing.

"Thank you, sir, but I can manage by myself." She kept her voice low and firm.

"My pardner's right," the one named Clint insisted. "A purdy little thing like you shouldn't have to carry a bag."

This was the one thing the cowboys had in common with Papa, the belief that ladies were weak. The fact that Alexandra had made it to Texas on her own proved they were wrong.

As Clint tried to wrest the valise from her, his hand brushed hers, reminding her of the way Franklin had grabbed both of her hands the night he'd demanded she marry him. Alexandra forced the memory away and fixed a steely gaze on Clint. Though it took every ounce of willpower she possessed not to recoil, she was determined not to let these men know how much their presence disturbed her.

"The answer is still no."

"All righty, folks. We're ready to board." The coachman opened the door and grinned at Alexandra. "Ladies first."

Ignoring the cowboys who stood so close that their rank odor made her want to hold a perfumed handkerchief over her nose, she began to make her way toward the coach. She was so intent on giving no sign of being aware of the cowboys' attention that she barely noticed the sudden hush or the sound of bootheels on the boardwalk. A second later, a man appeared at her side, brushing the cowboys aside as though he—not they—had every right to accompany her.

"Darling! I thought I'd missed you."

Alexandra looked around in confusion. There were no other unaccompanied women in sight, but this total stranger was giving her a smile that would have melted any woman's heart, one that lit a spark inside her. Did he somehow think she was his darling?

He was as tall as the cowboys, but that was where the resemblance ended. This man was dressed in what she recognized as a custom-made suit with a shirt as white as though it had been laundered only this morning. His dark brown hair was neatly cut, his eyes the deep blue of Aunt Helen's sapphire ring. The one detail that kept him from being the picture of a gentleman was the bump on his nose where it had obviously been broken.

"Play along with me," he murmured, "unless you want to sit next to them." His breath was fresh, not reeking of tobacco and cheap whiskey, his voice low and confidential, the kind of voice a woman would find difficult to resist.

"I assure you I have no ulterior motives," he continued. "I simply didn't like the welcome those two were offering."

Alexandra looked up at the stranger, wondering who he was and why he'd want to help her. He sounded sincere, but she had thought Franklin was sincere too.

"Why should I trust you?" She smiled and kept her voice so low that the cowboys could not overhear her. To a casual observer, she was a woman greeting her beau.

"Would you rather trust them? You have to sit next to someone. Why not me?"

Despite herself, Alexandra was impressed by his reply. He hadn't tried to convince her; he'd simply stated the facts, and they were compelling.

She broadened her smile and raised her voice. "Why, darling"— she emphasized the word, hoping the cowboys would accept it as sincere—"what a surprise. I wasn't expecting you."

The stranger gave her another of those heart-melting smiles. "You didn't think I'd let you travel all that way alone, did you?" Like her, he pitched his voice so not only the cowboys but all the men who'd gathered to board the stagecoach could hear him. "Now, let's claim our seats." Turning toward the cowboys as if he'd just now noticed them, he said, "Sorry, fellas, but she's mine."

When Franklin had said the same words, she had bristled and contradicted him. Now Alexandra simply smiled. This was a pretense, designed to separate her from the cowboys, and she'd do nothing to spoil the illusion.

She accepted the tall man's assistance as she climbed into the coach, then took the seat on the far side next to the window, stowing her valise beneath her feet. The man followed and settled onto the bench next to her. Unlike the train seats, this was unpadded, but at least it had a back. The bench in the center lacked that, making Alexandra certain those passengers would have an unpleasant ride.

"I'm flattered that you decided to trust me," the stranger said as he stretched his legs, seemingly staking a claim to the limited space between the benches.

"It wasn't exactly trust." Alexandra paused for a second. "I considered my choices and you . . ." She wrinkled her nose. "Smelled better."

When he'd managed to subdue his mirth, Gabe turned his attention back to his companion. No question about it: she was an amazing woman. She hadn't needed his help in dealing with the cowboys, but as he'd told her, she had to sit next to someone, and so did he. From the instant he'd spotted her standing between those two overly friendly men, her stance shouting defiance though she'd kept her voice well-modulated, he'd wanted to meet her.

He probably wouldn't see her again once they reached their separate destinations, but he couldn't deny the force that had propelled him toward her. And, though they'd spent only a few minutes in each other's company, he knew she was unique—a woman who could find humor in a less than amusing situation.

"So, you prefer bay rum to horse?"

Gabe was glad he'd had the chance to wash up last night. He'd bear some signs of travel when he reached Mesquite Springs, but he wanted to make a favorable impression on Calvin Tarkington or Calvin King, as he appeared to be calling himself these days.

"Bay rum and good manners," she said with another of those smiles that made Gabe's pulse accelerate.

"An unbeatable combination." As were her sense of humor and confident tone of voice.

She was prettier than she appeared at first glance. Not only did her face have a fine bone structure that would age well but, unless he was mistaken, that was padding, not fat, around her waist. Her hair was undeniably dusty, but the way the dirt clung to every strand made him suspect she'd rubbed the contents of a dustbin into her hair. It seemed the pretty young lady had deliberately tried to disguise her natural beauty. A wise move and one that raised her another notch in Gabe's estimation.

He also appreciated the way she didn't need to fill every second with conversation. Instead, she sat quietly, apparently assessing the other passengers. The cowboys seemed to have accepted that she wasn't available and had chosen seats on the other bench with a back, allowing an older couple to share Gabe and the pretty lady's bench. When the last passengers boarded and took their seats on the center bench, they chose to face the front of the coach, leaving Gabe and his companion facing their backs. That was fine with him, because it meant there'd be no need to deflect their conversation.

As the driver slammed the door shut, Gabe smiled at the woman by his side. "Since we're going to be sitting together for a while, we might as well introduce ourselves. I'm Gabe Seymour."

The saucy smile she'd plastered on her face faded, and she seemed to hesitate for a second. "I'm Alexandra Tarkington."

Was this what being struck by lightning was like? Gabe felt like his head was whirling, and all his senses seemed to have been heightened. He hadn't expected to meet the daughter of the man he was investigating. He'd been puzzled to find she lived in New York with an elderly relative while Tarkington had his offices in Cincinnati, but there'd been no reason to delve more deeply, since Tarkington's daughter wasn't part of Gabe's investigation. It was Tarkington he needed to find.

Phineas Drummond, Tarkington's junior partner, claimed not to know his partner's whereabouts. That had to be a lie. Fortunately, the woman who cleaned Tarkington's and Drummond's office had been more forthcoming and had overheard Tarkington saying something about a place in Texas called Mesquite Springs.

That had been the break Gabe had needed. It hadn't taken long to learn that a man calling himself Calvin King was opening a grand hotel there. Some might call it coincidence, but Gabe was convinced that Calvin King was none other than Calvin Tarkington, father to the woman seated next to him.

"I'm pleased to meet you, Miss Tarkington." More pleased than she'd ever know. Besides making this leg of the journey enjoyable, she could also be the key to getting close enough to Tarkington to uncover his next scheme before anyone was hurt.

The corners of her mouth lifted in a smile that Gabe doubted had anything to do with the bumpy start to their journey. The coach lurched forward, then listed to one side as it made its way across the rutted street.

Apparently unfazed, the woman who'd made him laugh continued to smile. "It's a long way from 'darling' to 'Miss Tarkington.' Why not call me Alexandra?"

"Only if you'll call me Gabe."

"That seems fair." For the first time since they'd boarded the coach, she seemed to relax, letting her spine touch the seatback. "Where are you headed, Gabe?"

"Most people haven't heard of it, but I'm going to a little town in the Hill Country. Mesquite Springs." He watched her carefully, wondering how she'd react to their common destination. As he'd expected, she was surprised, but he saw no concern in her eyes.

"I've heard of it. In fact, that's where I'm going." She paused for a second, probably deciding how much to share with him. "I want to spend some time with my father."

The father who lived half a continent away from her and who, if Gabe's information was accurate, saw her only once a year.

"Does he like living there?"

She gave a little shrug. "It's not really his home, but he's there on business for a while. I decided this was a good opportunity for me to see Texas and the Hill Country."

Others might not have noticed the way her explanation sounded rehearsed, but years of experience had taught Gabe to look beyond the words. Alexandra Tarkington was hiding something.

"So, this is your first trip out here." If he was going to discover her secrets, keeping her talking was his best approach.

"Yes. How about you?"

He nodded. "Me too."

Those blue eyes that had intrigued him from the first time he'd looked into them darkened as she spoke. "Am I being too forward if I ask why you're going to Mesquite Springs?"

Perhaps it would have been too forward under normal circumstances, but there was nothing normal about the way they'd met. Besides, her question gave Gabe a chance to practice his story. Alexandra wasn't the only one hiding things.

"No, darling." He winked as he pronounced the last word and was gratified by her grin. "You're not being presumptuous. I'm at a crossroads in my life." That much was true. "My parents died." That was true too, although their deaths weren't as recent as she might have inferred from his somber expression. "I had no reason to stay in Columbus, so I decided to explore different parts of the country."

The way her eyes filled with compassion told Gabe his story sounded plausible. That was good, because this was part of what he planned to tell her father.

"I've never been to Texas, and I've never lived in a small town, so when I read about a hotel opening in Mesquite Springs, it seemed like as good a first destination as any."

"Papa's hotel." Surprise and what sounded like wonder filled her voice.

"Really? You didn't mention that your father's business was running hotels."

"It isn't. Well," she said, obviously reconsidering, "it wasn't. This is his first hotel and his first business west of the Mississippi."

22

Tarkington was either expanding his reach or avoiding places where he'd perpetrated other frauds. He was also changing his process. The King Hotel appeared to be a real place, and there'd been no indication that Tarkington sought investors for it. So why was he building it and how did it fit into his plans to fleece investors? Those were the questions Gabe needed to answer.

"What an amazing coincidence." And a fortunate one for him. "We're both going to the same place in the same town. This must be my lucky day." Gabe wondered if Alexandra recognized the claim as the one the first cowboy had made.

"Mine too." The sparkle in her eyes told him she had.

"Because you don't have to sit between two overly friendly cowboys?" Oh, teasing her was fun.

"Because the smell of bay rum is infinitely preferable to horse."

"What about my scintillating conversation? Doesn't that count for anything?"

She raised a perfectly arched eyebrow. "What do you think?"

Three

*T*he gentle bantering continued, and as it did, Alexandra realized how much she appreciated Gabe, not only for his humorous side but because for the first time she felt that a man was seeing her as a person, not an heiress. The Tarkington name meant nothing to him. She was simply Alexandra, a woman on her way to visit her father. What a refreshing feeling!

Refreshed was not how she felt when the coach rumbled into Mesquite Springs. Relieved might be a better word, because Alexandra was tired and in distinct need of a bath after what had been the most taxing part of her journey. It had been uncomfortable and exhausting but also exhilarating, the last thanks to Gabe. Not only had he kept the cowboys from annoying her but he'd made the ride as pleasant as possible by engaging her in conversation. Now they'd reached their destination.

"The town looks prosperous," she said as the coach made its way down what was probably the main street. Neatly dressed residents strolled along the boardwalk past well-cared-for shops.

Alexandra hadn't known what to expect, because Papa's last letter had been written while he was still in Cincinnati. Unlike most of the missives that had accompanied her quarterly allowance, this one included Papa's concerns about the man he'd hired to oversee the building of a hotel in Mesquite Springs. "I haven't heard from him in a while, and that worries me. It appears I need to go there sooner than I'd expected. By the time you receive this, I may already be in Texas."

And now she was here too.

"I don't see any sign of a hotel." Gabe gestured toward the street. Several shops and a church were located on the right side; more shops, the post office, and a restaurant with a bright blue door on the left.

"Okay, folks," the driver said as he stopped in front of what was obviously the mercantile. "This here's Mesquite Springs."

Gabe disembarked, then helped Alexandra out of the coach. While the driver was unloading their luggage from the back, a man emerged from an office across the street. About the same height as Gabe, he had equally dark brown hair and classic features and walked with the same assurance, but as he approached, Alexandra saw that this man's eyes were brown, not blue like Gabe's.

"Welcome to Mesquite Springs," he said as the coach continued on its way. "I'm Wyatt Clark, honored to be the town's mayor. Are you visiting friends or family here?"

"Yes," Alexandra said at the same time that Gabe replied, "No."

The mayor appeared amused. "Well, what is it? Most newlyweds agree on simple things like that. My wife and I certainly do."

Newlyweds. Alexandra felt color rise to her cheeks. How embarrassing! It was one thing for Gabe to pretend they were sweethearts to keep the cowboys from annoying her, but this was different. She couldn't mislead the town's mayor.

"We're not married, Mr. Clark. We just happened to be on the same coach."

At her side, Gabe nodded. "Miss Tarkington is here to visit her father. I was planning to stay at the hotel."

To Alexandra's surprise, the mayor seemed not to recognize her name. Instead, he focused on Gabe.

"I'm afraid that could be a bit of a problem, Mr. . . ." He paused, waiting until Gabe introduced himself before he continued. "I'm sorry, Mr. Seymour, but the hotel's not finished, and the boardinghouse is full."

Two birds chattered loudly as they flew into the tree whose shade kept the Texas sun from scorching her. On the opposite side of the street, three women stopped to admire the contents of a shop window. It was an ordinary afternoon, but the sinking feeling in Alexandra's stomach was anything but ordinary. For the first time since she'd left New York, she questioned the wisdom of coming here. Where was Papa?

Gabe seemed oblivious to her concerns. "I'm sure we'll be able to work something out," he said, giving Alexandra a small smile. Turning back to the mayor, he asked for directions to the hotel.

"I doubt you'll find a room there," Mr. Clark cautioned him, "but if you're determined to try, I'd be glad to escort you."

Gabe shook his head. "There's no need, and I imagine you're busy."

Mr. Clark's lips curved into a wry smile. "The truth is, I do have a few pressing duties, but if you can't find a place to stay, come back here. I know my wife will have some ideas."

He pointed to the building with the bright blue door. "If you're hungry, you can't beat Polly's Place. I'm not bragging, simply stating facts, when I tell you that folks come from miles away to eat my wife's cooking."

The mayor reached for Alexandra's trunk. "You can leave your bags in my office until you arrange lodging." When everything was stowed, he turned toward Gabe. "Here's how you get to the hotel."

Though her heart was pounding with apprehension, Gabe appeared unfazed by the mayor's unfamiliarity with Papa's name.

"I imagine the answers are at the hotel," he said, apparently reading her thoughts. "Speaking for myself, it feels good to be stretching my legs and breathing fresh air."

"You're right." Alexandra smiled at the memory of how many

times she and Gabe had wished for fresh air while they shared the stagecoach with the rank-smelling cowboys and the woman who'd doused her wrists with perfume that was almost as offensive as the cowboys' odors.

As tension drained from her, Alexandra looked around. The town was even more charming than her first impressions had led her to believe. She and Gabe headed west on Main Street, then turned right onto River. The stone church seemed to beckon people inside, while the exuberant cries of children in the schoolyard told her that recess was their favorite part of the day, as it had been hers.

What impressed her most was the large house across the street from the school. Three stories tall, with verandahs on the first two and wide stone steps leading to a massive front door with a leaded-glass window, it rivaled some of the mansions she had seen in New York and Saratoga. When Alexandra had pictured Mesquite Springs, she had not imagined anything of this grandeur.

"That would make a good hotel," Gabe said as they passed it.

But it wasn't one. As they turned east on Hill, the sound of hammers and workers' shouts confirmed that they were approaching a construction site. Situated next to the town's park on a spacious lot were three tents, a two-story house, and a half-finished building of a style similar to the house. Though it had been framed and men were nailing shingles onto the roof, even to Alexandra's untrained eye, it was clear that the building was far from completion. This must be Papa's hotel, but where was he and why had the mayor, who appeared to know everyone in town, never heard of him?

As she and Gabe approached the older building, Alexandra stopped short when she read the sign.

The King Hotel.

"King? Not Tarkington?" Was it possible that Papa was here but using a different name? If so, why?

Gabe shrugged, seemingly unsurprised by the sign that had made Alexandra's heart stutter. "Maybe he chose that because it's shorter."

"Maybe." But she wasn't convinced. "There's only one way to know." Without waiting for Gabe, she climbed the steps. Since the door was ajar, she didn't bother to knock before entering.

Even in its current state of disarray, it was an attractive building. A wide center hall separated the parlor and dining room of what had obviously been a private residence, and a beautifully polished staircase led to the second story. As she glanced at the rooms on either side of the entrance, Alexandra saw workers stripping wallpaper.

One looked up and frowned. "Sorry, folks, but if yer lookin' for a room, we ain't ready yet."

Gabe, who now stood at Alexandra's side, nodded. "We understand that. We're looking for the hotel's owner."

She noted that he hadn't used Papa's name.

"Mr. King?" The worker jerked his head toward the rear of the building. "I reckon he's back there in his office. Last room on the left."

It was true. It had to be true. Papa was now calling himself King. Though her head was still reeling, Alexandra managed to thank the man before she headed in the direction he'd indicated.

"Would you like me to go with you?"

The cowardly part of her wanted Gabe's company, but Alexandra knew that was not the right answer. "Thank you, but this is something I have to do alone."

Her steps were firm as she walked along the hallway, although her mind was whirling. After passing what appeared to be a music room on the left and the kitchen and the servants' staircase on the right, she reached the closed door on the left.

"What's the problem now?" Her father's voice, unmistakable and angry, rang out after she knocked on the door.

"There's no problem." *Other than the fact that you've changed your name.* "I simply wanted to see you," she said as she entered the room.

Alexandra froze at the sight of the man seated behind the desk.

Though it had been only four months since she'd spent time with Papa, she almost didn't recognize this man. Papa had never been heavyset, but he now appeared emaciated, his once ruddy complexion pasty, his hair grayer than she remembered. Only his eyes, the same shade of blue as hers, were unchanged.

Papa rose, his shock seemingly as great as hers. "Alexandra! What are you doing here? Is Helen with you?" He glanced down at his desk, hastily shoving some papers into a large gray envelope.

She'd made a mistake. She'd hoped she would be safe here. More than that, she had hoped Papa would welcome her. But he had not.

"I'm alone." Though she'd planned to tell him about Franklin, Alexandra could not shake the impression that this man who looked and acted so differently from the father she'd known, this man who'd even changed his name, was not the one to keep her safe.

Papa shook his head, a shock of hair tumbling over his forehead, his expression grim. "I never thought you were foolish, but that was a foolhardy thing to do."

He pulled out a chair in front of his desk and waited until Alexandra was seated before he continued. "You've never visited one of my businesses. Why this one? Surely you can see that this is no place for you."

"Why not?" Other than Papa's coolness, Alexandra saw nothing wrong with Mesquite Springs. The mayor had been welcoming, and the town itself was attractive. Best of all, it was far enough from New York that Franklin was unlikely to find her.

Though there was a second chair in front of the desk, Papa did not take it. Instead, he'd returned to the other side of the desk, letting three feet of wood separate him from her.

"Why not?" He echoed her question. "Because I'm busy. I need to get this hotel finished. I had planned to open it on June 1, but the man I'd hoped would manage it died." Papa closed his eyes briefly, his sorrow evident.

When Alexandra expressed her condolences, he shook his head. "I can't change that, but now I'll be lucky to have it open by

Independence Day. Surely you can see that I won't have time to entertain you."

"I don't need to be entertained." Alexandra hadn't expected to be treated as a guest. She'd wanted to spend more time with Papa than his brief holiday visits had allowed, to become part of his daily life. "Maybe I can help you with the hotel."

"How? You're a girl." Papa frowned. "You need to return to New York. The eastbound coach leaves this afternoon."

Alexandra's back stiffened at the realization that she was being dismissed like an unruly child. She'd been concerned by the unusual tone in his last letter; now she was more than concerned. She was worried.

"I'm not leaving until I have some answers."

"Like what?" Another frown accompanied Papa's question.

"Like why you're calling yourself King." *And why you're so different than you were at Christmas.* He'd never been overly demonstrative, but he'd never been like this. If Alexandra had to choose one word to describe the man who sat across the desk from her, it would be hostile. And that was not the Papa she knew.

He was silent for a few seconds, his expression betraying unease, but when he spoke, his words were firm. "That's simple," he said. "This is Texas. Tarkington sounded too pretentious, but the King name is respected here. It's a good name for a hotel."

"But it's not your name or mine, either."

"A name is nothing more than a label. I saw no harm in shortening mine." There was a hint of defiance in Papa's statements, as if he disliked being questioned. "Besides," he continued, "your name won't be Tarkington once you marry."

He was changing the subject to one that made Alexandra cringe. "I won't be marrying anytime soon." Not unless she found a man who loved her for herself, not her inheritance, a man who recognized that she was not a fragile piece of china.

"Maybe you should. Helen won't live forever." As Papa grimaced, fear welled up inside Alexandra.

"Are you all right?"

"Of course I am, but I'll be better when you're safely back in New York."

"I can't go back." The instant the words were out of her mouth, Alexandra regretted them. She hadn't meant to tell Papa about Franklin. Not yet.

"Why not?" For the first time since she'd entered the room, her father seemed concerned about her.

"I'm too tired to think about traveling again." That was true, even though it wasn't the whole truth. "I want to spend time with you."

Papa's expression softened. "That's not possible until the hotel opens."

"Then I'll stay until then."

Something that might have been hope lit his eyes but was extinguished a second later. "Where? If the manager's house was finished, you could stay there, but we haven't even begun construction. I sleep on a cot upstairs. I'm sorry, Alexandra, but there's no place for you here."

At least he hadn't dismissed her again. "I'll find somewhere. The mayor said his wife would help."

Papa nodded. "Wyatt and Evelyn are good people. Right now, they can help you more than I can." Sorrow tinged his words. "I wish you'd return to New York."

"I won't." This time Alexandra was careful not to say "can't." "Not for a while." She needed to discover why Papa was acting so strangely and why he looked so ill. It might be nothing more than overwork and not taking care of himself. If she stayed, she would try to convince him to slow down. At a minimum, she'd do what she could to ensure that he ate properly. And maybe, just maybe, he'd see that she belonged here with him.

"You're stuck with me, Papa."

He nodded slowly, then rose and stood next to her, putting his hand on her shoulder. "I'm glad to see you, Alexandra. Don't doubt that. I only wish things were different."

CHAPTER

Four

onny hated trains. He hated travel. Most of all, he hated failing. But so far, that's what he'd done. The old man wouldn't be happy when he learned that Tarkington's daughter was no longer in New York and that this woman was refusing to tell him where she'd gone. Drummond hated delays, and so did he, especially when a rich reward was waiting for him.

"My niece's whereabouts are none of your concern." The tiny silver-haired woman's expression left no doubt that she considered Sonny beneath her notice. "Suffice it to say that she is not here now."

"It's important, ma'am," he said, trying his best to sound humble rather than angry. "I have a message from her father."

This time the woman raised an eyebrow and fixed her gaze on him for a long moment before she shook her head. "I doubt that. Calvin Tarkington does not send messengers."

But Calvin's partner did.

"I must see her." Sonny hated the desperation that crept into his voice.

"My answer remains the same." With another haughty look, the heiress's aunt closed the door in Sonny's face.

He stood there for a moment, knowing he would not go back to Cincinnati until he'd found Alexandra Tarkington and done what Drummond wanted. But how could he complete his mission—for that's what it was—when he had no idea where the gal was?

He spun on his heel, then stopped when he heard a woman call out, "Sir. Sir."

He turned and donned his most charming smile for the servant who'd opened the door of the aunt's house.

"Don't tell my mistress I said this, but I heard where Miss Al-exandra was going. She's in the Springs with her cousin."

Sonny grinned. Once again, he'd escaped failure.

The slump of Alexandra's shoulders as she emerged from the office told Gabe the reunion hadn't gone well.

"What's wrong?" he asked as he reached her side, intending to escort her wherever she was going.

Her shrug appeared casual, but the pain in those pretty blue eyes left no doubt of her anguish. "Nothing." She shook her head. "Everything. Being here isn't turning out the way I'd expected."

Choosing to misinterpret the reason for her distress, Gabe said, "It's a shame the hotel isn't finished. It'll be a showplace when it's done, something to rival that house on River Street."

While she'd been with her father, he'd followed the sound of hammering to the hotel's second story. There a worker had explained they were redoing the entire floor, constructing eight bed-chambers. The building next door, he'd learned, would be a twin to this one on the outside but would have six bedrooms on its first floor, eight on the second. It appeared that Calvin Tarkington was expecting a large number of visitors.

When Alexandra made no reply, Gabe wondered if she'd heard him or whether she was lost in her thoughts. "Will you stay here?"

"My father wants me to go back to New York, but I'm not going to do that. I plan to stay in Mesquite Springs until . . ."

When she did not complete the sentence, Gabe nodded. "Then it appears we both need the mayor's help." He bent his arm, inviting Alexandra to place her hand on it. "I imagine you're as hungry as I am. Let's see what the restaurant has to offer before we throw ourselves on the mayor's mercy."

A faint smile tipped the corners of her lips upward. That was progress, even though she said little as they retraced their steps.

When they reached the restaurant and he opened the bright blue door, the delicious aromas made Gabe's mouth water. There was nothing fancy about Polly's Place, but the contented expressions on the diners' faces confirmed that the food tasted as good as it smelled.

"Welcome to Polly's Place and to Mesquite Springs." The woman who greeted them was a few inches shorter than Alexandra, her hair a shade or two lighter, her eyes hazel rather than blue. Though Gabe suspected many men would find her attractive, in his opinion she paled next to Alexandra.

"Are you the mayor's wife?" Alexandra asked with a smile that matched the woman's. Either she had recovered from her disappointment or she was a good actress.

"I'm afraid not." The woman's slightly forced laugh made Gabe believe there was more to her answer than she was admitting. "As far as Wyatt's concerned, I'm nothing more than his sister's pesky friend. Evelyn's the lucky one."

Gabe's supposition was correct. This woman had once set her sights on Wyatt Clark.

"I should have introduced myself." This time her laugh was both self-deprecating and sincere. "I'm Laura Downey, and I work for Evelyn. We already know who you are." She looked around the room, then started toward an empty table. "I figure you're hungry, so I'll wait until you've finished eating before we talk about where you're going to stay."

It sounded as though everything had been decided. Gabe knew small-town gossip traveled quickly, but he suspected this wasn't a case of the rumor mill. "Wyatt must have told you about our possible predicament."

"He did. Now, would you prefer chicken and dumplings or pot roast? They're both delicious."

Laura did not exaggerate.

"These are the best dumplings I've ever tasted," Alexandra said a few minutes later after she'd swallowed her first bite.

Gabe couldn't disagree. "I've had a lot of pot roast in my life, but none as tender and flavorful as this." Not only was the food delicious, but to his relief, Alexandra was more relaxed than she'd been when they left the hotel, confirming the wisdom of insisting they eat.

"If everyone's as friendly and helpful as the mayor and Laura, I can see why Papa chose Mesquite Springs for his hotel."

If Jason Biddle was correct, there had been other motives, but Gabe had no intention of raising that subject with Alexandra. As far as he could tell, she had no idea her father might be involved in unscrupulous dealings.

"I agree. Maybe it's because it's a small town, but it feels comfortable." He hadn't expected Mesquite Springs to be so appealing. If he wanted to make his guests feel welcome, Calvin Tarkington had chosen well.

Laura emerged from the kitchen accompanied by a pretty blonde whose thickening waist told Gabe she was expecting what Ma would have called a blessed event. "I hope you're enjoying your meal," the blonde said when they reached the table. "I'm Evelyn Clark."

Alexandra smiled and laid down her fork. "The mayor's wife and the best chef in Texas."

"Half of that is true," Evelyn agreed. "I am Wyatt's wife, and it seems I'm also the town's hospitality committee." She lowered her voice to prevent eavesdropping. "Wyatt told me you might need a place to stay until the hotel opens. Here's what we suggest." She gestured toward Laura. "Laura's parents own the largest house in town. You passed it on your way to the hotel. They've invited Miss Tarkington to stay there."

"If you want to, that is," Laura clarified. "I hope you will."

Alexandra's relief at having temporary accommodations was palpable. "That's very kind of you, but are you sure? Papa said the hotel won't be open for another two months."

That was longer than Gabe had expected, but he was hardly an expert on hotel construction.

Laura nodded. "You're welcome to stay for as long as you like."

"Then I accept. Thank you."

Evelyn turned toward Gabe. "Although the Downeys have room for you, I'm not sure it would be seemly, since you and Miss Tarkington are not married."

"I can sleep in the livery if necessary." It wouldn't be ideal, but he agreed with Evelyn that propriety needed to be considered.

"That won't be necessary," Laura assured him. Though she appeared to want to say more, she let Evelyn continue the conversation.

"Sam Plaut—he's Mesquite Springs's attorney—just returned from some time in the East. He has rooms above his office and said he'd welcome a companion."

"Thank you." Gabe was amazed by the speed with which the women had arranged everything. It had been less than an hour since he and Alexandra had left the stagecoach. Somehow, though Evelyn and Laura had been greeting customers and serving meals, they'd also found accommodations for him and Alexandra.

Gabe didn't know if this was typical of small towns or unique to Mesquite Springs. He did know that his comfort with this small Texas town continued to increase.

He smiled at Evelyn. "Your husband was right when he said you'd find a solution."

"We try. We pride ourselves on being a friendly, peaceful town."

Was it only his imagination, or had Evelyn emphasized the word "peaceful"?

CHAPTER

Five

*A*re you sure you like the room?"

Alexandra turned from the trunk she'd been unpacking, astonished by Laura's question. She would have been happy sharing a small room, so long as it was clean. Instead, this was as large as her room at Aunt Helen's and just as well furnished. The only thing she was sharing with Laura was the bathing room, which had allowed her to wash away both the travel dust and the dirt she'd used to help disguise her hair.

"Of course I like it. It's beautiful, and the view from the verandah is wonderful." Though Laura's room was at the front of the house, Alexandra's faced the backyard, making it quieter and—at least in her opinion—more peaceful. "Why would you think I wouldn't be pleased with it?"

Laura seemed unconvinced. "I can tell you're used to nice things. The dress you were wearing when you arrived was out of style, but the fabric was expensive, and you must have bought this one in New York or Boston." She gestured toward the peach-colored frock with its apricot sash and piping. "I wasn't sure how my home would compare to where you lived before."

"I hadn't realized there would be such luxury in Texas." Whenever she'd thought of the Lone Star State, Alexandra had pictured the primitive log cabins she'd been told were normal on the frontier. She'd seen no log cabins in Mesquite Springs, and *primitive* was not a word anyone would apply to the Downeys' house. "Your home is beautiful."

Appearing more relaxed, Laura opened the armoire and laid the stack of Alexandra's shirtwaists on one of the shelves. "Texas is different from the East, isn't it? I'd never admit it to my parents, but it was a bit of a shock when they sent me to a finishing school in Charleston."

So that was where she'd developed her eye for fashion. Alexandra had wondered after Laura's comment about her black dress being out of date, since *Godey's Lady's Book* had featured a similar style earlier this year, declaring it a classic mourning gown.

"I wasn't prepared for the differences," Laura continued. "People were more formal there, and it took a while to make friends." She turned, her expression earnest as she looked at Alexandra. "I do hope we'll be friends. I need one right now."

And so did Alexandra. She'd hoped Papa would welcome her and that they could become friends as well as parent and child, but that hadn't happened. Laura's overture was as welcome as her parents' offer of a temporary home. Only one thing confused Alexandra.

"Isn't Evelyn your friend as well as your boss?" The interactions between the two women seemed to indicate a more than professional relationship.

"Yes, of course, but her life is changing now that she's married and expecting a child. Dorothy—she's the mayor's sister—was my closest friend, but she's getting married this week. And even if she weren't, she's so busy with the newspaper that we don't see each other as often as we used to. That leaves me the only old maid."

Laura appeared almost woebegone, making Alexandra determined to cheer her. "I'd hardly call you an old maid. You're probably younger than I am."

"I'm twenty-two."

Alexandra let out a soft hoot. "I was right. You're still a young-ster. I'm an ancient twenty-four, but despite my advanced years, I don't feel like an old maid, and you shouldn't either." Being single was far better than being married to someone who loved her inheritance, not her.

To her relief, Laura laughed. "You're making me feel better."

"And you've already made me feel better. The hot bath was just what I needed." That and the warm welcome both elder Downeys had given her. Mrs. Downey had wrapped her arms around Alexandra and announced that she'd always wanted a second daughter. Though Mr. Downey had been less effusive, his welcome had been genuine—so different from Papa's.

Alexandra shook herself mentally and tried to convince herself that the reason Papa had seemed so cold was that he'd been surprised to see her. By tomorrow, he'd be used to the idea that she was here and would be more welcoming. One thing was certain: she was not going to leave Mesquite Springs. She'd found a refuge here, and while it might be only temporary, she had no intention of abandoning it until she had a plan for her future.

"You can have a bath every day if you teach me how to arrange my hair like yours." Laura's words reined in Alexandra's thoughts. "I love those curls."

She wrinkled her nose, glad to be thinking about something other than Papa and the future that remained out of focus. "Someone should. I've spent most of my life trying to tame my hair, but nothing works."

Laura exchanged a sympathetic look with Alexandra. "And I've scorched my hair more times than I can count trying to make curls like yours. Mother tells me to be content with what I have."

"That's good advice."

"Did your mother say that too?"

Alexandra shook her head. "Mama died when I was seven. I don't remember her ever talking about hair." The memories had faded, leaving her with nothing but fragments, the most vivid of which was her mother reading her stories at bedtime before Mama became so ill that she could not leave her own bed. Alexandra remembered laughing at one of them, but though she'd tried desperately to recall the story itself, she had failed.

Laura reached out to lay her hand on Alexandra's, squeezing it in an attempt to comfort her. "I'm so sorry. I can't imagine what it must have been like to lose her. What did you do?"

"Papa sent me to New York to live with my aunt—my great-aunt, really. I've lived there ever since."

"And now you're in Mesquite Springs. Father said the man who's building the hotel is your father, even though his name is King, not Tarkington."

"He told me he shortened it to make it more Texan." Or maybe he, like Alexandra herself, was trying not to be found. As the thought popped into her mind, she blinked in surprise. Where had that come from? Surely Papa had no reason to hide.

"I agree with your father. King looks better on the sign than Tarkington would."

But appearance wasn't everything. Tarkington was her name, and Alexandra was proud of it. If the hotel were hers, it would bear her name. But it wasn't hers.

~~~~~

Jason spurred the horse. Normally, galloping helped calm him, but today nothing was working. Despite everything he'd done, everything he'd told himself, he was restless and worried. His brain told him he'd hired the best man for the job. Even though it took extra time, he'd known he couldn't approach a local investigator, because the Biddle name was well-known here in New York. He didn't want someone from Cincinnati, because there was no guarantee that that man wouldn't be one of Tarkington's cronies. Columbus had seemed like the ideal spot—relatively close to Cincinnati but far enough from New York that he ran little risk of being recognized.

Seymour was custom-made for the job. A young man with a sterling reputation for successful investigations. A man who worked alone. A man who was willing to travel. Jason had known the challenge would be convincing him to find Tarkington, but when one of Seymour's neighbors mentioned what had happened to his father, Jason knew the man would not be able to resist his story.

He'd paid Seymour in cash, asked for weekly reports, and told him not to expect replies. That way there'd be no record of where he was . . . or wasn't. What bothered him was the waiting. Jason knew it might take several weeks to track down Tarkington, but until he heard from Seymour, he couldn't suppress his worries.

What if he'd been wrong? What if the Tarkington heiress wasn't with her father? What would he tell Franklin? The man didn't tolerate failure. The mere thought of what he'd do if Jason failed turned his legs to jelly. If anyone learned that he was responsible for that death in Chadds Ford, he'd be sent back to Serenity House permanently.

He couldn't let that happen. He *wouldn't* let it happen.

CHAPTER

Six

I can't tell you how much I appreciate this." Gabe was surprised by the man who'd offered him a room. He'd thought Mesquite Springs's attorney would resemble the ones he'd known in Columbus, but Sam Plaut was more muscular than he would have expected for a man who spent his days behind a desk, and he lacked the swagger Gabe had come to associate with lawyers. What surprised him was the pain he saw in Sam's eyes. This man, who appeared to be a year or so younger than Gabe, had known his share of suffering.

"This?" Sam's raised eyebrow seemed to dispute Gabe's assertion.

While the apartment over the lawyer's office was small, consisting of two modestly sized bedrooms and a tiny kitchen, it was preferable to sleeping in the livery. Plus, the company was better. Gabe was accustomed to making rapid assessments of people, and his instincts told him Sam Plaut was someone he could trust.

"You're doing me a favor." Sam flicked his hand over his forehead, brushing away a stubborn lock of hair that was almost the same shade of brown as Alexandra's.

"I used to live on my parents' ranch, but after almost a year back East, I wanted more independence." The way his brown eyes darkened when he said "East" told Gabe that the pain he'd sensed was connected to that time in Sam's life. "Having you here gives me a good excuse for not living with them. Stay as long as you'd like."

"I'm the one who's benefiting." Gabe tossed his bag onto the floor in the room Sam had offered him. There'd be time to unpack later. Right now, he wanted to learn more about his host and whatever had caused the pain. Though he believed Sam was trustworthy, he had to be careful. "Where did you live in the East?" He made it sound like a casual question.

As Gabe had expected, Sam appeared uneasy and hesitated briefly before saying, "Outside Philadelphia. Where are you from?" It was clear that Sam wanted to shift the focus from himself. "You don't sound like an Easterner."

"You have a good ear. I'm from Columbus."

"What's it like?"

Gabe shrugged as he sought a way to divert Sam's attention. Like his host, he was unwilling to talk about himself. He leaned against the wall, feigning nonchalance. "It's a city."

"And now you're here in what no one will ever call a city. At least I hope not." A frown crossed Sam's face. "The town's been growing faster than some might like. Not everyone welcomes change."

"Like the hotel?" Gabe might not be able to delve into his host's past, but perhaps he could discover the town's feelings about Calvin Tarkington.

Sam nodded. "And the newspaper. It's fairly new. Brandon came while I was gone."

"What's the problem with the paper?" Knowing newspaper editors normally had their fingers on a town's pulse, Gabe planned to talk to this Brandon and wanted to be prepared.

"I've heard a few people complaining that their news wasn't given as much prominence as their neighbors', and others think the subscription rates are too high. There are even some who don't believe Dorothy should write for it once she's married, but they're a minority."

"Dorothy?" Experience had taught Gabe to collect every detail that was offered, then sift through them later.

"Dorothy Clark, soon to be Dorothy Holloway. She's the mayor's sister and is set to become Brandon's bride on Saturday. She's been writing for the *Chronicle* since the first issue."

Though Gabe wasn't aware of any women writers for the Columbus newspaper, he'd heard that lady authors sometimes adopted men's names.

"And people disapprove of her writing?"

Sam made a show of closing the shutters to keep the afternoon sun from overheating the room. "It's mostly old-timers who think a woman's place is at home, cooking meals and raising children."

As Gabe's mother had done. "What about the hotel? What are the complaints about it?"

"What you might expect—the noise of construction, the fear that there'll be more crime with temporary workers in town, the fact that the hotel's being built on Mrs. Lockhart's extra lots. Some folks liked them empty, because they made the park seem larger."

Nothing unusual there. "Who's Mrs. Lockhart?" If he was going to uncover Tarkington's scheme, Gabe needed to recognize all the players.

"The widow who used to own the house that's being converted. She had the only triple lot in town."

And that would have made her house ideal for Tarkington's hotel.

"Some folks think she's unhappy that she moved to the boardinghouse, but my mother says Mrs. Lockhart's probably relieved that she doesn't have to take care of a large house. My father claims it's the price of progress and that the hotel will be good for the town."

"What do you think?" It was more than an idle question.

"I'm not sure."

And until he learned more, neither was Gabe.

Despite Sam's protests that it wasn't necessary, Gabe made them a quick supper before heading out, determined to meet Calvin Tarkington. As he'd expected, the workers were gone for the day, but someone had left the front door ajar. Taking that as an invitation, Gabe entered Mrs. Lockhart's former home.

"Mr. King," he called, raising his voice so it would carry throughout the first floor.

Alexandra's father emerged from his office. If Gabe had been surprised by Sam Plaut's appearance, he was shocked by Calvin Tarkington's. The man's clothes looked like they'd been made for someone far larger, his complexion was pasty white, and his hair had more gray than Gabe would have expected for his age.

"That's me." Though Tarkington appeared frail, his voice was firm. "What can I do for you?"

You can tell me why you're really here and why you didn't welcome your daughter. "Name's Gabe Seymour. I was hoping you'd have a room for me, but I can see the hotel's not finished."

Tarkington shrugged, as if it were of little import. "We're behind schedule. Had some problems a couple months ago. That's why I'm here to oversee everything." The story could be true, but Gabe suspected there were other reasons for Tarkington's presence.

"What brings you to Mesquite Springs?"

The question gave Gabe the opportunity to begin spinning his own story. "I've been at loose ends ever since my parents died. I need to make some decisions about how best to honor their legacy."

As he'd hoped, Tarkington's eyes lit at the word *legacy*. Though Gabe hadn't claimed it was monetary, Alexandra's father had clearly made that assumption and had begun to view Gabe as a potential client.

"I understand," he said, ushering Gabe into his office and taking the chair next to him.

The room was an ordinary one, dominated by the desk and three chairs. Other than a small bookcase on one side, the walls were bare, giving no clue to its owner's personality.

"I was in a similar position a few years ago," Tarkington continued. "You don't want to squander your inheritance." Apparently, the man hadn't noticed that Gabe had said "legacy," not "inheritance." "You want to be a good steward."

Gabe nodded. "The problem is, nothing in Columbus felt right. I thought living in a new place for a few months might help clear my mind."

Tarkington gave him a calculating look. "You strike me as a sensible young man. I think we might be able to help each other."

"I don't see how I could help you." Gabe gestured in the direction of the unfinished building. "I'm not good at carpentry."

"You don't need to be. You came on today's stagecoach, didn't you?"

Though intrigued, Gabe wasn't sure where this was leading. "Yes."

"Then you must have met my daughter."

"I met a Miss Tarkington."

"That's my daughter. Alexandra. She has this fool idea that she wants to stay here."

"Because you're here." Gabe noticed that Tarkington hadn't bothered to explain the difference in names.

"That's what she says." Frustration colored the older man's voice. "Look around, Seymour. This is no place for a gently raised girl. The problem is, she doesn't see it that way."

Alexandra hadn't exaggerated. Her father was anxious for her to leave. The question was, why. Though the hotel might still be under construction, the rest of Mesquite Springs was suitable for what Tarkington called a gently raised girl. The only reason Gabe could imagine was that Tarkington feared his daughter would uncover whatever he was hiding.

"If you can't convince her to leave, I certainly couldn't."

Tarkington sighed. "No one can. Alexandra may appear biddable, but when she makes up her mind, there's no one more stubborn."

Gabe would have called her determined rather than stubborn, but he wouldn't argue with her father. "Then how can I help?"

"You can keep her occupied. Be her friend. Pretend to court her. Do whatever it takes to keep her away from here."

It was an odd request, but everything about this discussion had been odd. When he'd first heard about the hotel, Gabe thought it would be nothing more than a shell designed to convince investors to part with their money, but if that was the case, there was no reason for the second building or the work that was being done here. The hotel appeared genuine, leaving Gabe to suspect it was a front designed to mask Tarkington's true scheme.

"If I keep her away from here, what do I get out of this? You said we could help each other." Though the prospect of spending more time with Alexandra was far from unpleasant, Gabe refused to show any enthusiasm.

"I'm starting a new company." Which meant that Gabe had been right. The hotel was not the new venture.

"No one's heard about it yet," Tarkington continued, "because I'm still working on the legalities, but once it's open, it will be one of the best investments of the decade. Maybe even the century."

The litany was the one that had led countless men into poverty. Biddle had been right. Calvin Tarkington was indeed planning to defraud others, and by some small miracle, it appeared Gabe had arrived early enough to stop him.

That was good. What was not was that Alexandra would discover her father's shady dealings if she stayed in Mesquite Springs. No wonder Tarkington wanted her to leave.

Gabe pretended to weigh his choices. "That sounds intriguing, but I need to know more. What kind of company is it?" He doubted he'd get a straight answer, but it was worth a try.

Tarkington shook his head. "All in good time, Seymour. If you keep Alexandra busy, I'll sell you shares at half what other investors will pay."

That would be an attractive proposition if the company existed. "I like the idea of getting in at the beginning of a profitable venture, but I still need to know more before I commit to anything."

"Naturally." The way he said it told Gabe that Tarkington had no intention of revealing anything anytime soon. "As soon as the hotel is finished, I'll be able to tell you more. I'll even give you a free room here, if you help me with Alexandra." He extended his hand. "Do we have a deal?"

More time with Alexandra and a reason to stay close to the older man—Gabe couldn't have devised a better plan himself.

"We do."

CHAPTER

Seven

oday would be different, Alexandra told herself as she placed three cinnamon rolls in the napkin-lined basket. When she'd wakened refreshed after the first good night's sleep she'd had since she'd left New York, hope had bubbled up inside her. Instead of dwelling on his insistence that she leave, Alexandra remembered how Papa had said he was glad to see her. That's when she'd come up with the plan.

Now that Papa had had a chance to get over his surprise at her arrival, he would be more welcoming. She was certain of it, as certain as she was that the contents of the basket would help improve his mood. Aunt Helen claimed that Papa had a sweet tooth, and, giving thanks that Laura had said she was going to make cinnamon rolls for breakfast, Alexandra decided to exploit Papa's weakness. Fortunately, there'd been more rolls than she and the Downeys had wanted, and they'd been amenable to her suggestion of sharing the extras with her father.

She poured milk into a jug, then arranged the plates and glasses in the basket, covering everything with another napkin. It was time to leave. But as she closed the front door behind her, Alexandra's attention was drawn to the schoolyard across the street.

She laid the basket on the porch floor, then stood next to the railing, watching the children approaching the stone building. Some were eager to greet friends and vie for seats on swings. Others, like the blond boy and girl who clung to each other's hands, were obviously apprehensive.

Alexandra's heart ached as she studied the nervous children, guessing them to be no more than seven. The way they walked so hesitantly, seemingly oblivious to the other youngsters, reminded her of how she'd felt her first day at school in New York. She'd been a stranger trying to find her way in a world where everyone else knew each other, where alliances had already been formed.

Were they newcomers as she'd been? Though they looked as forlorn as she had when she walked up the steps to her new school, at least they had each other. She'd been alone.

Alexandra wanted—oh, how she wanted—to race across the street, hug them, and tell them everything would be all right. But she couldn't. No one could promise them that, least of all the woman who'd tried and failed to please her father.

Her earlier enthusiasm dimmed, Alexandra reconsidered her plan. Perhaps she should wait until tomorrow to approach her father. But the aroma of cinnamon and sugar convinced her to proceed. Once the teacher had rung the bell and the pupils filed into the school, Alexandra picked up her basket and headed down Hill Street.

As she'd expected, workers were practically running from one place to the next, giving her the impression of only slightly controlled chaos. One man appeared so focused on delivering the wood he'd just sawed that he almost knocked a tiny woman to the ground when he swung the board to avoid hitting another worker.

Alarmed, Alexandra raced to the woman and put her arm around her shoulders to steady her. "Are you all right, ma'am? This is a dangerous place."

The silver-haired woman, who couldn't have been more than five feet tall, looked up at Alexandra, her gray eyes misty. "It used to be so quiet here that Timothy claimed it was as silent as a graveyard."

"You certainly can't say that now." Though the woman was no longer in danger of falling, Alexandra was concerned by the quaver in her voice and the tears she was trying to blink away. When she swayed ever so slightly, Alexandra tightened her grip. "You appear a bit shaky. I'd be happy to go home with you."

"This is my home." The woman shook her head, the action releasing one of her tears. She wiped it away and shook her head again. "It used to be my home. Now it belongs to Mr. K."

Was there no limit to the names Papa had assumed? Dismissing that thought, Alexandra turned back to the woman. "It's going to be a beautiful hotel."

"That's what Phil said. He said I'd be helping the town and leaving a legacy if I sold my house."

Though Alexandra had never heard her father mention anyone named Phil, the woman's story suggested he was the person Papa had sent here, the one who'd died. Papa had said he'd expected that man to run the hotel, but if Phil was the same man, it appeared he'd also convinced this woman to sell her home.

"Are you sorry you agreed?" Aunt Helen would chide her for prying, but Alexandra wanted to learn everything she could about her father and his hotel.

The woman shook her head. "No. Phil was right. It was time. I'm too old to take care of such a big house. This way, many will be able to enjoy my home, even if it's only for a few days. My one regret is that Phil couldn't see it."

Though her words seemed to confirm that Phil was the man who'd died, she looked up at Alexandra, her eyes once again dry. "You don't need to worry about me, young lady. I'll make it back to the boardinghouse safely, but you'd best deliver those cinnamon rolls and whatever else is in that basket before one of the workers decides he should eat them."

The hint of humor in the older woman's voice reassured Alexandra, but she had to ask once more, "Are you certain?"

"Yes."

When Alexandra dropped her arm, the woman walked away, her steps as firm as someone a decade younger. It was only when she turned the corner that Alexandra climbed the stairs to the hotel and discovered her father just inside the door, a frown on his face.

"I saw you talking to Widow Lockhart. What did she want?"

"Nothing. Mrs. Lockhart"—it was good to know her name—"was simply feeling nostalgic about her former home." Though her little speech about the benefits of leaving her house had sounded rehearsed, Alexandra had heard sincerity in her voice. If she had regrets, they were few, other than Phil's death.

Alexandra gestured to the basket she still carried. "Let's go back to your office. I have something for you." Food and a proposal.

"I have work to do." Papa's frown deepened.

"Fifteen minutes won't matter."

The frown turned into a chuckle. "You always were stubborn. All right, Alexandra, let's see what you've brought."

When they reached his office, she pulled out the plates, glasses, rolls, and jug of milk, arranging them on one side of the desk so he'd have to take the chair next to her rather than on the opposite side.

The desk was neater than yesterday, the papers that had been scattered across it now arranged in a pile, almost covering a large gray envelope. What hadn't changed was Papa's expression. He seemed a bit wary as he glanced at the papers on his desk, making Alexandra wonder whether he was hiding something.

Trying to dismiss that thought and the worry that his pallid complexion aroused, she gestured toward the food she'd brought. "I didn't know whether you'd had a proper breakfast, but you need to eat more to make up the weight you've lost."

Though he sniffed the rolls appreciatively, Papa wrinkled his nose at the glasses. "I don't drink milk."

"Have you ever had it with cinnamon rolls? It tastes different when it's paired with the right food." Alexandra didn't have to own a restaurant to know that.

Papa pulled off a piece of roll, chewed carefully, then grudgingly took a sip of milk. "Not bad."

"That's high praise, coming from you. I'll tell Laura you enjoyed her baking. And, before you protest, you can expect to see me here every day. I've made it my mission to see that you eat more." Alexandra reached over and laid her hand on her father's. "I worry about you."

"Worrying's my job. I want you back with Helen so I don't have to worry about you in addition to everything that's going on here."

Alexandra had known she wouldn't escape without that particular admonition. Rather than argue about it, she countered with her own concerns. "It's clear you're working too hard. You need a helper. That's why I'm here."

It hadn't been part of her plan when she left New York, but when Alexandra had wakened this morning, she'd realized that Papa needed a helping hand as well as more food. She could provide both.

"You? Help?" Papa couldn't hide his shock. "You're a woman. Besides, you don't know anything about hotels."

Alexandra chose to ignore his first statement. "Unless I'm mistaken, you didn't know anything about hotels when you started here."

Her words appeared to hit their mark, because his lips twisted in what could have been anger. "Be that as it may, no daughter of mine is going to work here. You'd only be in the way."

Alexandra bridled at his supposition that she was helpless. "I'm certain there are things I can do."

"The answer is no." Papa took another large bite of roll, washed it down with a gulp of milk, then surprised her by asking, "Did you bring your paints?"

"Yes, of course."

"Then there is something you can do." He gestured toward the bare walls. "Paint something to brighten this room."

Though she did not see how that would help him, Alexandra could not refuse the request. "What would you like?"

"Whatever you think best. You're the artist in the family. I'm the one who needs to finish this hotel before the investors' meeting."

And painting would keep her from interfering. Alexandra bit back her anger. She'd been a fool to think anything had changed. Since she'd refused to return to New York, Papa had sought a different way to keep them apart. What he didn't realize was that she was no longer a child to be ordered around. She was a grown woman, a determined one.

She took a deep breath before seizing on the second part of Papa's statement. "Investors? Don't you usually have them before you begin a project?" Though he hadn't shared details of his past business ventures, Papa had told her that the first step in each was to arrange for investors.

"Of course. I didn't need any for the hotel. They're for my next project."

Alexandra blinked in confusion. She had thought Papa's sole reason for coming to Mesquite Springs was to build the hotel. Now it appeared he had more in mind. "What is it?"

"A secret right now."

"Even from your daughter?"

He nodded. "I need to be very cautious. I can't risk anyone hearing about it too early. My man was supposed to take care of everything, but he didn't."

The pieces were starting to fit together. "Phil?"

Papa looked as surprised as he had when he'd first seen her. "How'd you hear about him?"

"Mrs. Lockhart mentioned him. She said he convinced her to sell her home."

"He did more than that. He's the one who found Mesquite Springs for me. I had big plans for him, but now he's gone." Papa's face contorted in what appeared to be genuine sorrow before he drained the glass of milk, then rose, his actions saying more clearly than words that he would not discuss the man he'd once employed.

"Thank you for bringing me food. You were right. It tasted good, but now I have to get to work."

Alexandra placed the empty dishes in the basket and covered them with the napkin. "I'll be back."

"I know you will." Though there was an ironic tone to his words, Papa did not reiterate his demand that she leave. She was making progress.

Alexandra was still smiling when she descended the front steps and saw Gabe approaching from the east.

"Did you have food in that basket?" he asked as he reached her.

"I did. I brought some cinnamon rolls for my father."

"And he ate them all."

"We did. I knew he wouldn't eat alone, so I brought one for myself." Thankfully, the ploy had worked.

Gabe wrinkled his nose. "Sam and I had to content ourselves with scrambled eggs and toast."

"Those sound good too."

It was ordinary conversation, but Alexandra couldn't deny that she was enjoying it. The reason was easy to find: Gabe. The time they'd spent together on the coach had forged a camaraderie between them. While they didn't always agree, their disagreements had none of the tension that had characterized her time with Papa. Instead, their disagreements were like flint against steel, creating sparks that made her think differently. It felt good to be with Gabe.

When they reached the edge of the park, he stopped. "Shall we explore it?"

Part of her was eager to begin the painting Papa had requested, but the other part wanted to spend more time with Gabe. Unlike many men she'd met, he was not pretentious. He didn't fawn over her; he didn't treat her like an heiress. Instead, it seemed that they were friends. Alexandra nodded her agreement.

By New York standards, the park was not large, but what it lacked in acreage it made up in charm. Live oaks lined three of the four sides, making Hill Street the primary entrance to the central grassed area. Alexandra suspected that was the site of town gatherings, while the shaded areas beckoned casual visitors to linger on one of the benches.

"Do you have time to sit?" Gabe asked when they reached the northwest corner and a bench that looked particularly appealing.

Alexandra nodded again.

"You seem happier today," Gabe said as he brushed a few leaves from the bench. "Has your father agreed that you should stay in Mesquite Springs?"

If only. "Not exactly, although he did ask me to make a painting for him." Her heart warmed at the memory of Papa's request. Though he'd admired her watercolors in the past, she had always wondered whether his praise was perfunctory. The commission—for that's what it was, even though she wouldn't be paid—must mean he believed she had talent. If his only goal had been to distract her, he would have found another way.

"So you're going to use the crown jewels." Gabe waggled his eyebrows, making Alexandra laugh as she had the first time they'd disembarked from the stagecoach for a meal. Though the other passengers had left their hand luggage inside, she'd carried her small valise. When he'd asked whether it contained the crown jewels, she'd replied that the paints and brushes it held were almost as valuable to her.

"Once I decide on a subject, it'll be time to put the crown jewels to work. Maybe then Papa will realize I'm a grown woman. It doesn't seem to matter how old I am; he still views me as a child."

Gabe shrugged. "Maybe he's only trying to guide you."

"Is that what your parents did?" Alexandra remembered his saying they were both deceased.

"Yes. Ma was convinced she was the only one who could find the right bride for me, while Pa insisted I not settle for anything less than love."

As often as she'd deplored being the object of matchmakers'

attention, Alexandra hadn't considered that men might suffer from the same unwelcome efforts.

"It sounds like they wanted to see you settled, but they didn't succeed." She stopped, realizing she'd made an assumption. Gabe had never mentioned a wife, but that didn't necessarily mean there was none. "Are you married?"

"No, and before you ask, let me say it's because I never found the right woman, despite Ma's matchmaking."

Two birds perched on a branch overhead and squawked loudly, as if protesting Alexandra's and Gabe's presence. He waited until they'd flown away before he continued. "Let me turn the tables. Why isn't a beautiful woman like you married? You must have received proposals."

Beautiful. She'd heard the word so often that it had lost its meaning, but somehow this was different. When Franklin had called her beautiful, Alexandra had known he was flattering her, but there was no flattery in Gabe's voice. He made it seem like a statement, and the way he smiled made her wish it was true.

"I have received proposals," she told him, "but never from the right man."

"You had a busy day." Sam settled at the table, apparently accepting Gabe's declaration that he'd do all the cooking.

Gabe shrugged as he turned toward his friend. The potatoes he was dicing for stew could wait. "If you call walking around town being busy. Alexandra was busier. She started a new painting." Gabe hadn't missed the excitement in her voice when she'd spoken of it and hoped her father would appreciate the finished product.

"Alexandra, huh?"

"That's her name."

"So is Miss Tarkington."

Realizing he was being teased, Gabe sent a mock glare at Sam.

"Are you jealous because Miss Tarkington asked me to use her first name?"

"Not one bit. I just wanted to see how you'd react."

"So you treated me like a hostile witness."

Sam's innocent expression was clearly false. "I got my answer, or at least part of it. You find her attractive."

"So would any red-blooded man." The combination of those pretty blue eyes, curly brown hair, and flawless features made Alexandra's a face no man would forget. Gabe hadn't been exaggerating when he'd called her beautiful.

Sam grinned, his satisfaction at having riled Gabe apparent. "The question is whether you're planning to court her."

"It's a bit too soon for that, don't you think?" Gabe returned to dicing vegetables, not wanting Sam to study his expression and possibly realize that Tarkington's suggestion of courtship continued to echo through his brain. Gabe ought to have dismissed it unconditionally, but somehow the idea of doing more than keeping Alexandra occupied had taken hold of his imagination.

"I've just met her." Gabe turned to face his friend, determined to convince Sam that his interest in Alexandra was purely platonic. It was. Of course it was.

Sam's eyes narrowed, once again giving Gabe the feeling of being on the witness stand. "You don't need much time. When you meet the right woman, you'll know. It can happen in the blink of an eye."

"Are you speaking from personal experience?"

"That's a valid assumption." A lawyerly response if Gabe had ever heard one. "I have my eye on a special woman. And don't worry; it's not Miss Tarkington."

Though Gabe shouldn't have felt such a sense of relief, he did. "Who is she?"

Sam shook his head. "If you want to find out, you'll have to stay in Mesquite Springs a while longer."

"That's exactly what I have in mind."

CHAPTER

Eight

I'm sorry, sir, but Alexandra isn't here. She usually spends August with us."

And today was only early May. Though he was fuming internally, Sonny tried not to let his anger show. The redheaded chit who'd answered the door wasn't to blame, and while he didn't like her answer, he would not give up. It was possible she knew more than she was saying.

"I must have misunderstood." He gave her the smile that had never failed to charm impressionable girls. And this one was impressionable, no doubt about it. Sonny had seen the way her eyes widened when she'd caught sight of him and the extravagant bouquet he carried.

Ma had always claimed with a face like his, he could have any girl he wanted, that he wouldn't have to bother with the normal courting gifts of flowers, books, and candy, but Sonny wasn't taking any chances today. Too much was at stake. Alexandra Tarkington might not be here, but her cousin was, and the cousin held the key to finding the heiress. Sonny was sure of that.

He let his smile fade and adopted a hangdog expression designed to elicit sympathy. "A man shouldn't admit it, but I'm afraid I had too much champagne that evening. When I woke the next morning, all I could remember was your cousin's beauty and something she said about going to the springs. I thought she meant Saratoga, so I came here to tell her she'd stolen my heart."

That was all balderdash. Sonny had never met Alexandra Tarkington, but her cousin didn't know that, and—judging from the way she smiled at the notion of his stolen heart—she was as susceptible to sentimental drivel as he'd hoped.

"I wish I could help you, sir. If you leave your card, I'll send it to Alexandra in my next letter."

"That's most kind of you, but I wanted to surprise her." He looked down at the flowers. "Since she's not here, I hope you'll accept these."

The flush that colored her face made her freckles more prominent. Though Alexandra Tarkington was reputed to be a beauty, her cousin was not.

"Thank you, sir. They're beautiful." She sniffed the bouquet, then smiled at the fragrance.

"No more beautiful than you," he lied. "But remember now, there's no need to mention my visit. You wouldn't want to spoil the surprise."

"No, sir." She sniffed the flowers again. "This is so romantic."

It wasn't romantic at all. Either the servant had lied or she genuinely didn't know that Alexandra wasn't in Saratoga Springs. Oh, she'd boarded a train in that direction, but apparently she had never arrived.

Sonny strode down the street, his pace increasing along with his anger. He'd wasted time, first going to New York, now coming to Saratoga. Though he'd traveled hundreds of miles, all he'd learned was that Alexandra Tarkington was cleverer than old man Drummond realized. Sonny had no idea how, but she must have suspected she would be followed and had done everything she could to keep from being found.

He frowned. She might be smart, but so was he. Smart and

determined, especially since she was the key to his future. With all the money he'd have, he could leave Cincinnati and never work again. And, if she was as beautiful as he'd heard, the first part of Drummond's scheme might be downright pleasant.

Sonny pulled out his watch, his frown deepening when he saw he had an hour before the next train left this miserable town. An hour to curse the time he'd wasted. An hour to plan his next steps. The problem was, he had no idea what to do next. All he knew was that he couldn't return to Cincinnati without the heiress.

He turned the corner, then grinned at the sign he saw down the street.

"New to town?" the barkeeper asked as he entered the saloon.

"Yep. I'll have your best whiskey."

Ma had deplored the effect of strong drink, claiming it led men to do foolish things, but Sonny knew better. Whiskey wasn't responsible for his predicament. The blame lay squarely on a marked deck of cards. Whiskey deadened the pain.

The man plunked a glass of amber-colored liquid in front of him. "You came to the right place. The finest saloon in the town with the finest springs in the country."

Taking a large swallow, Sonny nodded as the man's words registered and the glimmer of an idea took hold within him. Saratoga might have the finest springs, but they weren't the only ones in the country. Maybe Alexandra hadn't lied to her aunt. Maybe she'd wanted the old woman to think she'd come here, when all the while she'd been headed to another springs. That made sense if she was as clever as Sonny was beginning to believe she was.

Which springs? There had to be a clue. Sonny wracked his brain, trying to think like a girl. Girls never grew up, did they? No matter how old they were, they needed to be protected. Sonny grinned as the pieces fell into place. If he was right—and he knew he was—she'd gone to her father.

Drummond had said that Tarkington was in Texas at some town with springs in its name. That had to be the place. What was its name? Something about a tree or a bush. Oak, pine, maple. That wasn't right. He took another swallow. It was something more western. Chaparral, sage. Still not right. He drained the glass and stared at the floor, searching for an answer. Mesquite. That was it! Mesquite Springs.

With a groan, Sonny ordered another whiskey. He'd need that and more to get through another long journey, but he wasn't going to admit defeat. No, sirree. Not with so much at stake.

"This is the first time I've attended a wedding without an invitation and without knowing either the bride or the groom." Alexandra touched the end of the tongs, testing their warmth before she began to curl Laura's hair. Though Alexandra had tried to convince her own hair to remain in a smooth chignon, Laura wanted ringlets framing her face.

"This is Mesquite Springs, not New York. Everyone knows everyone, and everyone's invited to everything." Laura kept her eyes averted from the long mirror, having told Alexandra she didn't want to see her reflection until the curls were in place. "The only reason you haven't met Dorothy and Brandon is that they've spent the week putting out a new issue of the paper and trying to decide where to live."

The first curl was done. "I'm afraid I don't understand." Every newlywed couple she knew had arranged for their first home well before the wedding.

"You wouldn't think it was complicated, but it is. There's more room in the apartment over Polly's Place. That's where Dorothy's been living," Laura explained, "but Brandon would prefer to stay in the same building as his office and printing press. There was some trouble earlier this year, so he's extra cautious. The problem with living there is that Dorothy has a dog."

Alexandra tried to dismiss the fear that Laura's casual mention of trouble had evoked. Perhaps it was simplistic of her, but she hated the idea that Mesquite Springs's peaceful appearance might be cloaking danger. Was the safety she'd felt since she'd arrived only an illusion? She hoped not.

"I suppose dogs don't mix well with paper and ink," Alexandra said as she formed a second curl.

"Exactly. They're planning to build a new house next door to the office, but they can't start until the hotel is finished. Your father's using all the workers. Now, let me see what you've done with my hair."

Laura turned to face the mirror and gasped. "You're a miracle worker. You've made me look almost beautiful."

"You are beautiful."

Laura shook her head. "I'm not, but you're sweet to say so. And now that I've seen what you can do with my hair, I'm more determined than ever that you can't leave. You need to make Mesquite Springs your home."

Her home. The thought was still bouncing through Alexandra's mind half an hour later as she and her father entered the church. Like her, Papa had been reluctant to attend the wedding of people he hardly knew, but he'd finally agreed to escort her.

Alexandra looked around. This small stone building was far different from the churches she'd attended in New York and Saratoga, with no vaulted ceiling, no stained glass, no intricate carving on the pews, and yet it gave her the same feeling of peace she'd always found in God's house.

She settled into the plain oak pew, and her eyes filled with tears as Dorothy walked down the aisle toward the man whose life she'd chosen to share. Her gown was simple but elegant, lacking the furbelows Alexandra had seen on many society brides, yet the simplicity served to highlight Dorothy's natural beauty, drawing attention to her radiant smile, a smile that brightened with each step she took.

If ever there was a joyful bride, it was Dorothy Clark, soon to be Dorothy Holloway. Alexandra heard several sighs and saw other women dabbing their eyes as Dorothy made her way toward her groom. Weddings had that effect.

The ceremony was beautiful, the looks Brandon and Dorothy exchanged along with their vows leaving no doubt of the love they shared. As the newlyweds walked slowly to the back of the church, holding hands and beaming with happiness, Alexandra felt a pang of longing. Would she ever know that kind of happiness? Would she ever find a man who loved her the way Brandon loved Dorothy?

She closed her eyes, willing her tears not to fall, and as she did, she pictured Gabe. In her imagination, he was standing in front of the altar and smiling as she walked toward him. It was nonsense, pure nonsense fueled by the emotions a wedding evoked, and yet Alexandra could not deny that she enjoyed Gabe's company more than she had any other man's. There had to be a logical explanation, but try though she might, Alexandra could not explain her feelings. They were friends, she told herself, simply friends, and to think otherwise was foolish. Alexandra Tarkington was not a foolish woman.

"Too bad there's not another exit," Papa muttered as they joined the crowd waiting to greet the bride and groom. "Never did like newspapermen."

"Why not?"

"Doesn't matter."

But it did, for there was no mistaking the way Papa stiffened as they approached the newlyweds.

"So, this is your daughter, Mr. King." Though Dorothy kept her left hand firmly in her husband's, she extended her right to Alexandra. "I can't wait for us to have a good, long chat, but I'm afraid that won't happen today."

"I should think not. You have far more important things to do than welcome a newcomer."

The bride nodded. "You're both invited to the ranch. Evelyn and Laura have made enough food for the whole county, and you won't want to miss either it or the dancing."

Without waiting for a response, Dorothy continued. "As much as I love this town, it could benefit from more women. That's one of the reasons I'm glad you're here. Evelyn, Laura, and I try to get together every week. Please say you'll come. It's Tuesday at 3:30 at Polly's Place."

The woman was like a whirlwind, knocking down any resistance Alexandra might have had. "Thank you," she said. "I'd like that."

It was time to congratulate the groom, a blond man with eyes almost as deep a blue as Gabe's and a smile as broad as his wife's.

Brandon turned toward Papa. "I want to echo my wife's invitation to join us at the Circle C."

Papa shook his head. "I'm afraid you'll have to excuse me from dancing. It's been so long that I've forgotten every step."

Alexandra doubted that. Mingling with her memories of her mother reading bedtime stories was the image of Mama and Papa dancing in the parlor. There'd been no music other than Mama's humming, but Alexandra could still recall the happiness that had lit their faces.

That was the answer. Alexandra felt a moment of triumph at having found the subject for Papa's painting. It might not be a conventional piece of art for an office, but it was the one she'd create.

"You may have forgotten how to waltz, but I'm sure you still remember how to eat. Please say you'll come with your daughter." Though Dorothy's smile was as warm as her words, Papa continued to hesitate.

"It's the bride's day," Brandon reminded him. "No one can refuse her requests."

"All right."

Brandon and Dorothy appeared to accept the less-than-gracious reply, but Alexandra did not.

"Why don't you like newspapermen?" she asked her father as they walked to the livery. "Brandon seems like a good man."

"You can't trust them. They make their living by creating scandals, printing exaggerated stories. I've seen them destroy men with their false allegations."

"But that's never happened to you, has it?" From the little Papa had told her about his past business ventures, they'd all been successful and praiseworthy. Some had faltered and even failed, but that was after he'd ceded control to someone else. Not once had he mentioned unscrupulous reporting.

"No," he admitted, "but I don't like taking unnecessary risks. That's the one mistake Phil made in recommending Mesquite Springs. There wasn't supposed to be a paper."

Alexandra had read only one issue of the *Chronicle*, but she'd seen no evidence of sensationalism in it. "Maybe the *Chronicle* is an honest paper."

"Maybe, but I still don't like it. Now, let's talk about something else. Have you thought about my painting?"

"I have, but it's going to be a surprise."

"All right."

His good spirits apparently restored, Papa spoke about the hotel and his plans for making it the finest in the whole Hill Country as they rode to the Clarks' ranch.

"You'll be proud of it," he told Alexandra.

She had no doubt.

The first sight of the Circle C made her realize that raising quarter horses was a prosperous endeavor. With its freshly painted shutters, the ranch house seemed to welcome visitors, as did the jugs of flowers on the long tables and the delicious aromas emanating from the kitchen. Though it would be more casual than the ones she'd attended in New York, Alexandra had no doubt that this would be a memorable wedding reception.

To her delight, Papa remained at her side as they mingled with the other guests, and the coldness he'd displayed while he'd been speaking to the bride and groom had disappeared, replaced by his normal friendly demeanor.

"It's important to make people trust you," he had told her more than once, "and a smile goes a long way toward trust." He was smiling now, impressing her with his memory of names. Who could fail to trust a man like her father?

But though she tried to keep her attention on the people she was meeting, Alexandra found herself looking around, searching for one particular person. Gabe must have been invited, but she hadn't seen him at the church, and so far there'd been no sign of him here.

Ah, there he was! Relief and something more, something that felt like anticipation, filled her as he approached her and Papa.

"Good afternoon, Alexandra. Good day to you, Mr. King," he said when he reached them.

Papa smiled at Gabe. "I trust you're here to invite my daughter to dance."

If she hadn't had years of training, Alexandra might have cringed. While it was true that she'd hoped to dance with Gabe, she'd wanted it to be his idea, not what sounded almost like a command from Papa.

Gabe nodded and gave Alexandra a small bow that would have been more appropriate in a formal ballroom. "Will you do me the enormous honor of granting me the first dance?"

This time Alexandra did cringe. Gabe's flowery words were unpleasantly reminiscent of Franklin's flattery. What had happened to the seemingly genuine man who'd made the stagecoach ride so pleasant? For a second, Alexandra was tempted to refuse to dance with him, but curiosity about his apparent change had her saying, "It would be my pleasure."

CHAPTER

Nine

It took every bit of self-discipline Gabe possessed to keep his expression neutral. He'd clearly made a mistake with his overly effusive invitation to dance, but he'd been so startled by Tarkington's less-than-subtle maneuver that he'd spoken without thinking of how his request would seem to Alexandra. Judging from her reaction, he must have sounded like one of her unwanted suitors. He'd have to undo the damage.

Relief washed over Gabe when he saw Mrs. Clark urge people toward the long tables filled with food. Once they were seated with others, perhaps Alexandra would forget his question.

"It looks like they're ready for us to eat. Shall we get in line?"

Tarkington shook his head. "You two go ahead. I want to talk to the mayor."

The hoped-for reprieve lasted only seconds. As soon as her father was out of earshot, Alexandra spoke. "Despite what Papa said, you don't have to dance with me."

"But I want to." That was the truth. It was also the truth that while he wanted to hold Alexandra in his arms, Gabe would have preferred their first dance to be his idea, not something he'd done to placate her father.

"I need to warn you, though, that I'm not a particularly good dancer."

Alexandra shook her head, releasing one of those curls that he found so attractive from her chignon. "It wouldn't be the first time someone stepped on my toes."

But he didn't. To the contrary, the dance they shared was the best one Gabe could recall. After only the briefest of hesitations, they began to move seemingly without conscious effort, their steps so perfectly matched they might have done this a dozen times. And that was good, because it allowed him to savor the pleasure of being close to Alexandra, of watching her curls bounce, of catching the sweet scent of her perfume.

When the dance ended and he'd given her the customary bow, he raised an eyebrow. "That was fun. Shall we do it again?"

"You were right," Alexandra said that evening as she rubbed her feet. Though Laura had made a pot of hot chocolate for them, she had yet to sample it. "It was a wonderful wedding." Releasing one foot and beginning to minister to the second, Alexandra added, "I never thought dancing on grass would be so enjoyable."

"It seems it might have been more enjoyable with a different pair of shoes, but I suspect that with the right partner, dancing on hot coals might be enjoyable." Laura smiled as she picked up her cup of cocoa.

"I doubt that." But Alexandra couldn't deny that the dances she'd shared with Gabe had been the best of the day and, if she was being honest, the best of her life. The momentary awkwardness had vanished, replaced by the easy camaraderie they'd shared on the stagecoach.

But Alexandra wasn't going to talk about Gabe. She fixed her gaze on Laura. "If you want to try dancing on hot coals with Sam, I'll watch."

"Sam?" Though she tried to sound surprised, the flush that

colored Laura's cheeks left no doubt Alexandra had been right about her friend's attraction to him.

"I saw the way you looked when you were dancing with him. You had stars in your eyes."

Laura busied herself refilling her cup, perhaps so she wouldn't have to meet Alexandra's gaze. "I did not."

Was it Shakespeare who said the lady doth protest too much? If so, he could have been speaking of Laura. "I know what I saw. There's something between you two. You could call it magnetism, but it looked like love to me."

"You're mistaken, Alexandra, sadly mistaken. I'm not in love with Sam, and believe me, I'd know if I were. I've been in love more times than I want to admit."

Alexandra took a sip of the hot chocolate as she tried to hide her surprise. "Truly? My aunt says people fall in love only once."

"She hasn't met me. It started with Wyatt."

"Evelyn's husband? The mayor?"

"Yes. He was the first. The last was Brandon."

"Who married Dorothy today."

Laura nodded. "Exactly. In between there were close to a dozen men I met in Charleston." She sipped her cocoa, then put the cup back on the saucer and turned to Alexandra. "It was always the same. When I'd see them, I'd start to shiver. I could hardly breathe because I was so excited, and in that instant, I knew this was the man I was meant to marry."

Though Laura's explanation was in perfect English, she might as well have been speaking Latin, for while the words registered, Alexandra had never experienced what Laura was describing.

"And then?" she prompted her friend.

Laura's expression turned sheepish. "A few weeks later, I couldn't imagine why I'd felt like that. The man I thought I was destined to marry turned out to be very different from my first impressions. I'd stop seeing him, and it would begin again with a new man."

Though Alexandra had known she and Laura were very different, until now she hadn't realized how great those differences were.

"I've never felt that way," she told her friend, "so I can't be certain, but it sounds to me like what you experienced was infatuation, not love."

"Perhaps. All I know is that I don't feel that way when I'm with Sam."

"How do you feel?" It was more than curiosity. Mama had died before she could tutor Alexandra in the mysteries of love, and Aunt Helen had never married. Perhaps understanding Laura's emotions would prepare her for the time when she fell in love.

"I'm not sure I can describe it. All I know is that Sam's different from the other men I knew." Laura shook her head and offered to refill Alexandra's cup. "Let's not talk about me. Haven't you ever been in love?"

The answer was simple. "No."

Laura appeared unconvinced. "But surely you've had suitors."

"Three so far," Alexandra admitted with a rueful laugh. "They all professed undying love and promised to cherish me forever and ever, but what they really loved was the prospect of my inheritance."

Laura gasped. "Fortune hunters?"

"Every one of them." Alexandra shuddered at the memory of Franklin and his threats.

"Not all men are like that. Gabe Seymour isn't."

"How do you know?"

Laura shrugged. "I just know. I'm not a matchmaker, but I know he's the man for you."

CHAPTER

Ten

*Y*ou're doing a good job." Tarkington favored Gabe with an approving nod as they climbed the stairs of the new building Monday morning.

It was still so early that work had yet to begin, and Alexandra wouldn't bring breakfast for another two hours. That was why Gabe had chosen this time to seek out Tarkington. He'd discovered the man liked to walk through both buildings at the beginning of each day, checking progress and making notes of mistakes that needed to be corrected.

"I wasn't certain at first," the older man continued, "because you didn't seem to be pursuing Alexandra, but you're doing all right now."

Though Tarkington's assessment rankled, Gabe kept his voice neutral as he said, "Your daughter doesn't strike me as someone who wants to be pursued. That sounds too much like the fox and the hounds, and you know what happens to the fox."

The man let out a chuckle. "You've got a point there, Seymour." He ran his hand along the top of the banister, nodding when it met his approval, then turned back to Gabe. "What do you say we drop the formalities? I'll call you Gabe, and you can call me Calvin."

"That's fine with me." Among other reasons, it avoided the question of whether to refer to him as Tarkington or King.

"So, no pursuit." Calvin appeared determined to continue discussing his daughter.

"I prefer subtlety."

This time the chuckle was more like a hoot. "If you call dancing with her three times when no one else got more than one, I agree. Saw you out walking with her yesterday afternoon."

"Yes, sir . . . er, yes, Calvin."

"Looked like the four of you were having a good time."

Had Tarkington—that is, Calvin—been spying on him? If true, it was ironic, since Gabe was the one being paid to investigate.

"We were," he told Alexandra's father. "Sam and I would have been fools not to want to walk with two lovely ladies."

Wyatt had invited Gabe and Sam for Sunday dinner, claiming it was his and Evelyn's way of welcoming Gabe to Mesquite Springs and showing Sam how happy they were that he was back. What it had shown Gabe was how different small towns were from cities. He had enjoyed the relative anonymity of Columbus, believing it gave him more freedom, but seeing the close ties among Mesquite Springs's residents made him wonder what else he'd missed.

Afterward when Gabe and Sam were walking off some of the meal, they'd seen Alexandra and Laura emerging from the Downeys' home and had suggested they accompany them. At first they'd conversed as a foursome as they strolled along almost every street in town, ending at the park, but soon they'd paired off, the alacrity with which Sam had moved to Laura's side leaving Gabe little doubt that she was the woman his friend fancied. He didn't object, for spending time with Alexandra was more pleasure than work as they discussed everything from the political situation in Washington to her plans for her father's painting.

"Your daughter's excited about having a painting in the hotel."

Calvin frowned at a misaligned strip of wallpaper, making a

note to have it replaced. "She's talented," he told Gabe. "Got that from her mother. I'm no artist."

"But you know how to turn a house into a hotel. That's a form of artistry."

The older man gave Gabe an appraising look, perhaps trying to decide whether he was sincere or merely doling out flattery. At last, he said, "Never thought of it that way."

It was time to see if he could learn anything this morning. "Is the next project going to be as beautiful?"

Calvin laughed. "Afraid not, but it'll be far more lucrative. The hotel's just a place for potential investors to stay."

"Then the next business is close by."

This time the man shook his head. "You're fishing for information, aren't you?" When Gabe shrugged, he continued. "I like initiative in a man. Maybe you ought to be my next partner. Drummond and I don't see eye to eye on everything."

Gabe wasn't surprised. Now that he'd met both men, he couldn't imagine their working well together. Though he and Bill Woods, the Cincinnati investigator Gabe had hired to help him, had interviewed a number of people, they'd been unable to learn why Tarkington had taken Drummond as his junior partner.

There'd been rumors that Tarkington had amassed substantial gambling debts less than a year after Drummond joined him, but Gabe had found no connection. What he'd discovered was that though the men were partners on paper, they appeared to work on different projects with Tarkington's being more successful, perhaps because he met with investors personally while Drummond relied on advertisements. How Tarkington benefited from the partnership was unclear, but it didn't matter.

What did matter was that Gabe had a new lead. The next venture was close to Mesquite Springs. All he had to do was figure out where.

Alexandra gripped the railing, trying to stop her knees from shaking. She shouldn't be so apprehensive. After all, the worst Miss Geist could do was refuse her offer. Still, she couldn't forget the excitement that had rushed through her at Laura's suggestion. Memories of the two blond children she'd seen approaching the school had flashed before Alexandra and refused to disappear. Would they be interested? Would what she was offering help them? There was only one way to know.

She'd waited until the morning recess so that the pupils would be occupied in the schoolyard and no one would overhear her conversation with the teacher. It would be the ideal time, if only her legs would cooperate.

Mustering every ounce of courage she possessed, Alexandra crossed the street. "Miss Geist?"

The woman was perhaps an inch shorter than Alexandra, her hair steel gray, her eyes a few shades lighter, her rigid posture declaring that this was indeed the town's schoolmarm.

"Yes, I'm Sarah Geist." Recognition lit her eyes. "You're Miss Tarkington. I wanted to welcome you to town when I saw you at the wedding, but you were always busy. It seemed every unmarried man in town wanted to dance with you."

"That's the hazard of being a newcomer."

It was because they were both newcomers that Gabe had danced with her three times, nothing more. But though she'd tried to dismiss Laura's claim that Gabe was the man she should marry, Alexandra had failed. The thought crept into her mind at all the wrong times, like right now. She forced her attention back to the schoolmarm.

"It's nice to meet you." Miss Geist extended her hand, then frowned at one of the schoolboys. "Bobby, let Hilda have her turn on the swing." Turning back to Alexandra, she sighed. "Children have so much energy. Sometimes I wish I could give them recess every hour, but they'd never finish their lessons that way." She sighed again. "Rainy days are the worst."

Though Miss Geist had no way of knowing it, she'd given Alexandra the opening she needed. "The school I attended used to have art on days when we couldn't go outdoors for recess."

"That's a good idea, and it's one I've considered. Unfortunately, my artistic skills are nonexistent. When an artist came to town last year, I hoped he might help, but he said he couldn't teach anyone, especially children. Now Phil's gone."

Phil? Alexandra tried to hide her curiosity. Was he the same man Papa had hired? It seemed unlikely, for what would an artist know about building a hotel, and yet how many newcomers named Phil could there have been in a town this size? Though she wanted to ask, Alexandra needed to concentrate on the reason for her visit.

"I paint a little—mostly watercolors, but I can sketch too. I'm going to be in town for a while, so I wondered if you'd like me to teach your pupils." Alexandra held out a sheaf of papers, grateful that when she'd left New York, she hadn't wanted to leave her favorite paintings behind. "Here's an example of my work."

The teacher studied them carefully before nodding. "These are wonderful." Her expression turned sober. "I'd like to hire you, but I can't afford to pay you very much."

Exultation raced through Alexandra. Miss Geist hadn't dismissed her idea; better yet, her appreciation of the paintings had been sincere. What a wonderful morning this was turning out to be.

"I didn't expect to be paid. I simply want to do whatever I can to help the children." Especially the boy and girl she thought might be twins. They'd looked as forlorn today as they had the first time she'd seen them.

"Are you certain you want to do this? If you start and then decide you don't enjoy it, the pupils will be disappointed. I don't want that to happen."

"I'm certain. Very certain."

As Miss Geist smiled, the crow's feet next to her eyes deepened. "Then you have a job. Can you start tomorrow?"

"Yes!"

Within minutes, they'd arranged the details. Since Alexandra might be leaving Mesquite Springs in a few months and both she and Miss Geist wanted the children to experience as much art as possible, instead of waiting for inclement weather, art would be part of each day's lessons. Alexandra would teach the younger children in the morning, the older ones in the afternoon. Miss Geist would order the supplies Alexandra needed; she would contribute the talent.

As she returned to the Downeys' house, Alexandra was filled with excitement and anticipation. Teaching the children felt right. As for Gabe . . . his role in her life remained to be determined.

Interesting. More than that, unexpected. Gabe's thoughts whirled as he left the hotel. When he'd come to Mesquite Springs, he'd suspected that Calvin Tarkington's current scheme was related to the hotel. Now it seemed he didn't expect men to invest in the hotel but in something else, something they would want to see before committing significant amounts of money.

He hadn't expected that. The research he'd done on previous schemes had revealed that they all involved bogus companies. There'd been a locomotive manufacturing plant, an iron foundry, an invention that would allegedly revolutionize printing, and a shipping company, probably the one that had bankrupted Biddle's father. In each case, the investors received piles of paper describing the expected profits, but there'd been no inspection of the factories. For good reason. Either the factories did not exist or they were so dilapidated that no one with an ounce of brains would invest a penny in them.

Gabe headed west on Spring Street, trying to make sense of what he'd learned, but he had no answers, only more questions. Why was this scheme different? Why would Calvin deviate from the procedure that had worked before? And why was he so adamant that his daughter be kept away from the hotel?

As he approached the building he'd been told housed the *Chronicle*, Gabe couldn't hide his surprise. Brandon Holloway, the man whose wedding Gabe had attended only two days ago, was standing on the front steps, staring into the distance.

"I thought you and your bride were on your wedding trip," Gabe said as he approached the ordinary-looking house.

Brandon, whose blond hair and blue eyes reminded Gabe of Jason Biddle, shook his head. "We've got a paper to put out. Dorothy and I can't disappoint our subscribers. Wedding or no wedding, they expect a new issue every Tuesday."

And today was Monday. "That must make Mondays your busiest days."

"Exactly." While Brandon had the same coloring as the man who'd hired Gabe, the similarity ended there. This man exuded confidence, and his square chin hinted at determination. "If you're wondering why I'm standing out here, apparently doing nothing, it's because I'm struggling with this week's editorial."

"What's it about?" Gabe had been impressed with the last issue's careful blending of local and national news and its thought-provoking editorial.

"That's the problem. I don't know. I usually have no trouble finding a subject, but this week is different."

Though Gabe didn't know the man well, he knew what had changed in his life. "Perhaps it's the distraction of being a newlywed."

"That's possible. I have to say that marriage is more wonderful than I'd expected." Brandon stared into the distance again, as if meeting Gabe's gaze would reveal even more than his words did. "Dorothy fills spots inside me that I hadn't realized needed to be filled."

A longing so deep that it threatened to overwhelm him flowed through Gabe's veins. Would he ever find a woman who made him feel like that? As Alexandra's image flitted through his brain, he brushed it aside. It was true that she intrigued him. It was true that she was the only woman who stirred his senses. But it was also true that he could have no lasting relationship with her until he'd uncovered whatever it was that Calvin Tarkington was planning. And when Gabe did, it was possible—more than possible, it was likely—that she'd despise him for revealing her father's crimes.

Brandon Holloway wasn't the only one who wanted to conceal his emotions. Gabe was glad the editor wasn't looking at him while he tried to corral his thoughts. "Why not write about marriage?"

Brandon turned to stare at Gabe. "Who'd be interested?"

"You'd probably be surprised, but since everyone was invited to your wedding, sharing your thoughts with them will keep them feeling involved in your life." Gabe doubted any Columbus newspaper editor would have entertained such an idea, but this wasn't Columbus.

"It's not a bad idea."

"Such high praise!"

Brandon chuckled. "Actually, it's a good idea. Thanks." He turned, apparently ready to return to his office and write his editorial. "If there's any way I can help you, just let me know."

Though he knew the man needed to work, Gabe wasn't willing to forgo the opportunity he'd been given. "I heard you're a relative newcomer. What are your impressions of Mesquite Springs?"

"It's a good place to live. We're growing but not too fast. Hardly anyone leaves."

Though the words were ordinary, Gabe's instincts told him there was a story behind Brandon's final sentence. "But some people do?"

Brandon nodded. "Other than a few deaths, the only ones since I've been here were three ranchers. Some man in Mississippi wanted a lot of land by the river and offered them a good price."

Three ranches sounded like more than most people would need. "What's he going to do with all that land?"

"The speculation is that he wants to raise a large herd of cattle, but he hasn't come to town yet. We're all a bit puzzled by that."

The wheels inside Gabe's brain began to turn. It didn't make sense, unless . . . Unless the man wasn't from Mississippi. Unless he was already here. Unless the land was somehow part of Calvin's next scheme.

Eleven

*B*oys and girls, I have a surprise for you. You're going to learn something new."

Whispers, groans, and a few muted cheers met the schoolteacher's announcement. From her spot in the back of the classroom, Alexandra tried to ignore the groans. Though she'd hoped for enthusiasm, she knew not everyone welcomed change. Even Gabe, who'd impressed her with his spontaneity, had seemed disgruntled when she'd had to decline his suggestion they ride to the river for a picnic. He'd claimed to share her excitement over teaching the children, but the claim had fallen flat.

"None of that." Miss Geist's stern look squelched the groans. "This will be fun. Miss Tarkington is going to teach you to draw." She beckoned Alexandra to join her at the front of the room. "Children, please welcome Miss Tarkington."

A chorus of dutiful "welcomes" echoed from the walls.

"I hope it will be fun," Alexandra said as she let her gaze move from one pupil to the next. Some appeared curious, others skeptical. Fortunately, she saw no overt hostility. Perhaps this would be easier than she'd thought.

"Painting is an important part of my life," she told her pupils. "I hope to show you why."

Miss Geist took a step forward, holding a rolled piece of paper in her hands. "We're very fortunate to have Miss Tarkington with us and even more fortunate that she has made a special painting for us." Though her fingers had itched to begin Papa's painting, Alexandra had decided this was more important.

As the schoolteacher unrolled the paper and displayed it to the class, cheers erupted, raising Alexandra's spirits. She had deliberately made the painting a simple one, wanting the children to see that great precision and detail weren't required. The picture she'd offered Miss Geist depicted the schoolhouse with pupils hurrying to enter as the schoolmarm rang the bell.

"This is a watercolor," Alexandra explained. "It's my favorite art form and what I plan to teach you. Miss Geist has ordered the supplies we need, but until they arrive, we'll make charcoal drawings." Not only did those eliminate the need for children to choose the right color, but they would give Alexandra the opportunity to assess her pupils' talents.

"All right, children." Miss Geist nodded to the first two rows. "Miss Tarkington will teach you this morning. The rest of you will be in the afternoon class."

Alexandra took the younger pupils to the back of the room and waited until they were seated on the floor. Though it would be more difficult for them to draw here than if they were seated at their desks, Alexandra wanted this first session to be a casual one.

"You know my name. Please tell me yours." She'd been introduced to Polly, the orphan the mayor and his wife had adopted, and her friend Melissa but needed to know the others' names. Obediently, all of the children gave Alexandra their names. The only exception came when she reached the two she thought were twins.

"She's Frieda," the boy announced.

"And he's Hans." His sister completed the introductions.

"What is your last name?"

This time they spoke in unison. "Gottlieb."

"They're twins and they're a whole month older than me," Polly told her, though Alexandra had not asked for ages. That made Frieda and Hans seven, which had been her guess.

She handed out the paper and charcoal. "Today is just for fun. Draw anything that's important to you."

Though the other children talked among themselves while they drew, the twins remained silent, their concentration evident in the furrows that formed between their eyes. Whatever they were drawing consumed their energy.

"Is everyone finished?" When they all nodded, Alexandra moved from one to the next, praising the sketches. She wasn't surprised when Polly's showed a young girl with a puppy, because she'd heard tales of how devoted Polly was to Buster. And her friend Melissa's depiction of two girls swinging was equally expected. More than once, Alexandra had seen the girls racing to the swings as soon as school was over, determined to be the first to play there. It was when the twins shyly showed her their art that Alexandra thought her heart would break.

"Is that your father?" she asked Hans, pointing to the stick figure of a man with tears falling from his eyes.

"*Ja. Vati* is sad."

Frieda's picture left no doubt of the reason for that sorrow. She'd drawn two children standing on either side of a man, each holding his hand, all three staring into a grave.

"*Mutti* went to heaven." Frieda's words confirmed Alexandra's fears. If her death was recent, and she suspected it was, it was no wonder the twins clung to each other. "We miss her."

"I know you do. My mother went to heaven when I was about your age." And though the pain had faded, Alexandra had never stopped wondering what her life would have been like if Mama had lived.

"She did?" A spark of hope lit Frieda's blue eyes as she realized that Alexandra might understand her sorrow. "Did your papa hold your hand?"

Knowing it was what the child expected, Alexandra nodded,

though that wasn't the truth. It had been Aunt Helen who'd tried to comfort her.

Polly, who'd remained silent during the exchange, grabbed Frieda's hand to get her attention. "Evelyn found me a new daddy. Maybe your daddy will find a new mama for you."

"I don't want a new mama," Hans declared. "I want *Mutti* to come back."

But she wouldn't, any more than Alexandra's mother would. The most the twins could hope for was what Polly had suggested, a stepmother. It wasn't unusual for widowers to remarry, particularly if they had children, but Papa hadn't. Why not?

Gabe frowned as he closed the last drawer. When he'd seen that none of them was locked, he'd realized the chance of finding any incriminating evidence was slim, but he'd still riffled through the files, hoping Calvin had left something—anything—that might show he was the owner of the three ranches and what he planned to do with the land. There was nothing.

Gabe straightened and left the office, glancing around as casually as if he were simply inspecting the workers' progress. Fortunately, Calvin was as much a creature of routine as his daughter and spent this part of each morning in the other building, returning shortly before noon to oversee the final preparations for the meal he offered workers as part of their pay. According to Sam, Calvin had hired two relatively young widows to cook the midday meal.

"I doubt their food is as good as what they'd get at Polly's Place," Sam had said, "but the women appreciate the extra money."

That was consistent with what Gabe had learned about Alexandra's father. Though there were the usual complaints that not everyone did his share of the work, he had heard no grousing about Calvin. According to the men he'd hired, he treated them fairly, even paying for the tents where those from more distant ranches stayed.

Biddle might not be happy when he received Gabe's report that everything about the hotel seemed aboveboard, but he owed his client honesty and the promise that he would keep looking, because—like Jason Biddle—Gabe did not believe Calvin Tarkington was innocent.

"I'm so glad you could join us. Now we're a quartet." Evelyn gestured toward the table where Laura and Dorothy were already seated. "Would you like coffee or tea? There's also leftover oatmeal pecan pie. Can I tempt you with a piece?"

"You definitely can. That's the best pie I've ever eaten." Alexandra's concerns about joining the other women evaporated under the force of Evelyn's welcome. She waited until her hostess had taken her seat before saying, "Thank you for inviting me. I feel like I've joined an exclusive club."

Dorothy hooted. "That's the first time I've heard us called that. Brandon jokes that we're like the three witches from *Macbeth*, stirring up trouble."

Alexandra smiled at the way Dorothy's voice softened when she pronounced her husband's name. "Is that why you wanted me to come—to prove he was wrong? I don't think Shakespeare had four witches in any of his plays."

"Wyatt says he refuses to speculate on what we discuss, but he's warned me that we're not allowed to choose the baby's name. He says that's for us to do as a couple." Evelyn laid a protective hand on her midsection.

"Let me guess. Each week you give him at least one outlandish name and claim that's the one you want."

Laura, who'd raised her cup to her lips, set it down with a plunk and pretended to glare at Alexandra. "Don't you dare make me laugh while I'm drinking. I can't be responsible for what happens if you do."

"What was so funny about what I said?" Alexandra had only ventured how she would have reacted to Wyatt's decree.

"Nothing, really." Dorothy twirled the gold band on her left hand. "We're simply trying to figure out how you knew we pick a name every week. This is our week for girls' names."

They were debating the merits of Hepzibah versus Lemuela when the door from the kitchen burst open and Polly rushed in, a puppy at her heels. "Wanna see what I did at school today?" She brandished a piece of paper. "Miss Tarkington taught us how to—" She stopped abruptly. "Oh, you're here. Do you wanna meet Buster? He's the bestest dog."

Alexandra reached down to pat the puppy. Of indeterminate breed, he was far from a handsome animal, and yet the woebegone expression in his eyes when he saw her slice of pie made Alexandra's heart melt. She looked at Evelyn. "Is he allowed to eat pie?"

Evelyn shook her head. "We're trying to train him not to beg. As you can see, he hasn't quite learned that lesson."

"That's cuz your pie is sooooo good. Please, Evelyn, can't Buster have a bite?"

Alexandra suspected Polly's pleas were harder to resist than the dog's, but Evelyn shook her head again. "You know the rules." When the child began to pout, Evelyn gestured toward the piece of paper Polly still held. "What do you have there?"

Her spirits rising as quickly as they'd plummeted, Polly grinned. "I drawed me and Buster. Look."

An hour later as she and Laura walked home together, Alexandra's smile was as bright as Polly's had been. Her first time teaching, combined with her first meeting with a trio of women friends, had made this a wonderful day.

Twelve

*I*f you're not too busy, do you want to go for a ride?" Gabe leaned against the doorframe of Sam's office, pretending not to notice the man's almost indolent posture. Mesquite Springs's attorney was leaning back in his chair, his feet propped on his desk, his hands laced behind his head.

"Do I look busy?" Sam lowered his feet to the floor and sat up. "Folks are still getting used to the idea that I've returned. As you can see, I don't have clients lining up outside my door."

"Did you use to?" Though he and Sam had spoken about a number of things, Sam's earlier life hadn't been one of them.

"No," he admitted. "There's not a lot for an attorney to do here. That's one of the reasons I ran for mayor last year, and I suspect it's the only reason Fletcher asked if I'd run for sheriff. Can you imagine me as a sheriff?"

Gabe couldn't, but he wouldn't tell his friend that. "Who's Fletcher?"

"Fletcher Engel's been Mesquite Springs's sheriff for twenty years. He's a good man and a good sheriff. Everyone thought he'd be our lawman for the next twenty, but he was helping build a house a month ago, and a wagon filled with stone tipped over. Fletcher had the bad luck to be underneath."

Gabe winced at the thought of the damage that had inflicted. "How serious was it?"

"The best thing I can say is that he's alive, but his leg was broken in so many places that Doc Dawson says he'll never walk without a cane. That might be enough for most men, but Fletcher knows he can't do his job that way. That's why he's looking for someone to take his place."

"What about a deputy?" Though Mesquite Springs was smaller than Columbus, Gabe thought it likely that the sheriff had help.

Sam shook his head. "There are two, but even Fletcher refers to them as the boys. Neither one's ready."

"So that leaves you. You know the law, and you have time."

"Time but no inclination. I'd rather be a barely employed attorney than a sheriff." Sam frowned as he stood. "Let's talk about something else. Anything else."

"What kind of work does a barely employed attorney do?"

Sam shrugged. "I can only speak of the past. Not many disputes were serious enough to need me, so I mostly wrote wills and handled land sales."

It was a casual comment, but it opened the door to what Gabe wanted to discuss. "Were you involved in selling the ranches out by the river? I heard they sold recently."

Sam shook his head, then reached for the coat he'd hung on the back of his chair. "That was before I came back. If I'd been here, I might have tried to convince the men to stay. I don't believe they'll find better land in Dakota Territory." This time he frowned, seemingly perplexed by the ranchers' decision. "Their ranches were so close to the river that they never had to worry about water. I don't know what story they were told, but I'm afraid they'll discover that parts of Dakota are mighty dry."

So were parts of Texas, but not this one. Flooding was more of a concern than drought. Like Sam, Gabe wondered what the ranchers had been told that made them leave. Had Calvin paid them so much more than the land was worth that they'd decided to take a chance on starting over in a new area?

"I haven't seen the river. What do you say we ride that way?" If his suspicions were correct and Calvin had bought the land, the river must have been the reason. Gabe had asked around and discovered other plots of land for sale, but they were farther inland. The river appeared to be the attraction, and it was his job to learn why.

Sam shrugged into his coat and grabbed his hat. "Let's go."

The road to the river headed north out of town, climbing and descending gentle hills. As far as Gabe could see, there was nothing that distinguished this side of Mesquite Springs from the others. The same trees and brush grew here. The same critters scampered or lumbered across the road. The same faint scents of flowers and grass tickled his nose. But when they reached the top of another hill, he understood why Calvin might have wanted to own land here.

The sun sparkled on the river, turning its surface to a ribbon of silver, making Gabe wonder if the stories he'd heard about lost silver and gold mines had their origin here. There was no telling what fancies a man whose head was clouded by whiskey might have had.

Even without the illusion of precious metals, the scene was a beautiful one, the river's clear waters contrasting with the rich earth on both banks. If he were settling here, this would be the spot he'd choose, but Calvin Tarkington wasn't planning to settle here, and Gabe couldn't imagine a scheme that involved ranching. What had made those three ranches so desirable?

Doubting he'd learn anything more today and hating the idea that his first report to Biddle would be so inconclusive, Gabe decided to focus on something—anything—else. He studied the pastoral scene, noting that the road forked as it approached the river. One branch crossed the river on a small bridge, while the other ran parallel to it. Though the bluebonnets were past their peak, a few patches of faded blue hinted at the beauty of the area.

"That looks like a nice place for a picnic," he said, pointing to the flower-dotted meadow.

"A picnic? What made you think of that?"

"My parents used to take me on picnics some Sundays after church. Of course, we only went to a park, but it always felt like an adventure." Those afternoons were among his most cherished childhood memories. "It turns out that Alexandra has never been on one."

If Sam was surprised by the mention of Alexandra, he gave no sign. "I suspect her family had formal teas rather than picnics." He stared into the distance for a second before adding, "I'm not sure Laura's picnicked, either."

His wistful expression told Gabe the idea had caught his fancy. "Maybe we should change that. If you wanted to make it a foursome, that is."

"What I want and what I can have are two different things."

"Why do you say that?" It was the first time Gabe had heard a melancholy tone in Sam's voice. Normally the man was a master at keeping it neutral, but now both his voice and the tighter grip on the reins bore witness to his emotions.

Though their horses neighed their impatience at the slower pace Sam had set, he ignored them and fixed his gaze on Gabe. "Do you think a lady like Laura Downey could overlook a man's imperfect past?"

The way Sam phrased it left no doubt of the answer he expected, but Gabe refused to give him that answer.

"I imagine that would depend on what those imperfections were." From what he'd observed, the attraction between Laura and Sam was mutual.

Sam was silent for a few seconds. "Can I trust you not to tell anyone what I'm about to say?"

"Of course. I'm good at keeping secrets." And ferreting them out.

When more silence followed Gabe's reassurance, he wondered

if Sam had reconsidered and would refuse to share his past. At last, his friend spoke. "Do you believe in demons?"

The question took Gabe aback. No one had ever asked him that, and outside of church, he'd never heard anyone discuss demons.

"I can't say that I've had any firsthand experience with them, but I've read enough about them in the Bible to believe they exist." Or at least that they'd existed in biblical times. "Why do you ask?"

"Because I used to feel like I had one." Sam paused, waiting for Gabe's reaction.

Though the idea shocked him, years as an investigator had taught Gabe to hide his emotions. He simply nodded, encouraging Sam to continue.

"There were times when my anger was so strong it felt like I was possessed." Sam paused, the pain of his memories evident in the way his lips contorted. "I did some awful things when I let my anger control me. It was bad enough that I could have wound up in prison."

"But you didn't." Gabe knew he would have heard about that if it had happened.

"I was fortunate that Reverend Coleman knew of a hospital back East that had success treating people like me. He'd heard that almost every patient improved, so he urged me to go there."

Gabe said nothing but nodded again.

"I spent close to a year at Serenity House. At first I thought the name was a joke, but by the time I left, I knew it wasn't. I feel like a different man now. The anger hasn't disappeared, but it's lost its power, because I've learned to control it."

Gabe looked at his friend with new eyes, realizing how little he'd known about the man who'd offered him a temporary home. He would never have guessed from Sam's calm demeanor that he'd suffered from bouts of anger stronger than the ones Gabe had experienced after his father's death. There had been times— many times—when Gabe had wanted to pummel the man whose lies had convinced Pa to invest in the Ellsworth Bank. Perhaps fortunately for both of them, he'd never learned who was behind the phony bank.

"That's an impressive story."

Sam nodded as if he concurred. "I couldn't have done it alone. The doctors taught me techniques, but the credit goes to God. Every day I pray for strength to overcome the anger, and he gives it to me."

Another impressive story.

"I'm hardly an expert on women," Gabe said, "but I believe you when you say you've changed. If Laura's half the woman I think she is, she ought to care about the man you've become. The past is the past." Even though it was often difficult to forget.

Sam's relief was palpable. "Thanks for the encouragement. I hope you're right, because I want to court Laura. The problem is, I don't know how to start."

"And you're asking me?" Gabe laughed. "I've never courted a lady."

"But you're interested in Alexandra. I can see that from the way you look at her."

Gabe wouldn't disagree with Sam's assessment. He *was* interested in Alexandra.

"I'm not ready to court anyone, but I enjoy her company." *And I'm supposed to be courting her or at least keeping her occupied.* Though Sam had been candid with him, Gabe would not share that arrangement with him or anyone.

"Those walks we've taken have been pleasant." Gabe looked forward to the nightly strolls almost as much as he did the time he spent with Alexandra each morning. Even though their morning walks as he escorted her from the hotel back to the Downeys' home were not lengthy, they had become the highlight of Gabe's days.

"If we continue to spend time with Laura and Alexandra, Laura will have a chance to get to know the new you." And Calvin would be happy. "Maybe we can even plan a picnic out here."

Sam grinned. "I've got a better idea."

*I*t's beautiful!" Papa's voice quavered ever so slightly, and he blinked back tears while he stared at the painting Alexandra had laid on his desk. "I don't know how you did it, but you captured the happiness your mother and I shared whenever we danced."

Alexandra could explain that she'd chosen pink for her mother's dress because that particular shade made her happy. She could say she'd shown them gazing into each other's eyes because that was the most romantic aspect of a waltz. She could tell him she'd blurred the background to let the viewer's imagination fill in the details. She could say all those things, but the truth was, she had painted with her heart. Everything she'd done had been instinctive.

"I'm glad you like it."

Papa picked up the painting and held it against one wall as if imagining it hanging there. "You couldn't have chosen anything better." He laid the watercolor back on the desk and moved to the other side, where Alexandra had placed their breakfast basket. "I'll ask Fritz Gottlieb to make a frame."

"The twins' father?" Though Alexandra had not heard his first name, she doubted there was more than one Gottlieb family in Mesquite Springs. "I thought he was a rancher."

"He's also a skilled carpenter. I've got him making the baseboards and door trims in the new building."

Papa spread jam on the toast that had been Alexandra's sole recourse when Laura had overslept and hadn't been able to make rolls for breakfast. "He said you were teaching his children to draw and paint."

The elation that her father's pleasure with the painting had engendered began to fade when she realized he'd apparently forgotten that she'd told him about her work with the schoolchildren.

"I enjoy teaching. Some of the older children have real talent, but it's the little ones who touch my heart."

Papa's smile was wistful as his gaze strayed to the watercolor. "You sound like your mother."

It was a morning for unusual occurrences. First, Laura's oversleeping, now Papa's uncharacteristic mention of Mama. Alexandra couldn't recall the last time he'd volunteered any information about her mother, but perhaps the painting had stirred memories.

"What do you mean?"

He chewed the toast carefully before speaking. "I thought you knew your mother taught school before we married."

If anyone had told Alexandra that, the memory was lost.

"She said the youngest children were her favorites. I guess you inherited that along with her artistic talent." Papa was silent for a second before adding, "Your mother loved children."

Aunt Helen had said the same thing.

When she'd found Alexandra crying one day because she believed no one loved her, Aunt Helen had dried her tears, then said firmly, "That's nonsense, child. I love you and so did your mother. If there was ever a woman who loved children, it was your mother. She once told me she wanted a dozen, but since God hadn't seen fit to give her more than one, she was glad she had such a perfect daughter."

Even then, Alexandra knew she wasn't perfect, for if she were, Aunt Helen would have said that her father loved her. The omission stung more than the thorn that lodged in her thumb when she tried to pick a rose for her aunt, only to learn that that particular rosebush was grown for its color, not its scent, and that Aunt Helen reserved it for formal arrangements.

Alexandra took a sip of the milk she brought each day, hoping it would help her father gain weight. It was too soon to know if the extra food made a difference, but she was determined to continue providing it.

"Why did you have only one child?" She'd never dared to ask the question, but Papa seemed more open to discussing the past today.

"It wasn't our choice. When the wasting sickness began, the doctor warned us that another child would sap her strength even more. That was the death knell to our hopes for a large family." Papa reached for a second piece of toast. "Your mother wanted you to have sisters and brothers, but I wasn't willing to take the risk."

Alexandra wondered what her life would have been like if she'd had siblings. Would they have remained together after Mama died? Would she have tried to comfort the others the way the twins did each other? There was no way of knowing.

"She died anyway."

His lips contorted with pain, Papa nodded. "After much suffering."

At the time, Alexandra hadn't realized how ill her mother was, because she'd been forbidden to enter the sickroom. Had Papa or perhaps Mama been trying to protect her? All she knew was that the house had been too quiet, and when she'd finally been allowed to see her mother, Mama had been lying in bed, unable to lift her head from the pillow.

Unbidden, the image of the twins' pictures filled her mind. Their father had held their hands; he'd shared their grief; he hadn't sent them away. Papa had been different.

Placing her glass back on the desk, Alexandra faced her father and asked the question that had haunted her for years. "Why did you abandon me when Mama died?"

The blood drained from his face. "I didn't abandon you," he said firmly.

"That's what it felt like. You wouldn't talk to me, and then you sent me away." Though the conversation was painful for both of them, it was years overdue.

"I did what I thought was best for you," her father insisted. "I knew I couldn't raise you by myself. When Helen offered to take you, it seemed like an answer to prayer." Papa had abandoned all pretense of eating and kept his gaze fixed on Alexandra. "She was good to you, wasn't she?"

"Yes, but it wasn't the same as having a mother." Before she'd become so ill, Mama had spent most days with Alexandra. She told her stories while she braided her hair. She let her peek into a robin's nest to see the blue eggs. She made Alexandra a dress from the same material as one of her own so they could be twins, or so she said. Though most of Alexandra's memories had faded, those remained vivid. Aunt Helen had been kind, but she hadn't been a mother.

"Didn't you ever think of marrying again?"

A look of sheer horror animated Papa's face. "Never! Oh, some ladies from the church told me I should. They even tried to play matchmaker, but I knew I could never remarry. Your mother was the love of my life."

In that instant, Alexandra understood why her father had sent her to New York. It wasn't because Aunt Helen had volunteered to raise her. What she'd feared was true: Papa didn't love her. He'd given all his love to Mama; there had been none left for her.

Perhaps if she'd been better, if she'd truly been the perfect daughter Mama had described, it might have been different. Papa might have loved her at least a little, but he hadn't, and he still didn't. The softness she'd seen had been triggered by his memories of Mama.

"I loved your mother with every fiber of my being. She was the only woman for me."

More than that, she was the only person he could love. The milk that had been refreshing a moment ago curdled in Alexandra's stomach. Why, oh why had she started this conversation?

Papa's eyes, the same shade as hers, were serious as he continued. "Love like that is rare, but it's worth waiting for. Be sure you feel that way about the man you marry."

The fears she'd tried to suppress, the worry that men cared more for her fortune than for her as a woman, came roaring back. "If I marry." Aunt Helen had said some women were not meant to marry. Perhaps Alexandra was one of them.

"You will. You'll be a fine wife and mother."

How could Papa be so sure? He hardly knew her. It was true Alexandra had dreams of marriage and children, but now she wondered whether that was the path God planned for her. One thing was certain, though. If she found a man who loved her and if they had children, those children would know as surely as the sun rose each day that she loved them, and she would never, ever abandon them.

It hadn't been a good morning. Gabe could tell by the slope of Alexandra's shoulders that whatever had happened between her and Calvin had not pleased her. Surely the man had not rejected her painting. Gabe didn't claim to be an artist or even an art critic, but he'd been impressed by Alexandra's portrayal of a couple waltzing. It was delicate yet not overly feminine, the scene so beautifully wrought that it made Gabe long to dance that way with Alexandra.

He couldn't undo whatever Calvin had done; he could only hope that his invitation would boost Alexandra's spirits.

"You look like you could use some cheering up." Perhaps he should have chosen a different greeting, but Gabe saw no reason to dissemble.

Fortunately, Alexandra did not appear insulted by his bluntness. "You're right, but how did you know?"

"You weren't smiling." It was more than that, but if he revealed how much he'd seen, she might wonder why he was so observant, and that was a question he wasn't ready to answer. Instead, he asked, "Didn't your father like the painting?"

She shook her head. "That's not the problem. He liked it enough that he suggested I paint scenes for the common areas in the hotel."

That should have made her happy, but it hadn't. Though he knew he wouldn't, Gabe was tempted to march back to the hotel and shake some sense into Calvin. Didn't the man realize how fortunate he was to have a daughter like Alexandra?

"If you want to talk about whatever's bothering you, I've been told I'm a good listener." And an even better investigator, but Gabe had no intention of mentioning that today.

Alexandra shifted the empty basket from one arm to the other, another sign of her distress, and when he started to turn into the park toward what both of them referred to as their bench, she shook her head. "Thank you, but no. It's something I need to work out by myself."

He'd expected that. Alexandra was nothing if not independent. Beautiful, strong, and determined, she was a remarkable woman.

"The offer stands. Whenever you want a friendly ear, I'm here. But that's not the reason I'm here right now. Sam and I wanted to invite you and Laura on a picnic."

"A picnic?" For the first time since she'd emerged from the hotel, those blue eyes brightened.

"When you said you'd never been on one, it struck me as a shocking gap in your education." Gabe emphasized the word *shocking*, hoping it would make her smile. "I want to remedy that as soon as possible. That's why I hope you're willing to have your first picnic on Saturday."

Though her mood seemed to be improving, Alexandra raised a skeptical eyebrow. "I heard it's supposed to rain then."

"Sam assures me that won't be a problem." His friend's suggestion had been an excellent one, providing shelter in case of inclement weather. "Will you come with me?"

Alexandra nodded and gave him a weak smile. "Yes."

As he left her at the Downeys', Gabe found himself wishing life were simpler. So far he'd failed to discover what Calvin was planning, and that failure made him wonder whether he ought to find another way to earn a living. For the first time, the excitement of the hunt had disappeared. Perhaps it was time for a change.

Fourteen

Saturday morning was dismal. Heavy clouds obscured the sun, and the moisture in the air told Alexandra rain was imminent. It was hardly the day she would have chosen for a picnic.

"It'll be all right," Laura assured her as she pulled a tray of cinnamon rolls from the oven. "If Sam said so, you can count on it."

Though the aroma of the freshly baked sweet bread was enough to make her smile, it was the expression in Laura's eyes when she spoke of the attorney that tilted the corners of Alexandra's lips. Laura might deny it, but she was attracted to Sam.

"I hope so. I've been looking forward to it."

The prospect of a picnic with three of her favorite people in Mesquite Springs had helped soothe Alexandra's bruised emotions. Though she'd refused to shed the tears that threatened to overwhelm her, the memory of her conversation with Papa and what he hadn't said had torn ragged holes in her heart at the same time that it strengthened her determination to win his love. She'd show him that she could help with the hotel, and if she did, maybe he would view her as a valuable part of his life.

The question was how to help. When she'd asked, Papa had

said the paintings were enough, but they weren't. She needed to find activities that would force him to spend more time with her.

As if that weren't enough to worry about, for two consecutive nights Alexandra had dreamt of Franklin. The locations had been different. What hadn't changed was his threatening posture. He'd leered at her, shouting that she wouldn't escape, that no matter where she went, he would find her. It was worse than that night in New York, her fear heightened by the gun he'd brandished. Both nightmares had been so vivid that Alexandra had wakened trembling, unable to shake the fear that Franklin had somehow tracked her to Mesquite Springs.

Fortunately, her time with the schoolchildren had helped banish the nightmares. Alexandra had thought it might be nothing more than her imagination that Hans and Frieda seemed less apprehensive, but Miss Geist had confirmed it, declaring that the art classes' effect on them had been an answer to prayer.

"We'll have fun." Laura's words brought Alexandra back to the present. "I can practically guarantee it, but now I need to get to work."

The picnic wouldn't begin until after the restaurant closed, which meant that Alexandra would have six hours to herself since there was no school today. Pulling out her watercolors, she began to paint a scene from the park. She hoped its combination of spreading live oaks, winding paths, and strategically placed benches that never failed to soothe her spirits would do the same for the guests, giving them a peaceful scene to contemplate while they enjoyed a meal in the dining room.

She and Papa had decided she should begin with six large paintings for the common rooms and hallways. If Alexandra had time when those were finished, he had agreed she could create smaller paintings, one for each of the guest rooms. But for now, she was focusing on the dining room. Papa had said he wanted guests to relax while they were in Mesquite Springs, and the softness of watercolors would help.

As always happened when she was painting, Alexandra lost track of time. She'd been so immersed in the pleasure of creating a scene that she'd forgotten to look at the clock. When she laid down her brush, finally convinced she'd captured the essence of the park, she was startled to realize that it was time to prepare for the picnic.

She had debated over what to wear. Silk was too formal, and so she'd chosen a blue printed calico. Though more casual than many of her dresses, its summery print was one she liked and one she hoped would brighten this gloomy day. Gabe's appreciative smile when he saw it told her she'd chosen well.

"I'm glad you rented a closed carriage," Laura said as the four of them descended the porch steps. The rain that had begun soon after noon was now coming down in torrents.

Sam pretended to remove his hat and make a sweeping gesture that would not have been out of place in a romantic novel. "Nothing but the finest for the most beautiful ladies in Mesquite Springs."

Though Alexandra wondered at the flowery words, she said nothing, merely watched Laura's cheeks color.

"That doesn't sound very lawyerly," her friend said as she took the arm Sam offered.

"I was speaking as a man, not a lawyer, and I was right, wasn't I, Gabe?"

"Definitely. I'm not as good with words as my friend, but he's right. We're fortunate to be with such lovely ladies."

The words that would have been commonplace and virtually meaningless in New York seemed sincere, and combined with Gabe's smile, they made Alexandra's heart race. She swallowed deeply, trying to understand her reaction. Her heart had not raced when other men complimented her. Her skin had not tingled when she laid her hand on other men's arms. Her breath had not caught when other men smiled at her. Yet all that was happening today. Why?

She felt comfortable with Gabe. She trusted him. And, yes, if she was being honest, she found him attractive. But, despite Laura's prediction, he wasn't a suitor. He was simply a very nice man who happened to be staying in the same town as she. It was a case of temporary proximity, nothing more.

There was going to be more of that temporary proximity as they drove, because Sam helped Laura onto the front seat next to him, leaving Alexandra to share the rear one with Gabe. There was nothing unseemly about it, no reason that her heartbeat should accelerate even more at the scent of bay rum and wool.

"Where are we going?" she asked, as much to distract herself as to learn their destination.

"South." Gabe's lips curved into a mischievous smile.

"I knew that." They'd turned south onto Mesquite and were heading out of town. "I was hoping for something more specific."

Sam joined the conversation. "You'll see soon enough."

When Laura said, "I think I know where we're going," Sam was quick to admonish her. "Don't spoil the surprise for Alexandra."

As they passed the entrance to a ranch a couple miles out of town, Laura turned to face Alexandra. "That's the Gottlieb ranch. You can't see the house from here, but it's one of the best built in the area."

Laura's comment confirmed Papa's assertion that the twins' father was a skilled carpenter and reassured Alexandra. She knew from what Miss Geist had said that some of the schoolchildren lived in little more than shanties. "Not everyone succeeds with farming and ranching here," she'd explained.

Several miles later, the gentle hills that surrounded Mesquite Springs gave way to flatter ground, and Sam turned the carriage onto what was obviously the entrance to another ranch, prompting Laura to murmur, "I was right."

Though the rain kept her from seeing too far into the distance, the carefully smoothed road and freshly painted fences told Alexandra the owners had prospered. That impression was underscored when they reached the ranch house itself, a sprawling one-story building with a wide front porch. Though it seemed an odd place to have a picnic, perhaps Sam intended for them to eat on the porch. It was certainly large enough.

Before they had a chance to climb out of the carriage, the front door opened, revealing a silver-haired woman leaning on a cane.

"I'm so glad to see you," their hostess said as she ushered them into the house. Though not as elaborately decorated as either the Downeys' home or Alexandra's great-aunt's, the parlor still bore witness to both the owners' good taste and their wealth.

"Welcome to Mesquite Springs, Miss Tarkington and Mr. Seymour," the woman continued, her smile as warm as her words. "Sam has told me so much about both of you. And, Laura, it's good to see you again. Freckles has missed you."

Sam chuckled. "In case you haven't guessed, this is my mother."

Alexandra hadn't guessed that. If anyone had asked her, she would have said this was his grandmother, for the woman appeared to be more than sixty years old. "It's a pleasure to meet you, Mrs. Plaut."

While Gabe greeted their hostess, Alexandra darted glances around the room, trying to find Freckles. Unless she was mistaken, Freckles was a dog. While they'd been laughing over outrageous names for Evelyn's baby, Dorothy had claimed it was easier to name dogs and shared how Nutmeg, the stray she'd adopted, had earned her name by knocking over a saucer of the spice Dorothy had carefully grated.

"Fortunately, I didn't have to name the puppies," she'd said. "Their new owners had that privilege." And one of those owners was Sam's mother.

As if on cue, a brown whirlwind entered the room and raced toward the newcomers, first sniffing Gabe's boots, then standing on his hind legs, his front paws reaching Alexandra's waist. What an adorable creature! Buster had tugged at her heartstrings, but this dog's combination of exuberance and a soulful expression touched her even more deeply than Buster had.

As Alexandra bent to scratch the puppy's head, Mrs. Plaut snapped her fingers. "Down, Freckles. You know better." His tail between his legs, the dog slunk to his mistress's side.

"I never thought I'd want a puppy," their hostess said, "but Dorothy's very persuasive. Now I can't imagine life without him. The challenge is teaching him who's boss."

"There's no question of who's boss." Sam's eyes sparkled with mirth. "Anyone can see that Freckles rules the roost."

Though the others chuckled, Sam's mother merely inclined her head. "Be that as it may, you didn't come here to play with a dog. It's time for your picnic."

Moving as regally as any of the society matrons Alexandra had met, Mrs. Plaut led the way through the long hallway that divided the house to a doorway on the southern side. When she reached the double doors at the end, she stopped, allowing Sam to open them.

"Enter, my friends," he said with a flourish.

As she did, Alexandra was transported to a different world. The air was moist here, not the result of rain but of the dozens of plants that filled the glass-sided room. Red, yellow, green—even blue and pale purple—it seemed that every color of the rainbow had found its way to this indoor oasis. Dozens of fragrances combined in an appealing perfume. And while rain beating on the top of the carriage had seemed threatening, the patter of raindrops on the glass roof was soothing. The room's beauty tantalized each of the senses.

"What an incredible conservatory!" Alexandra turned to Mrs. Plaut, wanting to share her delight with the woman who'd been responsible for it. "I didn't expect one in Texas."

She knew they were popular among the nobility in England, and a few wealthy New Yorkers had them, but Alexandra had not imagined finding one here. She looked around the room again, her fingers itching to paint the scene.

"I've always loved gardening," Sam's mother explained, "but there are times when nothing is blooming. That's why Adam—he's my husband—indulged me by having this built." She chuckled. "It was supposed to be nothing more than a simple greenhouse near the barn, but Adam never does anything by half measures. He wanted me to be able to enjoy my flowers without going outside."

Though her companions seemed less entranced by the beauty surrounding them, Alexandra was still marveling at it. She bent to sniff a rose, then moved to a gardenia, savoring the different fragrances.

"I like to serve tea here," Mrs. Plaut continued, "but Sam insisted on a picnic, so . . ." She led the way to the opposite side of the conservatory where the plants had been pushed aside, leaving room to spread a blanket on the floor. "This is your picnic spot."

"And here's our picnic food." Sam retrieved a large basket that had been left on the floor near the door. It appeared that his mother had provided more than the location for the picnic. "Ladies, if you'll take your seats, Gabe and I will serve you."

Though Laura complied, Alexandra remained standing. "Won't you join us?" she asked Mrs. Plaut.

The older woman shook her head. "These old bones don't take kindly to sitting on the ground. Besides, you don't need me. Freckles and I'll be in the music room next door."

Some might call the food ordinary—fried chicken, potato salad, cool tea, and peach turnovers—but Alexandra could not recall a meal she'd enjoyed more.

"This was a wonderful idea. Thank you, Gabe."

"Thank Sam. He's the one who offered his home."

"My parents' home." Sam was quick to make the distinction. "After being gone for months, this no longer feels like home." He turned to Laura, raising an eyebrow as he asked, "Did you feel that way when you returned from Charleston?"

Though the question was not overtly personal, the way Sam looked at Laura told Alexandra the answer was important to him. More than that, it told her Laura was important to him.

"No." There was no hesitation in her reply. "My parents' house still feels like home, which is good, since I expect to spend the rest of my life there."

"Until you marry." Gabe, who'd been silent, joined the conversation.

"*Unless* I marry." The firmness of her reply made it clear that despite or perhaps because of the number of times she'd thought she was in love, Laura did not believe marriage was inevitable.

Alexandra darted a glance at Sam, wanting to see his reaction to Laura's declaration. As she'd expected, he appeared uncomfortable. Perhaps, like her, he sensed that Laura still dreamt of being a wife and mother, and he longed to be the man who made that dream come true.

Wanting to ease Sam's discomfort, Alexandra pointed toward the door, where a faint scratching could be heard. "I think Freckles wants to join us."

Gabe shook his head. "He wants to join you. I saw the way he acted when we arrived. Freckles didn't care about anyone else. I think he recognized you as someone who loves dogs."

The thought was a novel one. "I never had a pet."

Gabe's eyes darkened. "No picnics, no pets. What did you have?"

"Art lessons." They'd been designed to fill the missing parts of her life, but they hadn't succeeded.

"How do you think that went?"

Gabe considered Sam's question as they headed toward his apartment. They'd taken Alexandra and Laura home, then returned the carriage to the livery. Now they were on the final leg of their trip, walking through the rain that had turned into nothing more than a drizzle.

"I enjoyed it. I think the ladies did too. What do you think about planning something for every Saturday?"

Alexandra's expression when she'd talked about her childhood had made Gabe realize how difficult it must have been to live with her great-aunt. He hadn't had siblings, but he'd had both parents, a dog, and half a dozen neighborhood boys as playmates. Art lessons were a poor substitute.

"Sounds like a good idea. What do you have in mind?"

Before Gabe had a chance to respond, he was distracted by Pastor Coleman emerging from the church, so intent on his thoughts that he was headed straight for them.

"Hello, Reverend," Gabe said as he and Sam moved aside to avoid a collision.

The minister raised his head, clearly startled by the greeting. "Oh, hello, gentlemen. I'm afraid I didn't see you."

That much was evident. The reason was not. "Is something wrong?"

Pastor Coleman nodded in response to Gabe's question. "One of my parishioners died. She has no family, so it's up to me to choose the hymns and Scripture readings."

Gabe hadn't considered that that might be a problem, but it was Sam who asked, "Who was it?"

"Mrs. Lockhart."

Though Gabe had not met her, he'd heard about the widow whose home was being turned into a hotel.

"She had a good life," the minister continued, "and I know she's in heaven now, but I'll miss her. She never failed to comment on my sermons—not always favorably, I might add."

Both men chuckled at Pastor Coleman's attempt at humor.

Pastor Coleman turned his attention to Gabe. "In case you're interested, there's a vacancy at the boardinghouse. I doubt it'll last long."

Though he'd once expected to live at the boardinghouse, now it held little appeal. Still, he couldn't continue to impose on Sam when there was an alternative. "Thank you. I'll head over there."

As the minister continued on his way, Sam clapped his hand on Gabe's shoulder, restraining him. "There's no need to do that unless you're tired of my company. You're welcome to stay with me."

Relief flowed through Gabe. He'd been in Mesquite Springs less than two weeks, but Sam's apartment had begun to feel like home. It was more than the room itself, although that was comfortable. What made the difference was Sam himself.

"Are you sure?"

"As sure as I am that it rained today."

"Then, I accept. After all, I wouldn't want you to have to eat your own cooking."

As Gabe had intended, Sam laughed.

CHAPTER

Fifteen

"How did you hear about Papa's hotel?"

Gabe raised an eyebrow, surprised by Alexandra's question. Saturday's rain had ended, and by Sunday afternoon everything was dry, making it an ideal time for another stroll around town and, it appeared, for unexpected questions. Sam and Laura walked a few paces ahead of them, so engrossed in their own conversation that they might have been in a different town.

"I saw an article in the *Chronicle*." The glowing description of the plans for the hotel might have intrigued other readers, but what had caught Gabe's eye was the name of the proprietor.

"The *Mesquite Springs Chronicle*?" Alexandra seemed as surprised by his answer as he'd been by the question itself. "But you live in Columbus."

"True." There was no reason to admit he'd been in Cincinnati when he'd read it. "Papers reach further than you might think, because the post office doesn't charge for mailing them. I was talking to a friend, and he showed me the article."

Another thing Alexandra didn't need to know was that the friend was Bill Woods, who'd helped Gabe trace her father. "Even he was surprised at how far the paper had traveled. Looking back,

I know it was God pointing me in this direction." No matter what happened, Gabe did not regret coming to Texas, not when it had led him to Alexandra.

He had a question of his own. "Why did you ask? Was it simple curiosity or something more?"

"Both. It felt like more than coincidence that we were on the same stagecoach, and I wanted to know more about that, but I'm also concerned about the hotel. It's important to fill as many rooms as possible, so I've been trying to think of ways to do that."

"Did your father ask for your help?" Gabe doubted that was the case, because Calvin was like many men and had firm ideas of what women could and could not do.

"No, but . . ." Alexandra's expression was somber as she let her voice trail off.

"You're going to help anyway."

This time she smiled. "Exactly."

Alexandra set the basket on the desk and began to unpack it, trying to dismiss her concern. Papa was always waiting when she brought breakfast, but today there was no sign of him, only—

Her thoughts were derailed by the sight of an envelope addressed to Aunt Helen. What had he told her? Though she knew she shouldn't pry, Alexandra picked up the envelope, letting out a sigh of relief when she realized it was empty. Papa, it seemed, had not yet had time to write the letter.

Alexandra smiled. This could be the opportunity she'd sought to reassure her aunt without alerting Franklin. If he had someone watching the mail that was delivered to Aunt Helen—and Alexandra wouldn't be surprised if he did—they'd see only an envelope with Papa's return address. She could include a note or even write the whole letter. Judging from the terse missives Papa had enclosed with her quarterly allowance, Alexandra knew he did not find writing letters enjoyable.

"Ah, there you are." Papa was grinning as he strode into his office and held out the object he'd been carrying under his arm. "Look at this."

Alexandra's breath caught at the sight of the newly framed watercolor. Papa hadn't exaggerated. The twins' father was indeed talented. Though the frame was wider than she would have recommended, the intricate carving did not detract from her painting, and the finished product was pleasing to the eye.

"Do you like it?" Papa asked.

Alexandra nodded. What she liked most was the obvious pride shining from her father's eyes. If he was happy with her work and Mr. Gottlieb's, that was all that mattered.

"I'll hang it as soon as we eat. What have you brought today?"

As they savored slices of what Laura called breakfast pie, a combination of eggs, bacon, and cream in a pie crust, Alexandra mentioned the envelope.

"I know you're busy. Would you like me to write to Aunt Helen?" As she'd hoped, Papa agreed. Now, if only he'd agree to her next suggestion.

"I've been thinking about the hotel."

Papa took a swig of milk before he said, "About the paintings."

"More than that. I know you want it to succeed."

"Of course I do."

"If that's going to happen, people need to know about it. I think you should place an ad in the *Chronicle*."

This time Papa's face reddened. "I told you I don't trust newspapers."

Alexandra had expected that reaction. "This isn't an article that the editor could slant—not that I think Brandon would do that. It's an advertisement. You'd be paying for it, so you'd control the wording."

"True, but what's the point of telling anyone in Mesquite Springs about the hotel? They live here. They already know I'm building it."

"That's true, but the *Chronicle* is like many newspapers. It's sent to other towns. It even travels as far as Columbus. That's how Gabe learned about the hotel."

Papa appeared thoughtful, then nodded again. "It's not a bad idea, but I don't have time to think about it."

"I could do it. Not alone." Alexandra had tried to anticipate every one of Papa's possible objections. "Dorothy helps others write their ads, so I'd work with her, and I'd show you what we're proposing before it's printed."

When he seemed dubious, Alexandra added a plea. "Please, Papa. I'd like to help you."

"Oh, all right."

It might be grudging, but he'd agreed. When she left the hotel, Alexandra's step was lighter than it had been in days.

This was the first time he'd attended a funeral for someone he'd never met. Gabe wouldn't have come, but Sam had insisted that—like Brandon and Dorothy's wedding—this was an occasion when the whole town was expected to be present, so here he was, sitting two rows behind Alexandra and her father.

"It's at times like this," Pastor Coleman said, "that we reflect on the legacy we may leave. Mrs. Lockhart's legacy was a fine one. Those of us who knew her well knew we could count on her unwavering honesty. We may not have liked everything she said, but she was never mean-spirited. Her criticisms—and I was the recipient of many—were meant to challenge us to be better."

The minister let his gaze move from pew to pew. "That was a fine legacy and one we could all try to emulate, but Mrs. Lockhart's legacy did not end there. Though she might have been more comfortable remaining in it, she sold her home because she knew that a hotel would benefit the entire town. I call that selfless love."

Gabe wished he could see Calvin's face. From what he knew of the man, *selfless* was not an adjective anyone would apply to him.

"Mrs. Lockhart knew she would not live forever," Pastor Coleman continued. "None of us does. Knowing that, she arranged for one final legacy. I'm not sure how many of you know this, but before she married, Mrs. Lockhart taught school. Though she was not blessed with children of her own, she believed that the future belongs to the young, and so she left her entire estate to the school."

The minister spoke for several more minutes, then asked the congregation to join him in a final hymn before they proceeded to the cemetery.

"Not everyone goes to the burial," Sam said as he and Gabe exited the church. "You don't need to."

But Gabe wanted to. Somehow, it seemed important to pay tribute to the woman whose actions were indirectly responsible for his coming to Mesquite Springs and whose eulogy had made him think about his own legacy. When he was laid to rest, would anyone believe he'd made the world a bit better the way Mrs. Lockhart had? Gabe wasn't sure of the answer.

He remained on the periphery of the crowd that gathered at the gravesite, his attention drawn to Alexandra and her father. Alexandra's lovely face was solemn, but it was Calvin's expression that surprised Gabe. Unless he was mistaken, that was genuine sorrow he saw etched on the man's face. Was he mourning Mrs. Lockhart's death, or was it something else? Perhaps he regretted being the reason she'd spent her final months in a boardinghouse.

Gabe watched as Calvin's lips moved in what appeared to be a silent prayer. It was then that he realized Alexandra's father was looking beyond Mrs. Lockhart's open grave to one on the far edge of the cemetery.

⁓

"What do you think?" Alexandra laid the ad she and Dorothy had crafted this morning on the table, wanting Laura's and especially Evelyn's opinion before she showed it to her father.

Evelyn looked at the sheet for a moment, then began to read aloud. "'More than a bed. Luxurious accommodations and fine dining await you at the King Hotel. Once you've experienced what this elegant establishment and the town of Mesquite Springs have to offer, you may never want to leave.' I like it." The warmth in her voice left no doubt of her sincerity.

"If I didn't already live here, I'd be tempted to book a room for Wyatt and me to see if it's as good as you claim." Evelyn laid her hand on her stomach and smiled. "Drusilla said she agrees."

Laura nodded emphatically. "You ought to do that. I'm sure Mrs. Clark would keep Polly for a night or two if you and Wyatt wanted a second honeymoon."

Dorothy's expression was thoughtful. "Brandon and I could do that too and then write about our experience. Most people in Mesquite Springs have never stayed in a hotel. They'd enjoy reading about it."

And that article, Alexandra knew, would benefit the hotel more than the ad. "You're all being so kind."

"That's what friends do." Dorothy turned to Evelyn. "What's today's pie?"

"Raisin. It's almost as popular as oatmeal pecan."

When Evelyn returned with four small slices and a pot of coffee, Alexandra addressed her biggest concern. "I'm worried that the hotel's restaurant will hurt your business."

The look Evelyn gave Laura told Alexandra they'd already discussed this. "I'm not worried." Evelyn's gesture encompassed the entire dining room. Though comfortable, no one would describe it as elegant. "We're not competitors. I heard the hotel was going to offer breakfast and the evening meal. Except for Saturdays, Polly's Place isn't open for breakfast, and we close by midafternoon, so I don't see how you'd be taking business from me. To the contrary, your guests will probably want a midday meal. Laura and I will be ready for them."

"You can stop worrying, Alexandra." Laura refilled everyone's cups, then raised an eyebrow. "Let's worry about important things like the baby's name. We can't let Evelyn call him"—she emphasized the word—"Drusilla."

Happiness bubbled up inside Alexandra as she looked at the women who'd offered her one of life's most precious gifts: friendship.

"You're wonderful." No matter what the future brought, she would never forget them.

He wasn't taking any chances. Jason Biddle leaned against the seatback and feigned sleep. Beyond the necessary pleasantries, he hadn't spoken to anyone since he'd boarded the stagecoach, ensuring no one would have a reason to remember him. He'd claimed his name was John Nelson and that he was very hard of hearing. Not only did that excuse him from unwanted conversation, but it provided a plausible explanation for why he didn't respond immediately when someone addressed him as Mr. Nelson.

Running a hand over his face, he tried not to frown. No one who'd known him back East would recognize him. He had exchanged his carefully tailored suit for a cheap, poorly fitting one and hadn't shaved in more than a month. A beard and longer hair completed the disguise that the shabby clothing had begun.

That was probably enough, but Jason wanted to ensure he was leaving no trail, so he planned to leave the coach in Fredericksburg, buy a horse there, and head west. It was only when he was certain no one was following him that he'd turn north.

When he reached Mesquite Springs, he'd be nothing more than a workman hired to help build the hotel. No one would have any reason to connect a somewhat disreputable looking laborer with Jason Biddle. Even Seymour, whose information had helped him get this far, wouldn't realize that his client was in the same town.

When he'd received Seymour's letter saying Calvin Tarkington was building a hotel in Texas, Jason knew that must be where

AMANDA CABOT

the girl had gone. Seymour hadn't mentioned her, but where else would she be? Jason already knew she hadn't gone to Saratoga. If she wasn't with her cousin—and she wasn't—she had to be with her father. He'd find her and he'd convince her to return to Franklin. And, if sweet talking didn't work, there were other ways to persuade her.

Jason bit back the laughter that threatened to erupt. It was the perfect plan.

CHAPTER

Sixteen

*I*t was a perfect day. The weather couldn't have been more different from last Saturday. Today the sun was shining, and the lightest of breezes kept the late May afternoon from being too hot. Perfect for a ride.

"It was very kind of Wyatt to offer us his horses." When Alexandra had mentioned that she hadn't yet seen the river, Gabe had declared that it would be an ideal destination for a ride, either in a carriage or on horseback. Alexandra had voted for the horses. Now she and Laura were dressing for the excursion.

"It does the horses good to experience different riders. Wyatt says this will help get them ready for the sale."

Alexandra smiled as she watched Laura dab a bit of cologne on her wrists. Though the animals wouldn't care, her friend was probably hoping Sam would notice the extra effort she'd taken with her appearance.

"Then they've decided to have one." Evelyn had mentioned that with the hotel's completion being delayed, there'd been a discussion of whether to have a home sale or whether Wyatt's head trainer Caleb should take the Circle C's horses to Fort Worth.

Laura nodded and reached for her hat. "Evelyn said Wyatt and

Caleb are planning on late September. They want to wait until the baby's born." As she secured the last of the pins, she turned back to Alexandra. "Do you think you'll still be here then?"

It was a question Alexandra had asked herself numerous times. "I don't know. It depends on what my father does, but I like Mesquite Springs." She felt safe here, so safe that entire days passed when she didn't think about Franklin and his threats. Perhaps she was being unrealistic, but she hoped Franklin had realized he had no chance of winning her hand.

"I hope you'll stay. You've become like a sister to me." Laura pirouetted in front of the long mirror, checking her reflection from all angles. Apparently satisfied, she continued. "I'm so fortunate. First Dorothy, then Evelyn, now you. Three friends who are more than friends."

"And then there's Sam, who wants to be more than a friend." Alexandra couldn't resist teasing her.

"Nonsense!" Though Laura's protest was vehement, the color in her cheeks put lie to it. "He never paid me any attention before he went East."

"But he does now."

"Maybe." Laura paused for a second, lost in her thoughts. "He seems different. Almost vulnerable." She let out a wry laugh. "It must be my imagination. Sam's more confident than anyone I know, so why do I feel that I should protect him? I'm being silly."

But she wasn't, and judging from the expression she'd seen in Sam's eyes, that desire to protect was mutual. Laura and Sam cared enough to want to guard as well as cherish each other. How fortunate they were! They both had loving parents, and now perhaps they'd have each other. She and Gabe weren't so fortunate.

Alexandra shook herself mentally. She wouldn't think about how she had hoped to establish a warm, loving relationship with her father, only to discover that he wouldn't or maybe couldn't give her what she needed. Longing for something she could never have would only spoil the day, and Alexandra wouldn't let that happen. Instead, she would think about the good things in her life.

She had friends, both men and women, for she counted Gabe and Sam as friends as well as the trio of ladies who'd opened their hearts to her. She had a comfortable life here. And then there was today. The weather was perfect; everyone was looking forward to the ride; and if Alexandra had anything to say about it, it would be a perfect ride.

Half an hour later, the four of them were heading north toward the river.

"You seem at ease on horseback."

Alexandra could have said the same about Gabe. From the moment he'd mounted his gelding, he had appeared to be one with the animal.

"I may have grown up in a city, but I did ride," she told him. "Admittedly, Manhattan wasn't like this." The trees and shrubs were different, their scents filling the air with a perfume that still seemed unusual to her. The rolling hills contrasted with the flat city streets where she'd once ridden. Though it might only be her imagination, the Texas sky seemed bluer than the one over New York, but it was when they reached the summit of one of the hills and she had her first view of the river that Alexandra's breath caught in her throat. While the Hudson was wider and some might say more majestic, the way this one sparkled made her heart sing.

Sam and Laura remained a few yards behind them, engrossed in their own conversation, but Gabe was giving Alexandra his full attention. "It's beautiful, isn't it?"

She stared at the water flowing smoothly below the small bridge and wondered where it was headed. Though there were days when she felt she was drifting aimlessly, rivers always had a destination.

"I'm glad I didn't miss seeing this."

Gabe's smile faded. "You sound like you're getting ready to leave. Are you?"

"No. I don't know why I said that other than that Laura and

I were talking about how long I might stay in Mesquite Springs. What about you? Are you ready to explore other places?" The thought was as disturbing as the idea of leaving the town that had welcomed her so warmly. In a perfect world, she and Gabe would stay here forever, their friendship deepening with each day. But the world was not perfect.

Unaware of the direction Alexandra's thoughts had taken, Gabe shook his head. "Not yet. I thought I'd stay at least until the hotel opens. I don't want to miss seeing your paintings on display."

Though the idea was flattering, Alexandra doubted it was the reason Gabe was staying. It was a frivolous reason, and Gabe Seymour was not a frivolous man. But rather than risk having her melancholy thoughts resurface, Alexandra adopted a teasing tone. "I think it's more likely you want to keep eating Evelyn's oatmeal pecan pie." Gabe had mentioned that he tried to get to Polly's Place early enough to have a piece whenever she served the dessert that had made her restaurant famous throughout the county.

As two birds flew overhead, squawking loudly as if to protest the humans' intrusion into their domain, Gabe grinned. "Evelyn's an artist with food, but you're being too modest if you don't realize how talented you are. Your father should be paying you a goodly sum for the paintings you're doing."

Money wasn't what Alexandra wanted from Papa. "I enjoy painting."

"And teaching the youngsters?"

"Yes, especially the twins." She had told him about Hans and Frieda and how painting seemed to be breaking through the shell they'd erected around themselves. "They'll never be artists, but somehow drawing helps them express their feelings."

Though it had been gradual, she'd seen more optimism in their designs. The last time Frieda had drawn her father, he'd no longer been frowning, leading Alexandra to wonder if soon she'd depict a smile. Alexandra hoped so, for she'd come to admire the man whose love for his children was apparent in everything he said and did.

When he'd come to the schoolhouse to take them home one afternoon, he'd stayed to tell Alexandra how much he appreciated the art lessons and how the children said they were the highlights of their days.

"*Danke, Fraulein*," he said. "This is good for them."

And it was good for Alexandra too. "Teaching the children makes me feel I'm doing something useful," she told Gabe. There was no need to say that it wasn't enough, that she longed to have a different relationship with her father. Seeing the new building taking shape excited her; so did composing the advertisement, but she wanted more. She wanted to be a permanent part of Papa's life.

"We all need to feel useful." The way Gabe stared into the distance made Alexandra wonder what he'd done before he'd come here and whether he had found it fulfilling. Though they'd spoken of many things, Gabe's past livelihood had not been one.

"Did you feel useful in Columbus?" Aunt Helen had impressed on Alexandra that a lady never asked a man how he earned his living. If he wanted her to know, he would tell her. So far, it seemed Gabe had not wanted Alexandra to know, because he'd made only limited references to his life prior to coming here.

He nodded. "Most of the time. Oh, I had days when I questioned whether I was doing the right thing, but I believed the services I provided were needed."

"Services?" The question popped out before she could censor it.

The frown that crossed Gabe's face disappeared so quickly Alexandra wondered if she'd imagined it, for his voice bore no sign of disapproval or discomfort. "I used to help people solve problems," he told her. "I would listen to what they said and try to find whatever they needed."

The man was even more intriguing than she'd realized. "I never heard of professional problem solvers."

"There aren't a lot of us," he admitted. "I suspect that's because the work can be boring at times."

"And not too many people like to listen." Particularly men. At least that had been Alexandra's experience.

Gabe chuckled. "You could be right about that."

Sam and Laura caught up with them as they descended the hill toward the river and began discussing the likelihood of catching fish in the river.

"Have you ever gone fishing?" Sam asked.

Both Laura and Alexandra shook their heads, prompting him to declare, "That's what we'll do next Saturday. I know the best spot to catch dinner."

Laura wrinkled her nose. "I'll cook the fish, but you need to bait the hooks. I refuse to handle worms."

The look Sam gave Laura left no doubt that he was not surprised that she didn't want to touch worms. "How about you, Alexandra? Are you as squeamish as Laura?"

"I don't know. I've never done it."

"But you'll try." Gabe was obviously trying to encourage her.

As Laura shook her head and muttered that she would regret it, Alexandra nodded. "I'll try . . . once or twice."

"That's my girl."

They were simple words, casually spoken, and yet they warmed Alexandra's heart more than the bright sunshine. She heard more than approval in his voice; she heard affection, confirming that Gabe was her friend. Her life might not be perfect, but coming to Mesquite Springs had brought new friends into it. That was good.

While Gabe and Sam continued to discuss the merits of fishing in the early morning versus the late afternoon and Laura continued to roll her eyes, Alexandra studied the sky, trying to decide how to capture its brilliance. She could start with a blue wash, but she'd need more than that, perhaps . . .

Before she could complete her thought, Gabe reined in his horse at what had once been the entrance to a ranch. Now blocked with an obviously new fence, it offered no welcome.

"That's odd," he told her. "That fence wasn't here the last time

Sam and I rode this way." He turned toward Sam. "What do you think's going on?"

His friend shrugged. "Maybe the man from Mississippi arrived and wants privacy. Let's see what the next ranch looks like."

Several miles down the road, they had their answer. Three men were in the process of constructing a fence that would block the way to the second ranch.

Gabe dismounted and strode toward the workers. "Afternoon, gentlemen. It looks like you've got your work cut out for you." He pointed toward the pile of wood that had yet to be turned into a fence. "I guess the new owner doesn't plan to use this entrance."

Alexandra noticed that he kept his voice friendly, as if he were engaging in a conversation rather than asking a question.

The oldest of the men, who appeared to be the leader, shrugged. "Don't know. We just do what Mr. King tells us."

"Mr. King?" Alexandra was unable to mask her surprise.

The man nodded. "Yep. He's the one what bought all this land."

And he hadn't mentioned it to her.

Seventeen

I thought I told you about it."

Papa was lying. Alexandra knew that; what she didn't know was why. Though she'd tried to pretend that nothing was wrong, Gabe had sensed her discomfort and suggested they head back to town. He'd used concern over the length of the ride as a reason, but she'd known he'd realized that she wanted to confront her father. And she had. She'd found him supervising the plastering of one of the rooms in the new building.

"There's something I need to ask you," Alexandra said when he'd looked up and acknowledged her presence. "Something private." And so they'd come to his office, where he'd proceeded to pretend there was nothing unusual about having purchased land and not mentioning it to her.

"If you did, I forgot." Alexandra decided to pretend this was a casual conversation. "What are you planning to do with all that land? Sam said you bought three ranches."

"That's right. I did." The slightest hint of defiance colored Papa's words.

"Why?" Though she'd tried, she'd been unable to find any reason why he'd want so much property.

"I'm tired of living in the city and having neighbors close. With plenty of land, I won't have to worry about anyone bothering me. I'm going to build a house and retire here. That way I can keep an eye on the hotel."

Alexandra's attempt at nonchalance failed as the implausibility of her father's explanations mounted.

"You've never done that before, have you? You told me you hired good managers to run your businesses once you got them started. Why is this different?"

Instead of meeting her gaze, Papa stared at the painting she'd given him. "Two things are different. First, I don't have a manager yet, and second, the hotel is the only business with my name on it. You could say it's my legacy."

The story made little sense. Alexandra repeated what she'd told her father the day she'd arrived in Mesquite Springs. "King isn't your name."

Papa swiveled to face her. "That's what he called me. That and Mr. K."

The tenderness she heard in her father's voice, a tenderness she'd rarely heard directed at her, caused sparks of jealousy to ignite within Alexandra. "Who?" she demanded. "Who called you Mr. K?"

"The man who was supposed to run the hotel. Phil."

Gabe wandered around the construction site, waiting for Alexandra to conclude her conversation with her father. As much as he'd wanted to accompany her and hear Calvin's excuses, he'd learn more if he waited and spoke to Calvin separately.

Gabe feigned an interest in wallpaper as a reason for being in the hotel. "Who chose the wallpaper?" he asked the man who was struggling with the long strips.

As the man began a litany of complaints about the difficulty of hanging this particular paper, Gabe let his mind return to what he'd discovered today. His instincts had been correct. Calvin was the man who'd bought three ranches along the river. The question remained why. The blocked entrances made Gabe suspect the land was meant to be more than a ranch. But what? It would be interesting to learn what Calvin had told his daughter and then what he'd tell Gabe.

Alexandra emerged from her father's office, her head held high, though the way she pursed her lips told Gabe she was trying to rein in her emotions. He took her arm and led her out of the hotel, waiting until they'd reached what he'd come to think of as their park bench before he posed his question.

Pain radiated from Alexandra's eyes. "He says he's planning to build a house and retire here so he can keep an eye on the hotel, but I don't believe him."

Nor did Gabe, though he suspected his disbelief had different roots than hers. As much as Gabe wanted to comfort her, discovering why she hadn't accepted her father's story had to come first.

"Why don't you believe him?"

"There are already three houses there. From what Laura told me, they're perfectly good houses. Why would my father need to build another one?"

It was an excellent question. "Maybe he wanted something bigger." Most of the ranch houses Gabe had seen were relatively small. And, though the Plauts' home was large, the original building had been modest, with new sections added over the years.

"Papa never cared about that. Our house in Cincinnati was small. Aunt Helen said that even when Mama received her inheritance and they could have afforded a larger home, he refused to spend any of her money. It was kept for me."

Gabe had walked by Calvin's residence when he'd started his investigation, knowing that a man's home revealed more than most people realized. Calvin Tarkington's appeared to reflect a man with simple tastes. Neighbors had told Gabe that was where

Calvin had brought his bride and that when she died, he'd refused to leave, even though he'd sent his daughter away.

"Maybe he wants more."

Alexandra's eyes darkened with confusion. "Why?"

"So you would feel comfortable living there. After all, you lived with a wealthy woman for most of your life. Maybe he wants you to have the same luxury here." Calvin had insisted that his daughter not share his modest accommodations in the hotel.

"I don't think so. He expects me to marry and set up my own household soon. There'd be no need for a fancy house here."

A valid point.

"Then there's the part about retiring." Alexandra's gaze turned steely in an apparent attempt to control her emotions. "He's only fifty-two years old. Why would he be thinking about retirement?"

"I don't know." That part of the story rang false to him too. "I'd like to tell you not to worry, but he's your father. It's natural that you'd worry." As Gabe had worried about his own father.

He pulled out his watch, calculating the time until supper. "Would it help if we walked to the spring?" Perhaps then he could learn what else Calvin had said and why Alexandra was so sad.

She shook her head. "Not today. When I feel like this, there's only one thing to do: paint."

⁓

"How's your courtship of Alexandra progressing?" Calvin demanded as Gabe entered his office. The angry tone told him the conversation with his daughter had disturbed Calvin as much as it had Alexandra and, though Gabe hadn't been part of it, he was a convenient target for the older man's anger.

He wouldn't react to Calvin's use of the word *courtship*, although he suspected that was the man's intention. Instead, Gabe settled into one of the chairs in front of the desk and said as mildly as he could, "It would have been better if you'd told her about the land by the river. That and your plans to retire came as a shock to her. A shock to me too."

Gabe chose his words carefully, needing to maintain the pretense that he wanted to be part of Calvin's new project. "I thought you were going to let me in on your next investment opportunity, but now I hear you're retiring."

The man nodded slowly, as if he'd expected that. "Don't worry about that. I haven't forgotten our agreement. The truth is, I'm not planning to retire. I don't know why I told Alexandra that, other than that she surprised me by asking about the land. Living there was the first thing that came into my head."

"Then you're not going to build a house."

"Nope." Calvin confirmed Gabe's suspicions.

"Then why buy the land?"

Alexandra's father leaned back in his chair, crossed his arms, and took a deep breath in what Gabe recognized as a delaying tactic. Calvin was choosing his words as carefully as Gabe had.

"I don't know how much my daughter told you about her situation. Her financial situation," Calvin clarified. "When her grandmother died, Alexandra's mother inherited a goodly sum of money from a complicated and unusual trust. In most cases when she marries, a woman's property becomes her husband's, but this trust kept everything for the women—first my wife, now Alexandra.

"It's a sizeable amount," Calvin added, "but I want Alexandra to have more. You can call it an old man's pride, but when I take my last breath, I want my daughter's legacy from me to equal what she received from her mother. That's why I bought the land."

Gabe's instincts told him there was at least a grain of truth in Calvin's story, but he was still suspicious.

As if he'd read Gabe's thoughts, Calvin said, "The land's a good investment. When there's a drought—and there will be one—ranchers will pay me well for access to the river. Their livestock won't survive without it."

Perhaps, although the land he'd bought wasn't the only access to the river. But if the land was merely an investment for Alexandra's future, what was the new business opportunity? All of Calvin's previous schemes had been short term. Not only was planning for something that might not happen for many years out of character for him, but investors wouldn't be interested in such nebulous prospects.

The way the man refused to meet his gaze told Gabe that Calvin Tarkington was lying and that the land was part of his next scheme. That was good news on several fronts. It gave Gabe a new focus for his investigation and also meant that when he sent Jason Biddle his weekly update, he'd have more to report.

"What do you know about Phil?" Alexandra had waited more than a day to ask the question that had haunted her since Papa had spoken so warmly of the man. Though there'd been numerous opportunities, she had wanted the cover of darkness so that Laura would be less likely to read her expression. Now they were sitting on the verandah outside Alexandra's room on an almost moonless night.

"Phil Blakeslee?" Laura seemed surprised by the question. "I didn't know him very well. I don't think anyone did other than maybe Mrs. Lockhart, because he kept to himself most of the time unless he was sketching someone." She turned toward Alexandra. "Why?"

"I'm curious. My father mentioned him several times." A gust of wind warned Alexandra that the storm Laura's father had predicted was approaching.

"They might have known each other, because Phil talked to Mrs. Lockhart about selling her home. After he died and your father arrived, there was speculation that they were working together."

"They were. Papa hired Phil." Alexandra saw no reason to hide that. "I simply wondered what kind of man he was. My father didn't say much." But the way he'd spoken had resurrected the hurt and anger she'd believed she had banished.

"You might want to ask Dorothy. There was a time when I thought he might be the right husband for her. I tried to convince her of that, but she wouldn't listen."

Alexandra couldn't help laughing at Laura's pretended outrage. "So you've been a matchmaker for a while."

The darkness wasn't deep enough to hide Laura's shrug. "Only because I want to see my friends happy. I wish I could take credit for Dorothy marrying Brandon, but Nutmeg had as much to do with that as I did."

"Upstaged by a dog?" Alexandra felt her melancholy mood dissipate as she laughed again. "How did you know that I needed to laugh?"

Laura shrugged again. "It must be because I'm such a wise woman."

This time they both laughed.

Papa stared at the painting Alexandra had laid on his desk, his expression inscrutable. Did he like it? She couldn't tell, but for the first time she could recall, Alexandra didn't care. She knew the painting was good.

She'd begun it Saturday afternoon when she'd been hurt, angry, and—yes—jealous and had needed a way to express her emotions. Though Laura had protested, she hadn't stopped for supper but had worked until it was too dark. By then, daylight was finished, and so was her painting.

When she'd looked at it the next morning, she'd smiled with satisfaction at the scene she'd created. The flowers from Mrs. Plaut's conservatory shone like jewels, their lush colors attracting the viewer's attention. They were the central theme of the painting and all a casual glance would reveal. Few would notice that peeking out between the petals of one of the peonies was a woman's face.

She was looking upward, searching for something in the sky, her expression radiating hope.

"That's you, isn't it?" Papa broke his silence with a question.

Alexandra nodded. "Yes, but it could be anyone." Alexander Pope had written that hope springs eternal, and as she'd put the finishing touches on the painting, Alexandra had felt her anger subside, replaced by the hope that somehow she would be able to win Papa's love.

"It's beautiful, Alexandra. Where shall we hang it?"

"I was thinking about the parlor."

Papa studied the painting again, then nodded. "Having your paintings on display was a good idea and will make the hotel even more appealing to visitors. Do you have any other suggestions?"

She did. Though she'd expected an argument when he heard the suggestion, Papa agreed she should be the one to write the invitations to the men he'd identified as potential investors for his next business.

"That will be a big help," he admitted. "When I first contacted them, I thought the hotel would be ready before this. Fortunately, I didn't give them an exact date for the presentation, but a nicely worded invitation in your fine penmanship will help allay any concerns they may have had about the delays. I'm glad you offered to help."

It was another step forward, another reason to hope. Alexandra was smiling when she left the hotel.

Gabe was not smiling when he rode back to Mesquite Springs. He'd spent the day on horseback, exploring the first of the three ranches Calvin had bought. Though it appeared prosperous enough with well-tended buildings and good grazing for livestock, Gabe saw nothing that would attract investors.

He planned to return tomorrow and the next day to inspect the other ranches, telling himself it was possible one of them would be different, but he doubted he'd find anything.

What was Calvin's scheme this time?

Sonny stared out the window as the stagecoach entered Mesquite Springs. From what he could see, it wasn't a bad town, if you liked small towns. He did not. But if he wanted the money, he needed to find Alexandra Tarkington. That's why when she hadn't been in Saratoga, he'd endured the long, dusty, and boring trip to a small town in Texas. Finding the heiress was the first step.

Sonny climbed down from the coach and waited while the driver unloaded his luggage. They'd stopped in front of a building whose plate-glass window proclaimed it to be the mercantile. A good spot to let passengers disembark.

Realizing his bags would be safe on the boardwalk, Sonny left them there when he entered the mercantile. If Mesquite Springs was like other towns, the owner would know everything that was going on.

"How can I help you, sir?" Sonny saw the admiration in the woman's eyes as she hurried toward the entrance to greet him. Though she was old enough to be his mother, it appeared she wasn't immune to his appearance. That was good, for it would make it easier to learn what he needed. For what had to be the hundredth time, Sonny congratulated himself that the good looks that had been the object of other boys' envy when he was in school had never failed to attract females, regardless of their age.

"It's a pleasure to meet you, ma'am," he said, adopting his most courtly tone. "May I tell you that you have an impressive supply of merchandise? I don't know when I've seen so many items displayed so well." The variety of goods was larger than he would have expected from a town this size, and the shop was clean and well lit.

To Sonny's surprise, the woman dismissed his blatant flattery. "We stock what our customers need."

He doubted anyone needed fancy china or cut-glass vases, but there was nothing to be gained by saying that. Instead, he told the truth, or at least the partial truth. "I'm thinking about settling here and need a place to stay while I'm looking around. Can you direct me to the hotel?"

She stared at him, perhaps assessing his honesty, then gave a short nod. "The hotel's not finished, but you're in luck, because there's a vacancy at the boardinghouse. It's Martha Bayles's nicest room, in fact."

"It seems this is my lucky day." And if the Tarkington heiress was here, it would be even luckier. Though Sonny wanted to ask the proprietress about Alexandra, he couldn't. When he met her, it had to appear to be a casual encounter.

"How do I find the boardinghouse?"

"It's easy, Mr. . . ." The woman let her voice trail off, obviously waiting for him to introduce himself.

"Lewis," Sonny said firmly, giving the name he'd decided to use here. "Martin Lewis."

Eighteen

Gabe wasn't accustomed to wandering aimlessly, but he found himself doing that this morning. Alexandra was teaching the younger children as she did each weekday morning. Teaching and painting gave her a purpose, but while Gabe had a purpose, he'd exhausted every idea he had on how to uncover Calvin's next scheme.

He believed the land was involved, which was why he'd spent most of the past three days exploring the ranches. Each day, he'd ridden to the river's edge and approached from that direction, bypassing the barricaded entrances. As he'd expected, there'd been no fences near the water, nothing to interfere with his search. He'd seen nothing more than three ordinary-looking ranch houses with an ordinary number of outbuildings. There'd been no sign of workers but no sign of anything else, either. And that was frustrating.

If the land wasn't part of Calvin's plan, why had he bought it? From everything Gabe had learned, Calvin Tarkington was not a man who acted on a whim. The fact that he'd pretended to be a man from Mississippi when he bought the ranches told Gabe this was carefully planned, but though he'd wracked his brain, he could not determine what role the land played.

The answer had to be somewhere, but where?

"Good morning, Emil." As he walked by the construction site, Gabe tipped his hat to the foreman. In his midforties, the man Calvin had put in charge of the workers had appeared serious when Gabe first met him, but he'd learned that Emil had a lighter side and didn't hesitate to joke with Gabe so long as Calvin wasn't around.

"Is it a good morning?" Emil wrinkled his nose. "Maybe for you, but the new man I hired isn't pulling his weight. If we weren't so far behind schedule, I'd fire him, but bad as he is, John Nelson's better than no one."

Though Gabe had spoken with the other workers, hoping to learn more about Calvin, he doubted a new hire like Nelson could provide any insights. There was no reason to look for him.

"What can I do to help? I don't have any experience with building, but I could try."

A look of genuine horror crossed the foreman's face. "I couldn't let you do that. The boss would have my head if I let a gentleman like you or the other guy who came to town yesterday work here."

Two new people in Mesquite Springs this week. No doubt about it, the town was growing.

"How did you hear about the newcomer?" Emil wasn't one to frequent the saloon, which was where news seemed to flow as freely as strong drink.

"He came poking around here. Said he wanted to see if the hotel was going to be as good as he'd heard, but when I told him to talk to the boss, he just shook his head and left."

There was probably no connection between this man and Calvin, but Gabe knew better than to ignore any possibility. His morning was no longer aimless.

"Are you sure I can't help you?" he asked Emil.

"Sure as blue northers bring cold winds, but it was good of you to offer."

Gabe wanted to do more than that. He wanted to erase the worry lines from Emil's face. "There must be something I can do."

The man grinned. "I wouldn't say no to a piece of oatmeal pecan pie if it's on the menu today."

That was something Gabe could do. "If it isn't on the menu today, I'll see if Evelyn will bake one tomorrow."

The foreman's grin widened. "Thanks, Gabe. You're a good man."

He hoped that was true, and he hoped the new man in town was nothing more than a casual visitor.

Alexandra frowned as her stomach rumbled. Thank goodness it hadn't done that when she'd been teaching the younger children. They were easily distracted, and a noisy stomach would definitely distract them. Though she'd eaten her normal breakfast, Alexandra was already hungry and looking forward to whatever Evelyn and Laura were serving. She quickened her pace as she crossed Main Street, then stopped abruptly when a man stepped in front of her.

"Excuse me, miss, but I believe you dropped this."

The stranger holding a woman's handkerchief and smiling at her was the most handsome man Alexandra had ever seen. Opal would have been enchanted. The combination of flawless features, dark brown hair, eyes the color of Evelyn's chocolate cake, and a strong physique turned this man into the personification of the heroes of the books Alexandra and her cousin used to share.

"That's the man I want to marry," Opal had declared when they'd finished reading a particularly romantic tale. "I want a man who looks like Horatio and who'll treat me the way he did Rosalind." The fictional hero had been almost too good to be true, but that hadn't stopped Opal from dreaming about him.

Now the man of Opal's dreams was standing in front of Alexandra. Her cousin might swoon with pleasure; Alexandra took a step backward, the hair on the back of her neck rising in alarm. This was far from her normal reaction to a stranger, but something about him made her wary.

"It's not mine," she said firmly. The handkerchief was an expensive one, boasting delicate lace trim. While she hadn't seen anything like it in the Downeys' mercantile, it was possible this was a newly arrived item that someone had lost. "Where did you find it?"

The man's smile broadened. "I saw it drop to the ground when you crossed the street."

He was lying. If that had happened, there would have been dirt on the fine linen, but there was none. Alexandra took another step backward, her instinct to flee warring with the manners that had been drilled into her. Manners won, and she continued to speak to the stranger.

"You must have been mistaken. It's definitely not mine. I suggest you take it to the mercantile." Alexandra gestured toward the store. "Mrs. Downey may know whose it is."

Though her tone was clearly one of dismissal, the man's smile did not falter. "Thank you. Who shall I tell her sent me?"

"Alexandra."

As his eyes registered a satisfied gleam, making her wonder if he'd expected her answer, a shiver slid down Alexandra's spine, increasing her distrust of the stranger. Was it possible that he already knew who she was and that the handkerchief was simply a ploy to give him a reason to talk to her? If that was true, there was only one reason Alexandra could imagine: Franklin had sent him to find her.

He didn't look like the kind of man Franklin would hire, but her final encounter with Franklin had shown Alexandra how little she knew about the man who'd courted her. This man could indeed be his emissary, but if he was, he would not succeed. Nothing would convince her to return to New York and Franklin.

"It's a pleasure to meet you, Miss . . ." The man let his voice trail off, obviously waiting for her to complete the sentence.

There was no reason to lie, not when anyone in town could tell him her full name. "Tarkington."

He nodded and slid the handkerchief back into his coat pocket. "Thank you again, Miss Tarkington. I'm Martin Lewis."

Franklin had never mentioned anyone named Martin Lewis, but that didn't mean there was no connection between the two men. Alexandra would take no chances.

"If you'll excuse me, Mr. Lewis, there's somewhere I need to be." Without waiting for his response, she hurried toward Polly's Place, hoping the man would not follow her. He did not.

"Is something wrong?" Laura asked as Alexandra entered the restaurant.

Though her heart was still pounding more than if she'd raced up two flights of stairs, Alexandra shrugged. "I don't know. I just met a newcomer." *A man whose lies and the way he looked at me frightened me.*

"A very handsome man?" Laura led Alexandra to the restaurant's sole table for one, as if she sensed this was not a day when Alexandra would want to make conversation with other diners.

"Most women would say so."

"Then it must be Mr. Lewis. Mother met him yesterday when he arrived on the stagecoach. He said he was considering moving here and needed a place to stay while he made his decision, so he rented a room at the boardinghouse."

"Oh." Alexandra hadn't realized how much she'd hoped the man was simply passing through town and that her reaction to him had been misplaced, but knowing that he intended to remain in Mesquite Springs sent a new round of shivers down her spine. For a few weeks, she'd felt safe. Now the fear was back.

Laura positioned herself so no one else in the restaurant could see Alexandra. "What did he do that bothered you?"

"Nothing, really." She didn't want to worry Laura. "It must have been my imagination." Perhaps if she told herself that often enough, she might believe it.

Nineteen

onny—No, he corrected himself, Martin. He needed to start thinking of himself as Martin—forced himself to keep smiling. Nothing had gone right since he'd arrived in Mesquite Springs. The truth was, nothing had gone right since his last meeting with Drummond. The Tarkington girl wasn't in New York. She wasn't in Saratoga. And now that he'd found her, she wasn't acting the way she was supposed to.

Martin stared at her back as she headed for the restaurant. She was even more beautiful than he'd expected. The old man hadn't described her, claiming all he knew was that Tarkington claimed she was a beauty, then reminding him that a father's judgment couldn't be trusted and that looks weren't important. All that mattered was getting her signature on two very important documents.

If this first encounter was any indication, that was going to be more difficult than Martin had expected. Not only did she seem immune to what Ma had called his irresistible appeal, but he'd caught a glimmer of fear in her eyes. She wasn't supposed to fear him—at least not yet.

He debated following her into the restaurant, then changed his mind as a man approached from the opposite direction. It was time to become acquainted with the fellow who'd been out walking with the heiress last night.

"Does this town have a saloon?" Martin noticed with satisfaction that while the man was tall, he couldn't match his own height.

To his surprise, the man appeared to be studying him as carefully as he had him as he said, "It's at the end of the next block." He pointed west. "You can't miss it."

He appeared ready to enter the restaurant, possibly to join Alexandra Tarkington for lunch. Martin couldn't let him do that. If he was competition, and the way he and the gal had looked at each other made him suspect they were more than casual acquaintances, Martin had to do everything he could to stop him. The heiress was going to be his.

He held out his hand, inviting the man to shake it. "I'm Martin Lewis, a newcomer to town. I sure would appreciate it if you'd have a drink with me and tell me a bit about Mesquite Springs."

"Gabe Seymour." Seymour's shake was firm. "It's almost noon. How about some food instead of a drink?"

Martin shook his head. "I was looking for a place with just men. Not that I have anything against ladies, but they can be a bit too friendly."

"All right."

The agreement came more easily than Martin had expected. Ten minutes later, he and Seymour had drinks in front of them, sarsaparilla for Seymour, surprisingly good whiskey for him.

"What brings you to Mesquite Springs?" Seymour asked.

Martin spun his tale.

"You don't have to cook breakfast and supper every day," Sam said as he entered the kitchen. "We could buy canned food from the mercantile."

It wasn't the first time Gabe's landlord and new friend had said that, but it appeared they needed to repeat the discussion. "I keep telling you it's the least I can do since you're letting me live here for free."

Besides, it helped distract him from thoughts of Martin Lewis, the newcomer who'd done his best to evade Gabe's questions. The man had claimed that he'd come here in search of a new place to live, but the story hadn't rung true, nor had his assertion that he was a banker.

After what had happened to Pa, Gabe had learned everything he could about banking. He knew the difference between a teller's and a manager's responsibilities, but Lewis had shown a remarkable ignorance of their duties. Lewis had also claimed to have spent most of his life in New Orleans, but his accent was not southern. If anything, Gabe would have said Lewis was a Midwesterner like him.

The man was lying. The question was why.

Sam gave an exaggerated sniff that wrenched Gabe's thoughts away from Martin Lewis. "You can say what you want, but I'm benefiting more from our arrangement. It gives me independence and the chance to be closer to Laura."

Gabe turned back to the stove and gave the stew a stir it didn't need so that Sam wouldn't see his smile. The protest about cooking had been nothing more than an introduction to Sam's favorite subject: the woman he loved.

"I wish I knew how to court her." Sam pulled one of the chairs away from the table and sank onto it.

"Did you ask your father?" If he had, the advice might help Gabe. Though Calvin had told him he was pleased that Alexandra's responsibilities at the school and her walks with Gabe kept her too busy to spend much time at the hotel, he'd also admitted he was worried about her future and that he wanted to see her married. "You'd be good for her," Calvin had declared. "Better than those spineless suitors she had back East."

Spineless was not a word anyone had applied to Gabe. He prided himself on taking action. The problem was, though he knew what he wanted, he also knew this wasn't the right time. He wanted more than a sham courtship or one suggested by her father. He hadn't expected it, but the curiosity he'd felt about Alexandra had turned into admiration, admiration had turned into attraction, and attraction had turned into the strongest emotion he'd ever felt for a woman.

When Gabe courted Alexandra—and there was no doubt he wanted to do that—it would be when he was free to tell her who he was and why he was here. But until he completed his work for Jason Biddle, he was not free. And when he was . . . Gabe's stomach clenched at the thought of what the revelation of Calvin's crimes might do to his daughter.

"My father had no suggestions." Sam's voice reflected his annoyance. "He said he knew he wanted to marry my mother the day he met her. She must have felt the same way, because two weeks later, they were married."

"What about your mother?"

Sam shrugged. "She told me ladies expect flowers, candy, and books when they're being courted. Mother offered me some flowers from her conservatory, but that didn't seem special enough for Laura, and if I want to give her candy or books, I'd have to buy them from her parents' store. There'd be no surprise in that."

For the first time since the conversation began, Gabe had something to offer. "Brandon mentioned that he bought Christmas gifts in Grassey." Grassey, according to the newspaper editor, wasn't as attractive a town as Mesquite Springs, but it had a good candy store, and its mercantile carried different merchandise.

"Did you ask him for help courting Alexandra?"

"Nope." Gabe decided not to address the courtship part of Sam's question. "He volunteered the information." They'd been discussing Calvin's land, with Brandon admitting that he was as unconvinced by the story of water access as Gabe had been.

Gabe pulled two plates from the cupboard and began to spoon the stew onto them.

"It sounds like we ought to take a trip to Grassey," Sam said when he'd offered thanks for the food.

"We?"

"We. You can deny it all you want, but I know Alexandra's caught your eye."

"She has." Whenever he thought of his future, Gabe envisioned her as part of it. And if that wasn't preposterous, he didn't know what was. What could he offer an heiress? Still, the picture would not fade. Instead, its appeal only increased the more he thought of it.

"You're right. Let's go to Grassey tomorrow."

Twenty

*E*verything felt off-kilter today. It had started when Alexandra had found Papa coughing uncontrollably when she arrived at the hotel. The coughing had subsided after she'd gotten him a glass of water, but though he claimed it was nothing serious, she could not ignore how unwell he appeared. Once the flush from coughing disappeared, his skin had seemed almost gray, a color Alexandra had never seen before in human skin.

She wanted to ask Gabe if he knew anything about illness, but he wasn't here today. When they'd walked after supper last night, he'd told her he and Sam were going to Grassey, something to do with Sam's business, though Gabe hadn't been specific.

Alexandra had merely nodded and told him she hoped the weather would cooperate, because Grassey was a couple hours' ride from Mesquite Springs. What she hadn't realized was how much she would miss Gabe. It was just one day, she told herself, but somehow the hours passed more slowly than normal. Another thing that was off-kilter.

The one thing that seemed normal was the time she spent with the children. Polly and Melissa had painted landscapes bearing no resemblance to reality, a fact that didn't bother them in the least, while the twins labored over what were supposed to be portraits of their favorite sheep. Their father, they'd informed Alexandra, was a sheep farmer, although he was now helping build the hotel.

"We need extra money," Hans confided. "Too many lambs went to heaven this spring."

And so the twins were immortalizing the lambs that had, according to them, joined their mother.

"I love you, Miss Tarkington." Frieda wrapped her arms around Alexandra's waist and hugged her after being complimented on her painting. "I wish you could be our new mama."

Alexandra's heart clenched at the thought of these children, whom she'd grown to love so dearly, being without a mother. But, as much as she cared for them, she knew Frieda's wish would never come true.

While the other children continued to paint, oblivious to Frieda's plea, Hans nodded solemnly. "Frieda and me told *Vati* we want you, but he said we have to wait for God to send us another mama."

"He said God might never do that." Frieda appeared on the verge of tears. "I don't wanna wait. Why can't you be our mama? Don't you love us?"

There was such anguish in the child's voice that Alexandra found herself wanting to weep. Oh, how she wished she could help the twins. "Yes, I do," she said, stroking Frieda's hair in an attempt to comfort her. "I love you very much, but your father and I . . ."

Alexandra paused, struggling to find a way to explain that she felt nothing more than mild friendship for Fritz Gottlieb. If there was a way, it eluded her.

Though ten minutes remained in the morning lesson, Miss Geist clapped her hands and approached the art class. "Children, it's time for you to put your paints away."

Relief flowed over Alexandra. Thanks to the schoolmarm, she'd been spared from giving an explanation that might have hurt the twins. When Miss Geist dismissed the children for recess, Alexandra waited until the schoolroom was empty before she spoke.

"Thank you for interrupting when you did."

The teacher shrugged, as if her action were of little import. "I overheard a bit of the conversation and wasn't surprised by it. You're filling a very important role in the twins' lives right now. It's only natural that they'd want that to be permanent."

"But I can't be their mother."

Miss Geist squeezed Alexandra's shoulder. "Of course not. That would be wrong for both you and Mr. Gottlieb. It's too soon for him, and you already have a suitor."

"But . . ." Alexandra started to contradict her.

"It may not be official yet, but I've seen the way you and Gabe look at each other. I can practically feel the sparks between you, and that makes my heart sing."

Alexandra's heart was not singing when she emerged from the schoolhouse and saw Martin Lewis standing only a few feet from the entrance.

"Good morning, Miss Tarkington." He doffed his hat in what some would call a courtly gesture, one Alexandra had always found pretentious. "I was hoping you would take pity on a stranger and do me the great honor of having lunch with me. A man doesn't like to eat alone, especially when there's a beautiful woman he'd like to get to know better."

The speech was one Franklin might have made, filled with flattery and false obsequiousness, and it did nothing to convince her of anything other than that she had no desire to spend time with this man. Though the fear that had assailed her yesterday had not returned, she saw no reason to dine with him.

"I'm sorry, Mr. Lewis." Alexandra wasn't sorry, but there were social proprieties to be observed. Aunt Helen had impressed on her the need to be polite to everyone, regardless of her feelings toward them.

"Call me Martin," he urged, "and I hope you'll let me call you Alexandra. Please don't refuse me."

Until he continued, she wasn't certain whether he meant his request to use her first name or his invitation.

"Think of lunch with me as your good deed for the day. We're all supposed to do good deeds, aren't we?" His pleading tone was so exaggerated that Alexandra was tempted to laugh. Franklin would never have gone to such lengths to convince a woman to dine with him. Perhaps she'd been wrong, and he wasn't one of Franklin's cronies.

"The next thing I know, you'll say it's my duty as a temporary resident of Mesquite Springs."

"Only temporary? Why would you leave a place like Mesquite Springs?" This time his questions seemed sincere. "You must tell me more, and what better way to get acquainted than to share a meal? Please say yes."

Alexandra's resistance began to crumble. Even if Franklin had sent Martin Lewis to find her, she'd be in no danger in the restaurant. Polly's Place was the safest spot in town, run by her friends and filled with people who believed in watching out for their neighbors. She would come to no harm there, and an extended conversation would give her the opportunity to learn why this man had come to Mesquite Springs and why he was showing such interest in her.

"All right." And so Alexandra found herself being escorted to Polly's Place.

Though Laura gave her a quizzical look, she said nothing, merely showed them to one of the tables closest to the kitchen as she explained today's menu choices. Theirs was not an ideal table, because sounds from the kitchen emerged each time the door swung open, but it was the safest spot. Alexandra flashed a grateful smile at her friend and let herself relax.

To her surprise, Martin proved to be an entertaining companion, recounting amusing stories of his time working for a bank. Unless he was lying, he'd never been to New York, which meant that her earlier suspicions that he knew Franklin had been groundless. Perhaps he was nothing more than a lonely man.

"What will you do here?" she asked when he said he hoped to

make Mesquite Springs his home. "There are no banks in Texas. I've heard there's a law that forbids them."

Though he looked startled, Martin shrugged, treating it like nothing more than a minor inconvenience. "I'll find something else. Maybe I can help your father run the hotel."

The roasted carrots that had been delicious a second ago lost their flavor as Alexandra's initial misgivings about the newcomer returned. How did he know that Mr. King was her father? It was hardly a secret, but the fact that he had apparently been asking questions about her made her uncomfortable.

Martin cut another piece of his roast beef as he said, "Let's not talk about me. I'm curious about why you're teaching here. You haven't done that before, have you?"

"No." Discomfort turned to alarm, increasing Alexandra's feeling that everything was off-kilter today. The only people in Mesquite Springs who knew this was her first experience teaching were her father and Miss Geist, and neither of them would have told a virtual stranger.

How did Martin Lewis know that, and why did he care?

Patient. He needed to be patient.

Jason took a bite of chicken and pretended to be interested in the discussion of last night's poker game. He didn't care who'd held which cards. All he cared about was making Franklin happy and returning to New York, but neither of those was going to happen this week.

"Take your time," Franklin had said. "Figure out the best way to convince her to marry me. That's what I need. That's what we both need."

Franklin had fisted his hands, and for a second, Jason had thought he would hit him, but he hadn't. He merely pounded the table before he said, "Don't do anything else unless you're sure she won't agree."

Jason wasn't sure of anything other than that he didn't like being in Texas and working as a common laborer. Those crazy doctors at Serenity House had believed that hard work was good for a man, that being hot and tired helped clear the mind. They'd been wrong, just as wrong as they'd been in thinking that painting was soothing and that prayer was more than a waste of time. The only things he'd learned at Serenity House were to be patient and to pretend.

Thank goodness he didn't have to send Franklin any reports. The man who held his future in his hands wouldn't like what Jason had found. He couldn't tell him that the investigator Jason had hired to find Alexandra had done more than find her. Gabe Seymour had not only gained her trust but if the way they'd been laughing together was any indication, Seymour and the gal who was supposed to marry Franklin were attracted to each other.

How was he going to convince the heiress to marry Franklin when she had eyes for another man? Jason had seen enough couples to know that unless this infatuation faded, Franklin had no chance of winning her hand. The question was, how was he going to convince Alexandra Tarkington that Seymour wasn't the man for her without Seymour knowing he was here?

And then there was the man who'd arrived in town the same day as Jason. He was staying at the boardinghouse, not sharing a tent with a dozen workers. He wore the same carefully tailored clothes Jason used to, not shabby overalls. He was leading a life of leisure, not getting splinters in his hands. Jason shouldn't care about him, and he wouldn't except that the newcomer seemed to have taken an interest in Alexandra Tarkington. That had to stop. If—no, when—Jason showed the heiress that Seymour was wrong for her, he couldn't risk having another man wooing her.

He piled more mashed potatoes on his plate as the bowl passed by, then returned to his thoughts. Making Franklin happy was turning out to be more difficult than he'd expected.

Patient. He'd be patient.

Twenty-One

G abe tugged on his hat, trying to shade his face. Yet, despite the sun that made him squint, it felt good to be away from Mesquite Springs and the feeling that someone was watching him, someone other than Martin Lewis.

The man who was not from New Orleans had made no secret of his interest in Gabe's activities. Though he hadn't accompanied him to Polly's Place but had stayed at the saloon after their conversation, that same evening Lewis had left the boardinghouse porch when Gabe and Alexandra had walked by and had tried to join them. The way Alexandra's hand had tightened on his arm told Gabe she was as unwilling as he to have the man's company on their nightly stroll, and so Gabe had been curter than he might have been otherwise.

But it wasn't only Lewis who'd been watching him. Gabe knew that, because his hackles hadn't risen when he'd seen Lewis in conversation with Wyatt. Instead, he'd been blocks away from Lewis when the prickling feeling had occurred The problem was, Gabe had been unable to discover who had more than a casual interest in him. He hoped the ride home would help him think more clearly than he had this morning.

"I can't believe I'd never been to Grassey." Sam's voice held a note of chagrin. "I've lived in Mesquite Springs my whole life, and it took two newcomers—you and Brandon—to get me to Grassey."

Having spent two hours in the neighboring town, Gabe saw no reason to consider that a tragedy. "Other than the candy store, there wasn't much reason to go to Grassey. The Downeys' mercantile has a better selection." With one notable exception.

"True. And the restaurant can't compare to Polly's Place."

There was no question about that. "It would be hard to beat Evelyn's cooking."

"And Laura's." A frown marred Sam's face. "I hope she likes the candy. I never thought to ask what flavor she prefers."

Gabe couldn't help laughing. "Since you bought three pieces of everything the store offers, her favorite is sure to be there." The proprietor had been thrilled with the size of Sam's purchase, admitting business had been slow recently.

"Unless she hates candy." Sam looked at his saddlebags, as if they could predict Laura's reaction.

"Stop worrying so much. You could give Laura sawdust mixed with cactus juice and she'd be happy."

"I hope so." Sam still sounded dubious. "It's easier for you. You know Alexandra will appreciate the brushes."

"If the shopkeeper didn't lie." The only thing of interest Gabe had found in the mercantile had been a set of art brushes. The store's owner alleged they were of the finest quality, and the price seemed to confirm that. With a rueful expression, the owner explained that a man had ordered them a few months ago but never returned to buy them.

"I should have asked him to pay in advance," the shopkeeper admitted, "but he seemed so honest." He picked up the box of brushes and handed them to Gabe. "If you want them, I'll give you a good price." And so Gabe had become the temporary owner of a set of six paintbrushes.

"I'm no expert, but they look good. Better than the ones at Serenity House."

Sam's reply did more than surprise Gabe. It shocked him. "You painted there?"

His friend nodded. "It was one of the things they tried. The doctor who's in charge claimed painting helped patients express themselves better than words."

"Alexandra says the same thing. She believes it's helping the twins whose mother died." And she'd told him painting was one of the ways she dealt with anger and disappointment.

Sam stared at the road for a moment before speaking again. "I don't know whether it helped me very much, but it was satisfying to cover a sheet of paper with black paint. A couple months later, I used light gray. I suppose you could call that progress."

Gabe was fascinated by the insights into Sam's past. Though he'd seen no evidence of the anger that once ruled him, Gabe did not doubt that it had been real. Sam did not tell lies or stretch the truth. Unlike Calvin Tarkington.

One of the things that had made Gabe a successful investigator was that he tried to understand the reasons behind others' actions. Typically, it wasn't particularly difficult, but Calvin was harder to read.

Gabe still had trouble envisioning him as a gambler, but Bill Woods's inquiries had confirmed that Calvin had once gambled heavily. As far as Bill could tell, the shady deals had begun soon after the gambling losses mounted.

Was he trying to recoup the money he'd lost, or was there another reason he had begun defrauding others? It was possible that feeling he'd been cheated when he gambled had made Calvin believe it was all right to cheat others. But that left the question of why he had started gambling in the first place. Now was not the time to try to unravel the mysteries of Calvin Tarkington's brain.

Gabe looked at his friend, who was staring into the distance, his expression inscrutable. "Serenity House sounds like a very unusual place with a very unusual doctor."

"You're right on both counts. As far as I know, it's the only place of its kind in the country. I was fortunate Pastor Coleman knew about it."

The hawk that had been soaring lazily overhead suddenly dove to the ground, apparently having sighted its prey. Sam slowed his horse slightly and turned to face Gabe. "What are you looking for in Mesquite Springs?"

The unexpected question left Gabe feeling like a squirrel caught in the hawk's talons, paralyzed by the ambush. Gabe knew his reaction was absurd. This was Sam, his friend, asking an innocent question. Still, he hesitated. "I was looking for a place to stay for a few months while I decide what to do next."

Sam shook his head. "That's a good story. Some may believe it, but I don't. It's like you're two different men. When we're alone in my apartment, you're one man—relaxed, almost at peace—but once we go outside, you become another person—intensely focused on something. I have no idea what it is, but I sense that you're searching for something . . . or someone."

Should he tell him? Gabe stared into the distance, trying to settle his internal battle. Part of him wanted to confide in the man who was both his friend and his ally. The other part reminded him that the more people who knew why he'd come to Mesquite Springs, the more likely his secrets would be revealed.

"I should have realized your training as an attorney would enable you to see beneath the surface."

"That same training also means I'm accustomed to keeping secrets. You can trust me not to reveal anything you say."

Trust. That was the key. Framed in those terms, the decision was easy. "I do trust you." And Sam obviously trusted him, or he wouldn't have discussed his stay in Pennsylvania. Gabe didn't expect Sam to help with the investigation, but it would be good to be able to ask his opinion. The man's insights differed from his own, and that different perspective might be helpful.

"You're right. I am looking for something. I'm an investigator."

Sam didn't appear surprised. "A Pinkerton?"

"No. I'm independent."

Again, Sam showed no surprise. "You've been successful."

Warmed by his friend's faith in him, Gabe smiled. "For the most part. This current case has been more of a challenge than I'd expected. My instincts tell me something is wrong, but I can't find any evidence."

Though Calvin had admitted he owned the three ranches, there had been no paperwork related to the land purchases in his files. That was odd. Very odd.

"I'm tempted to tell my client he was mistaken, but I can't do that, because my head tells me he's right."

Sam seemed to understand. "I know you can't divulge your client's name, but if I knew who you were watching, I might be able to help you. I suspect I hear things you don't simply because I was born here."

"I won't refuse any help. I'd like to get this resolved quickly. To be honest, I'm more frustrated than I've ever been." Gabe wasn't too proud to admit that. He raised an eyebrow as he looked at his friend. "I don't know whether you'll be shocked, but I'm looking into the possibility that Calvin Tarkington is a swindler."

Sam whistled softly. "And Alexandra has no idea what you're doing."

"Or what her father's been doing, at least not as far as I can tell. Ever since her mother died, Alexandra's lived in New York with her great-aunt. Until she came here, she saw her father only once a year around Christmastime when he'd go to New York for the holidays."

Sam was silent for a while, apparently digesting what he'd heard. "That doesn't sound like a loving parent, does it?" His question was rhetorical, and so Sam did not wait for a response. "I may not like or even understand why he treated Alexandra that way, but it doesn't mean he's a criminal. Calvin strikes me as a troubled man but not necessarily a dishonest one."

This was one of the many times when Gabe agreed with Sam. "I have no proof tying him to the previous swindles, but everything I could find points to him. If I'm right, he's destroyed men's lives as well as stolen their money."

Sam gave him a sympathetic look. "It's an awful situation, isn't it? You want to help your client, but you know that if he's right and you prove Calvin is a criminal, you risk losing Alexandra."

"I'd certainly lose any chance of winning her trust." Especially if she learned about the agreement he had with Calvin.

"You can't stop the investigation, because you gave the client your word."

"Exactly. It's a matter of principle. I owe my client a complete investigation, but there's more than that at stake. If he's right— and my instincts say he is—I owe it to dozens of nameless people to stop Calvin from hurting them with whatever he's planning now."

Sam let out another low whistle. "And I thought I would have a hard time wooing Laura. Your predicament is far worse. I don't envy you, my friend."

Gabe tightened his hands on the reins as he thought of all he was facing. "I wish there were an easy solution, some way to stop Calvin without hurting Alexandra, but if there is, it's eluded me."

Jason frowned as he brushed the sawdust off his pants. He hated the shabby clothes, the beard, and most of all, having to labor like a common worker. He had splinters in his hands from carrying boards and a blackened fingernail from hitting his thumb with a hammer. He ought to be back in New York, dining at a fine restaurant with a well-dressed woman. But, no, he was here in a small Texas town, pretending to build a hotel.

If only there'd been another way, but there wasn't. He couldn't run the risk of Seymour recognizing him. As it was, he was virtually invisible. No one looked closely at workers. Not Seymour, not the Tarkington heiress, not even that newcomer in the fancy suit, Martin Lewis.

He'd tried talking to Lewis, had pretended to bump into him accidentally, then apologized profusely, but the man hadn't listened. He'd shoved Jason aside with a muttered oath, then continued on his way as if Jason were no more than a gnat buzzing around his head.

He'd regret that. Jason would make certain of that. But first he had to figure out how to convince Alexandra Tarkington that Gabe Seymour was not the man he appeared to be. Once she learned that, Franklin would have a chance. And if Franklin had a chance, he'd be happy, and so would Jason.

Twenty-Two

*Y*ou have a new admirer."

Laura smiled as Alexandra rolled the dough, doing her best to keep it a uniform thickness. The two women were in the Downeys' kitchen, where Laura was attempting to teach Alexandra to make cinnamon rolls. Though this was something Laura normally did in the morning, since it seemed unlikely they'd see Gabe and Sam this evening, she'd suggested a cooking lesson as a way to pass the time.

"The next step is to spread the cinnamon mixture on the dough. Make sure you get it all the way to the edge." Laura took a step back and returned to her original subject. "I know you didn't trust him at first, but Mr. Lewis seems smitten. He couldn't take his eyes off you."

That was one of the aspects of the lunch they'd shared that had disturbed Alexandra. "That doesn't mean I liked it. Until I got him talking about himself, he was looking at me the way some of the men look at Evelyn's oatmeal pecan pie—like they want to devour it."

"And you don't want to be devoured."

Though Laura had laced her words with humor, Alexandra

found nothing humorous in the situation. "No, I don't. Would you?"

"Definitely not." Laura shook her head for emphasis. "I want a man who looks at me like Wyatt does every time he sees Evelyn—like his world suddenly became complete."

"And I want a man who loves me for myself, not my inheritance. Martin reminds me of men I knew in New York."

After Laura nodded her approval of the way Alexandra had spread the filling and showed her how to roll the dough, she said, "The men you came here to avoid."

Alexandra looked up, surprised by her friend's comment. "How did you know that?"

"A lucky guess. I know you came to see your father, but I always thought there was more than that. When you first arrived, you were wary. You'd look around, like you were afraid you'd see someone you knew. You don't do that anymore."

Alexandra began to cut the long roll into individual pieces and place them in the pan she'd prepared. "I hadn't realized it was so obvious, but you're right. There was someone in New York who frightened me. Getting away from him was one of the reasons I came to Texas."

"I wish you hadn't had that experience, but I'm glad you're here."

"So am I." Even though the reunion with her father hadn't been as satisfying as Alexandra had hoped, there were many wonderful things about being in Mesquite Springs—her friendship with Laura, her pleasure in teaching the children, the changes she'd seen in the twins, her . . . She paused, not sure how to define her relationship with Gabe. All she knew was that he was one of the reasons she was grateful she'd come here.

"Girls, you have visitors." Mrs. Downey poked her head into the kitchen. "I put them in the parlor." Her grin left no doubt of the visitors' identity, and Alexandra felt her pulse race at the prospect of seeing Gabe again.

"We'll be there in a minute," Laura told her mother. "The rolls are ready for their second rise."

As she looked at herself, Alexandra chuckled. "It may take more than a minute for me to wash off all this flour."

"Gabe wouldn't mind, even if your face was covered with it."

Alexandra had no intention of discovering whether Laura was right. "I'd mind. Aunt Helen would be horrified if I left this room looking anything but perfectly groomed."

"Your aunt's not here."

"True." Alexandra scrubbed her hands, inspecting her fingernails to be certain no dough remained beneath them, then ran a towel across her face before she removed her flour-coated apron. "How do I look?"

"Perfect."

When they entered the parlor and Gabe and Sam rose to greet them, Alexandra noticed parcels wrapped in brown paper by their feet. She wouldn't ask what they were—a lady would never be so bold—but they roused her curiosity. Never before had the men brought packages.

"Good evening, ladies. I'm sorry we're late for our walk, but Sam's business in Grassey took longer than we'd expected." Was it only Alexandra's imagination that Gabe had put a slightly sarcastic twist on the word *business*?

"Laura and I've been busy. We weren't certain you'd come tonight, so she bravely volunteered to teach me to make cinnamon rolls." Alexandra wrinkled her nose at the thought of her first attempt at baking. "They're a bit lopsided looking, but if you're as brave as she was, I'll offer you some when they're baked."

Knowing the men would remain standing as long as she did, Alexandra took a seat on the couch next to Laura.

"I'm game." Gabe wasted no time in replying. "What about you, Sam?"

"Of course. Cinnamon is one of my favorite flavors. Evelyn can attest to that. When she started serving Saturday breakfast, I was a regular customer the weeks she served cinnamon rolls. I'd even come into town early every Saturday to see what was on the menu. I could smell those rolls as I walked by."

Sam was uneasy. That was the only reason Alexandra could imagine for his prattling like that. Wanting to put him at ease, she asked, "Was your business in Grassey successful?"

He shrugged. "I don't know yet." He reached down to retrieve the package by his feet and handed it to Laura. "This is for you. I hope you'll enjoy it." The normally confident attorney appeared as nervous as if he were trying his first case.

Alexandra turned her attention to her friend, whose face was wreathed with pleasure. Whether the package held priceless jewels or shredded paper, she would cherish it simply because it was her first gift from Sam.

Her face flushed, her hands shaking, Laura unwrapped and opened the box, then smiled. "Candy! What a wonderful gift!" She displayed a box with more varieties of candy than Alexandra had seen outside a confectionery. Sam had chosen well, for only a few days ago, Laura had called Mesquite Springs's lack of a candy store deplorable.

Her face radiant, Laura looked ready to burst from happiness. "This is perfect, Sam. Absolutely perfect. I don't know how to thank you."

"You just did." As tension ebbed from him, Sam leaned forward, his grin as wide as the Mississippi River. "Your smile tells me I made a good choice."

"You certainly did." Laura held out the box. "Would anyone like a piece?"

Alexandra shook her head. "It smells delicious, but I need to save room for a cinnamon roll. If I won't eat one, I can't expect anyone else to."

Though the men declined the sweets, Laura popped one into her mouth and gave a contented sigh. "This is the best fudge I've ever eaten."

Sam's contented expression left no doubt that that was exactly the reaction he'd hoped for.

"The trip to Grassey was for Sam, but while we were there, I found something I thought you might like."

Alexandra had almost forgotten there was a second package until Gabe handed it to her.

"I know it's not a traditional gift, but when I saw this, I couldn't resist."

A thousand butterflies invaded her stomach, each flapping its wings. She and Gabe were simply friends, which meant she probably shouldn't accept anything from him, and yet Alexandra couldn't—she wouldn't—disappoint him. Slowly, she unwrapped the long rectangular box and lifted the lid, gasping when she saw the contents.

"Oh, Gabe, these are wonderful!" Inside the box were half a dozen of her favorite brand of paintbrushes. "How did you know I was going to ask Mrs. Downey to order some for me? I've been painting so much that my brushes are becoming worn."

Alexandra leaned forward, heedless of protocol, and laid her hand on Gabe's. "Thank you. This is the nicest gift anyone's ever given me." And she knew exactly how she would thank him.

Twenty-Three

We could have gone fishing."

Laura, who was still starry-eyed about the candy she'd received, patted Sam's arm. "We could have, but this will be better."

Before the men had left last night, Gabe had suggested they change their plans for the day and have a picnic by the springs rather than fish, a suggestion both Alexandra and Laura had endorsed, although for different reasons. Laura had already made her dislike of fishing known, while Alexandra hoped to incorporate the springs in the painting she planned to make for Gabe.

She envisioned a series of scenes that would remind him of the times they'd shared, beginning with a stagecoach on a dusty road. The park bench and Mrs. Plaut's conservatory would be the focus of two other scenes, but she wanted a fourth and hoped the springs would be as beautiful as everyone claimed.

"I'm looking forward to seeing the springs," Alexandra told her companions. "It's hard to believe I've been here for almost a month and haven't seen the town's namesake. Besides, it's the perfect day for a walk."

"That's easy for you to say. You're not carrying a basket filled with food. If we'd gone fishing, we'd have been on horseback, and the horse would be doing the work."

Alexandra wasn't certain whether Sam's complaints were genuine, but Laura seemed unwilling to let him continue.

"You're being such a grouch, Sam. Lucky for you, I know how to stop that." She reached into her reticule and pulled out a piece of fudge. After unwrapping it, she handed it to him. "There. That ought to sweeten your mood."

Gabe hooted. "You did it, Sam. I thought you were joking when you said you'd get Laura to give you some candy before we reached the springs, but you did it."

Though Alexandra laughed, Laura appeared indignant. "You mean that was all a ploy?"

Sam smacked his lips. "It worked, didn't it, sweetheart?"

Any protests Laura might have had melted at the endearment.

"Let's let them go ahead," Gabe suggested, slowing his pace until Sam and Laura were a few yards in front of them. "I want some time alone with you."

And Alexandra relished time with Gabe. "The paintbrushes are perfect," she told him.

"I'm glad you like them. I had to trust the storeowner when he said they were good quality."

"The best. The ones I ordered for the schoolchildren are very basic. Some of the bristles have already fallen out, but they don't mind."

"Because they're still learning. They're not professional artists, but you are."

Gabe's praise made her face warm. "I'm not a professional. No one has paid for my paintings."

"They should. When the hotel's guests see them, I expect some will want to buy paintings to take home. Have you considered that?"

She had not, but she couldn't help wondering what Papa would think of the idea. Would he encourage it? And if he did, was that only because it would keep her away from the hotel?

Alexandra brushed the depressing thought aside as they approached the springs. She hadn't known what to expect, but the scene before her was more beautiful than she'd imagined, with a palette of greens and grays vying for her attention. Tall trees ringed the pool of water, the bubbles in the center revealing the presence of the spring, while ferns and vines with huge, heart-shaped leaves partially hid the small waterfall that tumbled into the pool.

"I don't ever want to leave."

Alexandra hadn't realized she'd spoken aloud until Gabe said, "I hadn't expected to, but that's the way I feel about Mesquite Springs too. It seems more like home than Columbus ever did. I'm not sure whether it's Texans' friendliness or simply because it's a small town, but I like it."

"So do I." There were times when Alexandra missed Aunt Helen, but her newfound friendships more than compensated for those times. Friendships that included the man at her side.

Though at least a dozen other people were visiting the springs, their shouts and sometimes raucous laughter did not destroy the feeling of peace that descended on Alexandra as she and Gabe made their way to the spot Laura and Sam had claimed for their picnic. The scenery was far different from the interior of the Plauts' conservatory, but the companionship they shared was as welcome as it had been that rainy day. This was where she was meant to be.

When they'd devoured the last bites of peach turnovers, Gabe rose and extended his hand to Alexandra. "I need to walk off some of that food. Would you like to join me?"

She nodded and accepted his hand, smiling when he did not release it or place it on the crook of his arm. It felt good—so very good—to be walking hand in hand with Gabe.

"This is such a peaceful place," she said as they picked their way around the springs. Exposed tree roots and boulders made it difficult going in spots, but Alexandra wouldn't have traded this experience for anything.

"It is peaceful," Gabe agreed. "I keep thinking of my father and wishing he could see it. We didn't have anything like this in Columbus."

This was the first time Gabe had spoken of his father since they'd been on the stagecoach when he'd said that both of his parents had died.

"You must miss your parents terribly. I barely remember my mother, but I still feel like I have a hole inside me that only a mother's love could fill."

Gabe gestured toward a boulder large enough to serve as a bench, waiting until they were seated before he spoke.

"It's been over seven years since they died, but I feel the same way."

"Seven years." Alexandra paused, trying to recall what Gabe had said on the coach. "Somehow I thought it was more recent, but no matter when it happened, it must have been horrible to lose them both at the same time."

Gabe pulled one of the heart-shaped leaves from a vine and traced its outline. "Pa lived almost a year longer than Ma." He shook his head, correcting himself. "More accurately, Pa kept breathing for another eleven months after he buried her, but he wasn't really living. He was existing."

"Oh, Gabe." Alexandra laid her hand on his and squeezed it, hoping to give him at least a little comfort. "What happened?"

"Ma was very ill. The doctors had a fancy name for it and claimed her only hope was an exorbitantly expensive medicine. We didn't have that kind of money, but Pa was determined to save her."

Though his voice was so calm he might have been telling someone else's story, Alexandra ached at the pain she saw in Gabe's eyes.

"When Pa heard about an investment that was practically guaranteed to double his money in less than six months, he put every penny he had in it. Three months later, the investment collapsed, taking Pa's money. Ma died a month after that, and so did my father's will to live. He blamed himself for having believed the promise of quick riches."

Tears trickled down Alexandra's cheeks at the anguish she saw on Gabe's face. "It's a horrible story, but could anything have saved your mother?"

"Perhaps not, but the man who advertised the investment knew it was phony. If it hadn't been for him and his false promises, my father would still be alive. I can never forgive him for that."

Gabe refused to clench his fists, increase his pace, or do anything that might reveal his frustration. There was no question about it. Someone had been watching him. The feeling had disappeared when he'd wandered through the construction site, talking to workers and admiring the way they were turning Calvin's plans into reality. If the watcher was one of the workers, he'd blended into the crowd and turned his attention to something else so that Gabe wouldn't find him.

It hadn't been his imagination. Gabe was certain of that. Someone had been watching him, and now he was being followed. As improbable as it seemed, there were two people in Mesquite Springs with an interest in him, for Gabe's instincts told him that the follower wasn't the same person as the watcher.

He spun on his heel to confront the man who'd made no attempt to soften his footsteps but had remained a few paces behind him.

"Good morning." He greeted Martin Lewis, not surprised to discover that the newcomer who'd shown so much interest in Alexandra, even sitting next to her in church yesterday, was the one who'd shadowed him this morning. For some reason, the man wanted to talk to him again. If he were a betting man, Gabe would have bet that Alexandra was that reason.

"It is a good morning," the man agreed. He tipped his head to the side, silently gesturing toward the building that was close to completion. "It looks like the hotel has a chance of being finished by Independence Day."

Though he doubted Lewis had any genuine interest in Calvin's project, Gabe decided to play along. "Are you interested in hotels, Lewis?"

"I sure am. Unlike you, who's fortunate enough to be staying with the town's attorney, I'm stuck at the boardinghouse until the hotel opens. I sure wish it was ready now."

Lewis was talking too much, a clear sign that he wasn't as comfortable speaking to Gabe as he wanted to appear. The question was why Lewis had chosen the hotel and the boardinghouse as his subject. From everything Gabe had heard, the accommodations at the boardinghouse were excellent, but it seemed that this man, whose suit bore the hallmarks of a good tailor, wanted more.

"It looks like the rooms will be luxurious. Fit for a king." That was the slogan Calvin had told Gabe he was using for his advertisements.

"As good as any in Cincinnati." Lewis blanched as the final word escaped from his lips, telling Gabe he hadn't meant to admit he'd been to the same town as Calvin Tarkington. Gabe's initial instincts that this man had things to hide were heightened. Pretending he hadn't noticed Lewis's discomfort, he said, "I'm not very familiar with Cincinnati."

Lewis's lips curled in apparent disdain, although whether for the city itself or Gabe's lack of familiarity with it wasn't clear.

"I used to live there," he said, apparently realizing there was no point in denying that. "Some might call it a fine city, but it lacked one thing—women as pretty as Alexandra. She's one fine-looking lady."

Although Gabe was tempted to smile at the proof that he'd been right about the reason Lewis wanted to talk to him, the lust that shone from the other man's eyes made his stomach curdle. "She's also a very talented artist and, from what I've seen, a good teacher."

"I heard you were interested in her." Lewis lifted his chin and looked down at Gabe, emphasizing his greater height. "I'm giving you fair warning. I plan to court her, and I plan to win her hand. You don't have a chance."

Courtship. Who decided to court a woman he barely knew? Though the man's words shocked Gabe, he kept his voice neutral. "That remains to be seen."

Lewis merely laughed.

As he strode in the opposite direction, taking longer strides than normal to cool his anger, Gabe tried but failed to picture Alexandra with Martin Lewis. The man was undeniably handsome, and some women might find him charming, but Gabe sensed a ruthless core under the polished exterior. Fortunately, at least so far, Alexandra had shown no sign of being impressed with the man from Cincinnati.

Gabe wasn't one to believe in coincidence, and so he did not believe it was coincidental that a man who used to live in the same town as her father had suddenly appeared in Mesquite Springs, trying to court Alexandra. He could be a fortune hunter like the ones Calvin said had pursued her in New York, but how had he found her here? Even Calvin hadn't known Alexandra was coming to Mesquite Springs.

One thing was certain: Gabe needed to know more about Martin Lewis and what he'd done in Cincinnati. Half an hour later, he handed his letter to the postmaster, hoping Bill Woods would be able to find the answers he needed.

Alexandra was sitting on the verandah, enjoying the breeze that, while not cold by any means, felt cool compared to the temperature of her room, when the whirlwind hit. The human whirlwind.

"Oh, Alexandra, I'm the happiest person on Earth!" Laura practically shrieked the words as she raced across Alexandra's room to the verandah. "He did it! Sam asked my parents if he could court me, and they said yes." Laura skidded to a stop by the railing, her face flushed with happiness, her eyes shining as brightly as the river when it reflected the sun. "Oh, I'm so happy!"

And so was Alexandra. She rose to hug her friend, then urged Laura onto the wicker settee next to her. "This is wonderful news. It's obvious to anyone who sees you that you and Sam are meant for each other."

"I can't believe I ever doubted that." Wonder filled Laura's voice. "Sam's so different from the other men I knew. How could I have ever imagined I loved them? Wyatt and Brandon are fine men, but they can't compare to Sam. He's the only one for me." She reached for Alexandra's hand and squeezed it. "Please say you'll be my bridesmaid. I want you and Dorothy and Evelyn at my side when I become Sam's wife."

For a second, Alexandra was overwhelmed. She'd known Laura for such a short time that, while the news of her courtship was expected, this was not. Even though she considered Laura, Evelyn, and Dorothy friends, their friendship was still new and surely didn't merit an honor like this. But there was no way she would disappoint Laura. "I would love to be one of your bridesmaids, if I'm still here." Alexandra's future had none of the clarity of the spring's water.

Laura tightened her grip on Alexandra's hand. "You must stay. You must. Mother and Father want us to court for at least three months. Only then will they agree to an engagement, and that has to be at least three months too."

Though Laura was obviously not pleased by the delays, Alexandra suspected the older Downeys wanted to be sure Laura wouldn't lose interest in Sam the way she had with Wyatt, Brandon, and the men she'd met in Charleston.

"We could have a Christmas wedding," Laura continued. "Say you'll stay."

So much could happen in six months.

"I want to say yes, but I can't make any promises. Everything depends on my father." He'd seemed evasive recently, making Alexandra wonder what he was hiding from her, but—fortunately—he'd stopped insisting she return to New York. Perhaps he was finally realizing that she wanted to be part of his life.

"You must stay. You must." Laura was nothing if not persistent. "Send your aunt a letter and tell her you're going to live here. She can ship your belongings."

Though the idea was appealing, Alexandra knew it was premature. She seized on the simplest excuse. "I can't impose on your family for that long."

"They'd love to have you stay, but your father probably wants you to live with him. Why else would he be building that new home?"

If he was in fact planning to build a new home. Alexandra kept a smile fixed on her face, not wanting Laura to see her discomfort with the subject. While it seemed disloyal not to tell her friend that she doubted Papa had any intention of building anything on the ranches he'd bought, that was a story she didn't want to share.

There were times when Alexandra wished she hadn't told Gabe, but she'd been so upset that day that she had spoken without considering the consequences. And while she might have some regrets, she trusted Gabe and didn't want lies or omissions to come between them. He'd returned that trust, sharing his family's tragic story with her. His story continued to reverberate through Alexandra, making her wish there were some way the man who'd perpetrated the shady deal could be brought to justice. But that, she suspected, was a vain hope.

Alexandra kept a smile fixed on her face as she returned her attention to Laura.

"I'll see what Papa says." That was all she could offer, but her friend beamed as if she'd promised to become a permanent resident.

"Perfect!"

Half an hour later, Laura headed to her room, leaving Alexandra alone with the thoughts that kept bubbling through her brain. As wonderful as it was to see Laura so happy and so obviously in love, Alexandra couldn't dismiss the worry that she'd never find that kind of love. The men who'd sought to court her in New York hadn't touched her heart. And, though he acted like a would-be suitor, plying her with compliments and attempting to spend time with her every day, she felt no attraction to Martin Lewis.

The only man who made her heart race was Gabe. He was the one person she could picture marrying, but though they saw each other almost every day and though she'd shared parts of her life with him that she'd kept hidden from everyone else, other than the gift of the brushes, he'd done nothing that could be construed as more than friendly.

Why? She could imagine only one reason: there was something about her that made her unlovable. It would explain why Papa had sent her to New York and why he was so reluctant for her to stay here. What, oh what, was wrong with her?

CHAPTER

Twenty-Four

Alexandra straightened her shoulders as she entered the hotel the next morning, determined to learn how long Papa was planning to stay in Mesquite Springs and to make another effort to play a more important role in his life. If he saw how helpful she could be, surely he would realize she was worthy of his love.

"Good morning, Papa." She forced a cheerful tone as she opened the door and laid the basket of breakfast food on his desk.

"Oh, hello, Alexandra." He looked up from the paper he'd been studying, then turned it over, but not before Alexandra could see that it was a plan for the hotel's grounds, a plan that included a third building.

"What's that other building?" Her glance, brief though it had been, had shown her it was much smaller than the other buildings and that it was set apart from them.

Papa frowned. "That was supposed to be the manager's house. I thought Phil might marry one day and want some privacy, even though he'd need to be close to the guests."

Alexandra leaned forward to pick up the plan, studying the structure that had caught her eye. It was smaller than the house she'd shared with Mama and Papa, but it had more style. The gables and front porch seemed to beckon her to step inside, and while there was no indication of the interior, she pictured a parlor with ruffled curtains and two bedrooms enlivened by colorful quilts.

"I could be the manager." The words popped out seemingly of their own volition, but as she heard them reverberate in the room, Alexandra realized how much she wanted Papa to agree. Seeing the drawing of the house had awakened a longing deep inside her along with the conviction that this was what she was meant to do.

"You?" Papa stared at her as if she'd claimed she could single-handedly build the house. "You're a girl."

"I'm a woman," Alexandra countered. Though she didn't want to argue, she needed to convince her father that she was capable of doing more than he realized.

"Aunt Helen taught me to manage a household. I know how to direct servants, how to buy supplies and keep to a budget, how to entertain guests. Those are all things a hotel manager would do." As Papa opened his mouth to protest, Alexandra finished her argument. "I can do all of that and more."

Papa shook his head. "It's not seemly. My daughter shouldn't have to work."

"But I want to."

"You'll change your mind once you're married and have children." Papa took the plan from her and tossed it onto the floor. "The answer is no. It's one thing for you to paint. That's ladylike. But you will not get your hands dirty running this hotel."

Though Alexandra was tempted to tell him that none of the things she'd listed involved dirty hands, she held her tongue. There'd be no convincing Papa today, but at least she had planted a seed.

"I brought apple muffins," she said, pretending they hadn't just argued. "They're not as pretty as the ones Laura makes, but she said they weren't bad for a first attempt."

This time Papa smiled. It seemed that dirtying her hands with muffin batter was acceptable. "You'll make some man a good wife," he said after he'd swallowed his first bite.

That gave Alexandra an opening into another subject. "Laura's going to be a bride before me. She and Sam are officially courting now, and she's asked me to be a bridesmaid."

When Papa nodded as if the idea pleased him, Alexandra continued. "The wedding won't be until Christmas. Do you think you'll still be here then?"

As a shadow crossed his face, Papa shrugged. "I don't know. Possibly, but probably not." Before Alexandra could ask why he was so unsure, he said, "I don't want to talk about that. Have you finished any more paintings?"

They discussed her progress for a few minutes while they ate the muffins, then Alexandra said, "The town is excited about the hotel. Have you considered letting people tour it the day it opens? Some of them, especially the families that live far from town, might want to stay here occasionally."

As she'd expected, Papa looked skeptical, but then he nodded. "That's a good idea. Do you want to arrange the tours?"

Alexandra smiled. "Of course."

Gabe was not a fan of cemeteries. He'd visited his parents' graves a few times each year, but he'd never found the peace others claimed graveyards provided. When he wanted to feel close to Ma and Pa, he'd walk by the house they'd once shared. Gabe had sold it after Pa's death, not needing all that space and not wanting the constant reminder that his parents were gone. Now a young family lived there, their three boys frolicking in the yard where he'd once played fetch with his dog. That sight brought him more comfort than kneeling by his parents' graves.

On an ordinary day, Gabe would not have entered the cemetery, but when he saw Calvin making his way there and remembered how he'd stared at another grave during Mrs. Lockhart's funeral, Gabe decided to follow the man.

"Did you know him?" he asked when he reached Calvin. Alexandra's father stood in front of a simple wooden cross bearing the name Phil Blakeslee.

"He was the closest thing to a son I've ever had." Though Calvin was dry-eyed, genuine sorrow colored his voice. "He wasn't supposed to die. The hotel was going to be my gift to him, but now . . ." Calvin stopped short. "What are you doing here?"

"You looked like you needed a friend. I thought maybe I could help." He gestured toward a nearby bench. "Do you want to talk about him? Sometimes that helps."

For a moment, Calvin appeared torn. Then he nodded. "When I first met Phil, he was shining shoes and picking pockets, but I could tell that he'd been raised for a better life. I did what I could to help him, and he repaid me with unwavering loyalty." Calvin paused, apparently debating whether to say more. "I'd like to think he loved me."

The uncertainty in the older man's voice touched Gabe more than anything he'd said, and in that moment, he realized that for all the pain he'd wreaked on others, Calvin Tarkington had done some good. He might appear cold and distant, but he was capable of love. If only he could lavish that love on his daughter.

He had to do something to stop Seymour. Jason's palms itched at the thought of stopping him permanently. He shook his head. Killing Seymour now might make the gal too upset to think about marriage to anyone. He had to get her away from Seymour and back to Franklin. Only when that was done could he take care of Seymour.

There she was. Jason grinned. You could practically set a clock by her. She left the fancy house at the same time every morning, carrying a basket of food to her father. It was like one of those fairy tales the nanny used to read to him. They all blurred together, but he knew there was something about a girl carrying a basket of food in one of them. She met a bad end, didn't she?

He waited until Alexandra was in front of the new building, then descended the front steps and, pretending he didn't see her, backed down the walk as if he were studying the roofline. As she approached, he accelerated his pace, stopping only when he was directly in front of her. As he'd planned, she was unable to stop and bumped the basket into him.

Jason swiveled, feigning shock. "Oh, miss, I'm sorry. I didn't see you. I hope I didn't hurt you."

She shook her head. "I'm fine. I should have been more careful."

Up close, she was even prettier than he'd thought, although not the kind of gal he preferred. When he married, it would be a blonde. Mother always said that golden boys like him should marry blondes.

"It was all my fault, miss." That much was true. "I'm the one who should be more careful." When she started to walk away, Jason moved to block the path. "You seem like a nice lady. That's why I'm telling you this. I'd hate to see anything bad happen to you, but you're keeping company with the wrong man. You shouldn't trust Gabe Seymour. He's not what he claims to be."

Her look of shock mingled with a hint of fear made Jason's heartbeat accelerate. He hadn't lost his touch. Before she could ask him what he meant, he scurried up the steps to blend in with the other workers.

It had been more than three days since the strange man had warned her not to trust Gabe, and though Alexandra had tried to tell herself he was nothing more than a busybody, she could not forget the fervor she'd seen in his eyes. Crazy eyes, Aunt Helen would have called them. Alexandra had encountered that expression only once before—the night Franklin had threatened her.

Could this man have been sent by Franklin? It seemed unlikely, because Franklin associated only with members of society. The man with the shabby clothes and unkempt hair and beard would never have been invited to a society event.

She'd considered asking her father about him, but Papa had been coughing more than normal when she'd entered his office, making her unwilling to add to his worries. One thing was certain: she would not tell Gabe of the man's allegations, for they were patently absurd.

"I'm glad you and Laura still have time for this," Gabe said as he and Alexandra walked behind Laura and Sam. When they'd gone fishing on Saturday, Laura had mentioned that the mercantile had been busier than normal the past two Saturdays and that she might have to help her parents wait on customers next week after Polly's Place closed.

"I wouldn't miss our walks," Alexandra assured Gabe, "and neither would Laura. Now that she and Sam are courting, she's adamant that her evenings belong to him. You and I are permitted to accompany them."

Gabe lifted an eyebrow. "Like the king and queen's courtiers?"

"Something like that. You'll notice that we're following at a respectful distance." Though they occasionally walked as a foursome, the majority of the time they paired off. That was fine with Alexandra, for she enjoyed her time with Gabe.

She smiled at him, thinking about the painting Mr. Gottlieb had agreed to frame. "This is your best one, *Fraulein*," he'd said when she had handed it to him. Alexandra hoped Gabe would agree.

"It looks like some of the men are working late," Gabe said as they approached the hotel.

"Papa's still not happy with the progress," Alexandra explained. "He wanted it finished by June 1, but now he's hoping for Independence Day. He's planning to drape red, white, and blue bunting from all the windows."

Gabe's eyebrow rose another inch. "That'll be . . ." He paused, trying to choose the correct word. "Colorful."

Alexandra couldn't help laughing. "That's one way to describe it. I hope we can attract enough guests to make it successful."

"I imagine you will. Brandon said you've sent advertisements to all the newspapers in Texas."

"It took a while to convince Papa. We got some reservations from the ad we placed in the *Chronicle*, but not as many as I'd hoped, so I persuaded him to advertise in other papers."

"I'm surprised he needed persuasion. Most businessmen know the power of advertising."

Alexandra nodded. "I reminded him of that, but he said he had a bad experience with the ads he placed for a bank he was managing. He claimed some of the papers changed the wording, and he didn't get the investors he wanted." It had taken Alexandra longer than she'd expected to convince Papa that wouldn't happen again.

Laura laughed at something Sam was saying, but Gabe was not laughing. His expression was almost grim, and when he spoke, there was an odd tone to his voice. "Your father ran a bank?"

Alexandra nodded again. "For a short time. I know some men stay with the same company their whole lives, but my father had a lot of different businesses. It seemed there was a new one almost every year. When I asked him why, he said he didn't like being bored."

Gabe inclined his head, but his expression remained solemn. "Few of us do." Alexandra thought he was about to change the subject, but then he asked, "Do you remember the name of the bank?"

She had to think for a moment. "It's been a few years." She wracked her brain again, then smiled when a memory popped in. "Ells something."

"Ellsworth?"

"That's it." To her surprise, the blood drained from Gabe's

face, and he appeared unsteady on his feet. "What is it, Gabe? Is something wrong?"

He gazed into the distance and shook his head. "No. Nothing."

Gabe stared at the paper in front of him, the words he'd written blurring before his eyes. Though he had had no idea how he'd done it, somehow he'd gotten through the rest of the evening without anyone seeming to notice how much Alexandra's innocent response had shaken him.

Calvin Tarkington had been behind the Ellsworth Bank.

For a second—or perhaps it had been an hour—Gabe had been so shocked that he'd been unable to speak. Then shock had turned to anger, an anger deeper and more intense than any he'd ever experienced. He'd wanted to storm into the hotel, grab Calvin Tarkington by the neck, and shake him until his teeth rattled before demanding why he'd done what he had.

Reason had prevailed. Reason and the desire to protect Alexandra. Gabe had done his best to hide his anger until he was back in the apartment. Then he'd pulled out paper and a pen and had vented his emotions by writing exactly what he wanted to do to the man who'd defrauded Pa. It had taken three pages, but once it was done, he'd felt a sense of relief. He wouldn't do any of those things, but he was filled with a new resolve. Not only would he stop Calvin from defrauding others, but he'd do his best to ensure that he paid for his earlier crimes.

Gabe crumpled the sheets and tossed them onto the floor. He shouldn't have been shocked. After all, he knew from what Biddle had said and what he'd learned during his investigation that Calvin Tarkington had been part of—probably the instigator of—numerous shady deals. That same research had revealed that the majority of the companies Calvin had promoted had collapsed, taking the investors' fortunes with them while he appeared to have escaped unscathed.

Gabe shook his head, then retrieved the papers from the floor and began to rip them into tiny pieces. The fault was his. He should have been more thorough in his work. When he and Bill had delved into Calvin's businesses, they'd found only five years of records. The Ellsworth Bank had failed eight years ago.

What a fool he'd been! He should have realized that Calvin might have changed the way he operated, that he might have previously relied on advertisements, like the ones that convinced Pa to invest in the bank, rather than meetings with potential investors. Gabe should have realized or at least considered the possibility that Calvin could have been the man responsible for his father's losing his money, but he let his growing feelings for Alexandra cloud his judgment. He hadn't wanted her father to have been responsible for Pa's death, and so he'd ignored the possibility. He'd been a fool, but he was fooled no longer.

The question now became what to do. Should he confront Calvin? Though Gabe wanted nothing more than to cause Calvin the kind of pain he'd inflicted on others, he couldn't. Not yet. He needed to complete his investigation. Somehow, he had to continue to play a role, not letting Calvin know what he'd learned until he had the proof he'd promised Biddle and had stopped whatever scheme Calvin had planned.

When that was done, Gabe would need to address the most difficult questions of all—how to tell Alexandra just how dishonest her father was and that he'd asked Gabe to pretend to court her.

Twenty-Five

*W*hat's wrong?"

Though the rest of the younger students were happily dabbing paint on paper, Frieda appeared on the verge of tears, and Hans was frowning. It was clear the twins were upset.

Alexandra bit back a sigh, wondering whether there was something in the air that was making people unhappy. For the past few days, though he'd denied anything was wrong, Gabe had seemed distracted, at times almost distressed. And now the twins appeared to have reverted to the solemnity that had characterized them when she'd first met them.

"School's gonna end soon." Frieda scrubbed her hand across her face, wiping away the tears that had begun to trickle down her cheeks.

The response surprised Alexandra. Far from dreading the end of school, she and her classmates had always looked forward to summer and the break from classes.

"That's true," she said. "Summer's a busy time. As soon as school's over, we have the Founder's Day celebration, and before you know it, it'll be Independence Day." Laura had claimed those were the highlights of summer in Mesquite Springs, two events that brought the town together for food, fun, and fellowship.

Frieda's upper lip wobbled. "But we won't be coming here." She flung her arms to the side, apparently wanting to ensure Alexandra realized that "here" meant the schoolhouse. "I don't like Mrs. Fisher."

"She's mean." For the first time, Hans spoke.

"Who's Mrs. Fisher?" Though she'd been introduced to many of Mesquite Springs's residents, Alexandra could not recall having met anyone named Fisher.

"She's our neighbor." Hans began the explanation. "*Vati* said we gotta stay with her while he's working."

It made sense that motherless children needed someone to care for them during the day.

"She makes us hunt for eggs. Chickens bite."

Though Alexandra had never experienced it, she imagined hens would peck anyone who tried to take their eggs.

"That must hurt."

Frieda held out a hand and pointed to a tiny scar. "It does. Me and Hans don't wanna stay there."

Alexandra's heart ached for the children whose pain was far deeper than that inflicted by angry hens. "I'll talk to your father. Maybe someone else can help."

The grateful look the twins gave her strengthened Alexandra's determination to ensure that their summer did not involve caring for poultry. When school was dismissed and Mr. Gottlieb arrived to take his children home, she met him at the street and explained what she'd heard.

He nodded. "Mrs. Fisher means well, but she's not used to having small children around. Her sons are all grown."

"Isn't there anyone else?"

This time he shook his head. "I asked, but everyone's too busy to take on two more children. It was easier when I spent my days on the farm. They didn't spend as much time with Mrs. Fisher then, but I need the money your father is paying me."

A pang of remorse that she'd added to Mr. Gottlieb's workload by asking him to frame her painting washed over Alexandra. It was clear that he was doing the best he could. It was also clear that he needed help.

Alexandra did not consider herself an impulsive woman, but the words that came out of her mouth were based on impulse, not careful reflection. "If the Downeys agree, would you be willing to let Frieda and Hans stay with me? I don't have much experience with children, but I care about them."

Mr. Gottlieb's visible relief and the sense of rightness that filled her told Alexandra her impulse had been a good one. She would still have time to try to help Papa, and her evening walks could continue, but in between, she'd be making life a bit easier for three people who might otherwise have had a difficult summer.

"You would do that for me?" Wonder colored Mr. Gottlieb's voice.

"For you and the children."

A smile lit his face. "*Danke, Fraulein.* That would be good. *Sehr gut.*"

———

"I heard you're taking on new responsibilities," Gabe said that evening when they met for their walk.

Alexandra nodded. "I knew the Mesquite Springs grapevine was active, but I didn't expect the news to spread that quickly." It had been only a few hours since she'd made the arrangements with the Downeys. "Who told you?"

"Sam. He was in the mercantile looking for a gift for Laura and he heard her parents discussing it. They think it's very generous of you."

"They're the ones who are being generous. First, they invited me to stay in their home, and now they've agreed that I can entertain two small children there." Mrs. Downey had even suggested that the twins have supper with them, allowing Mr. Gottlieb to work without interruption until sunset.

"What are you going to do with them all day?"

"Besides paint? I have no idea. Do you want to help?"

"I might. It's been a while, but I haven't forgotten what I used to do to avoid boredom on summer afternoons."

As his lips curved in a mischievous smile, Alexandra's spirits rose. It must have been her imagination that something had been bothering Gabe. Thank goodness.

"Do you want to talk about it?"

"Is it that obvious?" Though Gabe usually enjoyed his nightly conversations with Sam, sitting at the kitchen table and drinking glasses of buttermilk after their walks with the ladies, it appeared this discussion would not be an easy one.

Sam shrugged. "Maybe not to everyone, but I see the anger you're trying to hide. When I look at you, I see the same expression that used to confront me every time I looked in the mirror." He took another swig of buttermilk before continuing. "I'm going to tell you what the doctor at Serenity House told me: you need to let go of the anger or it'll destroy you like one of those diseases that eats you from inside. Before you know it, there's nothing left. Anger's dangerous. Sometimes it erupts in flames, but sometimes all you see is the smoke. You need to get beyond that."

Gabe recognized the truth in his friend's warning. He refilled his glass before he spoke, choosing his words as carefully as Sam had. "I thought the anger was gone. When I first learned what had happened to my father, all I could think about was revenge. I wanted to see the man who was responsible suffer the way Pa did."

It had been an all-consuming desire, as hot and as dangerous as the flames Sam had mentioned.

"Pa stopped me, saying revenge was not the answer. He'd accepted responsibility for the loss, knowing he should have been wiser. It was then that I realized the best thing I could do was to stop dishonest men from hurting others."

"Which is why you became an investigator." Sam leaned back in his chair, apparently relaxed, but Gabe knew he was watching him carefully, waiting for the end of the story.

"Yes. I stopped looking for the man who cheated my father, because I knew I couldn't undo the past. Preventing others from becoming victims seemed like the best way to honor Pa."

Sam nodded. "Because at heart you're a protector, not an avenger."

"I never thought of it that way, but you might be right." Gabe couldn't deny how much he wanted to protect Alexandra. It was one thing to keep nameless citizens from being swindled. That was satisfying, but his desire to save Alexandra from the heartbreak of learning what her father had done was stronger, perhaps because it was so personal.

Sam nodded again. "Something has changed, and that's why you're so angry."

"You're right. Something has changed. I now know who convinced my father to invest money he couldn't afford to lose in the Ellsworth Bank." Gabe paused for a second, not wanting to reveal the truth but knowing Sam deserved to hear the whole story. "It was Calvin Tarkington. His were the ads that Pa saw and believed."

"Oh." His friend let out a long sigh. "That complicates everything, doesn't it?"

"It was complicated before. Now it's worse. I don't see how I can face Calvin, knowing what I do." Gabe took another slug of buttermilk before addressing the heart of the matter: Alexandra. "I'd started to believe Alexandra and I might have a future together, but when I think about Calvin as my father-in-law, my stomach turns."

Sam drained his glass, then placed it back on the table. "You wouldn't be marrying him."

"Maybe not, but he'd be part of my life." And Gabe wasn't certain he could handle that.

"Would he? From what you've said, he didn't spend much time

with Alexandra, and he certainly hasn't been a doting father since she came here."

"That's all true, but whenever I think about him, I become so angry I want to smash something. How do I stop that?"

"You pray."

Alexandra tried to tamp down her nervousness as she carried Gabe's painting to the park. Instead of wrapping it in paper, she'd sewn a simple flannel bag for it, reasoning that he would need a way of protecting it when he left.

As much as she hated the idea, she knew their time together was limited. Even if she and Papa stayed in Mesquite Springs, which was far from a certainty, eventually Gabe would leave. But she wouldn't think about that today. They were still here. They were still together. And, if she'd judged properly, Gabe would like the painting.

"This is a small thank-you for the brushes," she said as she handed him the package. He'd risen to greet her, the curiosity in his eyes saying he wondered what was in the bag, but she'd waited until they were both seated before she'd given it to him.

"You already thanked me." For some reason, he seemed reluctant to open the gift.

"Those were words. I wanted something more permanent." She gestured toward the tie. "Open it, Gabe. It won't hurt you."

"I know it won't. It's simply that I'm not used to receiving gifts. It's not my birthday or Christmas."

The nostalgia in his voice made Alexandra wonder whether anyone had celebrated those occasions with him after his parents died. Somehow, she'd learn his birthday, and if they were both still here, she would ensure that it was a festive day for him.

As a blue jay cawed, Gabe untied the package and withdrew the painting, the smile that lit his face leaving no doubt of his reaction.

"It's beautiful, Alexandra." Gabe held the painting at arm's length, as though trying to envision it hanging on a wall. "What a clever idea, making it look like a window."

Alexandra had painted what appeared to be mullions to separate the four scenes, and Mr. Gottlieb had used window casing for the frame.

Gabe grinned as he gazed at the painting. "It's like receiving four paintings."

Alexandra laughed. "It was only supposed to be one, but I couldn't decide which scene I liked best. This is what happens when my imagination goes wild."

"It's wonderful and much more than I deserve." She heard the humility in his voice and something else, something she couldn't identify. "All I gave you were brushes, but you gave me a part of yourself. Thank you, Alexandra." Gabe lowered his head and muttered something that sounded like, "I hope you don't regret it."

She shook her head, certain she was mistaken. How could she regret doing something for Gabe?

"When are you going to tell me about your next venture?" Gabe asked the question as casually as he could while he and Calvin walked through the new building, inspecting the rooms that were nearing completion.

Today was the first day in a week that he'd spent more than a minute with Alexandra's father. It had taken that long for his anger to subside, and while it wasn't completely gone, the fervent prayers he'd offered had helped him control his emotions. So too did reminding himself that, despite everything he'd done, Calvin was a man who had cared deeply for at least two people: his wife and Phil Blakeslee.

"Getting impatient, huh?"

"Wouldn't you be? It's been six weeks, and I still have no idea what the investment is." When Calvin did not reply, Gabe launched the argument he'd hoped would get a response from the other man.

"Sometimes I wonder whether there is one at all or whether you're simply using me to keep your daughter occupied."

Calvin did not take the bait. "It appears I don't need you for that. Alexandra seems to be taking care of that by herself—first teaching school, now volunteering to care for those twins all summer. She's even started helping me here. She seems to think she knows which rooms the guests might prefer based on what they said in their letters, so I'm letting her handle the reservations."

And that had pleased Alexandra more than almost anything Calvin could have done. She'd been bursting with excitement when she'd recounted the discussion she and her father had had and how he'd agreed to let her help. Why couldn't the man see what a treasure he had in his daughter?

Calvin glared at Gabe. "I'm not sure you're holding up your part of the bargain."

"She's busy. Isn't that what you wanted? Besides, who's to say I'm not responsible for what she's doing?" He wasn't, but Gabe had no intention of giving Calvin the upper hand.

"I can't argue with the results," Calvin admitted. "Once the hotel is open, we'll talk about what's next. In the meantime, you might want to keep an eye on that Lewis fellow. He seems to have a hankering for my daughter."

"I've noticed."

"Better stake your claim. I don't like the way he looks at her."

Gabe didn't, either. Though it wasn't charitable, he didn't care for Martin Lewis, and he didn't trust him. He hoped he'd hear soon from Bill Woods.

"Fletcher paid me a visit this morning."

Gabe looked up from the loaf of bread he was slicing, wondering why Sam had singled out that visit. He'd seen Wyatt leaving Sam's office, but his friend had made no mention of the mayor. "The sheriff?"

"He's the only Fletcher in town. Don't you want to know why he came?" Sam seemed miffed by Gabe's lack of interest.

"I imagine he wanted to convince you to become Mesquite Springs's next sheriff."

Sam leaned against the doorframe, feigning nonchalance, but the faint furrows between his eyes told Gabe this was anything but a casual conversation.

"It started that way," Sam admitted, "until he finally realized that it wasn't the job for me. We both agreed there's a much better candidate."

Gabe gave his friend a long, piercing look before he asked the question Sam so clearly wanted. "Who?"

"You."

Jason's frown turned into a scowl. Perhaps he'd made a mistake when he'd approached her wearing his worker's clothes. They'd served him well, keeping Seymour from noticing him, but they might have made her discount his words. Folks tended not to put much stock in things uneducated people said. Not that Jason was uneducated—no, sirree—but the Tarkington gal didn't know that.

It was too late to undo that. Now he'd have to try a different approach.

"Is something wrong?" She might be prying, but Alexandra couldn't ignore the way Gabe seemed distracted tonight. As often happened when they walked with Laura and Sam, they were a few paces behind the other couple, but tonight Gabe's replies to her comments seemed perfunctory, making her wonder whether he was listening to her. And that wasn't normal.

"I'm sorry it was so obvious, but since it was, I'm not going to deny it. I'm struggling with something Sam said today." Gabe slowed his pace and turned to look at Alexandra. "Maybe you can give me some advice."

The warmth that rushed through her surprised Alexandra with its intensity. How good it felt to be consulted, to have her opinion valued.

"Until I know what the problem is, I'm not sure how much help I can be, but I'll do my best."

Gabe nodded. "I know you will." He laid his hand on top of the one she'd put on his arm and gave it a little squeeze. "Try not to laugh, but Sam thinks I should run for sheriff."

Alexandra was silent for a moment. She'd heard rumors that Fletcher Engel wouldn't run for reelection this year, but there'd been little speculation over who might replace him. The image of Gabe wearing a star flashed through her mind, and as it did, she felt a sense of rightness.

"Do you want to?" She wouldn't try to influence him, but the more she thought of it, the more she liked the idea.

Gabe shrugged. "I don't know. It's nothing I've ever considered."

"But Sam believes you'd be good at it."

"So do Fletcher and Wyatt. They say the town needs someone who hasn't spent his whole life here, because he'd be more impartial." Gabe gave a self-deprecating scoff. "I think they're desperate because no one else is interested."

"I refuse to believe that's the case. You've told me you enjoy solving problems, and isn't that what a sheriff does? The real questions are whether you want to stay in Mesquite Springs—"

"I do," Gabe said before she could complete her sentence. "I'm sorry I interrupted you. You said questions, plural. What are the others?"

"There's only one other, and it's the one I asked you before: do you want to be the sheriff?"

"I still don't know the answer to that. One side of me thinks it might be the right decision, but the other side says I'm not cut out for that life. How do I know which side is right?"

"You wait for the answer. It may take a while, but you'll know when it comes. You'll have no doubts."

Papa hadn't agreed, and he might never agree, but from the moment she'd seen the drawing of the manager's house, Alexandra had known she was meant to stay here and run the hotel. And if Gabe stayed as sheriff . . . The thought made her want to skip from pure joy the way schoolchildren did when classes ended.

Instead of doing anything so unseemly, she kept her expression solemn as she said, "This is only my opinion and not advice, but I think you're the right man for the job."

Twenty-Six

The day had finally arrived, and Alexandra's mild anticipation had turned into full-fledged excitement.

"It'll be shorter than normal this year, but that won't stop us from having fun." Laura had explained that the schedule for Founder's Day would be abbreviated because June 21 was a Sunday. While some residents had suggested celebrating on the previous day, the majority had insisted that it was essential to have Founder's Day on the twenty-first, and so instead of having events in the morning, the festivities would begin after church. Families would gather in the park at noon for a picnic lunch followed by speeches. Interminable speeches, according to Laura.

To Alexandra's relief, Papa had accepted the Downeys' invitation to join them for the picnic and had appeared to enjoy talking with Laura's parents, not seeming to mind that she and Gabe and Laura and Sam were not a part of that conversation.

Now everyone was quiet, waiting for the speeches. Wyatt's was blessedly short, but Mr. McBride, the former mayor, spoke for more than half an hour, recounting in excruciating detail the stories of the people who'd established Mesquite Springs almost thirty years ago.

"Do you think he intends to speak for thirty years?" Gabe, who was seated on Alexandra's right, murmured.

"I hope not. The children are getting restless." She'd seen a number of them fidgeting and suspected it wouldn't be long before fidgeting turned to whining.

Fortunately, Mr. McBride exhausted his anecdotes, and the next two speeches were even briefer than Wyatt's.

"Ladies and gentlemen, boys and girls, let's give a big round of applause to thank these gentlemen." Wyatt gestured toward the former mayor and the other speakers. When the clapping subsided, he raised his voice again. "And now, it's time to play. Miss Geist tells me that the first game will be the three-legged race."

To Alexandra's amusement, the cheering wasn't limited to the children. It seemed the adults were as grateful as the youngsters that the speeches had ended and they'd be able to stand up and move around.

Within five minutes, Miss Geist had organized the races, with the youngest children being part of the first group.

"I remember how much fun these races were," Laura said as she and Sam rose and prepared to help the children slide their legs into the pillowcases. Though Alexandra had volunteered, Miss Geist had insisted that she had already done more than her share by teaching the children to paint.

"When I was their age, we had our legs tied together," Laura continued. "That seemed like more fun, but Miss Geist started using pillowcases instead of rope when someone tripped and broke a leg. She said it was safer."

"Did you use rope?" Sam asked Alexandra.

Before she could respond, Gabe said, "If I were a betting man, I'd bet that Alexandra never ran a three-legged race."

"You'd win that bet," she admitted. Girls at her school were taught to be demure and that running races was something only hoydens would do.

Papa, who'd apparently overheard the discussion, touched Alexandra's shoulder. "I'm sorry," he said, his voice gruffer than normal. "You missed out on an important part of being a child."

But these children weren't missing out, and Alexandra gave thanks for that. She smiled when she saw Hans and Frieda, each with a partner. It seemed the twins were going to compete against each other.

"It's a good thing you're doing, Miss Tarkington," Mr. Gottlieb said as he approached Alexandra after the race. Neither Hans nor Frieda had won, but that didn't seem to bother them. They now stood on the sidelines, their smiles radiant as they watched the next group of children compete. "My *kinder* are happy to be spending the summer with you."

"And I'm happy you can continue working on the hotel." Papa nodded at the twins' father, then wiped his brow. "You'll have to excuse me. I need to go back to the hotel."

Once again, concern for her father's health made Alexandra's heart clench. Each time she asked him, he claimed nothing was wrong. Still, she had to ask. "Are you ill, Papa?"

"No." He shook his head. "Just too much Texas sun. Besides, dancing is for you younger folks. You and Gabe enjoy it."

Seconds later, Brandon Holloway engaged Gabe in a discussion of the next issue of the *Chronicle*, leaving Alexandra alone.

"At last." Martin Lewis forced his way through the crowd and stood closer than she would have liked. "I've been trying to talk to you all day, but you have guard dogs."

"Guard dogs? I'd hardly call my father a guard dog."

"Let's not argue. It's too beautiful a day for that." If Martin's smile had been designed to charm her, it failed. "I was hoping you'd save the first and last dances for me."

"I'm sorry, Mr. Lewis, but all the dances are spoken for."

A quick intake of breath told her he hadn't expected that. "By Seymour?"

Not all, but several. Seeing no need to fuel his apparent animosity toward Gabe, Alexandra said only, "I'm certain you'll have no trouble finding your own partners."

"But they won't be as lovely as you. That gown is particularly attractive." Once again, he was trying to charm her. Once again, he failed.

"Thank you." The dressmaker had shown Alexandra a bolt of light blue muslin that she had declared would be perfect, but Alexandra had not wanted to wear red, white, or blue today. Instead, she'd chosen an emerald-green fabric with pale green trim that banded the sleeves and the neckline and formed a wide sash.

Alexandra was pleased with the results. Laura had declared it her most flattering gown. Even Papa had complimented her on it, claiming it made her look like her mother. Now Martin was praising it. She should have been happy, but though Gabe's eyes had widened when he'd first seen her, he had said nothing about her dress. Alexandra knew she shouldn't be disappointed—after all, not all men felt the need to comment on a woman's appearance—and yet she was. Gabe's was the opinion that mattered most.

"I suppose I shouldn't be surprised that all your dances are spoken for." When Martin moved a bit closer and his arm brushed her sleeve, Alexandra took a step in the opposite direction. Though she no longer believed he was one of Franklin's cronies, moving too close was something Franklin would have done.

Apparently unconcerned by Alexandra's silent rebuff, Martin continued. "Next time I'll have to ask you earlier. Meanwhile, if one of your partners can't dance—accidents happen, you know—I would be honored if you'd favor me with that dance."

Accidents. The emphasis he'd placed on that word sent a chill down Alexandra's spine. Franklin hadn't called them accidents. He'd referred to them as unfortunate events and had warned Alexandra that those unfortunate events would occur if she did not agree to marry him. Martin's words, though more discreet, held the same menace.

Anxious to put as much distance as possible between herself and Martin, Alexandra excused herself and hurried toward Miss Geist. It didn't matter what tasks the schoolmarm had for her;

she'd welcome any excuse to be away from Martin. She might have overreacted to him—she probably had—but Alexandra had no desire to spend more time with him.

Fortunately, the afternoon passed quickly, and before Alexandra knew it, the games were over.

"Thank you. I know I said I didn't need your assistance, but I was wrong. Having you here made the children better behaved than I'd expected."

Alexandra flushed at the schoolteacher's praise. "I was happy to help." And not simply because it kept her away from Martin. Watching the children's excitement fueled hers, making her grateful for the circumstances that had brought her to this small town. The alarm she'd felt had dissipated quickly, replaced by the satisfaction of being needed, even if it was only to tie shoelaces and help children line up for the next game. Laura had not exaggerated. Founder's Day was a special occasion.

"All done?"

Alexandra turned, her pulse accelerating at the sound of Gabe's voice. She'd lost sight of him while she was involved with the children, but he'd never been far from her thoughts.

"That was the last game," she told him.

"Good, because it looks like they're ready to serve supper. Shall we get in line?"

By the time they reached the heavily laden tables, the line had grown so long that Alexandra wondered if there'd be enough food. Her expression must have revealed her concerns, because Laura smiled as she and Sam joined them.

"Don't worry," Laura assured her. "They never run out before everyone's been through the line at least once." Her smile broadened. "It'll be nice to eat someone else's cooking."

The women who'd organized the meal had insisted that neither Evelyn nor Laura bring anything, claiming they deserved a break. But, while the women who ran Polly's Place had come empty-handed, almost every other woman in town had made at least one dish.

"Is there anything we should avoid?" Gabe appeared to be scrutinizing the dishes.

Alexandra stared at him in surprise. "What a peculiar question."

Sam came to his friend's defense. "It's a prudent one. There are always some people whose enthusiasm for cooking is greater than the results. And, sad to say, my mother is one of those. You wouldn't want to eat one of her pies. It's no secret that her crusts are tough."

"Is that why your family has a cook?" Laura's hazel eyes were filled with curiosity. "I thought it was because she wanted more time with her plants."

"That's the excuse my father gave, but we all knew the real reason. Father called it self-preservation."

As the others laughed, Alexandra looked around. "Are your parents here? I haven't seen them all day."

Sam shook his head. "Mother was having more pain than usual, so they left right after church. This will be the first Founder's Day they've missed."

"I'm sorry."

Laura echoed Alexandra's sentiments, adding, "I'll take her some pie tomorrow." That was Laura, always thinking of others.

Sam winked at Gabe, making Alexandra wonder whether this was another ploy like Sam's pretended grouchiness that had gotten him a piece of fudge on the walk to the springs.

When he gave Laura an appreciative smile and said, "Why don't we go together?" Alexandra suspected she'd been right.

As Laura had predicted, the food was plentiful enough that they could sample everything. And, as Sam had cautioned, some dishes were better eaten in small quantities. Very small quantities. But though one piece of chicken would have benefited from less pepper and an apple pie could have used more sugar, Alexandra wouldn't have changed anything. Somehow, the imperfections made the day more special. What mattered wasn't the food but the opportunity to come together to celebrate the town's history.

Once the meal was concluded, families with small children began to leave. Gabe rose and extended his hand to Alexandra. "It'll be another half hour before the dancing starts. Would you like to walk a bit?"

She nodded and took his hand, smiling when he kept hers longer than simple courtesy demanded. It felt oh so good to have her hand in Gabe's and to savor the warmth of his palm against hers. When he placed her hand on his arm, for a second she felt bereft. Walking this way was seemlier, but it wasn't as enjoyable.

They strolled the perimeter of the park for a few minutes, reliving the highlights of the day until Alexandra's attention was snagged by the sight of half a dozen men carrying bundles of wood.

"What are they doing?"

"Preparing the bonfire. Sam said it's traditional. No one knows how it started, but each year they light a fire before the sun sets."

Alexandra considered possible reasons. "Could it be an attempt to hold back the darkness?"

"Maybe. I can't believe it's because anyone wants more heat."

"I have to agree with that." The day had been far warmer than June in New York.

She and Gabe walked silently for a moment until he stopped and turned to face her. "It never seems to be the right time. Every time I got ready to say something, someone interrupted." He looked around, as if searching for possible interruptions. "I wanted to tell you how beautiful you look today." Gabe shook his head in apparent dismay. "That came out wrong, didn't it? It sounded like you're not beautiful every day. You are, but today you look more beautiful than ever. Is that better?"

Alexandra was grateful that Gabe was no longer holding her hand. How embarrassing it would be if he felt her pulse surge. "I wasn't insulted by your first attempt," she said, keeping her voice as steady as she could, "but you're right—the second was better. And may I say that you look particularly handsome today?"

"If ever there was an exaggeration, that was it, but I'll accept the compliment."

They were both still laughing as they approached the bonfire, which was now blazing. To Alexandra's surprise, though the day was still so hot that no one needed extra warmth, people were milling around, seeming to want to be near the flames.

"Shall we see what the attraction is?"

When Alexandra nodded, they approached the fire. It happened so quickly that she had no warning. One second, she was standing next to Gabe, admiring the reds and blues of the flames. The next, she was tumbling headfirst into them.

CHAPTER

Twenty-Seven

She felt the heat. She saw the flames. She knew she had to stop herself from falling, but she couldn't. The force had been too great, knocking her off her feet and propelling her forward. Though Alexandra flailed her arms, desperately trying to stop her descent into the fire, she continued to tumble toward the heat that even now scorched her face. In a second, she would be horribly burned, permanently scarred, or worse.

Please, God, help me. He was the only one who could. As her silent prayer winged its way to heaven, strong arms jerked Alexandra away from the fire. *Thank you, dear Lord, thank you.* The nightmare was over.

The roaring of the crowd and the crackling of the flames diminished, and for an instant Alexandra heard nothing but the pounding of her heart.

"What happened?"

Wordlessly, Alexandra turned toward the man who'd pulled her from the flames. Somehow recognizing that her legs would barely support her, Gabe drew her closer to him, his voice husky with emotion as he said, "I was afraid I wouldn't be able to catch you. What happened?"

The previously noisy crowd quieted as the magnitude of the near accident registered. Alexandra knew they were expecting her to speak, but the words stuck in her throat. All she could do was nod as she tried to erase the memory of the hand on her back and the flames in her face.

"You need to sit down, Miss Tarkington." A woman Alexandra had seen only from a distance touched her arm.

"She needs a glass of water," a second woman declared.

Gabe nodded. Keeping his arm wrapped firmly around her waist, he started to move. "I'll make sure she gets both, and then I'll take her home. Please let us through."

The crowd parted like the Red Sea as Gabe led Alexandra away from the bonfire toward the bench where they'd sat so many times, stopping only long enough to pick up a cup of sweetened tea from the refreshment table. People recounted what they'd seen and speculated about what had caused her to trip. None of that mattered. All that mattered was getting away from the fire. Her face felt the way it did when she spent too much time in the sun, and she suspected that the curls that had framed her cheeks were singed, but other than that, she had escaped with no physical damage, thanks to God and Gabe.

As if he understood that she was still too shocked to speak, Gabe said nothing more until they were seated. Though he was no longer supporting her, he sat close enough to catch her if she fell.

"You're safe now, Alexandra. You're safe."

She sipped the tea, trying not to shudder. The memory of those flames turning from beautiful to threatening as they reached up to engulf her was indelibly etched on her brain.

When she laid the now empty cup on the ground, Gabe wrapped his arm around her shoulders. "Do you remember how you tripped?"

The words that had been trapped in her throat broke free. "I didn't trip." Tripping would have been bad enough. She would have had no one to blame but herself. But what had happened was terrifying. Despite Gabe's assurance, she was not safe.

"Someone pushed me."

It was still light enough for Alexandra to see his doubt. "There were a lot of people there. It could have been an accident."

"It wasn't. I wasn't bumped; I was shoved. I felt someone's hand in the middle of my back, pushing me toward the fire. It was deliberate, Gabe. I know it was."

Doubt had turned to worry, and frown lines appeared between his eyes. "Can you think of any reason why someone in Mesquite Springs might want to harm you?"

She shook her head. "No one in Mesquite Springs, but a man in New York threatened me. That's one of the reasons I came to Texas."

Before she could explain more, Laura and Sam hurried toward them, the Downeys at their side.

"Are you all right?" Concern laced Mrs. Downey's voice. "We just heard that you tripped and almost fell into the bonfire."

The look Gabe gave her urged caution, and while Alexandra saw no reason not to admit her fears to her friends, she wouldn't argue with him. It was possible she wasn't yet thinking clearly. Besides, she didn't want to ruin the evening for Laura and Sam.

"Alexandra's still wobbly from the scare. I'm going to take her home."

"We'll come too." Laura's mother extended her hand and stroked Alexandra's hair gently. "You poor dear. I have some salve that will make your face feel better. After that, you need to rest."

But first she needed to tell Gabe about Franklin. Alexandra rose, relieved that her legs would once again support her. Managing a small smile, she turned toward Laura and Sam. "There's no reason for you to miss the dance. I know you were looking forward to it."

Laura gave her an appraising look. "Are you sure?"

"Yes. I'd feel awful if you couldn't dance a polka or two."

When Laura's mother nodded her approval, Laura gave Alexandra a quick hug, then linked her arm with Sam's.

Once they reached the mansion, Mrs. Downey made a pot of

tea and insisted everyone eat a piece of the dried peach pie Laura had made earlier that day. To Alexandra's surprise, the normalcy of sitting at a table with friends helped dissipate her fear. She would never forget what had happened, but her limbs no longer trembled.

"I'm sure this isn't the way you'd expected to spend the evening," Mrs. Downey said when Alexandra had eaten the last bite of her pie. "Leonard and I won't mind if you want to spend some time on the front porch. Leonard will make sure your father knows you're all right."

Alexandra nodded, grateful that she wouldn't have to tell the story again. When Mr. Downey left, she and Gabe settled onto the porch swing.

"Will you tell me about the man in New York?" Gabe asked.

"His name is Franklin Beckman, and he was one of my suitors." She stopped and shook her head. "It would be more accurate to say he was a man who wanted to be a suitor. I never encouraged him, because I knew he was more interested in my inheritance than he was in me."

"Foolish man."

Gabe's indignant reply made Alexandra smile, though the smile disappeared as she continued her story. "The night I told him I'd never marry him, Franklin threatened me. He said he'd make sure I had no choice but to marry him."

She'd been frightened then, but that fear paled compared to what she'd experienced tonight. Nebulous threats had turned to dangerous and potentially deadly actions.

Alexandra leaned back in the swing, hoping the gentle motion would ease her anxiety.

"I was worried," she told Gabe, "so I left New York and pretended to go to Saratoga Springs. Instead, I came here."

His eyes brightened with understanding. "That's why you attempted to disguise yourself with those ugly clothes and dirt in your hair."

"Yes. I knew Franklin would try to find me, so I wanted to make it difficult."

"And now you think he's found you."

She nodded. "I haven't seen him here, but it's the only thing that makes sense. I can't imagine anyone in Mesquite Springs wanting to harm me."

"It's a friendly town." Gabe wrapped his arm around her shoulders and drew her closer. On another night, it would have been a romantic gesture. Tonight Alexandra knew it was meant to comfort her.

"I don't understand how pushing you into the fire would convince you to marry him."

"Maybe he thought that if I was scarred, no one else would want me." It wouldn't have worked. No matter what happened, Alexandra had no intention of becoming Mrs. Franklin Beckman.

Gabe let out an exasperated sigh. "Only a cruel man with a twisted mind would think that way."

The description was so accurate Alexandra almost smiled. "That's Franklin. On the surface, he seems pleasant, but he has a violent streak."

"We still have the question of how he found you."

"I believed I was being careful, but I did send a letter to Aunt Helen. Papa had already addressed the envelope, so I thought I was safe enclosing a letter to reassure her." Though it seemed unlikely that he'd opened the letter, Alexandra couldn't discount the possibility. "Somehow, Franklin learned where I am. I haven't seen him in Mesquite Springs, but he could have sent someone I wouldn't recognize."

Gabe was silent for a moment. "The only newcomers have been some workers and Martin Lewis."

As the memory of Martin talking about accidents flitted through Alexandra's brain, she said, "Martin was unhappy that I wouldn't dance with him, but I can't picture him hurting me." Though she didn't like him, Alexandra's instincts told her he wasn't vicious.

"Unless he's not who he seems to be." Gabe laid his hand on hers and gave it a quick squeeze. "Be careful, Alexandra."

"I will, and now we need to return to the celebration. I promised you three dances."

Gabe didn't bother to hide his shock. "Are you certain? I'm sure no one's expecting you to come back."

"That's exactly why I need to go. I want whoever was responsible to know that I'm not scared so easily." She'd been frightened—terribly frightened—but this was a battle she was determined to win.

Gabe rose and drew her to her feet. "You're a remarkable woman, Alexandra Tarkington."

*T*hank you for not mentioning my accident in the *Chronicle*." It was Tuesday afternoon, and Alexandra had joined her friends for their weekly gathering at Polly's Place, this time enjoying a piece of chocolate cake as they discussed the Founder's Day celebration.

Dorothy shrugged. "I try to fill the Sociable column with positive news, and there was plenty of that. Parents were proud to see the names of everyone who participated in the games rather than only the winners."

"And the description of the food must have helped sell some extra copies," Laura speculated.

"It did. People like having their names in print. That's why the Sociable is often the most popular part of a paper." Dorothy chuckled. "How's that for alliteration?"

"Not bad." Evelyn refilled their cups before a mischievous smile brightened her face. "I've been thinking about boys' names and think I like Balthasar."

"One of the wise men?" Though Alexandra doubted Evelyn was serious, she decided to play along. "Balthasar Clark." She tipped her head to one side, considering. "I'm sorry, Evelyn. That doesn't sound right to me."

Evelyn pretended to be disappointed. "What would you suggest?"

"I was thinking of Shadrach, Meshach, or Abednego."

"From the book of Daniel?" Laura looked puzzled. "What made you think of them?" She was silent for a moment. "Oh, of course. God saved them from the fiery furnace, and he saved you from the bonfire."

"Exactly."

Thanks to God, Gabe had been in the right place to keep her from serious injury. Thanks to God, he'd been able to protect her, just as he would protect Mesquite Springs's citizens if he became sheriff. *When* he became sheriff. Though he had yet to make a decision, images of Gabe in that role continued to swirl through Alexandra's mind, each one strengthening her opinion that he would be a good sheriff. The question was, what would it take to convince Gabe that he was the right man for the job?

"You don't paint very good, Mr. Seymour."

Gabe was tempted to grin at Hans's understatement, but he feared the boy might be insulted. This was the fourth day he'd joined Alexandra and the twins for their daily painting lesson, and he'd intended to do nothing more than sit and watch as he had the other days. The first day, he'd claimed the Downeys' front porch was a pleasant place to spend an hour or two each afternoon. It was, but that wasn't the reason he'd come. By being here, he could watch over Alexandra. Though he doubted the man who'd tried to harm her on Sunday would attempt anything in broad daylight, Gabe was taking no chances. Keeping Alexandra safe was more important than uncovering Calvin's next scheme.

"It's good practice for when you're sheriff," Sam had teased him when Gabe had mentioned his plans. The idea still seemed preposterous to him, and yet there were times when he admitted that it intrigued him. Being sheriff would give him a reason to remain in Mesquite Springs and a future to offer Alexandra, but he still wasn't convinced it was the right job for him. Protecting Alexandra was one thing; protecting a whole town was something else.

Earlier this week Gabe had been nothing more than an observer, but today the twins had insisted that he paint. And so he had. Badly, as it turned out. The exercise had given him new appreciation of Alexandra's talent and added to his enjoyment of the painting she'd made for him.

Frieda reached over and patted his hand, leaving a blob of red paint on it. "You don't paint good, but me and Hans like you anyway."

This time Gabe did grin. "And I like you." Being with the twins had proven to be more enjoyable than he'd expected, and their antics had distracted him from his worries. The truth was, he was more concerned about Alexandra than he wanted her to realize.

The fact that she'd been threatened in New York and that danger appeared to have followed her to Mesquite Springs triggered Gabe's investigative instincts and made him wonder whether his sense of being watched was because he spent so much time with Alexandra. Had the watcher been seeking a time when she would be most vulnerable?

That was possible, but it didn't explain Sunday's attack. Gabe had been at her side by the bonfire, and there was no way anyone could have predicted they'd approach it so closely. Pushing her into it had to have been an impulsive act, not a premeditated one.

What had the man hoped to gain by injuring her? Even if Franklin was as cruel and devious as Alexandra claimed, surely he did not want a badly scarred woman as his wife.

The questions were endless, the answers elusive. This was one time when Gabe would have liked Calvin's opinion, but Alexandra had been adamant about her father not knowing the truth. She wanted him to believe that she had tripped.

Gabe hadn't agreed. Though he'd been the one to suggest there was no reason for the town to know what had happened, her father was different. If he knew the danger she faced, Calvin could look out for her, but Alexandra would not be swayed. "Papa has too many other things to worry about," she'd said. Things, not people.

That left Gabe as the sole person who knew the truth. He'd do his best to protect Alexandra, but he couldn't be with her every minute.

Alexandra bent over his painting and nodded. "That horse isn't bad."

Gabe laughed as Alexandra's judgment confirmed the twins' opinion of his talent. "It's not a horse. It's a sheep."

"Oh." Alexandra appeared embarrassed by his revelation. He could almost see her struggling between being polite and being honest.

The twins had no such problem. Both Hans and Frieda giggled as they inspected Gabe's attempt at art. "See, I tole you. You don't paint very good." Hans pointed to the four-footed animal in the center of the page. "That's not what sheep look like." He giggled again.

"It's not polite to laugh at others," Alexandra admonished the children.

But laughter was a powerful force and one not to be discounted. "I don't mind. Hans is only being truthful." Gabe had no illusions about his artistic talent. It was nonexistent.

"Maybe it is a sheep." Frieda, often the peacemaker, added her opinion. "It's just an ugly sheep."

The four of them were still laughing when Martin Lewis climbed the steps. "It looks like you're having fun. Can I join this party?"

Frieda frowned and shook her head. "It's not a party. It's a painting lesson. Miss Tarkington is gonna show us how to charge."

"That sounds too dangerous for little children."

The man smirked as he looked down at the twins, leaving Gabe wondering if Lewis realized that calling them little children would alienate them or whether he was deliberately unkind toward them.

"She says it's an important tek . . ." Hans paused, trying to recall the word. "Tek something."

"Technique."

"That's right." The boy nodded as Alexandra supplied the full word.

"Can I watch? You never can tell when I might want to paint something." Without waiting for a response, Martin pulled a chair close to Alexandra and settled into it.

Focusing her attention on the twins, she asked, "Remember how we made puddles?"

Frieda nodded. "First we dipped our brushes into water. Then we mixed the water with color on the palette."

"Exactly. When we charge, we mix the colors right on the paper. Like this." Alexandra demonstrated the technique while the twins watched closely. They might never be accomplished artists, but they were clearly interested in learning from her, leaving Gabe no doubt that she was as good a teacher as she was a painter.

"How come you do that?"

Instead of answering Hans's question, Alexandra posed one of her own. "You tell me. What's different between these two areas?" She pointed to the sky that she'd just painted and then to the ground. Even Gabe could see the difference, although he didn't understand what had caused it.

"There's no line there." Frieda's finger hovered over the two shades of blue in the sky.

"That's right. It's a smoother transition."

"Trans what?" Hans seemed more interested in learning a new word than a painting technique, while Lewis's interest was focused on Alexandra. The looks he was giving her were not those of a lovestruck swain. Instead, they seemed calculating. Whatever he wanted from Alexandra, it was not love, and that set Gabe's antennae to vibrating. Alexandra might not think Lewis was dangerous, but Gabe wasn't so certain.

After half an hour of watching the painting lesson, Lewis left, clearly bored. And then, because he wanted to go to the post office before it closed, Gabe rose.

"Bye, Mr. Seymour." Frieda gave him a quick hug, while Hans extended his hand for a shake.

"Sam and I'll be back this evening," he told Alexandra, his pulse accelerating when she gave him one of those sweet smiles that never failed to warm his heart. The hours until their walk would go quickly and maybe in the meantime he'd have a letter from Bill Woods.

He did. Though he was tempted to open it the instant the postmaster handed it to him, Gabe waited until he was back in Sam's apartment. He slit the envelope carefully and withdrew the single sheet of paper.

"I apologize for the delay in responding," Bill began. "It took longer than I'd expected to track down Martin Lewis, because there is no Martin Lewis in Cincinnati."

Gabe stared at the sheet of paper, trying to make sense of his colleague's words. When he'd cautioned Alexandra that Lewis might not be what he seemed, he hadn't expected this.

"It's good you sent a description," the letter continued. "Without that, I wouldn't have been able to help you, but men as good looking as you said aren't common. One who looks like your Martin Lewis has been seen with Phineas Drummond."

Gabe looked up from the closely written script as thoughts tumbled through his brain. It couldn't be coincidence that someone who knew Calvin's partner was here.

"I couldn't learn anything about the relationship, but my sources say he was seen entering and leaving the office Drummond shares with Calvin Tarkington several times over the years but never when Tarkington was there."

It was no wonder Calvin hadn't commented on Martin Lewis's arrival in Mesquite Springs. To him, he was simply another stranger until he started paying attention to Alexandra. It was only then that Calvin had taken notice of him.

"The rumor is the man racked up some high gambling debts and Drummond paid them. Could be your man owes Drummond for that."

Gambling. Gabe closed his eyes for a moment, letting his thoughts whirl. Calvin had also gambled heavily after he'd taken Phineas Drummond as his partner. Was there a connection? But even if there was, how did Martin Lewis or whatever his name was fit into the picture? If Drummond had sent him, why?

Gabe opened his eyes and continued reading, hoping Bill Woods would have some answers. "His landlady said he paid a month's rent in advance, something he's never done before. He didn't tell her where he was going, but if it's the same man, we know where he is. I didn't find anything that told me why he's there and why he's calling himself Martin Lewis. Folks here call him Sonny, but his name is Louis Martin."

CHAPTER

Twenty-Nine

"Oh, Papa, this is beautiful." When Alexandra had asked why he'd wanted her to come to the hotel at suppertime, he'd refused to say more than that he had something to show her. Now she had her answer. The dining room, which had been closed to her for the past week, was finished. And what a beauty it had become.

The patterned green wallpaper formed the perfect backdrop for her painting, while the lace curtains gave diners privacy without sacrificing natural light. Mrs. Lockhart's furniture had been polished to a brilliant shine, the dark mahogany contrasting with the pale walls and the thick carpet that would muffle the sound of dishes and voices. It was everything Alexandra had imagined and more, for the table was covered with a fine linen cloth, and two settings of the china Papa had ordered were arranged at one end.

"Let me get your chair." When she was seated, he continued. "I hope you're hungry. The cook I hired will be unhappy if we don't eat everything he's prepared."

"He's already here?" Alexandra had thought the chef was due to arrive on Monday. Today was Friday.

"I asked him to come early. With only a week before the hotel opens, I wanted to be sure he was as good as he claims. If he's not, I'll . . . well, I don't know what I can do other than throw myself on Evelyn's mercy. Meanwhile, I need your opinion. You know what ladies like."

Alexandra knew more than that. She knew how to supervise staff and plan menus that would appeal to both men and women, but though she had volunteered to help, Papa had refused, saying she was doing enough by handling reservations. His unwillingness to recognize her abilities was the reason she hadn't told him of the changes she'd made to the orders he'd placed with the Downeys.

When Mrs. Downey had questioned the number of sheets and pillowcases Papa had specified, Alexandra had realized he hadn't considered that some might become torn or stained. It hadn't taken long to confirm that he'd made the same erroneous assumption about the table linens.

Papa might have thought she was interfering when all she was doing was trying to ensure success and lessen his worries. That's why she hadn't told him about the changed orders or what had happened at the bonfire.

She could do more than taste food, but if that's what Papa wanted now, she'd do it. Alexandra nodded. Five minutes later, she nodded again, approving the first course. "This chicken soup is delicious." The delicately seasoned broth had bits of meat and tiny pieces of carrots and onion, giving it a pleasing texture without being too heavy.

"I thought we'd serve that the day the investors arrive."

Perhaps Papa used the plural pronoun to mean him and the chef, but Alexandra chose to believe he was including her in the plans. He seemed to appreciate her help with the reservations, and while she wouldn't call him enthusiastic about the opening day tours, he'd agreed that they might make the townspeople more welcoming toward the hotel's guests.

"Did I tell you the investors will be here for three days?" When she nodded, seeing no need to remind Papa that the schedule had been included in the invitations she'd so carefully penned, he continued. "Do you have enough gowns? If you're going to be my hostess, you need to impress them."

"I can order new ones." The investors' gathering had been scheduled for the last week of July, which would give the town's seamstress plenty of time to make three new dresses.

"Go ahead. I need you to keep the wives occupied while the men and I discuss business. You can do that, can't you?"

"Of course." As she'd told Papa, entertaining guests was one of the many things Aunt Helen had taught her that helped qualify Alexandra for managing the hotel. "I'll plan activities for the women. We can go to the springs one day." Her mind began to whirl. "I imagine Mrs. Plaut would be happy to let them visit her conservatory." Perhaps she could arrange afternoon tea there.

Papa beamed. "That's my girl. Always thinking."

"You know I'm glad to help, but won't you tell me what the investment is?"

Alexandra didn't understand the need for continued secrecy. It was one thing to leave potential investors guessing. The invitations had described an opportunity unparalleled in modern history, an investment so exciting it had to be seen to be believed, accompanied as it was by three days' free accommodations at the finest hotel in the Hill Country. That proposition would appeal to people in Aunt Helen's social circle, wealthy men who craved a bit of adventure.

Alexandra understood why Papa cloaked his invitations in mystery, but she did not understand why he refused to explain his plans to her. She offered the best argument she could marshal to persuade him to tell her more. "If I know more about the investment, I can talk to the wives about it. Their enthusiasm might help convince the men."

Alexandra had little doubt that she could generate enthusiasm. That was another social skill she'd learned. Unfortunately, her father seemed immune to her powers of persuasion.

His smile fading, Papa shook his head. "It's too soon for anyone to know. I don't have everything ready yet. Now, what do you think of the roast?"

While they'd been discussing Papa's plans, the waiter had silently removed their soup bowls, replacing them with the main course. Alexandra took a bite, chewing carefully before she replied. "It's almost as good as Evelyn's."

"I was afraid you'd say that. I want it to be better."

His disappointment was palpable, making Alexandra determined to assuage it. "Don't forget that food isn't the only thing you're offering." She let her gaze roam around the beautifully decorated room. "There's the ambiance. The elegance here is very different from the casual atmosphere of Polly's Place."

Papa still looked dubious. "I told investors this was the finest hotel in the Hill Country."

"It will be. It already is." Every time she entered either of the buildings, Alexandra felt a sense of belonging, that this was where she was meant to be, not simply for a few months but for the rest of her life. Not even the terror she had experienced at the bonfire had shaken that conviction. Sadly, Papa did not agree.

As they ate in silence, Alexandra watched her father. Surely it wasn't her imagination that he seemed distressed. She hoped it wasn't because she'd asked about the new project.

"Is something wrong? Don't you like the food?" The roast might not have the special spices that made Evelyn's distinctive, but the vegetables were tastier than any Alexandra had eaten.

"It's not that." For a second, she doubted he'd say anything more, but Papa laid his fork on his plate and turned his attention to her. "Sometimes I wonder whether I'm making a mistake."

"About the hotel? It's beautiful. A real asset to Mesquite Springs."

"I hope you're right about that. This is the most important project I've undertaken, but it's not what's troubling me." He cut another piece of meat and chewed it carefully. "Do you ever wish you could do your life over?" Without waiting for a response, Papa shook his head. "Of course not. You're too young to have regrets, but I do. I wonder what our lives would have been like if I hadn't sent you to Helen."

Alexandra let out a small gasp. This was the first time he'd expressed doubts about what he'd done. In the past, when she'd begged him to take her back to Cincinnati with him, he'd claimed that living with Aunt Helen was best for her, that Alexandra needed a woman to raise her. Had he been right? She wasn't certain.

Papa fixed his gaze on her. "Would we have been happier?"

Alexandra wanted to protect her father and alleviate his worries by saying no, but she could not. She owed him an honest answer. "I don't know. Aunt Helen was good to me. She did her best."

"But she wasn't your mother or father."

"No, she wasn't."

Papa bowed his head. "I'm sorry, Alexandra, but I can't undo the past. No one can."

Martin stretched out on the bed, ignoring Mrs. Bayles's warning that if his boots soiled the linens, she would charge extra for laundering them. God might have contented himself with ten commandments, but Martin's landlady had at least twice that many, and she was vigilant about enforcing them. "They're important," she declared.

So was what Martin was supposed to be doing. Unfortunately, he hadn't succeeded, and that was a problem. A huge problem. He couldn't tell the old man he'd made no progress, particularly when he didn't understand why he hadn't. He'd never before failed, at least not where ladies were concerned.

Both his mother and Drummond had told him his face was his fortune, insisting no one could resist it or his charming words. But Alexandra Tarkington had. She seemed oblivious to him and the compliments he'd lavished on her. Oh, she was polite enough.

The old lady in New York had raised her well, but Alexandra had given him nothing more than the common courtesy good manners demanded. There'd been no spark of interest, no admiring glances at his undeniably handsome face.

He might have thought her incapable of that kind of attraction, but he'd seen how she looked at Seymour. The man couldn't hold a candle to Martin, but the heiress didn't seem to care.

That wasn't the worst of it. This week had shown him it wasn't only Seymour who had captured her attention; so had those little brats. Why, she paid more attention to them than she did to Martin.

The afternoons he spent watching them attempt to paint when it was clear they had absolutely no talent were painful. How could Alexandra bear to spend time with them, listening to their sense-less prattle, praising their miserable artistic efforts? If the stakes weren't so high, he would not have returned after the first unpleas-ant afternoon. But the stakes were high.

Somehow, he had to convince the Tarkington heiress to marry him. That was why he was here. Once she'd signed over her in-heritance, she'd be the victim of an unfortunate accident. He'd be able to repay his debt to Drummond with enough left over that, as promised, he would be a rich man. Nothing and no one was going to stop him from accomplishing that goal.

Gabe woke with a start, his heart pounding as remnants of the dream lingered. He swung his legs over the edge of the bed and stood, trying to banish the memories that continued to swirl through his brain. He'd been running, although whether to or from something hadn't been clear. All he'd known was that lives—perhaps his—were at stake. He had to run. He had to! But then he stopped short, his way blocked by a man wearing a frighten-ing mask. The gargoyles that protected cathedrals were beautiful compared to it, and the manic laughter that emerged from behind the plaster sent shivers down Gabe's spine.

"Fooled you, didn't I?" the man behind the mask asked, his voice once more normal. And then he lowered the mask, revealing a face Gabe had seen every day for close to two months: Calvin Tarkington.

What did it mean, if anything? Gabe had never been one to believe dreams were portents, but this one disturbed him more than any he could recall. Was Alexandra wrong? What if Franklin Beckman wasn't behind the attack on her? What if it was somehow tied to Calvin? Gabe knew he'd never hurt his daughter, but Calvin might be the keystone, the piece that held everything together. The man had enemies. The fact that Biddle had hired Gabe was proof of that. Had one of them decided to punish Calvin by harming his daughter?

Calvin might not know any more than Gabe did, but one thing was certain: Gabe needed to talk to him.

"What do you know about Louis Martin?" As he'd waited for daybreak, Gabe had debated the best way to approach Calvin, finally deciding on blunt questioning. He sprang the question on him as they walked through the new building on Calvin's morning inspection tour.

"Do you mean Martin Lewis?" Calvin's voice held nothing more than mild curiosity.

"They're one and the same. When he lived in Cincinnati, he was Louis Martin. Now he calls himself Martin Lewis."

If Calvin was concerned by the man's change of name, he gave no evidence of it but continued to run his hand over the headboard that had been delivered yesterday, checking for possible splinters. "Changing your name isn't a crime. People do that when they want to start over. I did, and I heard the mayor's wife used an assumed name when she came here."

Though Gabe hadn't heard that story, he wouldn't pursue it, for he sensed that Calvin was trying to deflect attention from Gabe's original question.

"Let's talk about Louis Martin. Did you ever meet him in Cincinnati?"

"No." Calvin's voice rang with sincerity. "I meet a lot of people in my business. Most are forgettable, but I'd remember if I'd met him. No one forgets a man with that face."

Unlike Jason Biddle, who could blend in anywhere. Gabe blinked, wondering what had made him think of Biddle now.

"I still question why Martin's here." The story of a banker moving to a state with no banks had never rung true.

"Trying to court my daughter. She's a nice prize for fortune hunters. Between the money from her mother's side of the family and what I plan to leave her, she'll be an extremely wealthy woman."

The undercurrent he heard in Calvin's voice made Gabe study him. Gabe knew Alexandra was slated to receive the money from her mother on her twenty-fifth birthday, but he'd assumed it would be some time before Calvin gave her anything. Now he seemed to be implying that his demise was imminent.

"Are you ill?"

Calvin shook his head vehemently. "Of course not. I've never been better."

Though Gabe doubted that, there was another possibility: Calvin was being threatened by someone he'd defrauded, someone who'd seen behind his mask.

Was that the meaning of Gabe's dream?

CHAPTER

Thirty

lexandra smiled as she joined her father on the Downeys' front porch. The weather could not have been more perfect. The deep blue sky was dotted with a few puffy white clouds, and last night's rain had broken the heat, leaving the air cooler than normal for early July. Best of all, Papa had looked happy when he arrived to escort her to the park.

His gaze moved slowly from her hat to her hem and back again, his smile broadening as he said, "You look like your mother." He made a twirling motion with his finger. "Turn around and let me see all of your gown." When she'd complied, he nodded. "Very nice."

Alexandra reached for the accessory she'd propped by the door when she'd greeted her father with a hug. "I have a matching parasol." The dress itself had been made of what the dressmaker called flag-blue poplin and boasted a white collar and cuffs, with a red sash completing the patriotic theme, while the parasol was white with red, white, and blue ribbon trim around the edges and covering the handle.

Papa's smile turned into a grin. "All our plans are working out." He bent his arm and escorted her down the steps. "Some of the guests have already arrived. It seems they're eager to see where they'll be staying."

But they wouldn't be allowed to do that until later in the day. Papa had assigned four men to guard the two buildings' entrances, ensuring that no one entered until the designated time.

After the Independence Day speeches and songs were completed, the townspeople had been invited to tour the hotel. Alexandra, her father, and Gabe would lead groups through Mrs. Lockhart's former home, showing them all that had been accomplished. Afterward, everyone was invited to enjoy the chef's special spice cake and lemonade before returning to the park for the traditional activities of games, a community supper, and dancing. To Alexandra's relief, unlike Founder's Day, there would be no bonfire tonight.

"I'm glad you've rented every room." The last one had been filled a week ago; since then, she'd had to return reservation deposits with a note suggesting a later date.

His head held high, Papa said, "It will be a fine legacy."

They walked the short distance to the park, where most of the townspeople were already gathered. Wyatt had explained that Alexandra and her father would be seated on the small platform with him and other dignitaries and that they should arrive only a few minutes before the festivities began.

Mercifully brief speeches were followed by Miss Geist leading the schoolchildren in a medley of patriotic songs. When those concluded, Wyatt gestured toward her father, who rose and faced the audience.

"It is my very great honor to be part of Mesquite Springs," he said, his voice ringing with sincerity. "Building this hotel has been a dream of mine for years. It took a while to find the perfect location, but it's been worth the wait. Thank you for welcoming me and my daughter and accepting us as part of the town. Now it's time to return the favor and welcome you to the King Hotel. Tours will begin in fifteen minutes."

"May I have the first dance tonight?" Gabe asked when the last of the tours had ended and Alexandra found herself with a lull between greeting guests. Though his work for the day was completed, Gabe had stayed by her side, adding his welcome to hers as each of the guests arrived.

"You may." Alexandra could think of nothing she'd like more than to spend the final minutes of the day dancing with him. Though they'd danced together on Founder's Day, the memory of what had happened at the bonfire had kept her from enjoying those dances to the fullest. Tonight would be different.

Gabe raised one eyebrow. "May I have the last dance?"

"You may."

"And all of them in between?"

Alexandra couldn't help laughing at the hopeful note in his voice. "I'd like to say yes, but I don't want to scandalize the town."

"Then I'll have to content myself with only two dances." Gabe's eyes sparkled with mischief. "Maybe I should ask Miss Geist for the others."

Though she suspected he'd meant it as a joke, Alexandra liked the idea. "You should do that. Spinsters rarely have the chance to dance, and that's a shame, since Miss Geist is probably the most accomplished dancer in Mesquite Springs."

"You're joking."

"Not at all. She teaches deportment and dancing as well as geography and history."

"And those deportment classes teach young ladies not to favor any one man with too many dances."

"Precisely."

"And you listened to them." Gabe seemed surprised.

"I didn't need her lessons. The same rules were part of my schooling."

"And well-bred ladies never break rules." This time there was more than a hint of mirth in his voice.

Alexandra decided to encourage his laughter and made her voice overly dramatic. "The very framework of society might crumble if we broke rules."

As she'd hoped, Gabe chuckled. "I'm still amazed that after that prim and proper upbringing, you defied convention and came out here alone."

"I probably shouldn't admit it, but at times I can't believe I did that. It was the boldest, most daring act of my life."

She saw respect reflecting from Gabe's eyes. "You're a strong woman, Alexandra Tarkington."

"And you're the first person who's said that." The thought warmed her more than the afternoon sun, making her want to tell him how much she appreciated his approval, but the approach of an elderly couple stopped her.

"Good afternoon, Mr. and Mrs. McAllister. Welcome to the King Hotel."

The man blinked in surprise, while the woman's face flushed with pleasure. "How did you know who we were?"

Alexandra descended the steps so she was no longer towering over them. "It was easy. Mr. McAllister told me he'd married the prettiest girl in the state."

The older woman tapped her husband on the arm as her smile brightened. "You old coot, you always did know the way to my heart."

As she helped the couple register, then led them to the room she'd reserved for them, Alexandra felt a longing deep in her heart. What would it be like to have a man look at her like that, his expression filled with the love that had lasted half a century? Oh, how she wished for a life like that. The McAllisters didn't have much money—she knew that from his letter saying he'd been saving for years to give his wife something special for this anniversary—but what they had was infinitely more valuable.

Faster than Alexandra had thought possible, afternoon slipped into early evening and it was time to join the rest of the towns-people for supper in the park. Though the hotel would serve the evening meal each day beginning tomorrow, today the guests were invited to join Mesquite Springs's residents for food and friendly conversation followed by dancing.

Alexandra hooked her arm in Gabe's, laughing when he said he hoped he was as spry as Mr. McAllister when he reached that age. "Even my grandfather wasn't that active."

Alexandra, who had not known any of her grandparents, was saved from replying when Laura and Sam joined them.

"The hotel's even more beautiful than you said," Laura announced with a backward glance at the main building.

"Papa's pleased with it, and the guests seem to be happy. I heard one woman say she'd be willing to spend the rest of her life there."

Laura raised an eyebrow, as if she suspected a bit of exaggeration had been involved. "What about you? Could you picture yourself living there?"

"Not in the hotel." As beautiful as it was, it didn't provide the measure of privacy she craved. "But I could be convinced to live in the manager's house."

Sam, who'd been regaling Gabe with stories of some of the youngsters' antics during the afternoon's games, appeared to have overheard Alexandra's response. "The manager's house? This is the first I've heard of that."

"That's because Papa hasn't had time to build it yet." And when it was finished, Alexandra would need no convincing at all to move in. From the moment she'd seen the plans, she'd been unable to stop thinking about the house and envisioning herself living there. She'd even seen herself chasing two small children around the parlor, laughing when they ran to their father for protection. Their father, the sheriff.

Pulling herself back to the present, Alexandra continued the explanation. "Papa said he'd start construction once Brandon and Dorothy's house is finished."

Gabe looked like he wanted to say something, but he led the way to the supper line and helped Alexandra fill her plate. Conversation remained light while the four of them ate, then strolled around the park, waiting for the musicians to finish tuning their instruments. When the final note sounded, Gabe turned to Alexandra.

"That's our cue." He bowed formally, his lips curving into a small smile. "May I have this dance, Miss Tarkington?"

"You may, Mr. Seymour. It would be my pleasure."

And it was. Alexandra had danced with dozens of men. Some of them had been more accomplished than Gabe, but no dance had ever felt like this. It was wonderful. Simply wonderful.

Alexandra took a shallow breath as emotions overwhelmed her. If only this dance could last forever. If only she could spend the rest of her life like this, being so close to Gabe, feeling the warmth of his hand on her waist, smelling the combination of bay rum and the scent that was uniquely his, hearing the way his breathing hitched, telling her he was as affected as she. But the dance ended as all dances do. When they moved apart, she was left with a sense of loss and the irrational fear that she would never again experience anything as wonderful as this dance with Gabe.

"We have another one to look forward to," he said softly, making her heart pound with the thought that perhaps he was feeling the same way.

Alexandra nodded, her emotions still so close to the surface that she was unable to speak. She wanted to place her hand in Gabe's, to feel his touch again, but propriety forbade that.

Before she could say anything, Martin appeared at her side, a scowl marring his handsome face. It disappeared an instant later, replaced by the fawning smile he always gave her. "May I have the next dance?"

Gabe moved closer, as if to protect her, and the memory of Martin talking about accidents only minutes before someone had shoved her toward the fire flashed through Alexandra's brain. Though she'd tried to convince herself that there was no connection between her not dancing with Martin and being pushed, a tremor of fear made its way down her spine. She would not give in to it. She would not let fear reign.

"I'm sorry, but I promised that one to Sam."

"What about the one after that?"

The veiled anger in Martin's voice told Alexandra he would persist until she granted him a dance. She nodded. She did not want to be the cause of an unpleasant scene, but the determination to overcome her fear prompted her to agree.

"Yes, you may have that dance." It would be a lie to say she was looking forward to it or that it would be a pleasure, and so she said nothing more.

Dancing with Martin proved to be surprisingly pleasant. He danced as well as Gabe and kept the conversation flowing smoothly. It wasn't like dancing with Gabe, because Alexandra felt no attraction toward this man, but it wasn't the distasteful experience she'd expected, and she felt no twinges of fear. That could be because Gabe and his partner were never far away, but Alexandra suspected the reason was simpler. She might not like Martin, but she did not fear him.

When the final notes faded, he bowed. "May I have another dance?"

She shook her head. One dance had been enough to conquer her fear; she had no need of another.

"The rest are spoken for." Brandon, Wyatt, and several other men had asked to be her partner, and the last dance was already promised to Gabe.

Though he made no effort to disguise his disappointment, Martin's voice was calm as he said, "Then I'll have to content myself with memories of this one. Thank you, Alexandra."

Perhaps it was the anticipation of her second dance with Gabe. Perhaps it was something else. All Alexandra knew was that the evening seemed to fly by. This was unlike the parties she'd attended in New York. Instead of dancing on polished wood floors under sparkling crystal chandeliers, she was waltzing on grass under a star-spangled sky. Her gown was poplin, not the silk and satin she would have worn in New York. Her hair was drawn into a simple chignon rather than arranged in the elaborate style that used to take her maid an hour to complete. Aunt Helen might have shuddered at the informality, yet Alexandra had never enjoyed an evening more.

"At last!" Gabe placed her hand on his bent arm and grinned. "I've been counting the minutes until this dance."

As she had. "You looked like you enjoyed the others."

He shrugged. "They were better than I'd expected, but they couldn't compare to the one we shared."

"I felt the same way." It might be forward to admit that, but etiquette rules seemed out of place here, and she wanted Gabe to have no doubt about how much she'd enjoyed her time in his arms.

Though Alexandra hadn't thought it possible, their second dance of the evening was even more wonderful than the first, all her sensations heightened by the pleasure of being close to Gabe. She smiled so much that her face hurt, but she didn't care. All that mattered was that they were together.

Alexandra was so caught up in the magic of being in Gabe's arms that she hadn't noticed he was leading them away from the musicians. They kept moving in time to the waltz, but when it ended, she realized they were apart from the other dancers, standing in the shadow of an old live oak. Though others could see them if they looked in this direction, the separation made Alexandra feel that she and Gabe were in a world of their own.

She looked up at him, the almost-full moon casting enough light that she could see his face, his eyes shining, his lips curving in a smile.

"That was wonderful." Gabe's smile widened. "I can think of only one thing that would be better."

Slowly, he caressed her cheek, the touch of his fingers sending shivers of delight through her. Slowly, he moved his finger from her cheek to her lips, tracing their outline, intensifying the pleasure that radiated through her. And then, slowly and deliberately, he pulled her closer and pressed his lips to hers.

An explosion of sensations filled Alexandra—the feel of Gabe's lips on hers, firm and yet gentle; the scent of newly mowed grass beneath their feet; the sound of the breeze soughing through the leaves, forming a counterpoint to the beating of her heart. This was her first kiss. Alexandra had dreamt of it. She had wondered what it would be like. She had thought she knew, but she'd been wrong. This was better—far better—than anything she had dreamt or imagined. This was sheer perfection.

And then a man's voice broke the spell.

"Take your hands off her. She's mine."

Jason stood on the sidelines, watching as the scene unfolded. Though his foot had tapped in time to the music and he'd been tempted to ask one of the girls to dance, he hadn't dared. Ever since the day he'd tried and failed to scare Alexandra away from Seymour, he'd taken extra care to avoid approaching her. The last thing he needed was Seymour somehow recognizing him.

They'd danced together twice, looking like smitten fools both times. Franklin wouldn't like that, but Franklin would never know, not if Jason could convince the heiress that the only way she'd be safe was if she returned to New York. Franklin didn't need to know that Seymour had become a problem. By the time Jason was done, the problems would be resolved.

He'd give the man credit. It was clever the way he'd gotten Alexandra away from the others. And the way he'd kissed her had confirmed how smitten he was. But Seymour's cleverness had its limits. He'd been so intent on smooching the gal that he hadn't seen Martin Lewis until the man shouted, "She's mine!"

Jason retreated further into the shadows, his hands clenched into fists. It was tempting, so tempting, to wrap his hands around Lewis's throat and watch him struggle to breathe. He wouldn't do it. Not tonight. But one thing was certain: Martin Lewis would never marry Alexandra.

"She's mine."

The words echoed in Gabe's brain as disappointment and anger rushed through him. Keeping his arms around Alexandra, he glared at the intruder who'd spoiled the single most wonderful moment of his life.

"This is none of your business, Martin."

The man raised fisted hands in an unmistakable challenge. "I'm making it mine. What were you doing, accosting Alexandra?"

Before Gabe could respond, Alexandra turned and faced Martin. "He wasn't accosting me. He was kissing me. And I was kissing him."

It was a bold declaration, one Gabe doubted any other woman would have made. It made him want to smile, but this was not the time to smile, not with an obviously furious Martin hissing like a snake.

"You had no right to interfere." Though her voice was calm, Alexandra's anger was as apparent as Martin's.

"I had every right. I care about you." Martin took a step closer, extending his hand toward Alexandra. "Surely you can't be taken in by this smooth-talking charlatan. What do you know about him?"

Ignoring his hand, she said, "I know enough to know he's a better man than you. Leave us alone."

Martin stared at her for a long moment, seemingly unable to believe she'd dismissed him. Finally, he lowered his hand in apparent defeat. "I'll go now, but it's not over."

When Martin was out of earshot, Gabe laid his hand on Alexandra's shoulder, wanting to reassure her. "I'm sorry that happened. He ruined the evening."

She shook her head. "Only if we let him. I won't give him that power." She placed her other hand on top of Gabe's and gave it a quick squeeze. "Here's how I want to remember tonight."

And, before he knew what she intended, Alexandra rose on tiptoes and kissed him.

Thirty-One

Seymour wasn't going to win the prize. Martin drained the glass of whiskey and ordered another. He'd lost count of how many he'd had, but it didn't matter. Although liquor might dull some men's brains, it sharpened his.

The saloon was filling with men who appeared to want to celebrate their own version of independence—independence from their wives. Several had invited him to join them, but Martin had refused, preferring his spot next to the bar. He could think better here.

He downed his drink, then stared at the wall. Odd how he'd never noticed that crack before. And there was the stain on the ceiling where the roof must have leaked. Odd, the things he was seeing tonight.

What else had he seen tonight? Martin thought about the moment he'd asked Alexandra to dance. He'd caught a glimpse of something unexpected in her expression. What was it?

As he stared at the scarred surface of the bar, Martin grinned. Fear. That's what he'd seen. Maybe that was the answer. Charm hadn't worked. Fear might.

Someone was knocking on her door. Blinking sleep from her eyes, Alexandra glanced at the clock on the nightstand. Though the sun was beginning to rise, five thirty was too early for her to be awake. Apparently whoever was knocking didn't realize that.

"Come in." She sat up in bed, forcing a smile as Mrs. Downey opened the door.

"Mr. Gottlieb is here to see you."

Alexandra's smile faded with the realization that he couldn't be bringing good news. "I'll be there in a minute." Rather than waste time dressing, Alexandra threw on her wrapper and rushed down the stairs.

She found the twins' father in the parlor, holding his hat and turning it around and around in an apparent attempt to settle his thoughts. When he spoke, his accent was more pronounced than usual. "Will you help me, Miss Tarkington? Frieda, she is sick. I cannot leave her alone and Mrs. Fisher is afraid to be around a sick child, but I need to work."

"Of course, I'll help you." Alexandra knew how important each day's pay was to the struggling father. "Shall I call Doctor Dawson?"

"*Nein*. It is not that serious. If she stays in bed today, the fever will break by morning."

Though he sounded confident, Alexandra wasn't convinced. "How do you know?"

"Because Hans had the same sickness yesterday. He's much better today."

"That's why I didn't see you in church." The Gottliebs had been at the Independence Day celebration and had been vocal in their approval of the hotel as they toured it, but they hadn't attended church services.

"*Ja*. I cannot leave my *kinder* alone when they're ill. When they wake, they will need you."

Though she had no experience with sick children, Alexandra could not refuse. "Don't worry. I'll take care of them until you come home."

"*Danke, Fraulein.* You are a good woman."

Within half an hour, Alexandra had sent notes to her father and Gabe, explaining what had happened, had rented a horse, and was on her way to the Gottlieb ranch, carrying leftover roast chicken and some vegetables that Mrs. Downey had insisted would make a good soup for the sick child. "Cover it all in water and let it simmer," she'd directed. "It's easy. Much easier than cinnamon rolls," she added, obviously trying to reassure Alexandra that no special culinary skills were required.

Though she'd never visited the twins' home, Alexandra remembered the turnoff Laura had pointed out on the drive to the Plauts' and had no difficulty finding it. As she'd expected, the house was small but meticulously crafted. When she entered the house, she found Hans still asleep but Frieda moaning in her bed, her face flushed.

"Oh, Miss Tarkington, my head hurts."

Alexandra placed her hand on it, confirming a fever. "Let's see what we can do. I'll be right back." When she returned with a pail of cool water, she dipped a cloth in it and laid it on Frieda's head. "Does that feel better?" she asked a minute later.

"A little."

Though she doubted the cool cloth was reducing the fever, Alexandra gave thanks that it was comforting Frieda.

"I want you to lie quietly for a while. I'm going to make you a special tea." Mrs. Downey might consider chicken soup a panacea, but when Alexandra heard that Hans had had an upset stomach the previous day, she knew something else was needed and asked Mrs. Downey for some ginger root. Now she grated a bit to mix with hot water. A little honey would make it more palatable.

"What's that?" Hans wiped the sleep from his eyes as he entered the kitchen. If he was surprised by Alexandra's presence, he gave no sign of it.

"It's a tea for Frieda. She's sick today."

"*Vati* didn't make tea for me when I was sick." Hans cast a suspicious look at the pan. "Can I taste it?"

Alexandra wasn't certain whether Hans was trying to protect his sister or whether it was simple curiosity, but since the tisane would not hurt him, she would not refuse.

"You might not like it," she warned as she poured a small amount into a cup.

Hans's reaction did not disappoint her. "Yuck! That's medicine." He left the remaining swallow in the cup and shoved it toward Alexandra.

"It is," she agreed, "but we're going to tell Frieda it's special tea. Okay?"

Though Hans still appeared dubious, he nodded. "Okay." He glared at what he considered a foul concoction. "I'm glad I'm not sick anymore."

"Me too."

By the time Mr. Gottlieb returned that evening, Alexandra was exhausted. There had been times during the day when Frieda alternated between being violently ill and shivering, making Alexandra fear Mr. Gottlieb's assessment of his daughter's illness had been overly optimistic. She'd been tempted to send for the doctor, but since she couldn't leave Frieda, and Hans was too young to go alone, she was unable to call for help.

"We need to pray," Alexandra told Hans, who'd been hovering in his sister's room.

The boy nodded. "*Vati* did that for me. He asked Jesus to heal me." Hans raised his head and looked at the ceiling. "Jesus, you have *Mutti* and the lambs with you. Don't take Frieda too. You don't need her, but me and *Vati* do." He scrunched his eyes closed, trying to decide what to say next. "If you make her well, I promise I won't pull her braids again and I'll eat green beans. Amen."

Perhaps it was Hans's prayer; perhaps the illness had run its course. All Alexandra knew was that by early evening the fever seemed to be subsiding and Frieda was no longer whimpering in pain.

"You did good, Miss Tarkington," Mr. Gottlieb said when he laid his hand on his daughter's forehead and felt the cooling. "You will be a good mother."

Alexandra wasn't so sure. "I hadn't realized being a parent was so difficult." She couldn't remember ever worrying the way she had today. Were days like that the reason Papa had sent her to Aunt Helen? Had he feared he wouldn't know what to do when she was ill?

The twins' father nodded. "Sometimes it is difficult, but the joy *kinder* bring is worth the hard times." He smiled at his children, then turned back to Alexandra. "I know you must be tired, so I saddled Galahad before I came in. Thank you again. You were a fine nurse."

Moments later, as Alexandra bent to kiss Frieda's cheek in farewell, the girl wrapped her arm around Alexandra's neck and whispered, "I love you."

Hans, who'd been watching the exchange, extended his hand to Alexandra, then threw his arms around her waist. "Me too."

Mr. Gottlieb winked, as if to say this was what he'd meant. Alexandra was still basking in the glow of the twins' love as she mounted the horse and headed for home. Their father was right: the love children brought far outweighed any pain.

The sun had yet to set, the road was clear, and Alexandra was in a hurry to get home. She leaned forward. "Faster, Galahad. Faster."

The horse began to gallop, his powerful legs carrying her toward town. For a moment, she reveled in having the wind in her hair, of feeling that she was flying. And then, without warning, Galahad reared up.

Desperately, Alexandra tried to hold on, but she was no match for the gelding. As he bucked again, she was flung into the air. A second later, she hit the ground, and the world turned to black.

"She should be back." Gabe had paced in front of the livery for so long that he wouldn't be surprised if he'd worn a track into the boardwalk.

Caleb Smith, who'd been filling in for his brother today, was less concerned. "Alexandra told me one of the twins was sick. Maybe she's staying all night."

"The note she sent me said she'd be back once their father finished work. That was more than an hour ago." He might be overreacting, but Gabe was worried. "I want your fastest horse."

Within minutes, he had left Mesquite Springs. Though the horse was fast, it didn't feel fast enough, not when Gabe's instincts were shrieking that Alexandra was in danger. Dusk was falling rapidly, making it difficult to see the road, but he wouldn't slacken his pace. The dread that made Gabe's stomach clench told him it was imperative to reach her quickly, wherever she was.

"Where are you, Alexandra?" In his heart, he knew she was no longer at the Gottlieb ranch, which meant she must be somewhere on this road. But where? He strained, trying to see something—anything—on the deserted road, but there was nothing. Then the horse whinnied, his superior eyesight spotting what Gabe had not: a dark mass at the side of the road.

"Alexandra!" Gabe jumped off the horse and raced toward the woman he loved. Lying on the ground, curled into a ball, she cradled her head in both arms and moaned.

"Oh, Gabe, I'm so glad you found me." Another moan escaped as she tried to sit up, then slumped back to the ground "I don't know what happened. One second I was riding, the next I was lying here. I must have landed headfirst."

Gabe tried not to shudder at the thought of how serious her injuries could be. At least she was alive and coherent, and though she was obviously in pain, she wasn't suffering from the shock that had left her speechless after she'd been shoved toward the bonfire.

"Don't move. Let me take care of everything." He looked around for her horse, but there was no sign of the animal.

As gently as he could, Gabe gathered Alexandra into his arms and carried her to his horse, settling her on the saddle before he mounted behind her. "I know it hurts, but lean back against me. I'll keep you safe."

She started to nod, then whimpered at a new onslaught of pain. "Try not to move," he cautioned. "It'll hurt less that way." He hoped that was true. All Gabe knew about head injuries was that they were dangerous. With his arms wrapped around Alexandra, he turned the horse toward Mesquite Springs. It would take far longer to get there at a slow walk, but the less jarring Alexandra endured, the better.

"I don't understand what happened," she said, her voice stronger now. "I've ridden Galahad before, and he was always gentle."

"Something must have spooked him." Gabe wondered why he hadn't encountered the horse as he'd ridden here. Normally, an animal would return to its home, but he hadn't seen Galahad.

"I didn't see or hear anything unusual before I fell."

Alexandra was still trying to make sense of what had happened. Afraid that speculation might excite her and make her head ache more, Gabe tried to reassure her. "The horse may have seen something you didn't, but let's not worry about that now. I'm going to take you to Doc Dawson and then get your father."

She shuddered. "Don't do that. I don't want to worry Papa." Though he couldn't see her face, Gabe could picture Alexandra's frown.

"You need to see the doctor, and your father needs to know you were injured. He'll worry more if he hears about it from someone else. You said he wasn't happy that Mr. Downey was the one to tell him about the bonfire."

Alexandra sighed. "You're right. I hate to admit it, but you're right."

When they reached Mesquite Springs, Gabe carried her into the doctor's office, explained what had happened, then headed for the hotel. Doc Dawson would give Alexandra the care she needed. What her father would do remained to be seen.

Gabe wasn't surprised to find Calvin in the dining room, regaling guests with stories that were undoubtedly exaggerated. If he was concerned that Alexandra had missed dinner with their guests, he gave no sign of it. Not wanting to alarm anyone else, Gabe drew Alexandra's father aside to explain what had happened. The man blanched, muttered a curse, then left for the doctor's office. Knowing there was nothing he could do for Alexandra right now, Gabe rode his rented horse back to the livery.

"Did you find her?" Caleb demanded, his tone anxious.

"Yes. Galahad threw her. She hit her head and is bruised, so I took her to Doc Dawson." Gabe recited the facts as calmly as he could when all the while his heart was still pounding over the memory of seeing Alexandra lying on the road and hearing her moans.

Caleb clapped him on the shoulder to comfort him. "Thank God that's all that happened." His voice was husky. "I've been praying ever since Galahad came back without Alexandra."

"The horse is here?"

"He arrived soon after you left. I don't know exactly where he went, but he had leaves and twigs in his mane like he'd run through a treed area."

"Something spooked him. I wish I knew what it was."

"You don't need to wonder." His expression ominous, Caleb reached into his pocket and held out a small object. "I found this under Galahad's saddle."

For a second, Gabe stared, speechless with horror. Then anger, more powerful than he'd ever experienced, filled him. He'd told himself Alexandra's fall was an accident, something that could have happened to anyone, but the small, sharp-edged rock in Caleb's hand said otherwise.

"This was deliberate."

CHAPTER

Thirty-Two

*H*ow do you feel?"

Alexandra looked at the doctor, who'd helped her sit up after he finished examining her head. Though his expression was serious, his freckles—the bane of many redheads—made him look younger than the thirty-five she knew him to be.

"My head hurts." Had it been less than twelve hours since Alexandra had been the one asking the question and receiving the same response from her patient? Now she was the patient, her injuries serious enough that she was in the doctor's office with her father looking on anxiously. And, while it was true that her head hurt, her entire body ached from the impact of hitting the ground. Fortunately, sitting no longer made her dizzy.

Doc Dawson stood at her side as she swung her legs over the edge of his examining table. "You've sustained a serious contusion. Or, to put it more simply, that's a large bump on your head. Fortunately, your hat and all that hair you ladies pile on your heads protected you a bit. You'll be sore from that and the bruises, but there's nothing to worry about. No permanent damage." He nodded at her father. "Make sure she sits here for a few more minutes before you take her home."

When the doctor left the room, Papa moved closer. "What happened, Alexandra? All Gabe told me was that you'd been thrown from the horse."

"I'm not sure. Something spooked Galahad." She had tried to remember whether she'd seen anything unusual, but she'd been so intent on returning to Mesquite Springs that she hadn't paid much attention to her surroundings. The fall had happened almost as soon as she'd left the Gottlieb ranch and headed north toward town.

"Maybe he heard a javelina in the brush. One of the workers said he'd seen one a few days ago."

"It wasn't a wild boar."

Alexandra turned toward the door, startled by the sound of Gabe's voice. She hadn't expected him to come back, but she felt a rush of pleasure that he had, pleasure that was quickly extinguished by the worry she saw in his eyes.

"How do you know it wasn't a boar?"

"Because Caleb discovered what happened. Someone put a sharp rock under Galahad's saddle. We know Mr. Gottlieb wouldn't have done that, so someone else must have been at the ranch waiting for an opportunity. If the rock had been there this morning, Galahad would have thrown you then. Caleb said the cut was deep enough that any horse would have reared up, even one as gentle as Galahad."

As the blood drained from Alexandra's face, she gripped the side of the table, willing herself not to faint. In the two weeks since Founder's Day, she had tried to convince herself there would be no further attacks. She'd been wrong.

"Franklin," she whispered. "It was Franklin."

Though Gabe nodded, Papa appeared confused. "Franklin Beckman? Isn't he the man Helen said wanted to court you?"

"Court my money is more like it. Franklin's the reason I left New York. He threatened me when I told him I'd never marry him. Maybe this is his way of convincing me to come back. He may think that if I'm frightened, I'll return to New York, and he'll be able to court me again."

Papa's confusion deepened. "I don't understand. Why didn't you tell me?"

Though Alexandra did not want to hurt her father, she was unwilling to lie. "I planned to, but when I arrived, you kept insisting I should go back to New York. I wasn't sure you'd believe me. You might have thought I was inventing an excuse."

"You didn't feel you could trust me." The pain in Papa's eyes wrenched Alexandra's heart. This was her father, and no matter what had happened between them, she loved him.

"I'm sorry, Alexandra. I should have been a better father."

Gabe took a step closer, perhaps realizing how difficult the conversation was for both of them and wanting to ease their discomfort. "We can't change the past, but we need to make certain that if Franklin is behind this, whoever he hired can't hurt Alexandra again. The attacks seem to be escalating."

Papa blanched. "This wasn't the first time?"

"No." Gabe didn't give Alexandra the chance to respond. "What happened at the bonfire wasn't an accident."

Alexandra looked directly at her father and nodded as she confirmed Gabe's statement. "I didn't trip. Someone pushed me."

"But you didn't tell me."

"I didn't want to worry you. You were so busy with the hotel that you didn't need more problems." And, while she wouldn't admit it here with Gabe listening, there was another reason she hadn't told Papa: the fear that he didn't love her enough to care.

Papa laid his hand on hers and squeezed it. "I'm your father, Alexandra. It's my right to worry about you."

Once again, Gabe intervened. "What matters now is keeping Alexandra safe. We know Beckman isn't here, because Alexandra would have recognized him, but someone clearly wants to hurt her." Gabe stopped addressing Papa and turned to her. "I don't think you should go anywhere alone."

"I agree." Papa nodded vigorously.

"I wasn't alone on Founder's Day when he shoved me."

"That's true," Gabe agreed, "but that was before we knew someone wanted to harm you. Everything is different now."

It was indeed. Alexandra knew the pain of her bruises would fade, but she suspected it would take longer for her fear to disappear. "I won't go out of town alone, but I can't imagine anyone bothering me if I walk from the Downeys' to the hotel or Polly's Place. I'll be safe here."

Jason raised the hammer, cursing his decision to work on the newspaper editor's house. He should have done what he'd first planned and moved out to that land near the river. But when he'd seen the activity there, he'd known that wasn't the right choice. Besides, he needed to stay close to the heiress. That was the only way he could do what Franklin wanted.

The problem was, he didn't know how much longer he could tolerate working like this. Even when the doctors at Serenity House had forced him to punch sandbags, saying that would release his anger without hurting anyone, he hadn't sweated like this.

Jason did not like sweating. But he'd be sweating from fear if he didn't finish Franklin's assignment. Franklin had told him not to return until he'd accomplished it, one way or another, and Jason wouldn't. He couldn't, not with the threat of Chadds Ford hanging over him.

Even though Franklin was his friend, Jason knew that friendship had limits. Why else would Franklin have forced Jason to sign a confession, then warned him that if he didn't return or if something untoward happened to Franklin himself, his attorney would give the police the confession? Jason couldn't—he wouldn't—let that happen.

If only it weren't taking so long. He slammed the hammer onto the board, splitting it.

"Careful there." The foreman shouted his command, though he was only a few feet away. "We ain't got extra wood."

Jason stared at the hammer for a second, forcing himself to relax his grip on it when what he wanted was to use it to pound the foreman's face. "I guess I don't know my own strength."

"Just make sure it don't happen again."

"It won't." Jason continued working, keeping his hat pulled low over his face. Though Seymour hadn't recognized him, he couldn't take any chances.

"Did you hear what happened to the Tarkington gal?" One of the other workers wiped the sweat from his brow before he picked up another board. "Seems she fell off her horse. Hit her head mighty bad."

"That's a shame." Another man joined the conversation. "She's a fine gal. Treated me and the missus the same as those fancy guests when we was at the hotel."

The first man nodded. "She's a real nice lady. I cain't figger out why she ain't married yet."

"I heard the Seymour fella's courting her. Reckon we'll hear wedding bells soon."

But they wouldn't, not if Jason had anything to say about it. And he did.

"Maybe this will take the frown off your face," Gabe said as he handed Emil a piece of oatmeal pecan pie. Knowing that the foreman who'd built Calvin's hotel and was now constructing a new home for Brandon and Dorothy favored the dessert, Gabe had made it his business to buy a slice each time Evelyn put it on the menu. Hard work deserved to be rewarded, and no one worked harder than Emil.

Though the man normally smiled when he saw Gabe approaching, today he was clearly disgruntled. "What's wrong?"

"I got trouble with one of the workers." Emil shook his head in obvious disgust. "Man disappeared yesterday right before supper—didn't tell anyone where he was going, just up and left. When he showed up this morning, he claimed he ate some bad meat and was sick. Could be true, but I don't think so." Emil shook his head again. "If I didn't need workers so bad, I'd fire him. Reckon I'll give him one more chance, but I'm gonna keep my eye on him."

Gabe's hackles rose as he considered the foreman's words. It might be nothing more than coincidence, but his instincts said otherwise. A man disappeared yesterday. Someone planted a rock under Galahad's saddle yesterday. There had to be a connection.

"What's the man's name?"

"John Nelson."

"You look pretty good for someone who was thrown off a horse less than a day ago." Evelyn studied Alexandra once she'd served everyone a piece of spice cake. "I thought you might be spending the day in bed."

Laura laughed. "My mother tried to convince her to do that, but Alexandra's too stubborn."

"I needed to take care of the twins." Fortunately, they'd been less rambunctious than usual today, though they'd been eager to spend an hour playing on the schoolyard swings with Gabe so that Alexandra would not have to miss her weekly time with her friends.

"Mr. Seymour's fun," Frieda had declared.

"Even if he don't paint good," her brother had added.

Alexandra had agreed with both sentiments. Gabe might not be an artist, but he was more than fun. He was kind, caring, and everything she most admired in a man.

"They could have come here. Polly would have been happy to have playmates."

Though Alexandra appreciated Evelyn's offer, it was one she would not accept, especially since Evelyn had once admitted how challenging she found the days Polly's friend Melissa spent here. Most of the time, Melissa's mother cared for both girls, but occasionally she needed a respite.

"You'd be surprised how much trouble two little girls can get into," Evelyn had said after one of those days.

Alexandra didn't want to consider how much mischief three children and a puppy left alone in the apartment over the restaurant might wreak.

"We had a quiet day," Alexandra told the others. "I didn't hear everything Mr. Gottlieb said, but I suspect he warned the twins not to bother me."

The man had been shocked when he heard what had happened and kept apologizing, even though Alexandra had assured him he was in no way responsible. He didn't need to know that someone had snuck onto his ranch and planted a rock under Galahad's saddle.

"I still don't understand how it happened." Dorothy looked thoughtful. "Galahad is one of our calmest horses. That's why Caleb chose him for the livery."

"But even a calm horse can be spooked. It was an accident." That was the story Alexandra was telling everyone.

After Gabe had revealed what had caused her fall, he'd gone around the corner to fetch Sheriff Engel. The sheriff had been alarmed, particularly when he learned the truth of what had happened at the bonfire, and he agreed with Gabe that it was wisest to pretend her injuries had been caused by Galahad shying at some unknown thing, possibly a javelina.

"We want to keep whoever's responsible believing we don't know it was deliberate," Gabe had said. "If he becomes overconfident, he's more likely to make a mistake. Meanwhile, we'll make sure you're safe."

"I'm so thankful your injuries weren't any worse." Evelyn refilled her cup, then turned her attention to Laura. "You've been unusually quiet all day. Is something wrong?"

A radiant smile crossed Laura's face as she shook her head.

She looked at Alexandra, her eyes pleading for understanding. "I didn't want to say anything last night. It seemed wrong after what had happened to you, but I had a wonderful night. You and Gabe weren't there, so Sam and I walked alone." Laura's eyes grew misty. "We went into the park, and then he . . ." She paused, and a blush colored her cheeks. "He kissed me. Oh, ladies, it was wonderful."

She would be safe, Gabe told himself as he mounted Galahad. If John Nelson was the man Franklin Beckman had hired, he wouldn't have a chance to harm Alexandra during the day, because Emil was keeping a close eye on him. Gabe would ensure her safety at all other times. Besides, he'd only be gone a few hours today, and since Alexandra had the twins with her, it was unlikely anyone would approach her, much less attempt to hurt her. Oh, Martin might join them if they sat on the porch, but the children's obvious dislike of him would drive him away within a few minutes.

She would be safe while Gabe rode to her father's river property. He'd seen no need to return sooner, since there had been nothing unusual other than the fencing, but now that Calvin was spending his days there, it was time to learn why.

It was a cloudy day, not a day Gabe would have chosen for a ride with Alexandra, but his ride was not for pleasure. Although his greatest worry since Monday evening had been Alexandra's safety, he could not neglect his responsibilities to Jason Biddle, especially since the threat to Alexandra might be connected to her father's activities.

Despite Alexandra's conviction that Franklin Beckman was behind the attack, Gabe couldn't ignore the possibility that Calvin was involved. The man had hurt so many people that others besides Biddle might have discovered the truth and want revenge.

When he reached the first of the ranches, Gabe turned Galahad toward the river. Today was a reconnaissance mission, its goal discovering what was happening here, and for that to succeed, Gabe needed to avoid being spotted by Calvin or his workers. Since he had no doubt that the man would lie about whatever Gabe found, the key was to uncover incontrovertible evidence, then confront Calvin with it.

As he approached the river's edge and began to ride along the bank, the wind wafted the unexpected sound of metal on rock toward him. Gabe dismounted quickly, then approached on foot, staying inside the small grove of trees that grew close to the river. It would be difficult to explain why he was sneaking onto the land, but Gabe had no intention of being caught. He would learn what he could today, returning later if needed.

He climbed a small rise, then squinted to see more clearly. A solitary man was digging what appeared to be a deep hole only a few dozen yards from the river. A well? That made no sense, since the river would provide all the water a family needed. A root cellar? Possibly, but each of the three ranches Calvin now owned had a root cellar. The foundation for a house? Unlikely, given the proximity to the river. A house this close would be subject to flooding whenever the river rose.

The man tossed the shovel to the ground, appeared to wipe his forehead, then turned, revealing his face. Gabe knew he shouldn't have been surprised, and yet he was. Why was Calvin Tarkington, the man who hired others to do all the heavy labor at the hotel, digging a hole? And why was he alone?

As he retraced his steps, Gabe knew two things: it was too soon to confront Calvin, and he needed to come back. The next time would be different. He'd use the front entrance, and he wouldn't come alone.

Thirty-Three

"Are you sure you feel well enough to ride?"

Alexandra gave Gabe a reassuring smile. "Yes."

Not only did her head no longer hurt but she had no responsibilities this morning, since Miss Geist had insisted she would care for the children today and every Saturday until school resumed.

"You need a rest," the schoolmarm had declared, "especially after your accident."

Though Alexandra still felt a bit guilty about letting everyone think it had been an accident, she trusted Gabe's judgment.

"I thought we might ride to the river," Gabe said as they walked toward the livery.

"I'd like that." Not only did that mean she wouldn't travel the road where she'd been thrown from Galahad but the destination was one she wanted to visit.

"I'd like to see Papa's land again. He's been out there every day, doing something. Let's surprise him."

"That's a good idea." Though the words were innocent, something in Gabe's tone made Alexandra wonder if that had been his intended destination. She put that thought aside and focused on enjoying their time together.

Though the sun was hot, the ride was pleasant. To Alexandra's relief, being on horseback again did not trigger memories of her last ride, perhaps because it was full daylight, perhaps because she had Gabe at her side. He'd said he would do his best to keep her safe, and he appeared to be doing exactly that.

"Do you think we're being followed?" she asked as he glanced behind them for what seemed like the hundredth time.

"No, but I won't take any chances." Gabe's smile was meant to reassure her, and it did.

"I wish we knew who was responsible. I keep thinking it must be someone Franklin hired, but I don't know who."

"What about Martin? He wasn't happy when he saw us together. Besides that, he's a liar."

"What do you mean?"

The idea startled Alexandra. She might not like Martin, but she hadn't thought he was lying to her.

"He told you his name was Martin Lewis, didn't he?" When Alexandra nodded, Gabe continued. "I don't know which is his real name, but when he lived in Cincinnati, he was Louis Martin."

"How do you know that?"

"I haven't trusted him from the first day I met him, so I asked a friend in Cincinnati to see what he could learn about him. He's the one who discovered that Martin Lewis called himself Louis Martin there."

Alexandra remained silent for a moment, absorbing what Gabe had said. "Just because people change their names doesn't mean they're liars. Look at Papa. He's calling himself King. It might not be his full name, but shortening it doesn't make him a liar."

Gabe turned to look behind them before he said, "I still don't trust Martin Lewis or Louis Martin or whatever his name is. The fact that he arrived not long after you did and that he's paying you a lot of attention makes me think he's the man behind what happened to you."

"You could be right, but I'm not convinced. The pieces don't fit together. How would Franklin have found Martin? He's never been to Cincinnati."

"Martin could have gone to New York and met Franklin there."

As a light breeze freshened the air, Alexandra considered Gabe's hypothesis. "I suppose that's possible. Martin did claim that he'd once lived in New Orleans, so he might have also lived in New York or at least spent some time there. The problem is, I can't picture Franklin having anything to do with him."

"Why not?"

"Because Martin is too handsome." Incredulity marked Gabe's face until Alexandra continued her explanation. "Franklin is vain. He wouldn't want to be associated with someone who'd outshine him. I can't imagine him even shaking hands with Martin."

"I've never met Franklin, so I can't dispute that, but if it's not Martin, then who's responsible?"

Alexandra had no answer. The idea that some unknown man was determined to hurt her had kept her awake Monday night until she'd finally surrendered her fears to God, trusting him to watch over her. It was time to do so again.

She and Gabe rode in silence until they reached the main entrance to Papa's river property, each lost in thought. The peace that had descended onto Alexandra dissipated at the sight of two guards with shotguns patrolling in front of the gate.

There had been workers before, constructing the fence that Papa had claimed was needed to keep casual visitors off his land, but he'd never mentioned hiring guards. Why were they here?

The look Gabe gave her said he'd handle this. Acting like armed guards were normal in a place where people didn't lock their houses, Gabe gave the men a wide smile. "Good morning, gentlemen. We'd like to ride around Miss Tarkington's father's ranch."

Though his eyes widened in surprise at Alexandra's name, the first guard shook his head. "Cain't do that. Mr. King said no one could come in."

That was ridiculous. "I'm not just anyone. I'm his daughter."

And Alexandra had every intention of seeing Papa and whatever it was that brought him here each day. There had to be a reason for both his secrecy and this level of security.

"Sorry, ma'am, but I gotta follow orders."

"Surely you can make an exception for us." Gabe's voice was pitched to persuade the guards.

It didn't work. "Nope. The boss said no one, and I ain't gonna go against him."

"Is my father here today?"

The guard shrugged. "I cain't say, ma'am."

Short of forcing their way past the guards, there appeared to be no way to get onto the land. This was the only road.

"It's my fault," Alexandra said as she and Gabe turned around. "I should have told Papa we'd be riding out this way. He would have told the guards to let us in."

Though Gabe looked dubious, he said only, "Don't blame yourself. You didn't know I'd suggest a ride today."

That was true, but it didn't alleviate Alexandra's discomfort with the whole situation. "I really wanted to see Papa. He's been distracted all week, and I don't think it was because Galahad threw me. He has breakfast with the guests, then he leaves and doesn't return until almost dinnertime. He said he's been spending the days here, but now I wonder if that's true."

Gabe did not seem to share her opinion. "The guard said he couldn't say whether your father was there. That could mean he didn't know, but it could also mean he had orders not to tell anyone where your father was."

If that was true, it made the situation even more difficult to accept. "I don't understand the need for secrecy, but you can be sure of one thing: I'm going to ask Papa what's going on out here."

Alexandra wondered if this was what it meant to be an actress—smiling, pretending nothing was wrong, all the while hiding her feelings. She played her usual role of hostess as she joined Papa for dinner at the hotel. Normally she enjoyed spending time with their guests, but today she was anxious to talk to her father, and so when the last bite of dessert had disappeared and the diners began to depart, she tucked her hand in the crook of her father's arm.

"Let's go to your office."

Concern etched his face, but he waited until they were in the hallway and would not be overheard before he spoke. "Is something wrong? Did someone try to hurt you again?"

"The answer to the second question is no. I'm not sure about the first." When they reached the office and had closed the door behind them, she continued. "Gabe and I rode out to your land today. I wanted to surprise you, but the guards wouldn't let us in. They said those were your orders."

Papa seemed to relax. "They were right. It's a dangerous place, Alexandra. I don't want anyone on it until the foundation is in place. There's too much risk."

His explanation did not ring true, leaving Alexandra to wonder what he was trying to hide and why he had hired guards. The foundation for a house involved only a small part of the property. Even if there were trespassers, which seemed unlikely, the odds of their finding the excavated area, much less hurting themselves, were slim.

"They could have told you we were there, and you could have guided us around the dangerous spots."

Rather than face her, Papa gazed at the painting she'd given him, then rose and straightened the frame before he spoke. "But I didn't know you were coming."

Recognizing that this was not the time to confront him about the guards, Alexandra said, "If we tell you in advance, will you show us around?"

"Maybe."

And that, she knew from past experience, meant no.

Gabe signed the letter, folded it, and slid it into the envelope. As much as he hated telling Biddle he still had no proof that Calvin was up to something illegal, that was the truth. He had suspicions—many of them—but no evidence of anything other than that Calvin Tarkington was a liar.

The story he'd spun about the dangers of digging the foundation of his new house was a blatant falsehood. First of all, there was no house. Calvin had told Gabe he had no plans to build a house on the river property, though he continued the charade with Alexandra. Secondly, there was no foundation, just that one hole.

Gabe knew there had to be a reason for the digging, especially since Calvin was doing it by himself rather than hiring laborers as he had for the hotel, but even though he'd wracked his brain, the only thing Gabe could imagine was mining, but this wasn't California. As far as he knew, there was no gold or silver in this part of Texas. And so, once again, he had no news to send to Biddle.

Grabbing his coat, Gabe headed for the stairway, determined to get this letter to the post office today. As he slid his arm into the sleeve, he bumped his elbow against the wall.

"Ouch!" The involuntary cry echoed down the stairwell as pain radiated up Gabe's arm, momentarily paralyzing him. He watched helplessly as the envelope he'd been clutching fell out of his grip and fluttered toward the floor.

"Hey, man, you okay?" Sam came out of his office and looked at Gabe, who'd made his way down the stairs.

"Just hit my elbow. It's better now."

"Good." Sam looked down and spotted the envelope. "What's this?" He picked up the letter, studied the address, then fixed his gaze on Gabe. "How do you know Jason Biddle?"

The concern in his friend's voice told Gabe this was not a casual question. "He's the man who hired me."

Lines of worry formed between Sam's eyes as he fingered the envelope. "Let's sit down. We need to talk."

He led the way into his office, then turned the sign to "closed."

When they were both seated, he laid the envelope on the desk in front of them. "Where did you meet Biddle?"

"He came to my office."

"In Columbus?"

"Yes. I thought it was odd when he said he lived in New York, but he claimed he wanted someone closer to Calvin Tarkington and that he didn't trust anyone in Cincinnati, since they might be in Calvin's pay."

Gabe thought back to the one time he'd met Jason Biddle and wondered if he'd made a mistake in accepting him as a client. It would have been the first time he'd refused a case, but for an instant, he'd been tempted to do that.

"I almost turned him down," he admitted, "but when I heard his story, I couldn't, because I understood exactly how he felt."

"What was the story?" Sam's voice was warm and friendly, encouraging Gabe to continue. If this was how he treated witnesses, Gabe suspected he had no trouble uncovering their deepest secrets.

"When Biddle's father lost all his money in one of Calvin's swindles, he killed himself. Biddle knew he couldn't do anything for his father, but he wanted to stop Calvin from ever doing that again."

"I see." Sam leaned forward, his expression earnest. "When did this happen? When did Mr. Biddle die?"

"January."

"And Jason Biddle was very convincing when he told the story."

Though he didn't like the direction the discussion was going, Gabe nodded. "He was."

Sam's eyes radiated concern as he shook his head. "Unfortunately, what he told you is all lies. Jason Biddle's father is alive and well, or at least he was in April. I saw him when he visited Serenity House."

The sinking feeling that had settled in Gabe's stomach intensified as he recognized the name. "That's the place where you recovered."

"Yes. The senior Mr. Biddle is a major donor and for a good reason. He was paying them to ensure no one knew his son had been a patient there."

Gabe knew Serenity House had helped Sam overcome his anger, but the way Sam spoke made him fear that the younger Biddle's stay had not been as successful.

"I never met him," Sam continued, "but I overheard one of the doctors saying he was their greatest failure. Eventually, they released him because there was nothing more they could do and no proof that he was a killer, but they were convinced he hadn't been cured."

A killer. Though he'd had momentary doubts about taking Biddle as a client, not once had Gabe thought the man might be a killer.

"Jason Biddle is a very dangerous man."

His mind reeling in horror, Gabe gripped his head with both hands. "What have I done?"

CHAPTER

Thirty-Four

I see your guard dog is gone."

Alexandra paused with her hand on the door as she prepared to leave the Downeys' house, trying not to frown at the sight of Martin waiting at the foot of the steps. Ever since Gabe had told her about Martin's two names, she had looked at him differently, suspicion tingeing her already ambivalent feelings toward him.

She'd told Gabe it was no crime to change one's name, and she believed that, but she also wondered why Martin had done it. Just as she wondered why he referred to Gabe as a guard dog. He'd used the term before. It had annoyed her then, and it annoyed her now. Still, she'd accomplish nothing by challenging him.

"I don't mean to be rude," Alexandra said as she descended the steps, "but I need to greet the hotel's guests before supper is served."

Martin nodded as if he'd expected that, making her wonder whether anyone in Mesquite Springs was unfamiliar with her routine. He bent his arm in a wordless invitation for her to place her hand on it. "I hope you'll allow me to accompany you on your walk. I heard about your accident and wouldn't want anything more to happen to you."

Ignoring the proffered arm, Alexandra focused on the way his lips had curved when he'd pronounced "accident." Had she been wrong? Was Martin the man Franklin had sent? Was he taunting her by hinting that he knew her fall had been no accident?

Though she was uncomfortable walking with him, Alexandra told herself nothing could happen between here and the hotel. It was a short walk, it was still light outside, and she'd never be out of sight of others, for the park was a popular spot at this time of day.

"All right." The acceptance wasn't gracious, but it was all she could manage.

Martin lowered his arm and seemed to content himself with walking at her side. "How is the hotel doing? Is it making a profit?"

Once again, Alexandra tried to bite back her annoyance. He was sounding like Franklin, concerned about money. "We've had full occupancy since we opened, and a large group is coming next week. Papa's pleased, and so am I."

"Good, good. I'm glad to hear it's doing so well. Not all partnerships are as profitable as your father's."

It was no secret that Papa had a partner, but it was also not something everyone in Cincinnati knew. The fact that Martin was aware of Papa's business arrangement aroused more suspicions, making her wonder if Gabe had been right and that Martin's arrival in Mesquite Springs had been a deliberate attempt to meet her, perhaps because Franklin had sent him. Though she'd once thought it improbable, Alexandra could no longer ignore the possibility.

"So, profits are good?" Martin's interest in the hotel's finances increased Alexandra's discomfort.

"I wouldn't know. Papa doesn't discuss that part of the business with me." Even though she handled reservations and had overseen ordering of some supplies, he had not given her access to the books.

"And he shouldn't. That's men's work. Ladies like you shouldn't be bothered with matters of money." Martin's smile radiated approval. "What you're doing is right. You're greeting guests and making them feel welcome. Those are skills that will serve you well when you marry."

Alexandra increased her pace, anxious to reach the hotel and be rid of Martin's company. His patronizing tone grated on her even more than his interest in the hotel's profitability. Though she'd done her best to ignore his other comments, she couldn't dismiss this one. "What I do when or if I marry is none of your concern."

"What if I want it to be? What if I ask your father for permission to court you?"

The thought made Alexandra shudder. "He'd refuse, and so would I."

Martin's eyes narrowed as he shook his head. "That's where you're wrong. He'll agree, and so will you."

"Never."

Alexandra let herself into the Downeys' house, grateful that the evening was coming to a close. She was later than normal returning from the hotel, because several of the guests had engaged her in conversation after dinner and she hadn't wanted to discourage them. The truth was, she enjoyed getting to know the guests. Some were only passing through Mesquite Springs, but most had come for at least a week's stay, attracted by the advertisement Dorothy had helped her write.

That was good. What wasn't was the darkness that had fallen by the time she was ready to leave. With the memory of Martin's threat—for that was the only way she could describe it—fresh in her mind, Alexandra had asked her father to accompany her back to the Downeys'.

She'd told herself that Martin couldn't force her to do anything, that his words were most likely the result of bruised pride at the thought that anyone could resist his good looks, but she wouldn't take any chances, and so she'd asked Papa to escort her. He'd agreed readily, declaring that he relished the opportunity to spend more time with her, but had declined when she'd invited him to come inside for a few minutes.

When Alexandra poked her head into the parlor, she was surprised to see only Mr. and Mrs. Downey enjoying a cup of coffee. "Isn't Laura back yet?" The others had continued their nightly walks, agreeing that if Alexandra hadn't returned by their usual time, they'd go without her. Other than the night Galahad had thrown her, that had happened only once before today.

Mrs. Downey set her cup on the table. "Laura's home. She said she was tired and was going to bed early. Would you like some coffee?"

Alexandra shook her head. "I think I'll read for a while."

But when she reached the top of the stairs, she saw that the door to Laura's room was open. Though the lamps were extinguished, the light of the half-moon coming through the open window revealed Laura curled up on the settee.

"Come in, Alexandra. I left the door open so you'd know I wasn't asleep."

Alexandra closed the door behind her, crossed the room, and took the seat next to her friend. "Your mother said you were tired."

Laura shook her head. "That was an excuse. I needed time to think."

"Are you all right?" Something was different about Laura tonight, but Alexandra couldn't identify it.

"I'm more than all right. My heart is so full of love that I feel like it'll overflow."

And Sam was the reason. Alexandra had no doubt of that. "Did Sam kiss you again?" The first time he'd kissed her, Laura had been almost giddy with happiness.

"Yes." Laura nodded vigorously. "It was wonderful, but he did more than that. He shared his deepest secrets with me."

There was a moment of silence, perhaps because Laura was trying to decide how much to share with Alexandra. Then she said, "I'd heard rumors about what happened when he ran for mayor, but I never knew the things Sam did to try to win, how he let anger control him, or all that he went through to overcome his anger." She shuddered. "It was a horrible story, but it had a happy ending, because Sam—my Sam—is a different man now."

When Laura's gaze met hers, Alexandra saw tears in her eyes. "Sam didn't have to tell me, but he did, even though he was afraid that I might hate him for what he'd done."

"But you don't hate him."

"I could never hate Sam. If anything, I love him more. We all make mistakes, but only strong people admit their mistakes and make sure they don't repeat them."

Alexandra nodded, thinking of the mistakes she'd made and hoping she had the strength to avoid repeating them. "Sam is strong," she told Laura. "He's also wise, because he knew there should be no secrets between people who love each other."

Laura flung her arms around Alexandra and hugged her fiercely. "I love you, Alexandra. Will you stay with me a bit longer? I need your advice about a few other things."

As she nodded her agreement, Alexandra felt the clouds that had shrouded her future lifting, erasing her doubts. She would stay—not simply for the few minutes that Laura needed her to-night but permanently. No matter what Papa decided or where he went, she would remain in Mesquite Springs.

She had friends here. More than that, her life had a purpose here. If Papa agreed, she would manage the hotel. If he didn't, she would continue teaching art. She would build a life for herself here, a life free from fear, a life that—if dreams came true—included Gabe.

Alexandra smiled at the prospect of a future filled with friends, filled with promise, and most of all, filled with love.

"Yes, I'll stay," she told Laura. "For as long as you need me." And even longer.

CHAPTER

Thirty-Five

*G*abe stood in the corner of the verandah, grateful that shadows from the live oak tree helped hide him. Though Sam had offered to help him keep watch, he'd refused. He'd made Alexandra's safety his responsibility, and so he'd come here each night since her fall.

As he had so often in the past when he'd been searching for people, he'd tried to put himself into the mind of whoever had sought to harm her. The attacks were escalating, indicating the man—for his instincts told him a woman would have used different methods—was becoming more desperate.

The wide verandahs that made the Downeys' house so beautiful also made access easy, particularly since the one on the rear where Alexandra's room was located boasted an exterior staircase. Even if she locked the French doors leading to the verandah, Gabe doubted the locks were particularly sturdy, meaning it would be simple for someone to enter her room when she was most vulnerable. Ensuring that didn't happen was why he was here.

He leaned back against the railing, then straightened when he saw a man climbing the stairs. Gabe's pulse accelerated at the realization that he'd been right. Something was driving Alexandra's attacker, forcing him to act tonight rather than wait for the greater darkness of a new moon. He must have bet he'd not be noticed approaching the back of the house. Still, the man was taking few chances. His movements were stealthy, and the dark hat pulled down over his face obscured his features.

Gabe waited until the dark-clad assailant reached the verandah, then matched his stealth, sprinting silently toward him, his brain registering the fact that Alexandra had been right. This was not Martin Lewis, but a much shorter man.

Stopping two yards away from the man who was heading for Alexandra's door, Gabe said, "I don't imagine the lady is expecting visitors at this time of the night." Gabe drew his gun but hoped he wouldn't have to use it.

The intruder had no such compunctions. He swiveled and pointed his weapon at Gabe. "You think you can stop me? I'm mighty fast with this."

The shabby clothes and the beard were new, but Gabe recognized the voice, and as he did, dread surged through him. "Jason Biddle."

"That's right." Biddle straightened his shoulders and glared at Gabe, his grip on the gun never wavering. "I've been working on the hotel for weeks, and you never knew it." His laugh was almost a cackle, reinforcing what Sam had said about Jason Biddle's stay at Serenity House. The man had serious problems that even the doctors there had been unable to cure, and now he was here, threatening Alexandra.

"You called yourself John Nelson."

"Yep. That's right. You're easy to fool." Biddle's voice rose to an almost maniacal level. "You believed my story, and you never saw me, even though you passed by me most days."

So the feeling that he'd been watched hadn't been Gabe's imagination. Knowing that his instincts had been accurate was no consolation when he was faced with a madman with a gun. Somehow, he had to keep Biddle talking until he found a way to disarm him.

"How did you learn what happened to my father?" It was more than an idle question. Ever since Sam had revealed the truth about Biddle, Gabe had been trying to piece the puzzle together. Biddle had spun an intricate and irresistible story to convince Gabe, one that had been carefully planned. What wasn't clear was why.

The man preened. "It wasn't hard. Neighbors talk when you offer them the right incentive."

Gabe could only hope that the incentive had been money rather than fear, although Biddle's laugh made him suspect the worst.

An owl hooted; a rodent scurried along the ground. For them, it was a normal night. They neither knew nor cared that Gabe was standing on the verandah, desperately seeking a way to protect Alexandra.

"None of your story was true, was it?" he asked as casually as he could while his heart was pounding with the realization that Alexandra's life depended on him.

Biddle shook his head. "The part about wanting to find Calvin Tarkington was. I figured Columbus was far enough from Cincinnati that you wouldn't know anything about him, so you'd believe my story of shady deals."

Another question was answered. Gabe had wondered how Biddle had learned of Calvin's involvement in the scheme that had supposedly bankrupted his father, since Calvin and his partner had been careful to keep their names from all official paperwork. That part of Biddle's story had been as false as the rest. As far as Biddle knew, Calvin Tarkington was an honest businessman.

"I had to find the gal," Biddle continued. "When she disappeared from New York, I figured she'd go to her father. You saved me having to search for him myself."

Gabe had been wrong about so many things. Calvin hadn't been Biddle's target. It had been Alexandra all along.

"What does she have that you want?"

"Nothing."

That made no sense. "Then why are you here?" Gabe gestured

toward the door to Alexandra's room, hoping Biddle's attention would be diverted. It wasn't.

Biddle let out another cackle. "You asked the wrong question, Seymour. It's not what I want. It's what Franklin Beckman wants."

Beckman. Of course. He'd hired Biddle to find Alexandra, and Gabe—gullible Gabe—had helped him. Now a presumed murderer, a man with more than a touch of insanity, was determined to harm Alexandra. All because Gabe had believed him.

He couldn't undo the past, but he could—and he would—do everything to ensure that Biddle did not succeed.

"Who's Franklin Beckman?" Gabe feigned ignorance.

"A powerful man. A dangerous man." For the first time, Gabe heard a note of fear in Biddle's voice. Beckman must have threatened him.

"Franklin needs money," Biddle continued, "and the Tarkington gal is going to have plenty of it. She was supposed to marry him, but she refused. That was her first mistake." Biddle's lips curled in a sneer. "Franklin doesn't like anyone saying no to him. When she did, he told me that if I couldn't convince her to marry him, I had to make sure she didn't marry anyone else."

Alexandra's opinion of Franklin Beckman had been more accurate than Gabe's assessment of Biddle. She had seen beneath the veneer of lies while he had not.

"Did you think shoving her into the bonfire would accomplish that?" Not only did Gabe want to keep the man talking, he wanted to confirm that Biddle had been behind the attacks on Alexandra.

"It would have worked. It would have frightened her enough that she'd go back to New York and Franklin if you hadn't charmed her. It's all your fault. You weren't supposed to do anything more than find her." Biddle's anger was now directed at Gabe as well as Alexandra.

"I suppose you planted the rock under her saddle." If Gabe stoked the anger, Biddle was more likely to make a mistake.

"You'll never prove that, Seymour, because she won't be the only one to meet her maker tonight."

Biddle laughed again, a sound that sent shivers down Gabe's spine, for it was the laugh of a madman. Gabe had to stop him before Alexandra returned to her room, but how? He said a silent prayer for wisdom and felt his fears begin to subside. God was in control. He would show Gabe the way.

When Biddle started to take a step toward Gabe, he thought this might be the break he sought. One more step and Biddle would be close enough that Gabe might be able to grab his gun.

The man stopped in midstride, clearly recognizing the possible danger. "The question is, who gets the first bullet."

No bullets would be fired tonight if Gabe had anything to say about it. He needed to disarm Biddle, and he needed to do it quickly. From the corner of his eye, Gabe spotted motion in Alexandra's room and knew the time for action had arrived. If she heard voices, she'd come out to investigate, giving Biddle what he sought—a clear shot at her.

"Stay back, Alexandra!"

The genuine fear in Gabe's voice did what his feint toward the door had not. Biddle turned, his attention momentarily distracted, giving Gabe the opportunity he needed. He lunged forward, placing himself between Biddle and the house and knocking the gun from Biddle's hand. Gabe almost smiled when he saw it fly over the railing. There'd be no shooting tonight.

"You—"

Before Biddle could complete the epithet, Gabe tackled him, but the man was stronger than he'd expected. Despite the shove that should have knocked him to the floor, he remained standing.

"You won't win." Biddle punctuated his words with a punch to Gabe's face that left him reeling. "You won't be so pretty when I get done with you." He raised his fist again.

This time Gabe was ready. In the instant it took for Biddle to begin the punch, Gabe lowered his head and butted his assailant in the stomach. Biddle's arms flailed for a split second as his back hit the railing. Then—perhaps in an attempt to steady himself—he grabbed Gabe. A second later, they were both in the air, propelled over the railing by the force of Gabe's attack.

When they landed on the stone walkway beneath, Gabe heard a sickening crack. *Dear Lord, no.* But when he scrambled to his feet, he knew his prayer had not been answered. Biddle lay there motionless, his neck at an unnatural angle.

Alexandra took a sip of the overly sweet tea Mrs. Downey had insisted she drink, claiming it was the best remedy for shock. Though her trembling had subsided, she knew the image of the two men lying on the ground was indelibly etched on her memory. Now she sat in the parlor with all three Downeys, Sheriff Engel, her father, and the man who'd saved her from harm, perhaps even death.

"You say you met this man before." Fletcher Engel was making notes on a piece of paper.

Gabe nodded. "He came to my office and asked me to help him find Calvin. It turns out he really wanted to locate Alexandra."

"Franklin sent him." Alexandra knew that without Gabe's confirmation.

He nodded. "I'm afraid so."

"And he admitted to putting the rock under the horse's saddle." The sheriff made more notes.

"Yes. He also pushed Alexandra toward the bonfire."

Laura and her parents gasped in unison.

"Those weren't accidents?" Laura's voice was filled with horror. "Why didn't you tell us?"

Alexandra knew her friend was trying to understand the reason for her pretense. "After the bonfire, I didn't expect anything more to happen, and I didn't want to worry my father. When Galahad threw me and we realized it wasn't an accident, the sheriff agreed with Gabe that it was best not to tell anyone the truth. We hoped whoever was responsible would become overconfident."

"And he did." Gabe's gaze moved from Laura to her parents. "It wasn't that we didn't trust you. We were simply being cautious."

Mr. Downey nodded. "I understand. It's hard to keep secrets, particularly in Mesquite Springs, but I hope you know we'll do everything we can to protect Alexandra if anything like this happens again."

Tears welled in Alexandra's eyes at the love the Downeys continued to shower on her. "Thank you, but there won't be a next time. The threat is gone."

Though she mourned the man's death, Alexandra could not deny her relief. Surely Franklin would admit defeat now and find another heiress to pursue.

Half an hour later, the sheriff and Papa left, and Mrs. Downey gestured toward her husband and Laura, urging them to stand. When they did, she turned toward Alexandra and Gabe. "I imagine you two want some time alone to talk about what happened. I'm leaving the door open and will be back in ten minutes."

Once everyone had gone, Alexandra rose and moved to Gabe's side, laying her hand on his face. "Your poor cheek. That's quite a bruise." She could only imagine what the rest of him looked like after falling from the verandah. Even though Jason's body had cushioned some of the impact, she suspected Gabe would be as sore as she'd been after being thrown from Galahad.

Gabe covered her hand with his, the warmth providing as much comfort as his nearness did. "It's nothing compared to what could have happened to you. I've never been so frightened in all my life. I couldn't let Biddle hurt you."

"Instead, he hurt you." Alexandra was still marveling at the knowledge that Gabe had stood watch outside the house each night since her fall.

"Bruises heal. Broken necks don't."

She nodded slowly. "I hate to see a life end, even when the man has done so much wrong." She'd been shocked by the story Gabe had recounted of Jason's past and wondered how Franklin had found him. That was something she'd probably never know, for she had no intention of ever seeing Franklin again.

"You have a tender heart," Gabe said. "I'm not feeling that charitable yet."

"You will. You're a good man, Gabe. You risked your own life to save mine." She paused, trying to control the emotions that bubbled so close to the surface. "I don't know how to thank you."

A wry smile curved his lips. "I have an idea."

"What is it?"

"This." He opened his arms, and she moved into them, raising her lips to his. Many moments later, when they were both breathless, he broke the kiss, then smiled. "Shall we try that again?"

Thirty-Six

*A*lexandra took each of the twins by the hand, wondering who would be the first to comment when they turned right instead of left at the bottom of the porch steps. The park, which was their usual destination for their daily walk, was a poor choice today because it was too close to the cemetery and the grave that was being dug.

Alexandra wanted no further reminders of what had occurred last night. Though she'd tried to cling to the memory of Gabe's kisses, she'd wakened multiple times as images of Jason Biddle's lifeless body invaded her dreams. Each time, she'd prayed for the strength to forgive him and Franklin; each time, she had failed to extinguish her anger. Now she prayed that her heart would soften enough for her to attend the funeral.

Papa had claimed Alexandra was making a mistake by even considering going to the funeral, but a voice deep inside her told her this was one thing she must do. Sheriff Engel was sending Jason's parents a letter explaining what had happened and that he would be buried here.

"*Vati* said a man went to heaven last night." Hans tightened his grip on Alexandra's hand, seeking her confirmation.

Though she hoped Mr. Gottlieb was right, only God knew what had been in Jason's heart. "Umm," she said, noncommittally. "I thought we'd do something special today."

"Is that why we're walking the wrong way?" Frieda cast a longing look at the park.

"This isn't the wrong way. It's a different direction, because we have a different destination." Just as they were deviating from their normal routine by walking in the opposite direction, Alexandra's life had pivoted and she was now headed into uncharted territory.

"Is the desti . . ." Hans paused, trying to recall the word she'd used.

"Destination."

He nodded. "Des-tin-a-shun. Is it a good one?"

"I think so." Dorothy had made the offer several weeks earlier, saying it was valid any day other than Monday. Today was Thursday, but to Alexandra it was the day after. The day after a man had sought to kill her and the day after Gabe had kissed her so tenderly that for the moments she'd been in his arms, the horror of what had happened only an hour earlier had faded.

As they turned onto Spring, Hans's eyes widened. "Are we gonna help build Mr. Holloway's house?" The excitement in his voice echoed the eagerness in his expression, and he tugged on Alexandra's hand, trying to get closer to the workers who were busy framing Brandon and Dorothy's new home. There was one fewer man working today, although from what Gabe had said, Jason Biddle had been at best a lackadaisical laborer.

"I don't wanna build." Normally cheerful Frieda was pouting.

"We won't be building anything today. What we're doing is something even more special. Mr. Holloway said he'd show you how he prints his paper."

To Alexandra's relief, both children appeared intrigued, and within minutes they were happily following the town's newspaperman into the pressroom.

"How are you feeling?" While her husband entertained the

twins, Dorothy led Alexandra into the room on the opposite side of the hall and gestured toward the chairs in front of the desk.

"Shaky and numb at the same time."

Dorothy nodded as she took the seat next to Alexandra. "I'm not surprised. That's how I felt when Phil died. Violent death is never easy to accept."

Though Papa had never discussed the details of Phil Blakeslee's death, Alexandra knew it had disturbed him. Perhaps that was why he'd advised her not to attend Jason's funeral.

"I only met Jason Biddle once, and it wasn't a pleasant encounter. He tried to warn me away from Gabe, saying he wasn't the man he appeared to be. That's ironic, isn't it, considering how much he was hiding?"

Dorothy nodded again. "We never really know what's in another person's heart. We only see what they want us to see." She darted a glance at the pressroom, where the twins' excited cries mingled with Brandon's calm explanations. "It took Brandon and me a while to trust each other enough to share our secrets."

"But look at you now—happily married."

"I can't imagine life without him. It feels like he's the other half of me." Dorothy shook her head. "You didn't come here to talk about my marriage. What else is on your mind?"

Alexandra wasn't surprised that Dorothy had guessed she had several reasons for coming here today. Like her husband, Dorothy was a reporter, good at ferreting out people's secrets. "Did Brandon agree not to print the story?"

Last night Alexandra and Gabe had told the others they thought it best to say only that Jason had fallen over the railing. They knew people would speculate about the reason he'd been on the verandah at night, but nothing good would be served by putting the details in writing. Alexandra preferred that the citizens of Mesquite Springs remain ignorant of her would-be suitor's anger and Jason Biddle's unfortunate past.

"Of course." Dorothy was quick to reassure Alexandra. "We

can't stop people from talking, but the excitement will have died down by the time the next issue comes out. Five days is a long time for gossip to thrive." She gave Alexandra a speculative look. "I was hoping we'd have something new to distract everyone."

"We might." It might not be what Dorothy was expecting, but the possibility for good news had helped buoy Alexandra today. "When I left them this morning, Laura and Sam were trying to convince her parents to let them announce their engagement now."

Once again, Dorothy nodded as if she understood the reason for not wanting to delay. "Sudden death changes people's priorities."

"Are you speaking from personal experience?"

Dorothy's face softened as she glanced at the pressroom. "Yes, but that story will have to wait for another day. Unless I'm mistaken, my husband needs help with the twins."

My husband. A longing so deep it startled Alexandra by its intensity pierced her. Would she ever say those words?

Three hours later, Alexandra and Gabe stood at Jason Biddle's gravesite listening to Pastor Coleman recite the words of the funeral service.

"Earth to earth, ashes to ashes, dust to dust." The minister's voice was solemn, yet it rose as he spoke of the hope of eternal life, which he called more than a hope. It was, he declared, a promise from God to all who believed, the gift paid for by Jesus's death on the cross.

"'Let not your heart be troubled,'" he said, quoting from the gospel of John. And, as she listened to the words that had been spoken countless times over the centuries, Alexandra felt peace descend on her.

"Father, forgive them," she prayed silently as tears slid down her cheeks.

Gabe winced as he slid his arms into his coat. His body ached from Biddle's blows and the fall, but that pain paled compared to the ache in his heart. Unless he agreed to run for sheriff, he no longer had a reason to stay in Mesquite Springs. The man who'd hired him was dead and buried; the story that had led him here was bogus. Logic said he ought to leave. His heart said otherwise.

He settled his hat on his head and descended the stairs. His instincts told him Calvin was involved in another shady deal, and though he owed Jason Biddle nothing, he owed it to Pa to prevent others from being cheated. That was a powerful reason for staying. The problem was, it was in direct conflict with his even more powerful desire to be with Alexandra.

Gabe took a deep breath as he closed the door behind him. Last night had solidified his belief that Alexandra was the one woman in the world for him. As he'd battled with Biddle, he'd realized that he would do anything, even sacrifice his own life, to keep her safe. She was the dearest, most precious thing in his life. The kisses they'd shared had deepened his conviction that she was the only woman he would ever love, and when he'd stood beside her at Biddle's gravesite, her courage and compassion had shown him she was one in a million.

Gabe loved her. He wanted them to build a life together, to forge a marriage as filled with love and happiness as his parents', but before that could happen, he needed to tell her the truth. The future could not be built on anything other than a foundation of truth and trust.

All day long Gabe had agonized over when and how to tell her what he knew about her father. The coward in him said she wasn't ready and that he should delay. The other part, which had prevailed, warned him he might have waited too long, that he should have revealed the connection between her father and his.

Her tears over Biddle's coffin had convinced Gabe he should delay no longer. Perhaps the mercy she'd been able to grant Biddle would extend to him. And so, now that dinner at the hotel would soon be over, ending Alexandra's duties as hostess, Gabe was on his way to see her and possibly break her heart.

"Gabe!" Alexandra's sweet smile when she saw him standing outside the dining room made his heart stutter. If only she'd still be smiling when the evening was over. "I didn't expect you."

As guests strolled along the hallway, chatting about dinner and their plans for the evening, Gabe tried to match her smile but failed. "I hoped we could talk privately. There are some things I need to tell you."

Her smile faded. "That sounds ominous. You're not planning to leave Mesquite Springs, are you?"

"That depends. Shall we go to the park?" They'd be less likely to be overheard there, and the peaceful setting might help soothe her, for Gabe was under no illusion that she would easily accept what he had to say.

He waited while Alexandra retrieved her shawl and draped it over her shoulders, then escorted her outside. After his attempts at casual conversation failed, Gabe decided to remain silent until they reached the bench they'd claimed as their own.

"You're worrying me, Gabe," she said as she took her seat. "I've never seen you like this."

Oh, how he hated the tremor in Alexandra's voice. "I didn't mean to worry you, but what I have to say is important."

She clasped her hands together to stop their trembling. "Is it related to Jason?"

"Partially. You know he claimed the reason he wanted to hire me was because he needed to find your father."

"When he really wanted to find me." Alexandra shuddered, perhaps remembering the bonfire and Galahad.

"I almost refused to take him as a client, but the tale he spun convinced me I couldn't refuse." Even now, Gabe could not regret agreeing to help Biddle, because the story, as false as it was, had introduced him to Alexandra. Even if she refused to believe him and wanted nothing more to do with him, he'd still have the memory of their time together.

Alexandra's eyes narrowed. "It had nothing to do with Franklin, did it?"

"No. I would never have agreed if I'd known his real motive was to hurt you. Biddle was clever. What he told me was so close to what happened to my father that I felt I had no choice but to help him." Gabe took a breath, exhaling slowly before he continued. "You know my father lost the money he'd counted on to pay my mother's doctor's bills in an investment that failed and that his will to live died along with my mother."

The bare recital of facts hid the emotional toll that had resulted. Years had passed, but Gabe could not forget the pain of watching his father wither away, of feeling that he'd lost both parents months before his father's body had been consigned to the earth.

Alexandra unclasped her hands and laid one on his, obviously trying to comfort him. Gabe could only hope she would feel the same when she'd heard everything.

"What happened to your father reminded me of my father after Mama died. He didn't die, but he was a different man afterward."

Gabe suspected that had been the turning point, the beginning of Calvin's dishonest activities.

He took a quick breath and willed his voice to remain calm as he finished his story. "What I didn't tell you was that my father lost his money when a bank collapsed."

Gabe paused, not wanting to tell her that her father was a man who preyed on others, who lured them with false promises, not caring that he might be destroying lives. Gabe prayed that his next revelation would not destroy her.

He fixed his gaze on Alexandra and said firmly, "It was the Ellsworth Bank."

Thirty-Seven

Shock rolled through Alexandra. Gabe had to be mistaken. She stared at him, willing him to take back the words that still echoed through her brain.

"The Ellsworth Bank? One of Papa's projects?" She shook her head, trying to clear it. "I don't understand. He told me it was one of his best investments."

"It probably was, *for him*."

Alexandra saw the pain in Gabe's eyes, though she didn't completely understand its cause. Her instinct told her his distress was caused by more than the memory of his father's death, that somehow—though she couldn't imagine how—it was connected to her.

"What do you mean?"

He turned the hand she'd been covering so that their palms were touching, then threaded his fingers through hers. "Please believe me when I say I wish I didn't have to tell you this. The truth is, there never was an Ellsworth Bank. It was all a sham. People invested based on false advertising and extravagant promises, believing they'd reap enormous profits. The only ones who benefited were the ones who set up the scheme."

Shock turned to horror, leaving Alexandra's heart pounding, her breath coming in rough pants. "You think my father did that?" She tugged her hand loose from Gabe's, not wanting any contact with the man who would make such heinous claims. "You think Papa deliberately cheated people?" Though Gabe's implication had been clear, Alexandra needed to hear him say the words.

"I have no proof," he admitted, and for a second, her spirits rose. She'd been right; Papa was innocent. But then Gabe continued. "Whoever arranged the schemes was very careful to cover his tracks. The closest thing to proof I found was a list of company names and records of large bank deposits that your father made just before each of the bogus companies failed."

Alexandra gasped as the final words registered. Companies. Gabe had said companies. She laid her hand over her heart, willing it to resume its normal pace, trying to convince herself that this was some great mistake.

"You mean there was more than the Ellsworth Bank?"

Gabe nodded slowly. "As far as I can tell, there was one almost every year. Sometimes your father's partner appeared to be responsible—those schemes were less profitable—but most of the time, it was your father who placed the advertisements in various papers or met with investors, claiming he'd just learned about a promising venture. That was the only connection besides the bank deposits that I could find."

Alexandra seized the glimmer of hope. "Perhaps he was doing a favor for someone."

"Once, perhaps, but not multiple times. I wish it were otherwise, but everything I've discovered points to your father being responsible."

He might believe it—and Alexandra could tell that he did—but she could not.

"You're wrong, Gabe. Papa is an honest man. He'd never hurt people like that." She wanted to shout, as if raising her voice would change Gabe's opinion, but she kept her voice low as she asked, "Why would he do something so dishonest?"

Gabe's eyes darkened with what Alexandra hoped was compassion, not pity. She neither wanted nor needed pity.

"You said your father changed after your mother died. Maybe the fraudulent schemes were part of the change. I heard he gambled heavily for a while. Bilking investors may have been a way to repay his gambling debts."

Bilking. If it weren't so childish, Alexandra would have covered her ears to block out the despicable word. As it was, she closed her eyes, wishing she were somewhere—anywhere—else. Surely this was a nightmare. Surely she'd waken and discover that she was lying in bed and that this conversation was nothing more than a bad dream.

Resolutely, she opened her eyes and faced Gabe. "Papa wasn't a gambler. He told me more than once that only fools gamble, that it was dangerous."

Alexandra heard the booming voice of one of the hotel's guests followed by feminine laughter. The Schraders were having a pleasant evening in the park. She was not.

"Perhaps he was speaking from personal experience." Gabe extended his hand, silently urging Alexandra to take it, but she could not. As much as she needed reassurance, Gabe was not the one to provide it. Not tonight.

"I won't believe that." She shook her head vehemently, then stopped as fragments of a conversation assailed her. Papa and Aunt Helen had been in the parlor, unaware that she was in the hallway outside and could hear them.

"Did you repay your debts?" her great-aunt had asked.

Papa's reply had been uncharacteristically long. "You don't need to worry, Helen. I won't gamble again. That's for other men." He'd lowered his voice, but not so much that Alexandra couldn't hear him. "My investors will be the gamblers."

As she relegated the memory to the back of her brain, Alexandra told herself there could be—there must be—an innocent explanation. She rose, knowing what she had to do.

"I don't want to believe anything you've said. I know you believe it, Gabe, but I can't. Not until I hear my father's side of the story."

When he nodded his understanding, she placed her hand on Gabe's arm, gratefully accepting the support, for her legs felt shakier than they had last night when she'd seen Jason's broken body. She had to talk to Papa. She had to learn what he had done, and that meant returning to the hotel.

Leaving Gabe to wait for her in the parlor, she made her way to her father's office, hoping he would still be there. He was.

"Alexandra." Papa stood, his surprise obvious. "I didn't expect to see you again tonight. What's wrong? You look upset."

"We need to talk." Alexandra sank into one of the visitors' chairs, hoping her father would take the one next to her, but he did not. Instead, he remained behind the desk.

She swallowed deeply, trying to muster the courage to ask the most troubling question. "Did you know that people who invested in the Ellsworth Bank lost their money?"

Papa stared at her for a moment, his expression inscrutable, before lowering his gaze. "The Ellsworth Bank? Where did you hear about that?"

That wasn't the response she'd expected. Once again, Papa was being evasive. In the past, she'd accepted it. Not tonight. Tonight there would be answers. "You mentioned the bank on one of your trips to New York. You said it was a good investment."

"It was." Papa tipped his head to the side, as if searching for a memory. Or was he searching for a plausible explanation? Alexandra hated the doubt that had crept into her.

Her father's voice was firm. "I heard the bank failed, but that was after I sold my shares."

It sounded credible, but was it true? "Then there really was a bank and you weren't responsible for its failure." She made it a statement rather than a question.

"Of course not." It was clear Papa did not like the direction this conversation had taken. A flush colored his face, and his voice held a note of defiance. "Who's been filling your head with nonsense like that?"

Was it nonsense? Alexandra wasn't certain. Papa's reaction to her questions had not been that of an innocent man. "Gabe's father lost everything when the Ellsworth Bank collapsed."

"And he thinks I was responsible." Papa's anger and the glint she saw in his eyes made Alexandra glad she had refused to let Gabe accompany her. This was a mood she'd never encountered, one that revealed how little she knew about her father.

"Yes." No matter how it infuriated him, she would not lie to her father.

"That's preposterous!" His face contorted with anger, Papa pounded the desk with his fist. Seconds later, he schooled his features and softened his voice into what sounded like a plea. "I'm your father, Alexandra. You must know I'd never do anything like that."

She stared at him, her heart warring with her mind. "I want to believe you, but I'm not sure I know the real you." The doubts Gabe had planted were taking root. "I only saw you for two weeks each year."

They'd been wonderful times, two glorious weeks when they explored New York and celebrated the holidays together, but as wonderful as they'd been, they were only two out of fifty-two. Other than the brief letters that accompanied his quarterly allowance checks to her, she'd had no other contact with her father.

Papa stretched out his hand in a conciliatory gesture. "You've been here for more than two months. You know me now."

Remembering all the times he'd evaded her questions, Alexandra shook her head. "I'm not sure I do."

The pain that crossed his face appeared genuine, but his next words were harsh. "So you'd trust a man you've known for only a few months instead of your own father? What kind of daughter are you?"

A confused one. "I don't know who to trust."

Papa rose and moved from behind his desk. Standing behind her, he laid a hand on her shoulder. "Trust me, Alexandra. I want only what's best for you. Everything I've done is for you."

She twisted, trying to see his face, to see if the emotion she heard in his voice was reflected in his eyes, but the angle was wrong. "I want to believe you, but . . ."

"You believe Gabe because he's young and attractive and fills your head with romantic nonsense." Papa tightened his grip on her shoulder, making her think he was trying to restrain rather than comfort her. "I see you aren't trying to deny it. Tell me, Alexandra, when that young man was spinning his stories, did he tell you I'm paying him to court you?"

For a second, the words bounced through Alexandra's head, making no sense. Gabe. Pay. Court. The allegation was ridiculous. She knew Gabe. She trusted him. What Papa claimed could not possibly be true.

Alexandra wrenched out of her father's grip and turned to face him. "You're lying. Gabe would never do that."

"Ask him."

Thirty-Eight

He might lie to her. He might give her evasive answers the way Papa had. He might simply refuse to answer her questions. Or he might tell the truth. Though Alexandra's brain warned her that any of the four possibilities could happen, her heart clung to the fourth. More than that, she clung to the hope that Papa had been lashing out in anger and that what he'd claimed about Gabe was nothing more than a lie.

Surely the kind words, the attention he'd paid her, and those sweet kisses had not been pretense. Surely the man she'd learned to trust, the man who'd become so dear to her that she'd started to weave fantasies of a life together, had not been lying. But if he wasn't, Papa was.

Alexandra marched down the hallway, her head held high, and entered the parlor, determined to learn the truth. By some small miracle, the room was almost empty. Two of the older guests sat in one corner, apparently undisturbed by Gabe, who seemed to have been pacing.

He approached her and started to say something, but she held up a hand to stop him. Only when she'd perched on the chair at one side of the fireplace and waited for him to take the one opposite her did she speak.

"Tell me the truth. All the truth, not just a part of it. Did my father hire you to court me?"

The pained expression that crossed Gabe's face told Alexandra her words had hit their mark. "Not exactly."

More evasion. She had thought her anger had reached its peak, but she'd been wrong. It had merely been simmering. Now it was boiling over. She gritted her teeth and glared at the man who'd starred in her dreams. "You sound like Papa, giving me half an answer. What does 'not exactly' mean?"

"Your father hasn't paid me anything, and courting you was only one of the things he suggested."

Though Gabe sounded sincere, the way he kept his gaze fixed on her to gauge her reaction made Alexandra suspect he was telling her only half the truth. When the couple at the other side of the room glanced at her, Alexandra realized they'd heard her exasperated sigh. She needed to be more careful.

Lowering her voice but refusing to mute her anger, she said, "It must be all the time you've spent with Sam, because you sound like a lawyer, arguing fine points. What *exactly* did you and my father agree to?"

The furrows between Gabe's eyes told her he was searching for the right words to convince her of his innocence. On another day, she might have given him her unconditional trust. Tonight, she was wary.

"It happened the day you and I arrived here. You know Biddle hired me to find information about your father, so I went to the hotel that night to introduce myself and see what I could learn."

Gabe's words continued to ring with truth, and Alexandra felt herself begin to relax. Perhaps she could trust him. Perhaps Papa had exaggerated. Perhaps Gabe hadn't misled her.

"What did you learn?"

"Your father said he was starting a new company and offered to sell me shares at a reduced price if I kept you busy. He didn't want you spending time at the hotel—said it was no place for you."

"Because I'm a woman." Alexandra made no effort to hide her bitterness. "He thinks girls should do nothing more than serve tea, play the piano, and—in my case—paint. It felt like just short of a miracle when he agreed that I could write invitations to potential investors and handle the hotel's reservations."

Alexandra shook her head, realizing she had let herself become distracted. Was that what Gabe had intended?

She seized on the incentive Papa had offered. "Did you plan to invest in my father's next venture? I can't believe you'd want to have anything to do with it after what happened to your father."

The furrows between Gabe's eyes deepened. "You're right. I wouldn't have accepted the shares even if he'd given them to me."

"Then why did you agree to court me?" The thought that everything they'd shared had been false hurt more than Alexandra had believed possible. When would she learn that men didn't care about her for herself? Franklin had wanted her money, and Gabe had his own ulterior motives.

He nodded slowly, as if he sensed her distress and wanted to ease it. "I agreed because I needed to learn more about your father and what he was planning."

He'd confirmed everything she feared. Alexandra's anger, which she'd tried desperately to tamp down, flared again. "And I was the way to do that." She glared at Gabe, wondering whether the sparks of anger that had become a conflagration were reflected in her eyes. "I thought you were sincere, that you saw me for who I was, that you cared about me—Alexandra Tarkington, the person, not the heiress, not Calvin Tarkington's daughter—but I was wrong." And that hurt. Oh, how it hurt.

When Gabe made no effort to deny her allegations, Alexandra continued. "You're no better than Franklin. You only wanted what I could give you—access to my father and his approval."

Gabe's lips thinned, and he took a deep breath, exhaling slowly as he tried to control his temper. "It wasn't like that."

"Wasn't it? Wasn't it *exactly* like that?"

"No." He fisted his hands, then released them. "It's true that I agreed to your father's scheme because it would help me. I won't apologize for that, because it was part of my job. But I didn't have to spend as much time with you as I did to keep him satisfied." Gabe paused. "I was intrigued by you from the moment I saw you waiting for the stagecoach. You made what could have been a boring ride enjoyable, and with each mile I found myself more impressed. Even if your father hadn't suggested it, I would have sought reasons to spend more time with you."

Gabe's eyes shone with emotion. "If anything, your father's suggestion was the means to the end. You were the end. I wanted to get to know you better, and he gave me an excuse to do that. The more I learned about you, the more I cared for you. You're the woman I fell in love with."

Alexandra's heart wanted to believe everything Gabe had said, but her brain warned her to be cautious.

"Do you expect me to believe that?" It was true that he sounded sincere, but Gabe himself had told her he was good at convincing people to trust him. "Those are pretty words, but how do I know they're not as false as Franklin's?"

That was the problem. Alexandra couldn't trust Gabe to tell her the truth, and—even more importantly—she couldn't trust herself to recognize falsehoods. The events of the past day crashed over her, overwhelming her with their intensity. Jason's death, the funeral, Gabe's allegations about her father, Papa's claim that he'd hired Gabe—it was all too much. Since she didn't know whom she could trust, the only answer was to trust no one.

Alexandra rose, knowing she had to end this conversation. "I'm sorry, Gabe, but I can't trust you, and without trust, we have no future. I think it's best if we don't see each other again."

❧

"She means it," Gabe told Sam as he scrambled eggs for their Sunday breakfast. He'd hoped Alexandra's anger would fade, but it hadn't. She'd acted like he wasn't there when he'd tried to accompany her to the Downeys' home, and the only words she'd spoken to him Friday morning when he'd joined her and the twins on the front porch were, "I'm certain you have more important things to do, Mr. Seymour." Then, as if he had suddenly become invisible, she'd resumed her conversation with the children.

"What did you do to rile her?" Sam arranged silverware and napkins on the table, the only tasks Gabe would allow him to perform.

"I told her the truth. I'm not sure what angered her more, my saying her father was a crook or learning that he'd asked me to spend time with her." Gabe wouldn't tell Sam that Calvin had gone so far as to offer him a financial incentive to pretend to court Alexandra. There were things even Sam, whom he considered a close friend, did not need to know.

"So now you're *persona non grata*."

"You can skip the Latin, Sam. Plain and simple, Alexandra hates me."

His friend grabbed two mugs from the cupboard. "I doubt that. She's hurting, and she needs someone to blame."

There was some logic in that. Though he'd suffered physically in his fight with Biddle, Alexandra's spirit must have been pummeled, first by the extent of Franklin's fury, then by Gabe's revelation of her father's crimes. When Calvin had tried to turn the tables and paint Gabe as the villain, it was little wonder Alexandra had been both confused and angry.

"I made a good target," Gabe admitted. Didn't ancient kings kill messengers when they didn't like the news they brought? "I can't blame Alexandra for being angry, but I'd hoped she would understand."

While Sam poured the coffee, Gabe pulled the bread he'd been toasting from the oven, laid two slices on each of the plates, then spooned the eggs onto the other side of the plates.

After Sam blessed the food, he fixed his gaze on Gabe. "You're asking a lot from Alexandra. It's not easy when parents fall off the pedestals we've made for them. In her case, the pedestal may be teetering, but since you don't have proof of her father's schemes, she still wants to believe in Calvin's innocence. And, while she may have feelings for you, she's only known you a few months. If she's forced to choose between you and her father, he has the advantage of time."

Again, Sam made sense. "I don't have proof yet, but I'm convinced there's evidence at the river property."

He'd ridden out there yesterday afternoon, trying to fill the hours that would normally have been spent with Alexandra, Sam, and Laura. Afterward, Sam had reported that Alexandra had remained inside the Downey home, supposedly painting. "Laura said she's been crying a lot," Sam had added.

Gabe wasn't one for tears, but he'd found himself close to weeping when he'd looked at the painting Alexandra had given him. Was that all he'd have to remind him of the woman who'd captured his heart?

He wrenched himself back to the present. "There are more guards now than before, and there's a fence by the river with guards next to it." The fence had surprised Gabe and deepened his belief that whatever Calvin was planning was tied to his land. "I have to discover what he's doing."

Sam nodded as he spread jam on a slice of toast. "Want some help?"

"Sure." Gabe had hoped Sam would volunteer, because he valued his friend's insights. "Tuesday's the new moon. I thought I'd ride out there once I was sure everyone would be asleep. I can't imagine there are many guards at night, and they wouldn't expect anyone to be coming in from the river side."

"You're probably right," Sam agreed.

Ten minutes later when they'd devoured every bite of their breakfast, Sam rose. "What do you suppose Pastor Coleman will choose for his sermon today?"

"Anger."

As the minister leaned his arms on the pulpit and let his gaze roam, Alexandra wondered if he was trying to determine which of his parishioners suffered from that sin. She wouldn't cringe; she wouldn't give any sign that her heart was filled with what Aunt Helen had called a deadly sin.

"Anger is a normal human reaction," Pastor Coleman continued. "Some would say that it's wrong, but some, including the apostle Paul, would disagree. Here's what he wrote to the Ephesians. For those of you who want to follow along, we're reading chapter 4, verse 26. 'Be ye angry, and sin not: let not the sun go down upon your wrath.'"

He laid the Bible on the pulpit and looked out at his congregation again. "We've all heard the second part of that verse, but what about the first phrase? Paul doesn't condemn anger. Instead, he seems to say that the sin is hanging on to it. I believe that's why he also wrote verse 31, to encourage us not to let anger consume us."

There was a slight pause as the minister raised his Bible. Although Alexandra suspected he had the verses memorized, he made a show of reading them. "Paul urges us as follows, 'Let all bitterness, and wrath, and anger, and clamour, and evil speaking, be put away from you, with all malice.' He knew that anger, like bitterness and evil speaking, can destroy us from the inside. Our Lord doesn't want that, and Paul, who had more than his share of anger when he persecuted the Christians, knew that. That's why we have verse 32. 'And be ye kind to one another, tenderhearted, forgiving one another, even as God for Christ's sake hath forgiven you.'"

Pastor Coleman was silent for a moment, letting the words resonate through the sanctuary before he spoke again. "As we begin this week, let us follow Paul's advice. Let us put anger aside and forgive each other. It may not be easy—forgiveness often is not—but with God's help, we can do it."

Alexandra closed her eyes, willing the tears that filled them not to fall. Had Pastor Coleman seen into her heart? Did he know of the anger she harbored against her father and Gabe? Was that why he'd chosen this passage for his sermon?

Paul was right. Alexandra knew that. She needed to forgive, and yet when she thought of what Papa and Gabe had said and done, the anger that had been simmering began to boil again. She wasn't ready to forgive. Even worse, she wasn't certain she ever would be.

Thirty-Nine

You have a visitor, Alexandra." Mrs. Downey stood at the door to Alexandra's room, where she'd retired after the midday meal. Though Sam and Laura had invited her to join them as they strolled around town, she'd refused, knowing they would prefer the time alone and not wanting any reminders of the walks she'd taken with Gabe. Sometimes they'd laughed; sometimes they'd disagreed, but there had never been discord between them. Until now.

Laura's mother's eyes were filled with concern as she said, "I've shown him into the parlor."

It wouldn't be Gabe. Of course, it wouldn't. Alexandra had told him he wasn't welcome, reinforcing that with her silence every time she saw him. Today, though he and Sam had sat in the pew opposite her and the Downeys, for the first time since that horrible evening when her dreams had been shattered, Gabe had made no effort to greet her. It seemed he'd accepted her decision to end their relationship. She ought to be relieved, but as she descended the stairs, Alexandra could not ignore the seed of hope that had taken root inside her.

She entered the parlor, her spirits plummeting at the sight of

Martin standing next to the fireplace, a bouquet of flowers in his hand. He was undeniably handsome, a man whose arrival in Mesquite Springs had made many women's hearts flutter. Hers had not been one of them. Despite his undeniable good looks, Martin had never aroused even a spark of interest in her, much less a spark of attraction. Yet here he was, looking like a man who'd come courting.

Courting. How she hated the word!

Alexandra fixed a smile on her face and nodded at Martin.

"Good afternoon, Alexandra. You're looking more beautiful than ever."

It was a lie. She had circles under her eyes from the sleepless nights she'd endured, and she knew her face was too pale.

"There's no need for false flattery." Just as there was no need to invite him to sit. She would do nothing to prolong this visit.

Martin shook his head. "It wasn't flattery. To me, you're the most beautiful woman on Earth." He extended his arm, offering her the flowers. "I hope you'll accept these."

Though they were beautiful, she wanted nothing from Martin. And yet, as she remembered Pastor Coleman's sermon, Alexandra knew it would be unkind to refuse them. Perhaps kindness was the first step toward forgiveness. If she could show kindness to Martin, perhaps her heart would open enough that she could forgive Papa and Gabe.

"Thank you. The flowers are lovely."

"No more so than you."

After she laid the fragrant blossoms on a table, Martin dropped to one knee and reached for her hand. Alexandra tried not to frown. First the flowers, now the classic pose. There was little doubt of Martin's intentions. Though Alexandra kept both hands at her sides, hoping to discourage him, he did not seem discouraged.

"I can't wait any longer to tell you how I feel. My love for you knows no bounds."

His voice resonated through the room, reminding Alexandra of one of the plays she and Aunt Helen had seen. The man who'd played the star-crossed hero had spoken with the same fervor.

"When we're apart, I'm an empty shell. Only when I'm in your presence do I find any happiness." Martin looked up at Alexandra, his eyes imploring her to believe him. "I need you to make my life complete. Will you do me the honor of becoming my wife?"

It was not the first proposal she had received, but it was the most eloquent. The words Martin had uttered were as beautiful as the flowers. Perhaps they, combined with his handsome face, would convince another woman to say yes, but they made Alexandra want to recoil, for they sounded false. The ease with which he spoke told her Martin had rehearsed his speech, and the extravagance of the sentiments made her suspect he'd found them in a book. At least when Gabe had pleaded for her understanding, he'd been sincere.

Alexandra took a step back, seeking to distance herself from Martin and his unwanted suit. Aunt Helen had schooled her in the proper way to refuse a proposal. "You don't want to hurt him," she'd insisted, "so you must say, 'I am honored by your offer of marriage, and it is with deep regret that I must decline it.'"

Just as Martin had memorized his proposal, Alexandra had memorized her response. She knew what was expected, and yet she could not utter the words, knowing them to be false. She was not honored, nor did she have any regrets about refusing.

She straightened her shoulders and looked down at Martin, hoping plain speaking would make him understand. "No, Martin, I will not marry you. I told you that before, and nothing has changed since then."

He rose and faced her, confusion and something else—perhaps anger—clouding his eyes. "But something has changed. You're no longer keeping company with Seymour. That means I have a chance."

Alexandra wasn't surprised that the Mesquite Springs grapevine had noticed that she and Gabe had not accompanied Laura and Sam on their nightly walks, but she hadn't expected Martin to take that as encouragement.

"Nothing between you and me has changed. I don't want to be cruel, but it would be worse to give you hope when there is none." Alexandra waited until Martin met her gaze again before she said, "I don't love you, and I will never marry you."

"But you must." His expression changed, and though Alexandra knew she had to be mistaken, she thought she saw fear in his eyes. "You're meant to be my wife."

As memories of Franklin saying similar things flashed through her, Alexandra tried not to react. Martin was an annoyance, not a threat.

Refusing to respond to his assertion, Alexandra turned toward the door. "It's time for you to leave."

Martin stared at her for a long moment before beginning to move. "I won't give up, Alexandra. I can't."

"I'm glad the rain stopped."

Gabe seconded Sam's sentiments. Rain had fallen all afternoon but had stopped at dusk. "Now if only the ground isn't too slippery."

His plan was to ride along the river, leave the horses at the fence, and try to get inside. Muddy terrain would slow their progress, but he didn't want to wait another day. The moonless night would help hide them, and the rain may have convinced any guards Calvin had posted to seek shelter in drier areas.

Once they left the town limits, he and Sam rode in silence. Gabe had no idea what was occupying his friend's thoughts, but his were filled with the conflicting wishes that he'd find proof of Calvin's dishonesty and that he would not. Despite everything he'd learned about him, Gabe felt a grudging admiration for Calvin. The man had done a good job turning Mrs. Lockhart's home into a showcase of a hotel. In doing so, he'd provided gainful employment for men who'd been struggling. And, despite what she considered his neglect of her and his refusal to recognize her strength, he appeared to love his daughter. A man like that couldn't be all bad.

The ground was as muddy as Gabe had feared, but the horses had no trouble traversing it, and before he'd settled the battle that raged inside him, they'd reached their destination.

"Here we are."

Sam whistled softly. "When you said he'd fenced this area, I expected something like the fence along the road." That was constructed of posts and rails. "This is almost a stockade."

Gabe gestured toward the six-foot planks that formed a solid barrier on all four sides of an expanse perhaps a hundred feet square. "Calvin doesn't want anyone to see what's going on." Gabe wondered if the guards had been inside the enclosure.

This was where he'd seen Calvin digging earlier in the month. At the time, he'd known Calvin was not constructing a home and suspected the excavation was somehow tied to the investors' meeting next week. The obvious desire for secrecy confirmed Gabe's belief that whatever was inside was important and possibly illegal.

He dismounted, looping the reins over a tree branch, then beckoned to Sam. When they heard nothing beyond ordinary nocturnal sounds, Gabe nodded. "Let's find a way inside. There's got to be one."

He walked along the riverside fence, testing the strength of each section, while Sam inspected the eastern perimeter. A minute later, Gabe grinned when one section wobbled. "I found what we need," he called out to Sam. "Either the fence isn't finished or it's designed to be temporary."

Sam joined him by the river, pushed on the next part of the fence, and found a similar weakness. "The whole thing is unsightly. If Calvin's planning to impress investors with something out here, he needs to get rid of the eyesore before they arrive." He moved to Gabe's side. "Let me help you. Together we can probably shift this section."

They did, their job made easier by the day's rain. While the fence posts were driven into the ground at least a foot, the planks appeared to be held upright by nothing more than dirt piled next to them, confirming Sam's supposition that they would be removed before the investors were escorted to the site. And, thanks to the rain that had softened the dirt, while the section of fence they dismantled was unwieldy, removing it was not difficult.

As Gabe had surmised from the absence of unusual sounds, there were no guards either inside or outside the enclosure.

"I think it's safe to light the lantern." He retrieved it from his saddlebag, lit it, then looked around, nodding when he recognized a tree with a distinctive bend to its branches at the far corner. "This is the area where I saw Calvin digging."

He led the way, stopping abruptly when he remembered the fleeting thought he'd had about mining. What had been nothing more than a hole had turned into a tunnel, its entrance outlined by posts.

"What do you make of this?" he asked Sam. "It looks like a mine entrance to me." Though he'd never been inside a mine, Gabe had seen sketches of them in newspapers, often as part of advertisements.

"Probably is." As Sam approached, he picked up a rock that had caught his attention. "Look," he said, pointing to the edge that gleamed in the lantern light. "Gold."

Gabe whistled softly. A gold mine. No wonder Calvin was keeping this a secret. There was something almost primeval in the appeal of precious metals, something that made normally rational men leave their families, give up everything they'd once prized, and travel thousands of miles, lured by the hope of finding gold. If word got out, this piece of property would be stampeded by treasure seekers. But Calvin had kept the secret, telling no one, not even his daughter. There'd been no hint of his discovery.

"Gold?"

Sam shrugged. "That or something that looks enough like it to fool the unwary."

Gabe's heart sank at the realization that Sam was probably correct. "You don't think Calvin discovered gold, do you?"

"It's unlikely, and I'm not saying that because of what you've told me of Calvin's past. There've been rumors of rich veins of gold for decades. Some claim the Spanish found gold in this part of Texas years ago, but as far as I know, if there was any gold, it was insignificant. It's as much of a fable as the cities of gold."

Sam's explanation confirmed Gabe's doubts. This had the hallmarks of a Calvin Tarkington scheme to defraud investors.

"But people from the East wouldn't know that it's a fable."

"Especially if they saw more evidence like this." Sam held the shiny rock closer to the lantern. "If it is genuine gold, I doubt it came from here."

"Even if it is genuine, I wonder whether that would be enough to convince people." Gabe tried to recall everything he knew about mining. "It might lure them, but they'd want to see an assay that claims there's a rich lode here. Where would someone go to get a rock like that assayed?"

Sam shook his head. "I don't know, but I can find out. It might take a day or two."

"It probably doesn't matter. If I'm right, Calvin has a false assay. He'll bring the investors out here, let them find a shiny rock or two, then take them back to the hotel. That's where he'll show them the assay as he convinces them to buy shares in his mining company."

It was a more complicated scheme than any of the previous ones, but Gabe had few doubts that that was what Calvin planned to do. Chances were good that he'd concocted the elaborate charade, including bringing the potential investors to Texas to see the mine itself, because the price of shares in the goldless mine venture would be far higher than any previous scheme. Calvin hoped to bilk investors on a grand scale this time.

Sam slipped the rock into his pocket. "Your theory's possible, even plausible, but where's the proof?"

"I don't know, but I'm going to find it."

Forty

lexandra tightened the shawl around her shoulders. Perhaps it was foolish to be here, but she hoped the fresh air would clear her head. In the past, she'd enjoyed being on the verandah outside her bedroom. Sometimes Laura would join her, and they'd sit in the growing darkness, confiding the secrets of their hearts. Other nights, Alexandra would pace the length of the verandah as she debated the subject for her next painting. Still others, she'd stood at the railing, staring into the distance and trying to picture her future. The verandah had been a peaceful refuge, but now it held too many painful memories. That was why she'd come to the front porch.

Everyone else had retired for the evening, giving her the solitude she craved. She felt like a tightly coiled spring, ready to snap. Papa hadn't seemed to notice—he was preoccupied by whatever it was he was doing at the ranch—but both Evelyn and Dorothy had commented on her uncharacteristic tension when they'd met this afternoon. Even Evelyn's assertion that if the baby was a girl, she planned to name her AlexandraDorothyLaura with no nicknames allowed hadn't made Alexandra laugh. How could she laugh when her insides were tied in knots?

It had been two days, and the words from Pastor Coleman's sermon still echoed through Alexandra's brain. Anger. It all came down to that. Though she'd tried, she had not been able to curb hers. She knew the minister was right; she needed to put her anger aside, but oh, that was difficult. It was time to make one more attempt. She settled back in the chair and closed her eyes.

Lord, I can't do it alone, she prayed silently. *I need you to wash anger from me the way you've washed away my other sins. I need to accept that no one is perfect.*

"*Including you.*"

Alexandra's eyes flew open and she looked around. There was no one else on the porch, and yet she'd heard the words as clearly as if someone were standing next to her. Aunt Helen claimed that God spoke to her, but Alexandra had never heard his voice. She'd felt the warmth of his love surround her; she'd sensed his peace descend on her like a mantle, but she had never had an audible response to her prayers. Until now.

Including you. Was that the answer? Was her anger caused because deep inside she knew she wasn't perfect even though she'd tried so desperately to achieve perfection?

Alexandra wrapped her arms around herself, trying to chase away the chills that made her shiver as memories coursed through her. Though it had been warm, she'd shivered the day, only a month after Mama's funeral, when she and Papa had arrived in New York and he'd told her she was to stay there.

"I'll be better, Papa. I will," she'd cried as servants unpacked her belongings in the room Aunt Helen had declared would be hers. "I promise."

Alexandra had pleaded with her father to let her return to Cincinnati, but he'd refused, saying her home was now with Aunt Helen. The next day he'd left, promising to return for Christmas.

Each Christmas Alexandra had followed her aunt's advice and had been on her best behavior, believing that if she was a good daughter, Papa would love her enough to take her back with him.

It had never worked. Each time when the two weeks were over, he left. Each time she wept, then clenched her fists and resolved to be better.

Had that been anger, not sorrow and disappointment?

Lord, forgive me for believing I could be perfect. Only you are perfect. Forgive me for expecting perfection from others. We're all sinners, me most of all.

She sat silently, her head bowed, hoping to hear the voice again, but there was only silence. Still, as her tears fell, the weight on Alexandra's shoulders lightened.

She didn't know how long she sat there, but when the silence was broken by the sounds of horses' hooves and men's voices, she looked up. Yesterday she would have retreated to the house rather than greet the men, but today, she descended the steps and walked toward the street. This was no coincidence, she knew. God had given her an opportunity to make amends.

"Gabe and Sam, what are you doing out so late?"

"I could ask you the same," Gabe replied.

The two men exchanged undecipherable looks before Sam gestured toward Gabe's horse. "I'll take him to the livery."

As soon as Sam was out of earshot, Gabe turned to Alexandra. "Why are you outside?"

She heard the hesitation in his voice and knew it was the result of how curt she'd been the last time she'd spoken to him. "I was praying." Though she hadn't meant to say that, when the words slipped out, Alexandra found she didn't regret them.

She took a step toward Gabe, wanting to lay her hand on his arm but not daring to be so forward. "I hope you can forgive me for my anger. You didn't deserve it. You only told me what you believed was true."

He nodded slowly. "I hope you can forgive me for being so blunt. I should have found a gentler way to tell you what I suspected."

"You did nothing wrong." After all the years of believing it was her failures that kept her father from her, she would not allow anyone else to suffer from the same fears. "I reacted poorly, and I'm sorry for that."

The silence began to grow uncomfortable, as if they were both hesitant to speak and possibly destroy their newly forged truce. Alexandra knew it was up to her to take the first step.

"Were you at Papa's ranch tonight?" That was the only reason she could imagine for Gabe and Sam to have been traveling from that direction.

"Yes."

"Did you find anything?"

"Yes." Another single word, but this time it seemed that Gabe was reluctant to say it. "Are you sure you want to hear what we found?"

An hour ago, Alexandra might have had a different answer, but now she knew what was important. "There's a verse in the Bible about the truth setting us free. I need to know the truth."

Gabe gestured toward the porch and waited until they'd both taken seats before he spoke again. "It looks like your father has the beginning of a gold mine out there. Sam and I saw what appears to be the entrance to a mine shaft, and he found a shiny rock."

Alexandra released the breath she hadn't realized she was holding. "That's good news, isn't it? The mine must be why he invited potential investors to come here."

"It would be good news if it were true."

Gabe's tone left no doubt that he didn't believe that, and for a second, Alexandra wished she had not asked what Gabe had found. She squashed the cowardly feeling, reminding herself that truth was the only thing that mattered.

"Why don't you think it's true?"

Gabe stretched his legs, trying to relax. "When did you send out the invitations?"

Alexandra thought for a second. "Almost two months ago. Late May."

Her reply turned Gabe's expression grim. "There was no digging until two weeks ago. I've been riding out there every couple of days, hoping I was wrong and that the land wasn't part of your father's next business venture, but other than the fence and the guards, I saw nothing unusual. If your father had discovered gold before he sent the invitations, there should have been signs of excavation long ago."

Gabe's explanation was both logical and deeply disturbing. "You don't believe there's any gold, do you?" Oh, how she hated the idea that Gabe was correct and that Papa was involved in shady deals.

Gabe shook his head, confirming her fears. "Sam said it's unlikely there's any in this part of Texas. Apparently, there've been rumors of rich gold deposits for many years, but Sam says they're nothing more than rumors. Add that to the fact that your father invited people before the mine shaft was dug, and I'm suspicious."

He shifted in his seat, as if the discussion had made him uncomfortable. It was certainly making Alexandra uncomfortable.

"I have to be honest," Gabe continued. "I have no real proof yet."

But he expected to find it. Alexandra knew that, just as deep in her heart she knew he was right. Papa had done all the horrible things Gabe had claimed, and he was planning to commit at least one more crime. The reason Papa had refused to tell her the nature of the next investment was that he had feared she'd ask questions he didn't want to answer.

Alexandra stretched her hand out, wanting the comfort of Gabe's touch. When he clasped it, she began to speak. "I don't know anything about mining, but I imagine investors would want more than just a shaft and a rock or two. They'd want an assurance that the mine had a substantial amount of gold."

Gabe nodded. "They'd expect an assay. That's an expert's assessment of the amount of gold ore. Your father would need one of those to convince them. Sam wasn't sure how long it would take, but since the investors are scheduled to arrive next week, your father probably already has one. After all the work he's done so far, I can't imagine him waiting until the last minute for something that important."

Once again, Gabe's logic was irrefutable. "Then it must be in Papa's office." And maybe—just maybe—it would prove that he hadn't been lying, that there really was gold in his mine.

"I imagine you'll find something," Gabe agreed, "but I'm afraid it'll be a false assay. I've tried to work out the timing, and everything points to this being another phony investment."

"Like the Ellsworth Bank."

Gabe stroked Alexandra's hand. "Possibly. Probably. Your father bought the land well before he moved here. According to Sam, there were never any rumors of gold near Mesquite Springs, so why did he choose that land?"

"Phil arranged everything. Papa told me he sent Phil to Texas to find the perfect spot, and he chose Mesquite Springs."

"Phil Blakeslee?"

Alexandra wondered at the tone of Gabe's question. "I never met him, but it seemed my father trusted him."

There it was again, the word *trust*. Alexandra closed her eyes, wishing she could block the suspicions that whirled through her as easily as she could block the starlight, wishing she could once again trust her father. "Even though I know it's likely, I don't want to believe Papa plans to defraud those people. As far-fetched as it may be, I want to believe there's some innocent explanation for everything."

Gabe squeezed her hand. "Of course, you do. He's your father. You want to believe he's honorable."

And loving and trustworthy and so many other positive attributes. "I want that," she admitted, "but I need to learn the truth. I'll look for the assay. I can ask Miss Geist to care for the twins tomorrow. Then when Papa leaves for the ranch, I'll search his office."

"I did that once and didn't find anything."

Alexandra supposed she should have been shocked by Gabe's admission, but she wasn't. As an investigator, he would have done whatever he thought was necessary to find the truth.

"Your father probably has stock certificates as well as the assay report. The problem is, I don't know where he's keeping them."

Alexandra remembered the large envelope she'd seen Papa fingering several times and the way he'd slid papers into it when she entered his office, almost as if he were afraid she'd read them. Though she hadn't seen the envelope recently, if it was as important as it had seemed, she doubted Papa had destroyed it.

"Papa must have a hiding place. I'll find it."

"I can help."

She shook her head. "Thank you, Gabe, but this is something I need to do alone."

Martin spread jam on a piece of toast, pretending to care about the conversation that was going on around him when all the while his thoughts were whirling. He couldn't wait any longer. He'd hoped the girl would agree to marry him, but she'd been more stubborn than he'd expected. Now he had no choice. He didn't like the idea of force, but if he wanted the money—and he did—he'd do whatever was necessary to get her signature on the marriage license, then on the documents transferring her inheritance to him, her lawfully wedded husband.

Alexandra might not want to marry him, but by the end of the day, she would agree. She'd be a fallen woman with no alternatives. Even her father wouldn't protest when he learned what had taken place. All Martin had to do was find the perfect time and place.

It might not be the perfect time, but it was as good as she would find. Breakfast was over; the guests had gone out for the day; Papa had left for the ranch; the kitchen staff had finished cleaning up and wouldn't be back until afternoon. With the hotel virtually empty, no one would notice Alexandra going into Papa's office, and if someone did, they'd assign no importance to it. After all, she was the owner's daughter.

Still, she hated the need for stealth. If only Papa had told her the truth, this wouldn't be necessary. But he'd refused to confide in her, and so she had no choice.

As casually as she could, Alexandra entered the office and closed the door behind her. Once inside, she abandoned all pretense of nonchalance, strode to the desk, and began opening drawers. When she realized they were unlocked, she knew it was unlikely Papa kept any important papers there, but she still had to search. Ten minutes later, she shook her head in frustration. She'd found no assays, no stock certificates, no mention of a gold mine.

They had to be somewhere, and if she were a betting woman, she would have bet they were in the envelope he'd handled so carefully. Where would Papa hide it?

It could be in his bedroom, but that was cleaned daily, while this room was not. He might be carrying the papers with him, but if it was the same envelope she recalled, it was bulky and would be difficult to hide under his clothing. For a second, hope surged through her. Perhaps the reason she couldn't find the papers was that they didn't exist. A second later, Alexandra's hopes faded. There would be no reason for the mine shaft if Papa didn't plan to convince investors he'd found precious metals here.

The envelope must be here. She turned the chairs over, thinking something might have been affixed to their bottoms. She picked up the edges of the rug and looked underneath. She pulled books from the bookcase and shook them to see if something had been hidden among the pages. Nothing. But the envelope had to be here. It had to.

Alexandra stood in the middle of the office, looking for a hiding place she might have missed. She'd opened every drawer, looked in every book, even crawled beneath the desk to see if something had been tacked to its underside. Nothing. Though her instincts shrieked that Gabe was right and that those documents must exist, she had failed to find them.

Biting back disappointment, Alexandra reached for the lock of hair that had come loose and tucked it back in her chignon. She wouldn't leave this room with anything awry, not like . . .

Her eyes widened at the sight of the painting she'd made for Papa. Why hadn't she noticed that it was askew? She must have knocked it when she'd gone to the bookcase. If Papa, who liked everything to be precisely aligned, saw it, he'd know someone had been in his office.

As Alexandra touched the bottom corner to straighten it, she realized the painting was unevenly weighted. She hadn't bumped the frame; it had been crooked when she entered the room, but she'd been so focused on finding the envelope that she hadn't noticed.

With trembling hands, she removed the painting from the wall and laid it upside down on the desk. There, wedged in the back of the frame, was the envelope.

She stared at it for a long moment, torn between wanting to see the contents and fearing they'd confirm Gabe's suspicions. Finally, she pried the envelope from the frame and opened it. It took only seconds to see that it contained the documents Gabe had predicted: stock certificates for the King Gold Mine and an assayer's report indicating that the vein of gold on Calvin King's property was a major one.

The assay looked official and even had a seal affixed to one corner, but as she studied it, Alexandra's heart sank. There was no doubt that it was false, for it was dated last December when the land still belonged to the three ranchers. Gabe was right. Her father was a swindler.

"Oh, Papa, what have you done?" Her involuntary cry echoed through the room.

"That's the wrong question."

Startled, Alexandra spun around, her heart pounding with

alarm at the sight of Martin in the doorway. Unlike Sunday, when he'd appeared courtly, today his posture was cocky. Unlike Sunday, when he'd carried a bouquet of flowers, today he held a gun in his right hand. Most alarming was the sneer that marred his handsome face.

"The right question is, what *will* your father do? The answer is, he'll insist you marry me."

Wanting something—anything—between her and Martin, Alexandra moved behind the desk. "He won't." Papa would never, ever force her to marry a man like this.

"That's where you're wrong." Martin kicked the door shut, then strode toward her, his grin so malevolent that it made Alexandra shudder. "When I'm done with you, he'll have no choice."

She had made a mistake in believing there was no reason to fear Martin. She had made an even greater mistake in moving behind the desk. Now she had no way to escape from the man who was stalking her as a cat did a mouse. Alexandra glanced around the room, looking for something—anything—that would help her escape. Shouting would do no good, for there was no one else in the hotel. The sole weapon she had close at hand was the picture she'd painted, but its frame was no defense against a gun.

"Give up, Alexandra," Martin taunted her as he strode toward the desk. "There's nothing you can do other than enjoy it." The leer that twisted his lips left no doubt of his intentions. In one swift move, he breached the distance between them, and she felt the pressure of the gun on her back as Martin pulled her toward him, smashing his lips to hers.

No! She couldn't let him do this! Alexandra struggled with all her might, but with her arms pinned to her sides, she could not break Martin's hold. She kicked, but he held her so close that the kicks had no power behind them. She bit his lip, taking an instant's satisfaction when he howled, but the satisfaction faded when he knocked her to the floor and landed on top of her.

"Help me, dear God. Help me!"

Forty-One

hy was Calvin coming back now? Gabe rose from the bench when he saw the horse and rider turn onto Hill Street. Normally Calvin stayed at the ranch until mid-afternoon, but here he was, riding toward the hotel. What could have brought him into town so early? Gabe thought he and Sam had done a good job replacing the fence section, so unless Calvin noticed the missing rock, there should have been no indication that anyone had seen the mine. And, even if he'd realized there had been an intruder, it was unlikely Calvin would report it to the sheriff. That would require too many explanations.

Why he was here wasn't as important as the fact that it was too soon. Alexandra wouldn't have finished her search yet. Though she hadn't wanted him to accompany her, Gabe knew she planned to go to the hotel after breakfast was completed. He'd arrived at the park only a few minutes ago, wanting to be close enough to join her when she left. So far, he'd seen only a few guests strolling around town, but now Calvin was approaching. Gabe couldn't let him surprise Alexandra.

If she found the incriminating documents, she would need time to prepare herself for the confrontation with her father, and—no matter how she might protest—that was one time Gabe intended to be with her.

He sprinted toward the hotel, reaching it as Calvin dismounted.

"Calvin!" This was the first time he'd spoken to the man in almost a week.

"What are you doing here?" Calvin's hostility was no more than Gabe had expected. "After what you told my daughter, I thought you'd know you weren't welcome on my property."

"She's forgiven me." No matter what it took, Gabe wasn't going to let Calvin enter the hotel alone. He needed to alert Alexandra to their approach.

"Ha! That's a likely story." Calvin's lip twisted in disbelief.

"It's the truth." Gabe mounted the steps at Calvin's side, deferring to the older man only long enough to let him pass through the doorway first.

"Help me!"

The scream that came from the back of the building, a scream that was undeniably Alexandra's, made Gabe's blood run cold. Knowing Alexandra was in danger, he pulled his gun and began racing toward her, Calvin following close behind.

Please, God, let me be in time to help her. The silence that followed Alexandra's scream was even more terrifying than her cry had been.

Gabe flung open the door to Calvin's office, and for an instant, the rage that burned inside him threatened to consume him. This was far worse than the night he'd found Biddle on Alexandra's verandah. Gabe had been able to protect her then; today he was too late. Alexandra was pinned to the floor, struggling with her assailant.

His fury changed to steely determination to prevail. He would not let this man do any further harm. If he could have shot him without endangering Alexandra, Gabe would have done it, but they were moving too much for him to risk it.

"Stay away from Alexandra!" Calvin shouted the words, his own gun drawn but shaking.

"Papa, you came." Though Alexandra's voice was weak, hearing it sent waves of relief flowing through Gabe. They weren't too late. Between him and Calvin, they'd be able to stop the attacker.

The man scrambled to his feet, dragging Alexandra in front of him, his gun pointed at Calvin. For a second, he was silent, letting them register both his identity and the way he was using Alexandra as a shield. Martin Lewis, Louis Martin, whatever his name was, was not a fool. He had no intention of letting either Gabe or Calvin shoot him.

"You've got a choice," Martin said. "If you agree that Alexandra will marry me, I won't kill you."

He must be after her inheritance. That was the only explanation Gabe could find for his behavior. They'd all been wrong, believing that the threat to Alexandra had died along with Jason Biddle.

As Gabe watched, Alexandra took a shallow breath, then managed to give her father a reassuring smile. What strength she had, to be held hostage but still worry about others. And what dignity she displayed. Her dress had been ripped, but she stood as proudly as a queen.

Though he did not lower his weapon, Calvin's posture softened ever so slightly. "Go ahead and shoot. You'll be doing me a favor. I've only a few months left, anyway."

Alexandra's gasp filled the room. "Papa, what are you talking about?" To Gabe's amazement, she darted a look at him, seemingly seeking his reassurance. If only he could tell her that everything would be all right, but he could not. He couldn't reassure her about her father's health, and he couldn't promise that he could disarm the man who kept an arm firmly around her. He could only continue moving ever so slowly, hoping that Martin did not notice.

"I have cancer. Last year the doctor said I had a year and a half at most. That time's up." Calvin spoke calmly, as if he'd long since accepted the diagnosis, and in that moment, so much became clear. Calvin's focus on legacies, his determination to make the current scheme his most successful so that Alexandra would have a large inheritance—it all made sense for a man whose days were numbered.

While Alexandra's face paled, Martin's reddened. "Why didn't you tell Drummond?"

"Phineas Drummond?" The way Calvin's eyes narrowed as he stared at the man who held his daughter's fate in his hands confirmed Gabe's belief that Calvin was unaware of the connection between Martin and his partner. There was still the question of motive, but Gabe had little doubt about that.

"Yeah." Martin tightened his grip on Alexandra, his smirk saying he was taking pleasure from her gasp. "He had everything planned. 'Sonny,' he said, 'I don't like being the junior partner.'"

"You're Sonny?" Calvin made no effort to hide his surprise. "The way Phineas talked, I thought you were a youngster."

Martin glared. "I'm his assistant. His best assistant. He trusted me with the important deals. That's why he sent me to find Alexandra. He had it all figured out. He knew she'd be getting her inheritance soon. I was supposed to marry her. A couple months later, Alexandra would have an unfortunate accident and I'd be rich." Martin's chuckle held little mirth. "He saw how lost you were when your wife died and was betting you'd be worse this time and that it wouldn't be hard for him to convince you to give him your share of the company."

Gabe had been right. Money had been the common factor in everything—Franklin Beckman's rage which had sent Biddle here, Phineas Drummond's greed that had led Martin to this moment, even Calvin's desire to provide Alexandra with a large inheritance. But money was nothing compared to human life.

Though his mind was whirling, Gabe kept his gaze fixed on Martin, hoping he'd loosen his hold on Alexandra enough that Gabe could disarm him, but the man remained vigilant.

Calvin took a step toward Alexandra, then retreated when Martin gave him a threatening look. "I'm afraid Phineas will be disappointed. A man does a lot of thinking when he knows he's going to face his maker. When I realized Phineas was the one who set me on the wrong path, I knew what I had to do."

Calvin's lips twisted, telling Gabe this was not an easy revelation for him to make. "It wasn't all his fault. I should have been stronger and resisted him, but I didn't."

"Quit jabbering, you old fool, and tell me what you meant. Why is my boss going to be disappointed?"

Martin was so fixed on Calvin's story that Gabe suspected he'd almost forgotten he was in the room.

"Because I changed my will." This time Calvin's voice resonated with satisfaction. "When I die, he won't inherit a penny. It all goes to Alexandra. Not Phineas and not her husband. I've done the same thing her grandmother did when she set up the trust and made sure it'll be Alexandra's to do with as she sees fit."

"No!" Martin's cry sounded like that of a wounded animal. "I was supposed to get that money!"

Gabe stared at Alexandra, willing her to look at him. The last remaining color had fled from her face, as if her father's obvious confidence in her judgment had leached it away. *Please, Alexandra, look at me.* Gabe hoped the revelation hadn't shocked her so much that she would faint. He needed her to remain alert.

Alexandra. Gabe sent another silent plea. At last, she turned her gaze toward him, her eyes widening when he gestured toward the floor. He could only hope she understood.

"It looks like you're the fool." Gabe filled his voice with contempt, determined to snag Martin's attention.

It worked. Martin swung around to face Gabe, inadvertently loosening his grip on Alexandra. It was the moment Gabe had been waiting for. As Alexandra dropped to the floor, Gabe pulled the trigger, shooting the gun from Martin's hand. In the instant when Alexandra's assailant stared at his bleeding hand in disbelief, Gabe lunged forward, forcing Martin back against the desk. The awkward position combined with his injured hand rendered him unable to do much more than flail his legs.

From the corner of his eye, Gabe saw Calvin snatch Martin's gun from the floor, then wrap his arms around Alexandra.

"You'll pay for this." Martin spat the words at Gabe. "You can't destroy a man's gun hand and not pay for it."

Though still bleeding and undoubtedly painful, Martin's hand was far from being destroyed. As relief that Alexandra was safe washed over him, Gabe was tempted to smile at the man's melodrama.

"It seems to me you're the one who's going to pay. Juries don't take kindly to men who assault ladies." Gabe darted a glance at Alexandra and was reassured by the return of color to her face. "Martin could probably use a bandage while we wait for the sheriff." Though the man was fuming, he'd stopped struggling, perhaps realizing the futility of trying to escape.

"I'll get a towel from the kitchen."

"And some rope," her father added. "Better tie him up before we send for Sheriff Engel."

By the time Gabe had staunched the bleeding and Calvin had tied Martin's legs together, the sound of bootheels and a cane thumping the floor told Gabe there was no need to summon the sheriff. Alerted by the gunshot and discovering a crowd gathered in front of the hotel, Fletcher had rushed inside.

If he was surprised that a second man had tried to hurt Alexandra within a single week, he gave no sign, merely listened to the story, advised Martin to stop shouting his innocence when three witnesses were ready to testify that he was anything but innocent, then asked Gabe, Alexandra, and her father to come to his office that afternoon to make formal statements. Within minutes, Martin was being led toward the town's jail cell.

The worst was over, but Gabe knew there'd be an aftermath. Once the initial shock faded, the combination of Martin's attack and Calvin's revelation would take its toll on Alexandra.

"How do you feel?" he asked when the sheriff and his prisoner were gone.

Alexandra had draped a shawl over her shoulders, hiding the damage Martin had done to her dress. The only sign of her trauma was the way she'd practically fallen onto one of the chairs once Fletcher had led Martin away.

"I've never been so scared in all my life," she admitted. "My legs are still wobbly, and my heart is pounding, but thanks to you, I'm safe."

The look she gave Gabe was filled with more than gratitude, its warmth causing his pulse to accelerate. But no matter how deep his emotions were, this was not the time to tell her how he felt. They had to reconcile the present before they could address the future.

As if she'd read his thoughts, Alexandra retrieved an envelope from the floor and looked at her father. "We need to talk."

Forty-Two

As Papa stared at the envelope, then darted a glance at the now-straight painting, a flush colored his face, leaving Alexandra torn between not wanting to do anything that might worsen his health and needing the truth. She was still reeling from the knowledge that their time together was so limited, but though part of her wanted to do nothing more than savor every minute they had, the other part knew she could not dismiss what she and Gabe had found.

"I saw the assay and the stock certificates, and Gabe says you have what looks like a gold mine on your land."

Though she'd thought he might deny it, Papa spun around and glared at Gabe. "How did you find it? No one was supposed to be let onto the ranch."

"Even the best guards need to sleep. Sam and I rode out there last night." Gabe paused, letting Papa absorb what he'd said before he continued. "It's all a sham, isn't it?"

After a moment of hesitation, Papa looked at her, the regret in his eyes serving as silent confirmation. "I never wanted you to know about my businesses."

"Is that why you sent me to Aunt Helen?" Once again Alexandra sought reassurance that her banishment—for that was how she regarded it—had not been her fault. "Were you cheating people even while Mama was alive?"

"No. It started later." As if his legs would no longer support him, Papa sank onto the chair next to her. "After she died and you were gone, nothing seemed to matter. I lost interest in the business, so I took on Phineas as a junior partner. We worked well together for a while, but then Phineas and I started gambling."

Gabe had been right about that too.

"You told me gambling was wrong."

Papa sighed. "I learned the lesson the hard way. For a while, it seemed luck was on my side. I kept winning, and because I did, I kept wagering more. Then I lost it all." He dropped his gaze to the floor, his embarrassment evident. "I knew I'd been cheated, but I couldn't prove it. That's when Phineas suggested a way to get my money back."

"By cheating others, like Gabe's father." Though she tried to keep the condemnation from her voice, Alexandra failed. He might be her father, but what he'd done was wrong. "The difference was, when you lost your money, you knew you were gambling. They didn't."

Anger surged through Alexandra, startling her with its intensity. Though it was one of the most difficult things she'd ever done, she pushed it aside, and as she did, sadness took its place. She'd known him all her life, but in that moment, Alexandra felt that she was seeing her father clearly for the first time. Papa wasn't the strong man, the giant of integrity she'd believed him to be. Instead, he was a weak man who took advantage of others' weaknesses.

She looked at Gabe and then back at her father. "Gabe's father died believing he was a failure, but he wasn't. He was an honest man who loved his wife and son. Everything he did was for them."

"I loved your mother and you."

Alexandra stared at her father, searching for signs of sincerity. He'd said the words she'd longed for all her life, telling her for the first time that he loved her, but she couldn't help wondering whether he truly meant it. Was this another instance of Papa misleading someone for his own benefit?

The vulnerability in his expression said he was telling the truth. In his own way, Papa had loved her. It wasn't the kind of love she'd wished for, but it was all he had to give.

"The gold mine was for you. I knew it would be my last venture, so I wanted it to be the most profitable. It was supposed to be a legacy for you. I never thought you'd come here and discover what was happening. All I wanted was to give you more money than you'd ever need."

How could he think she wanted that? He didn't know her at all, but how could he when they'd never talked about anything important?

"A legacy of stolen money and shame is not what I want. If you want to give me something, give me this hotel."

The request clearly startled him. "It was supposed to be Phil's." Sorrow etched Papa's face. "I wanted him to have a way to make an honest living, but now he's dead, and I don't know what to do."

"You could give it to me," Alexandra repeated.

Papa shook his head. "How would you run it? You're a woman. Women don't run hotels."

Before Alexandra could reply, Gabe spoke. "That's where you're wrong. Alexandra is as capable of managing this hotel as any man."

Gabe turned his gaze to her, his eyes radiating honesty, his belief in her chasing away the pain of Papa's doubts.

"Alexandra's stronger than you realize—maybe not in physical strength but in everything that counts. She has good ideas, and she's willing to use those ideas to make the hotel a success."

This time Papa nodded slowly, his expression thoughtful. "It sounds like you know my daughter better than I do."

"Maybe, or maybe I simply see her more clearly."

Had Gabe's eyes been opened the way hers had, or had he always viewed her that way? Alexandra didn't know. All she knew was that his defense of her was more wonderful than anything she'd ever heard. Other women might crave pretty words, but Gabe's assertion that she was strong and capable filled holes deep inside her, making her determined to prove him right.

Sensing that Gabe had said all he planned to, Alexandra turned to her father. "Even if you don't agree about the hotel, you can't go forward with the gold mine. I don't want to see you in jail." If his illness was as severe as he claimed, Papa would die there, and that was a prospect Alexandra could not bear.

Gabe nodded his agreement. "There's no crime in having a false assay. The only crime would be using it to defraud investors."

His brow furrowed, Papa looked at Gabe. "What would I do with the investors? They're probably already on their way here."

"When they arrive, you say the early promise of gold didn't pan out. You can show them the mine shaft and tell them the truth: there's no gold there."

Though Gabe's suggestion was a good one, Papa seemed dubious. "They'll be angry."

"Not as angry as if they lost money." Alexandra thought about the plans she'd made for the meeting. "We can still entertain them and show them what a wonderful town Mesquite Springs is."

Papa nodded but didn't appear convinced. "What about my past crimes?" he asked Gabe, his voice cracking when he pronounced the final word. "What about the people I hurt, like your father?"

Gabe's response came so quickly that Alexandra wondered whether he'd expected the question. "There's nothing you can do to erase the pain you've caused or the lives you changed. I can only speak for myself when I say I've forgiven you. The rest is between you and God."

"What about you, Alexandra? Can you forgive me?"

"I already have. I love you, Papa."

He was silent for a moment before he once again uttered the words that warmed her heart. "And I love you."

"It's over," Gabe said as he walked into Sam's office. "Alexandra found the assay report and the stock certificates and convinced her father not to go forward with the scheme."

Sam turned over the papers he'd been reading, then rose and clapped Gabe on the back. "That's good. I would have done my best to defend him if it had come to that, but I'm glad it didn't."

"Me too." Gabe knew he'd never forget the sight of once-proud Calvin broken under the weight of his sins. "He says he has only a few more months to live. I hope that'll give him and Alexandra enough time to heal." Though they'd spoken words of love, she and her father needed more than that to mend the wounds that had developed over a lifetime.

Sam gave Gabe another pat on the back. "Seems to me you can help with the healing process."

"What do you mean?"

"You know what I mean. Show Calvin that Alexandra has a happy future ahead of her. You know she wants to stay here, and so do you. Give her a reason to stay. That'll bring him peace."

"If she'll agree."

"There's only one way to know."

Alexandra stared at her reflection in the mirror. The bruise where Martin had hit her was turning blue and would last for days, like the bruises Gabe had received in his fight with Jason. They were both wounded, and yet she felt victorious. A hot bath had washed away Martin's touch, leaving her feeling renewed.

As difficult as the conversation with Papa had been, it had helped her recognize the truth and, as the Bible said, that had freed her. And then there'd been Gabe's declaration.

Gabe, wonderful Gabe. The man she loved, the man she hoped would share her life, the man who'd sent a message, asking if she'd take a walk with him. She'd go anywhere with Gabe, but oh, how she hoped they had a future together in Mesquite Springs.

"You're beautiful," Gabe said as she joined him on the porch.

And he was handsome. Those blue eyes that reminded Alexandra of a summer sky sparkled. Those lips that had formed the sweetest of kisses curved in an irresistible smile. Those hands that had given her both comfort and caresses reached out to clasp hers.

Before she laid her hands in his, Alexandra touched her cheek. "I'm a bit bruised, but it'll heal."

"Even with a bruise, you're still the most beautiful woman I've ever seen and the strongest."

Beauty faded, but strength remained. At least she hoped it would. "Thank you again for saying what you did in Papa's office. I'll never forget it." Though her father hadn't agreed to give her the hotel, he'd agreed to think about it.

"I only spoke the truth. I have more to say, but I thought we might go to the park, if that's all right with you."

Keeping one hand in his, Gabe escorted her to their bench. When they were seated, he reached for her other hand, and Alexandra gave it freely, loving the way the warmth from Gabe's hands traveled up her arms, making her feel both safe and cherished.

"Have you made your decision? Are you going to run for sheriff?"

"Yes. It took me a while, but I finally realized you were right when you said I'd know if it was the job for me. What happened this morning showed me that I want to protect people, and I can do that as the town's sheriff, but that's not what I wanted to talk about."

Gabe gave her a wry smile as he said, "Sam told me I should have rehearsed a speech, but I knew I'd forget every word, so I'm apologizing in advance. This won't be poetic, because I'm not a poet. I'm a man who loves you with every fiber of his being."

He lifted her hand to his lips and placed a kiss on it, the touch sending shivers of delight through Alexandra. This was the man she loved, saying the words she'd longed to hear.

"I love your strength, your kindness, your caring, your honesty. I love everything about you, Alexandra, and I want to spend the rest of my life showing you how deep and strong that love is."

Gabe paused to take a breath. "Will you make my dreams come true? Will you marry me?"

Her heart overflowing with happiness, Alexandra nodded. "I used to wonder if anyone would love me for me—just me, not my inheritance. I was afraid that wasn't possible, but you proved me wrong."

Repeating Gabe's gesture, she raised his hand to her lips and kissed it. "I used to dream of meeting a man I'd love enough to want to share my life with him, but I never dreamt I'd meet him waiting for a stagecoach."

Alexandra smiled at Gabe, hoping he'd see the love shining from her eyes. "You've made my dreams come true. You've taught me what true love is. Yes, my darling, I'll marry you."

Epilogue

"I should hate you; you know that, don't you?" Laura fisted her hands on her hips and pretended to glare at Alexandra. "You're getting married today, and I'm . . ." She paused, then grinned as she whisked the sheet off the cheval mirror, allowing Alexandra her first view of herself in her wedding gown. "I'm so happy for you!"

Alexandra's eyes filled with tears as she stared at her reflection. When Aunt Helen had heard about the engagement, she'd asked whether Alexandra wanted to wear her mother's wedding dress, saying it was the one thing she'd insisted Calvin give her. "I always hoped you'd want to wear your mother's gown," she'd written.

Alexandra, who'd had no idea it existed, had been thrilled. Though the style was old-fashioned, nothing could have pleased her more than being able to wear something of her mother's on this special day. Combined with the lace veil Laura's mother had given her, it was the perfect wedding ensemble, something old and something new.

"It's beautiful," Alexandra said softly.

"You're beautiful," Laura countered.

"All brides are." Alexandra smiled at the woman who'd become

323

the sister she'd always wanted. "It'll be December before you know it, and I'll be at your side just the way we planned."

"But you'll be my *matron*, not my maid, of honor." Laura punctuated her sentence with a false pout.

"You know why we couldn't wait." That was the only cloud in the seemingly bright sky of her life. When Alexandra had convinced Papa to consult Doc Dawson, the doctor had confirmed that Papa would probably not see the new year. Both she and Gabe had wanted him at their wedding, so they'd begun preparations the next day, buoyed by Papa's decision to give the hotel to Alexandra.

"Even if you want to help her run it, you'll be too busy once you're sheriff," he'd told Gabe. "This is my gift to Alexandra. Hers will be the only name on the deed."

With their future in Mesquite Springs secure, the next question had been their home. Fortunately, Dorothy and Brandon's house had been close to completion, allowing the workers to begin building the hotel manager's house. They'd put the final touches on it yesterday, just in time for the newlyweds to begin their life together there.

Laura made a minor adjustment to the back of the dress, though Alexandra had seen nothing wrong. "I'm glad your father is able to walk down the aisle with you."

He'd had some days when the pain had prevented him from leaving his bed, but Papa had rallied this past week, insisting nothing would keep him from escorting Alexandra to her groom.

"Don't forget Aunt Helen," Alexandra reminded Laura. It might not be traditional, but Alexandra, who'd wanted to share the moment with the woman who'd raised her, had asked her to walk on her other side.

"How could I forget your aunt? Father claims she reminds him of his own mother. He and Mother are trying to convince her to make Mesquite Springs her home."

Alexandra doubted that would happen, but she shared the

Downeys' wish. Her thoughts were interrupted by a furious pounding on the door.

"You gotta let us in." There was only one person in Mesquite Springs who combined a childish voice and an imperious tone.

Alexandra smiled at the thought of Polly demanding entrance. Though she hadn't expected to see the little girl until she reached the church, Alexandra was like most of the town's residents and could deny her nothing.

When Laura opened the door, Polly rushed in, followed by Evelyn carrying her week-old son.

"I'm sorry we're interrupting, but Polly and I wanted to see you before the ceremony. I wasn't sure whether you had something borrowed, but—"

Before she could finish the sentence, Polly held out a strand of pearls that rivaled any Alexandra had seen in New York. "Do you wanna wear these? Papa Wyatt found them when we went to my old home. My mama wore them on her wedding day."

When Alexandra had first tried on her mother's gown, both Laura and her mother had declared that the one thing it needed was jewelry, but though Alexandra had agreed, she had found nothing she thought did the dress justice and had decided to leave it unadorned. Polly's mother's pearls would be perfect.

Overwhelmed by the child's generosity, Alexandra brushed the tears from her eyes. "I would be honored." She bent down and hugged the little girl. "Thank you, Polly. These are just what I need."

Evelyn shifted the baby in her arms and turned to Laura. "If you hold Will, I'll fasten them for Alexandra."

As Laura cradled the sleeping child, Alexandra smiled. "So you finally chose his name."

Evelyn laughed. "That's one of them. Wyatt says Wilson Herman Bartholomew Clark is too big a name for such a small boy, so I keep reminding him that he'll grow into it. He's named after three men who would have enjoyed watching him grow up: Wyatt's father, mine, and Polly's."

Laura peeked into the swaddling blanket. "What will you do for the next one if you've used up all the boys' names on him?"

"She'll just have to be a girl. Polly's already told me she wants a sister. And, speaking of sisters"—Evelyn smiled—"guess who I saw walking toward the church with the twins?"

"Eugenia Duncan?"

Evelyn's nod confirmed Alexandra's guess. Papa had sold two of his ranches, one to a family with an unmarried sister whose frequent appearance with the Gottliebs had Mesquite Springs's rumor mill predicting another wedding.

"Me and Hans like her," Frieda had told Alexandra. "*Vati* does too. He said God sent her to us."

As he'd sent Gabe to Alexandra.

When Will began to fuss, Evelyn reached for him. "That's our cue to leave."

"Mine too." Laura gave Alexandra's veil one final tweak.

Two minutes later, Alexandra descended the stairs, tears filling her eyes again when she saw her father's reaction to her gown.

"You look so much like your mother," he said, his eyes glistening. "For a second, I thought she was coming down the stairs, and it made me feel young again."

Alexandra felt old, dreading the separation she knew was coming. Then she brushed her melancholy aside, resolving to enjoy every day she was given, and linked her arm in Papa's.

"Are you happy, Alexandra?" Papa asked as they walked slowly down the street.

"So very, very happy."

In less than an hour, she would be married to the man she loved. In less than an hour, she would be the new owner of the hotel. And in less than an hour, the hotel would have a new name. When she'd told Gabe she wanted to have the new sign in place before the guests arrived for the wedding reception, he'd arranged for everything, including paying workers extra to keep the secret.

She didn't know how Papa would react when he saw it, but

Alexandra felt deep satisfaction over changing the King Hotel into Tarkington House. It was more than a change of name; it was a change of purpose. She wanted guests to feel that they were staying in a house, not a commercial establishment. Just as importantly, she wanted the building to honor her father.

Papa squeezed her hand. "Your mother would be proud if she could see you today, almost as proud as I am." His rapid blinking made Alexandra wonder if he was trying to hold back tears. She certainly was.

"I haven't said it often enough, but I love you, Alexandra. Never doubt that."

His reassurance was the final piece she needed to make today perfect. Her heart filled with joy, Alexandra walked down the aisle, hand in hand with her father and Aunt Helen, her eyes fixed on Gabe.

Papa and Aunt Helen were her past; Gabe was her future. He'd changed her life in so many ways, he'd kept her from harm, he'd seen and encouraged her strength, he'd shown her the meaning of love.

The past with all its fear and anger was over. In its place lay the future. There would be challenges; there might be heartaches, but Alexandra knew the love she and Gabe shared was strong enough to surmount the challenges and survive the heartaches. Theirs was a love forged by adversity, strengthened by difficulty, a love that would last a lifetime.

Author's Letter

Dear Reader,

I hope you enjoyed your time in Mesquite Springs as you got to know Evelyn and Wyatt, Dorothy and Brandon, and Alexandra and Gabe. I had so much fun creating this little town and its residents that I'm reluctant to leave it, and yet I know it's time to move on to a new town, one that's caught my fancy just as much as Mesquite Springs did.

Sweetwater Crossing is a bustling town in—where else?—the Texas Hill Country. On the surface, everything seems peaceful, but there's plenty of tension and more than one mystery to be unraveled.

To the casual visitor, the town appears to resemble many others in the Hill Country except for the plantation-style mansion that seems decidedly out of place. Finley House, as it's called, has secrets of its own. Built by a man named Finley before the Civil War, it's been home to the minister, his wife, and their three daughters ever since. We'd call them a blended family, but to the residents of Sweetwater Crossing, *they're simply the Vaughn girls, three sisters who love each other dearly . . . most of the time.*

I don't want to give away too much, but if you'd like a sneak peek at the beginning of Emily's story, turn a couple pages. In the meantime, if you haven't read the first two Mesquite Springs books, now might be the perfect time.

Though she would not have thought it possible when her home burned, Evelyn's happily-ever-after came Out of the Embers, *and both Dorothy and Brandon found their* Dreams Rekindled *when he came to Mesquite Springs, determined to build a life far different from the one he'd left behind.*

I also encourage you to visit my website, www.amanda cabot.com. You'll find information about all of my books there as well as a sign-up form for my monthly newsletter. I've also included links to my Facebook and Twitter accounts as well as my email address.

It's one of my greatest pleasures as an author to receive notes from my readers, so don't be shy.

Blessings,
Amanda

Turn the Page to Read
the First Chapter of Amanda's
Newest Historical Romance Series!

COMING SOON

AUGUST 19, 1882

Everything looked the same. The live oaks in the park still shadowed this block of Main Street, providing a welcome respite from the early afternoon sun. In the schoolyard, two boys vied to see who could swing higher, while another scuffed his feet, impatiently waiting for his turn. Beulah Douglas was hurrying down the street, moving faster than Emily remembered, probably because she'd spent more time than usual with Father's horse and knew her parents would be looking for her. Other than Beulah's uncharacteristic speed, nothing appeared to have changed, but Emily Leland knew otherwise. Everything had changed.

Or perhaps it was only that she was different.

She guided her horse onto Center Street, trying not to frown at the memories the sight of the small church sent rushing through her. All those Sundays sitting sandwiched between her two younger sisters in what everyone called the preacher's pew, not daring to fidget even when Father's sermon lasted for what seemed like hours. The Christmas and Easter services when well-meaning parishioners pinched her cheeks and told her mother she was the prettiest of the Vaughn girls, that her blonde hair made her look like an angel.

She was no angel, but she'd been a happy girl. And when she'd left Sweetwater Crossing, she'd been a bride smiling at her groom and dreaming of the life they'd share. Now . . . Emily adjusted the sleeves of the black dress she'd found in the attic and had hastily altered to fit her, ensuring that neither the sun nor prying eyes would see her skin.

Mama had insisted that the hallmark of a lady was her lily-white complexion. Mama had said . . . Emily bit her lip. She wouldn't cry. After all, tears solved nothing. If there was anything she'd learned in the last year, it was that.

She kept her gaze fixed firmly ahead as she approached the corner of Creek, refusing to look at the cemetery. The wrought iron gates would be open; the cypress trees had probably grown an inch or two, and somewhere within the fenced area was a new grave. Since it was too soon for grass to have covered it, it would be what Mama called a raw grave. The grave wasn't the only thing that was raw. So too was Emily. This was far from the homecoming she'd dreamt of.

"We're here." There was no need to tell the horse, for Blanche's ears had perked and she'd tossed her head in apparent delight as they'd approached town. While Emily dreaded what faced her, Blanche was happy to have returned. For her, the barn behind the house that still looked out of place in this small Hill Country town was home. Blanche was probably anticipating a reunion with Father's horse, never questioning her welcome, while Emily wondered what awaited her within the stone mansion.

She looped the reins over the hitching post on the side of the house, then returned to the front. Fourteen months ago, she would have entered through the closest door, but today she felt the need to climb the front steps as if she were a visitor. For she was. She wouldn't knock on the door, but she also would not use the entrance that had been reserved for family. The harsh tone of her sister's letter had made her cautious.

As she stepped inside, Emily took a deep breath, savoring the familiar scents of floor polish mingling with the lavender of Mama's sachets. The house was blessedly cool compared to the summer sun, the silence normal for a Saturday afternoon when everyone spoke in hushed voices lest they disturb Father while he was writing his sermon.

For a moment, Emily let herself believe that everything would be fine. Then, mustering her courage, she called out, "Father! Joanna!

Louisa! I'm here." By some small miracle, her voice did not tremble, nor did it reveal the grief that threatened to overwhelm her.

There was no sound from the library that had been turned into Father's office, but Emily's youngest sister emerged from the kitchen, an apron tied around her waist, a frown on her normally pretty face.

"I wasn't sure you'd come." Louisa's voice radiated anger, sorrow, and something that might have been fear.

"I left as soon as I received your letter." Emily chose a conciliatory tone as she stared at her sister, wanting nothing more than to gather her into her arms, hoping that a warm embrace would lessen their grief. Louisa's expression stopped her. If she wanted comfort, Louisa would have to take the first step. As it was, she stood there stiffly, her hands clenched into fists.

Emily glanced around the spacious foyer whose twin staircases mirrored those of the house's exterior. Mama had once confessed that she found it all a bit ostentatious, but Father would not consider leaving the home he'd promised his closest friend he'd watch over.

"We owe it to Clive," he'd told Mama. She'd nodded, her resignation apparent. She would nod no more.

The enormity of the situation hit Emily with more force than she'd thought possible, turning her legs to jelly.

"I can't believe it's true," she said, her voice no longer steady. "Father always said he'd be the first to go."

"But he wasn't." Louisa shook her head, loosening a strand of medium brown hair from her chignon. Four inches taller and with more curves than Emily, Emily's half-sister shared only one characteristic with her: deep blue eyes, a legacy from their mother.

"Father's lost without her," Louisa continued as she led Emily into the parlor. In the past, they might have sat in the kitchen, sipping cups of coffee as they talked. Today, however, Louisa appeared to want more formality. She perched on the edge of one of the least comfortable chairs in the room and gestured toward the one facing it, telling Emily this would be a confrontation, not two sisters comforting each other.

"He walks around in a daze, and when he leaves, he doesn't tell me where he's going." Louisa glanced through the open doorway into the hall. "He must have gone out again. It's awful, Emily, awful. He won't even sleep in the room they shared."

She closed her eyes for a second, clearly attempting to control her emotions. "It's been horrible trying to be strong for him." And that was a role Louisa, as the youngest, had never needed to assume.

"Where's Joanna?" Though their sister had sometimes seemed capricious, declaring nothing was as important as playing the piano, she'd also helped Mama keep the house spotless. The layer of dust on the spinet made Emily wonder whether Joanna's grief was so deep that she, like Father, was in a daze.

Louisa's eyes flew open, sorrow replaced by anger. "As if you care!"

Emily cared. Oh, how she cared. She'd written letters to the family every week, asking about each of them, hoping their lives were happier than hers, but there'd been no response.

"Joanna's in Europe with her grandmother." Louisa's voice was harsh. "Her dreams are coming true, just like yours did. You got a handsome husband, Joanna's studying music with a master, and I'm stuck here alone." Louisa glared at Emily, her anger escalating into fury. "You should have been here. Mama asked for you at the end, even though she knew you wouldn't come."

The words ricocheted through the room before piercing Emily's heart. "Why would she think that?"

Louisa's upper lip curled in disgust. "Don't pretend you don't know. That letter George wrote for you was very clear. You may have scalded your hand, but that didn't stop you from telling us you were a Leland now and didn't need any of us Vaughns."

Emily bit down the bile that threatened to erupt at the evidence of George's cruelty. She'd known something was wrong when she'd found Louisa's letter in his pocket—*"I'm not sure you'll care,"* her sister had written, *"but I thought you should know that our*

336

mother died"—but she hadn't realized the extent of her husband's depravity.

No wonder she had received no response to the letters she'd written each week. In all likelihood, George hadn't mailed them. It was probably only chance that he hadn't destroyed Louisa's last letter. Or maybe he'd meant to torment Emily with it, promising she could visit her family once she gave him what he wanted. She'd never know.

"Mama was devastated," Louisa continued, "and Father looked like he'd been bludgeoned. You know he always tried his best not to treat you differently from his real daughters."

Emily winced. She was the offspring of Mama's first marriage, while her middle sister Joanna was Father's daughter from an earlier marriage. Only Louisa had been raised in a home with both of her parents. Even though Joseph Vaughn was the only father Emily remembered, for as long as she could recall, she'd known he wasn't the man who'd sired her. Most days it hadn't mattered, but when one of the girls was angry and wanted to hurt her sisters, parentage was a convenient weapon.

Louisa wasn't through. "Joanna and I weren't as shocked as Mama and Father. We knew you thought you were special because you were the oldest."

Emily hadn't thought she was special. In fact, there were times when she'd wished she hadn't been the oldest, but now wasn't the time to say that. Instead, she seized on the most damning of Louisa's accusations. "I didn't write that letter."

Her sister's eyes flashed with anger and disdain. "Of course you didn't. George wrote it, but you dictated it."

She hadn't. She would never have written anything like that, for it was as far from the truth as east was from west. Surely her family knew that. Even if her sisters had questioned her love, her parents should have recognized the falsehoods. But it appeared that whatever George had written had convinced them that Emily no longer wanted to be part of the family.

Knowing she had only one defense that Louisa would accept, she held out her hands, turning them so her sister could see both sides. "Look. There are no scars. I never scalded my hand."

Though Louisa studied Emily's hands, she still appeared dubious. "You must have said those things. Why else would George have written them?"

Because he wanted me totally dependent on him. Even though it might exonerate her, Emily wouldn't say that. When she'd left the ranch that had been her home for over a year, she had vowed that no one would know the truth of her marriage. Some things were too horrible to put into words. Besides, she didn't want pity or even sympathy. All she wanted was to forget.

Louisa raised her head and met Emily's gaze. "Where is George? I'm surprised he'd let you travel alone."

He wouldn't have. He hadn't even let Emily go into town unless he accompanied her, and by telling everyone she had delicate nerves and was easily disturbed by visitors, he'd ensured that the neighboring ranchers' wives stayed away. Visits, he'd told her, would be her reward when she fulfilled her mission. But she hadn't. Fortunately, George could no longer control her life.

Emily squared her shoulders, knowing there was no need to cower. "George is dead."

"Dead?" The blood drained from Louisa's face as the word registered.

"He was killed in a fight at the saloon." The anger that his hopes for a son had been dashed again had been more intense this time than any other month, leaving bruises that had yet to fade. Emily thought he'd gotten himself under control before leaving the ranch, but it appeared he hadn't, for the sheriff said he'd started the fight.

Louisa shook her head, dumbfounded. "I don't know what to say other than I'm sorry."

I'm not.

"Food."

Craig Ferguson smiled when his son's stomach rumbled, confirming his hunger. Though the boy frequently claimed to be hungry, perhaps because eating helped alleviate the boredom of their journey, this time the need was real.

"You're right, Noah. It's time to eat." Craig nodded when he saw a row of trees ahead. They'd provide welcome shade from the August sun, and if his assumption that they lined the banks of a stream was accurate, he and Noah would also have a source of water. This part of Texas might be cooler than Galveston, but it was still hot, and fresh water was always welcome.

Even if there was no stream, stopping would give Noah a chance to run. That too would be welcome. Craig knew it was hard for a boy his age to sit in a wagon for so long. It was also hard for him. Being a schoolmaster might not involve heavy labor, but it kept him on his feet most of the day. The extended periods of sitting involved in traveling halfway across the state were difficult for both of them, but the result would be worth it: a new home, a new beginning.

"Me eat?" Noah darted an anxious look at the back of the wagon when Craig brought it to a stop.

"We'll both eat"—and so would their horse, thanks to the lush grass—"but let's see who can reach those trees first." Craig lifted Noah and set him on the ground, knowing his son needed to release some energy. Noah had slept better since they'd been on the road, bolstering Craig's belief that the change which many had considered extreme would hasten the healing process, but that extra sleep meant the boy had an even greater need for activity.

"Me! Me run!"

As Noah scampered toward the trees, Craig grabbed the bag that contained their food and followed at a leisurely pace. Noah might fall in his hurry to win the race, but the thick grass meant he wouldn't hurt himself, and he'd feel independent. Rachel would have been proud. She had claimed that the most important things parents could do were to ensure that their children knew they were loved and give them the freedom to make mistakes.

"They'll learn from them," she'd declared.

"Who's the teacher here, you or me?" Craig had asked, feigning annoyance, though he'd known Rachel would see through his pretense. They'd rarely argued, and when they had, it was usually because Craig thought she was being too impulsive. But there'd been nothing impulsive that day, simply a shared desire to raise their soon-to-be-born child the best they could.

"We'll both teach our baby," she'd said. "That's the reason God gave children two parents."

But now Noah had only one, and though he'd tried his best to fill the void, Craig knew that wasn't enough.

"Water, Pa, water!" Noah shrieked in delight.

Craig, who was only one step behind him, moved to his side, ready to catch him if he seemed likely to tumble into it, then smiled when he realized the stream was only a few inches deep. It would provide water to wash down the bread and cheese he'd bought in the last town but wouldn't be a threat to his son's safety.

"Me wade."

Craig's smile broadened at Noah's use of the word he'd learned the day before they'd left Galveston. "I thought you were hungry." He rubbed Noah's stomach, then bent down to listen to it. "Yep. You're hungry. Let's eat first, and then you can wade."

He wouldn't deprive his son of the simple pleasure of splashing in a creek, particularly when there was no need to rush. The journey had taken less time than he'd expected, and unless they encountered a major delay, they'd arrive in Sweetwater Crossing two days earlier than he'd arranged with Mrs. Carmichael. He hoped that wouldn't create a problem, but if she wasn't ready for them, he and Noah could sleep in the wagon as they'd done every night since they'd left home.

"Good." Noah reached for the bag of food, confirming Craig's priorities.

What was good was that his son had not had a single nightmare since they'd left Galveston, nor had he burst into tears at the sight of a brown-haired woman who wasn't Rachel.

"He'll forget," the minister's wife had told Craig a week after Rachel had been laid to rest. "Children that young forget quickly."

But Noah had not. He still cried for his mother. He still refused to be separated from Craig, even though he was too young to spend his days in a schoolroom. He still woke screaming almost every night . . . until they'd left the house that held tragic memories. The difference had been dramatic, proof that God still answered prayers.

Craig hoped that would continue once they reached Sweetwater Crossing. The gently rolling hills with their sandstone and limestone outcroppings, the roads canopied with live oak branches, and the open fields carpeted with wildflowers filled Craig's heart with joy and the sense of peace that had been missing for too long. That and the hope that Noah had begun to heal made him more confident that the decision to come to the Hill Country had been a wise one.

Though part of him had balked at the thought of leaving the home he and Rachel had shared, he'd known he couldn't continue to live mired in memories of the past and had prayed for guidance. His prayers had been answered sooner than he'd expected. Only days after he'd first prayed about his future, the minister had mentioned a letter he'd received saying a town in the Hill Country would need a new schoolteacher because the current one was about to marry.

In less time than Craig had thought possible, everything was arranged. The decision makers had been impressed with his credentials and had offered him the position of schoolmaster, a position that included room and board as well as a small salary. Craig and Noah would board with a widow who claimed to love children and whose house was catty-cornered from the school, and since the widow was old enough to be Noah's grandmother rather than the mother he still searched for, perhaps he'd be content to spend his days with her. Perhaps they'd both find peace in the Hill Country.

———

"I'm surprised Father's not back yet," Louisa said as she glanced at the wall clock.

So was Emily. In the past, unless one of his parishioners had an emergency, their father spent most of Saturday writing and rewriting his sermon. In the past, he would not have left without telling someone where he was going. But this was not the past, and according to Louisa, their father was greatly changed.

"Do you want to help me make supper?" Louisa rose and smoothed her apron. It wasn't only Father who was changed; so was Louisa. The Louisa Emily knew would not have left the kitchen without removing her apron. But, then again, the Louisa Emily knew would have acknowledged their shared sorrow, not treated Emily like a stranger. "You always were the better cook, and you know how Father depends on a hot meal served precisely at six."

"Of course I'll help." Emily accepted the olive branch her sister had extended. Perhaps if they worked together, they could regain at least a semblance of the closeness they'd once shared.

As they passed the library, Emily glanced inside. The desk was cluttered with papers, the two chairs in front of it turned sideways, evidence the guests had left in a hurry. Both were common occurrences. Father's absence was not.

As if she'd read Emily's thought, Louisa paused and stared at the empty desk chair. "He's different. Nothing's been the same since Mama . . ." Louisa's voice broke, and tears filled her eyes.

"How did it happen?" Like her sister, Emily wouldn't pronounce the word *died*, but she needed to know. While Emily and her sisters had had measles, chicken pox, and other ailments, she could not recall Mama ever being ill.

"Doc Sheridan claimed it was a virulent fever. He bled her,

but that didn't do any good. She just kept getting worse." This time Louisa shuddered, her grief visible. "Oh, Emily, it was awful watching her waste away. I tried to help, but no one would listen to me."

Hoping her sister wouldn't reject her attempt to comfort her, Emily wrapped her arms around Louisa. "I'm sorry I wasn't here. There's nothing I could have done to save her—you know far more than I do about healing—but I could have helped in other ways. I could have . . ."

Emily stopped, her thoughts arrested by the unexpected odor wafting through the hallway. She'd closed the front door, but all the windows were open in an attempt to cool the house. She sniffed the air again. "It smells like smoke." And fire was one of the town's greatest threats. Though many of the houses were made of stone, others and almost all the outbuildings were wooden structures.

Their grief shoved aside for a second, the sisters ran to the front porch, searching for the source. It wasn't difficult to find, for billows of dark, acrid smoke rose from Center Street, turning the clear blue sky an ominous gray.

"It's either the church or Mrs. Carmichael's house." Louisa stared at the sky, appearing frozen by shock.

"We've got to help." Emily touched her sister's arm. "They'll need water. You take the kitchen pail." At this time of the day, it was sure to be almost full. "I'll get another from the barn and will join you there. Hurry!"

The urgency in Emily's voice seemed to break through Louisa's shock, and she ran to the kitchen, then rushed toward the fire while Emily raced to the barn.

Still debating whether she could carry two pails, Emily flung the barn door open and ran inside, pausing for a second to let her eyes adjust to the darkness. She blinked once, twice, then a third time. When she opened her eyes again, she stared in horror, praying that her mind was playing tricks on her, knowing that it wasn't.

"No, Father! No!"

Acknowledgments

You may think that writing is a solitary pursuit, and it is, but publishing is a very different story. It takes a team of talented professionals working together to turn a raw manuscript into the book you're holding in your hands.

I am extremely fortunate to have an outstanding team working on my books. Without exception, the staff at Revell are both talented and dedicated to making each book the best it can be. Each one of them cares about their authors, but—more importantly—they care about you, the reader, and strive to make your reading experience a rewarding one.

There are countless people who work behind the scenes, and if I listed them all, this book would rival *War and Peace* for length. I would, however, be remiss if I didn't single out the women who form the nucleus of what I consider to be the dream team.

It's been more than fourteen years since Executive Editor Vicki Crumpton bought my first manuscript. I was thrilled then, and the thrill has not waned. Vicki's belief in my stories gets me through the dreaded middle-of-the-book doldrums, while her gentle editing that combines constructive criticism with very welcome humor strengthens each of my manuscripts. I give thanks each day that I have the perfect editor—Vicki.

Few authors look forward to revision letters, but that's because they don't have Managing Editor Kristin Kornoelje on their team. Kristin's incredible attention to detail and her thoughtful analysis of characters' motivation have given me new perspectives on my own work and made me a better writer. She's a true blessing.

Senior Marketing Director Michele Misiak does so much more than her title might imply. In addition to constantly looking for new ways to promote my books, a job that she does exceedingly well, she serves as my gateway to Revell, answering myriad questions and educating me about the constantly changing world of publishing and social media. I've learned so much from Michele.

I'm convinced that Karen Steele doesn't sleep. She wears several hats, including Senior Publicist. In that role, she's on what seems like a perpetual search for ways to spread the word about my books. Radio and print, interviews and reviews, blog tours, social media—Karen's got them all covered, and not just covered but covered well. I couldn't ask for a better publicist.

I also want to thank Audrey Leach for going "above and beyond" to ensure that I receive cover flats for each of my books. She knows how much I enjoy having them framed and hanging over my desk, and so nothing—not even a pandemic—stops her from getting them to me.

Each day I give thanks for Vicki, Kristin, Michele, Karen, Audrey, and the rest of the Revell staff. They're the best!

Amanda Cabot's dream of selling a book before her thirtieth birthday came true, and she's now the author of more than three dozen novels as well as eight novellas, four nonfiction books, and what she describes as enough technical articles to cure insomnia in a medium-sized city. Her stories have appeared on the CBA and ECPA bestseller lists, have garnered a starred review from *Publishers Weekly*, and have been nominated for the ACFW Carol, the HOLT Medallion, and the Booksellers Best awards.

Amanda married her high school sweetheart, who shares her love of travel and who's driven thousands of miles to help her research her books. After years as Easterners, they fulfilled a longtime dream when Amanda retired from her job as director of information technology for a major corporation and now live in the American West.

Don't Miss the Other Books in the
MESQUITE SPRINGS SERIES!

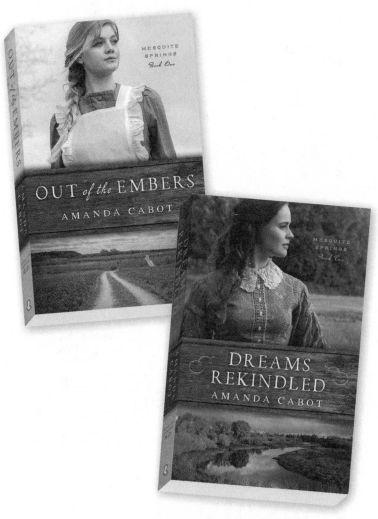

"Such beautiful words flow from Amanda Cabot's pen—words that lead characters from tattered situations to fresh beginnings and culminate in tender story endings that make a reader sigh in satisfaction. I've never been disappointed by a Cabot tale."

—Kim Vogel Sawyer, bestselling author

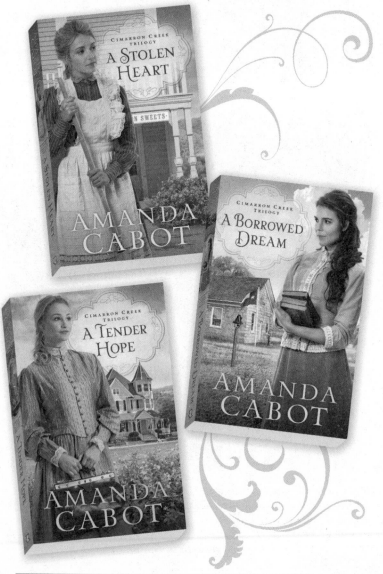

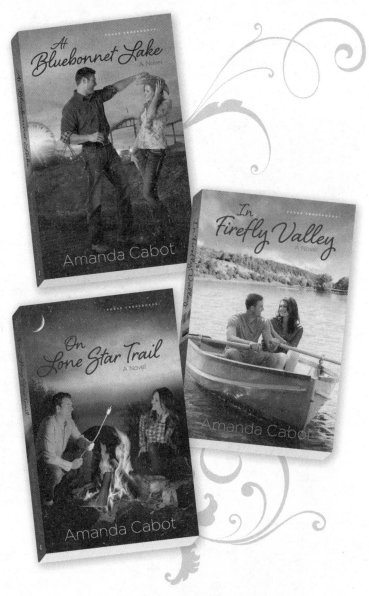

"Cabot engages and entertains in equal measure."

—*Publishers Weekly*

"One thing I know to expect when I open an Amanda Cabot novel is heart. She creates characters that tug at my heartstrings, storylines that make my heart smile, and a spiritual lesson that does my heart good."
—**Kim Vogel Sawyer, bestselling author**

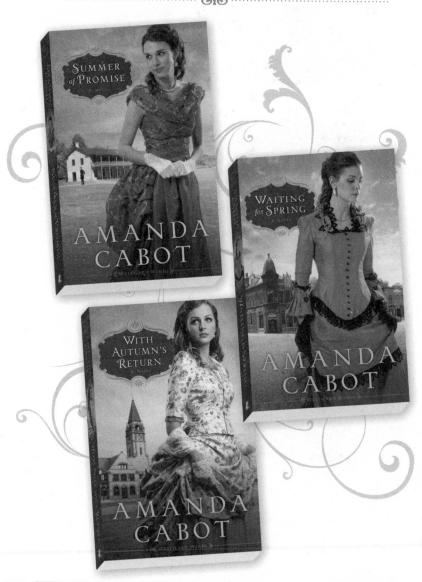

MEET
Amanda Cabot

VISIT
AmandaCabot.com

to learn more about Amanda,
sign up for her newsletter,
and stay connected.